PRIMITIVE PASSIONS

John M. Cahill

PRIMITIVE PASSIONS

*To Silvia,
for her support and encouragement*

PART I

October 1681 – June 1684

There are only six primitive Passions...
wonder,love, hatred, desire, joy, and sadness...
--René Descartes

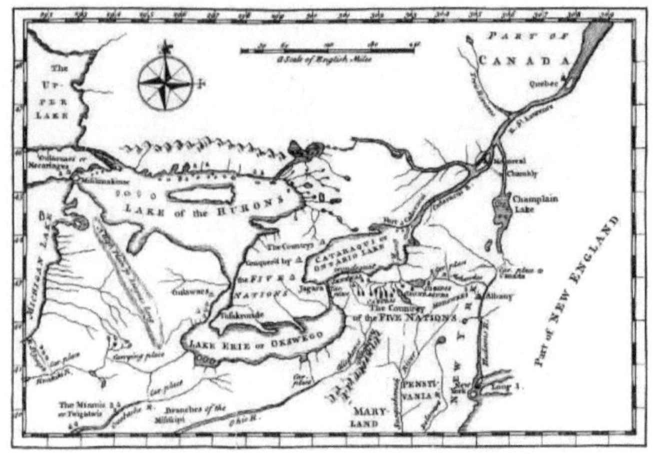

A map of the Country of the Five Nations, belonging to the Province of New York; and of the Lakes near which the Nations of Far Indians live, with part of Canada. This map appeared in the 1749 edition of Cadwallader Colden's **The History of the Five Indian Nations.**

Chapter 1

As H.M. Frigate *Expeditious* rode peacefully at anchor within the Mole at Manhattan Harbor, Sean O'Cathail leaned against the gunwale, daydreaming. Since they had arrived the day before, Sean had found himself drawn to the landscape. However, it wasn't the small but substantial town that interested him. Rather, his thoughts focused on the forest that lay just to the north.

It's so green, he thought. Almost as green as Ireland... But wild... Much wilder than Ireland.

Imagine, the sixteen year old reflected, the opportunities that lay in that wild, new country. It looks like a place where a man could become whatever he had the strength, courage or desire to be. Not like in Ireland, where the best I could hope for would be to become a tenant farmer like my father. Despite my education

with the hedgerow priests, reading and writing
Irish, English and Latin, I could never be more
than a tenant farmer. Or a priest! Nay.
Imagine life as a priest! How boring that would
be.

And, life in this new land would have to
be better than serving in the English Navy!
Here I've spent the last four years of my life, and
what do I have to show for it? I'm still just a
common seaman with only the coins sewn in the
waistband of my breeches. True, I've got a share
of the prize money coming from our capture of
that pirate ship. But my share certainly doesn't
make me rich. If I stay in the Navy, nothing will
change. I'll be just as poor as I was when I left
Ireland. I'll have no money, no trade, no future...

"Sean!"

"I say, Sean!"

The insistent voice of Dick Fielding, an
eleven-year-old powder monkey who looked on
the tall, red-headed Sean as both friend and role
model, finally broke through the young man's
reverie.

"What, Dick? What is it?"

"Sean, ye were staring at the town. What
did ye see?"

"Oh, nothing... I was just thinking about
my future. I think it's time that I had one.
When we get back to Portsmouth, I'm leaving the
ship."

"Really? Why?"

"I want to make something of my life. I've
got grander dreams than just being a sailor."

"But, what will ye do? I can't think of anything I'd rather do than be a sailor!"

"Really, Dick? Is that truly all ye want from life? Well, it's not enough for me. I think I'll return here, to the Americas, and seek my fortune. With the money I'll have when we finish this voyage, I should be able to pay my passage and get a fresh start in this new land."

"But... what will ye do once you return? What do ye want to be?"

"I don't know. All I know is... it would have to be better than this... But... what did ye want, lad?" Sean finally asked.

"I wanted to know if ye knew where the others are. I haven't seen Cox or Smithers, or Lieutenant Ambler for that matter, in some time."

Sean and Dick were part of a five-man detail that had remained on board while the rest of the crew enjoyed the attractions of the town. Their turn for shore leave would come the following day while the ship was being loaded with provisions. Under the command of the third mate, Lieutenant Ambler, the detail included two other seamen, Jeremy Cox and Alan Smithers.

"Come to think of it," said Sean, "I haven't seen them, either. I imagine that Lieutenant Ambler is in the mates' quarters, and I'll wager that Cox and Smithers are below, sleeping. Stay here, Dick, one of us has to be on deck at all times. I'm going below to put them out of their hammocks!"

"Aye, aye, Sean," said the boy, snapping to attention.

Sean went below decks and, as he ducked to enter the companionway leading to the fo'c'sle, he heard the voice of Lieutenant Ambler, "Keep looking! There has to be more! We've only found a fraction of what's hidden in here!"

Peering into the crew's quarters, Sean saw Cox rummaging through a sea chest while the third mate watched. What the bloody hell are they doing? Wait... They're stealing from the crew! How dare they! If a man can't trust his shipmates, or officers for that matter, who can he trust?

"Hey! What are ye about?" he yelled as he burst in and made a grab for a canvas bag Smithers had been digging through. "Give me that!"

Smithers pulled the canvas bag out of Sean's reach as Ambler ordered, "Grab him! We'll make him tell us where he's hidden his money!"

Quickly, Cox came up behind Sean and wrapped his arms around him, pinning Sean's arms to his sides.

Ambler advanced, taking a piece of rope, knotted at the end, from the pocket of his coat. He swung the weapon at Sean's face. In response, Sean turned his head enough so that the knot only glanced off his cheek. As the mate started his backswing, Sean leaned his weight against Cox and, bringing both feet up, kicked the officer in the chest, knocking the wind out of him and sending him to the deck. The force of the kick threw Sean and Cox to the deck, as well. Lying on top of Cox, Sean threw his head back as hard as possible, butting Cox on the forehead. Stunned, Cox released his hold on Sean and rolled away as Sean regained his feet.

For the moment, it was just Sean and Smithers. Smithers threw the canvas bag at Sean and drew his knife. Sean knocked the bag away and drew his own knife as the two men began to circle, each seeking an opening. Smithers slashed wildly at Sean, but Sean easily deflected it. Smithers slashed again and, this time, knocked Sean's knife from his hand. They resumed circling until Smithers lunged at Sean's mid-section. Sean feinted and, as his opponent leaned in, grabbed Smithers' arm, twisting it until the knife fell from his hand. Continuing to twist the arm, Sean pulled it behind Smithers' back and grabbed him around the neck in a headlock.

Holding Smithers in front of him as a shield, Sean turned and found Ambler and Cox coming at him from two sides. Just as Sean was thinking that he may have overreached, Dick Fielding appeared and leaped onto the lieutenant's back! Wrapping his legs around Ambler's midsection, the boy dug his fingers into the mate's eye sockets.

"Arrrgh!" groaned Ambler as he tried to pry the boy loose.

Seeing that Ambler was occupied, Sean turned his attention to Cox. Cox grasped a stool with two hands and swung it wildly. The stool struck Smithers' head with such force that it cracked his skull open! Burdened with Smithers' deadweight, Sean pushed the body at Cox, dropped to the deck and, rolling away from Cox, felt for and found his knife. Sean rose to his feet just as Cox came at him again, swinging the stool. Sean slipped under the stool and jabbed at Cox's face, stabbing him in the left eye. Reflexively, Cox's hands flew to his face. He dropped the stool and, with blood seeping through his fingers, collapsed.

Sean turned and saw that Ambler had pulled Dick from his back and had thrown him to the deck. The officer was kicking the youngster in the ribs and, when he raised his boot to stamp on the boy's skull, Sean threw his knife. The knife lodged in Ambler's thigh, and he fell to one knee. Sean jumped on him, and the two men wrestled, rolling about the deck until the bigger man managed to pin Sean down. Grabbing Sean by the ears, Ambler began to beat the young man's skull against the planking.

Despite having his head slammed repeatedly against the deck, Sean managed to kick at the knife impaled in the mate's leg, causing Ambler to grunt in agony. When it finally tore loose, Ambler gave a cry of pain and released Sean. Sean pushed the mate off and quickly stood. Ambler got up slowly and roared with anger as he advanced again. But Dick, still lying on the deck, stuck out his foot and tripped him. Ambler stumbled out of control toward Sean and Sean punched him in the face as hard as possible, breaking his nose and loosening some teeth. Ambler reared back, spitting blood and teeth at Sean, and attacked once more. Dick found Sean's knife and, regaining his feet, came up behind Ambler and stabbed him in the back. The boy stabbed the officer again and again, and kept stabbing even after the man had crumpled to the deck.

Sean gently pulled Dick away from Ambler's body. He pried the bloody knife from Dick's trembling hand, wiped it on Ambler's coat and returned it to its sheath. Then, he looked at Dick. The lad was covered in Ambler's blood and crying.

"Why didn't ye stay up on deck? I told ye to stay there!" Sean said harshly.

"B- b- but I was worried. Ye were gone so long," replied the youth, sobbing.

Mustn't be hard on the lad, thought Sean. He's been through a lot in the past few minutes.

"Well, I am in your debt," said Sean. "Thank ye, Dick! Ye saved my life!"

"Did I? Really?"

"Aye, lad, ye did!"

"B-b-but... what happened, Sean?"

"They were robbing the crew's sea chests! I couldn't stand by and let them do it!"

"Oh, my God! I've killed a superior officer!" Dick said with sudden realization. "What will happen to me? I'll be hung as a mutineer!"

"Aye. We'll both hang."

"Not you, Sean. You didn't kill Mister Ambler. Anything you did, you did in self-defense!"

"It doesn't matter that Ambler was a thief and a bully. He was an officer. An officer is dead and you and I are the only ones still alive. A court martial will find us both guilty of mutiny."

"What do we do?"

"I think the most prudent action would be to jump ship."

"J- j- jump ship? You mean, desert?"

"They'll hang us if we stay. If we run, they can hang us only if they catch us. By running, we give ourselves a chance."

"I g- g- guess ye're right. B-b-but, I'm scared."

"Ye're right to be scared, lad. Truth be told, I'm scared as well. But, if we stick together we might just get through this. Now, do ye trust me?"

"I do, Sean."

"Right, then! We have work to do. We have to make the fo'c'sle look like nothing happened here today."

"How do we do that? Look at this place! Look at me!"

"First, go wash the blood off and get some clean clothes. Then, come back here. We need to dispose of the bodies. Oh, bring your bloody clothing back with ye and get three shrouds from the sail maker's cabinet."

While Dick was doing that, Sean selected nine, nine-pound cannonballs from the gun deck and, making three trips, brought them topside. He and Dick returned to the fo'c'sle at the same time and discovered that Cox was gone!

"I thought he was dead. Where could he have gone?" asked Dick.

"We don't have time to find out," said Sean. "Come, let's hurry and finish this so that we can get away before anyone comes back."

Together, he and Dick carried Ambler's and Smithers' bodies up to the main deck. There, they stuffed them into the shrouds, along with the cannonballs and Dick's bloody clothes. Then, one by one, they dragged the bodies to a gun port on the starboard side, away from the town, and pushed them through.

"Hopefully, the shot will keep the bodies from surfacing," said Sean. "At least, until we're far away," he added. "Quick, now, we need water to wash the blood from the fo'c'sle deck."

Once that was done, they returned to the main deck and crossed to the port side, where they looked toward the town. After determining that no one was yet returning to the ship, Sean put his arm around the boy's shoulder and said, "There's America, Dick. As good a place as any to start a new life."

"I- I- I suppose so," said Fielding, not sounding at all convinced.

"Come, Dick," said Sean, leading him back to the starboard side. "See those rocks? That's the Mole. It's not too far away. We'll swim... Ye can swim can't ye?"

"Aye, I can."

"We'll swim to the Mole and," continued Sean, pointing, "follow the Mole to the wharf. Then, we'll just lose ourselves in the streets of the town. Are ye ready?"

"I- I- I suppose so," the lad stuttered as Sean helped him climb onto the gunwale.

With one last look at the ship, Sean announced, "Well, then, we'd best be leaving." And, holding hands, they jumped into the water.

They lost touch when they hit the water, but both swam to the Mole and pulled themselves up onto the rocks.

After they had caught their breath, Sean said, "Let's go. Quickly now, but mind your step. The rocks are slippery."

Barefoot, they made their way around the harbor without attracting attention. When they reached the wharf, they ran, as fast as possible, into one of the streets that led away from the harbor.

Shadows in the narrow streets were lengthening as they hurried, trying to put distance between themselves and the wharf. But, as he turned a corner, Sean ran headfirst into Lieutenant Allworthy! The lieutenant, with a group of armed seamen, had been charged with finding "volunteers" to make up losses in the ship's company. After visiting the town's more disreputable taverns, they were taking four, obviously drunken men back to the ship.

"God's blood! You ragamuffin, watch where you're going," the officer yelled, pushing Sean away. Sean stumbled backwards and fell on his bottom. That was when Allworthy recognized him.

"O'Cathail! What are you doing ashore?"

Sean picked himself up. Thinking quickly, he touched his forelock in a salute and said, "Captain's compliments, sir. He says that ye should return to the ship straight away with whatever men ye have. He wants to sail on the tide."

The lieutenant started to respond, "Very well, then..." But, seeing Fielding standing behind Sean, he exclaimed, "Fielding! Why...?"

At that, Sean yelled, "Run!" and began running with Dick hot on his heels. Behind them, Sean heard the officer order some of his men to give chase.

The two young men ran for all they were worth! They dodged people and carts! They leapt over dogs and puddles and children! But, even over the pounding of the blood in his ears, Sean could still hear the pounding of the pursuing sailors' boots on the pavement.

Sean led the way, twisting and turning through the narrow streets. He ran, not knowing where he was going, until he heard Fielding cry, "Sean!" Turning, he saw the boy lying face down on the cobblestones.

"C'mon, Dick," he yelled.

"I can't" Fielding cried.   "I've hurt me ankle!"

Sean ran back and, drawing Dick's arm over his shoulder and around his neck, lifted the boy to his feet. Just then, a shot rang out! Sean saw the ball strike a nearby wall.

"Go on, Sean!   Save yourself!" Dick insisted.

Seeing that there was only one sailor in sight and that he was reloading his pistol, Sean carried Dick into an alleyway. The first door he tried was unlocked. Opening it, he helped Fielding inside and, as Dick slid to the floor, said,

"Stay here. Lean against the door. Don't open it except for me. I'll be back for you." Then, he closed the door.

Going back to the corner, Sean allowed himself to be seen by the sailors who had clustered around the one who had fired. Spying Sean, they took up the chase. Certain that they had seen where he had gone, Sean ran back into the alley, past the door behind which Dick was hiding.

Sean ran through the alley and, making sure that his pursuers were still on his trail, turned left at the next street, then right and right again. Rounding the last corner, he found a cart full of straw. Quickly, Sean climbed onto the cart and burrowed into the straw. He tried to catch his breath. Soon, he was able to control his breathing enough so that he could hear running footsteps in the street.

Peering between the stalks, Sean watched as Lieutenant Allworthy and four men trotted past. Eventually, their steps grew fainter. After a few moments, Sean screwed up his courage and, poking his head out of the hay, looked in both directions. No pursuers were in sight. He left his hiding place and quickly walked back to where he had left Fielding. After checking the alleyway, he went to the door and knocked, "Dick, it's me, Sean, open the door."

Dick opened the door, smiling broadly as he saw Sean. "I think I can walk now," he said.

"All right, let's see how ye do," responded Sean, supporting the boy.

Fielding walked carefully for a few steps and said, "It's much better now."

"Good. Then, let's get moving."

Walking as quickly as Fielding's ankle allowed, they headed away from the direction in which their pursuers had gone. They continued to walk until they were far from the docks and had lost themselves in the warren of streets.

"Sean, do ye know where we're going?" asked Fielding.

"Well, maybe not specifically, but I'll know it when we get there," Sean responded.

Soon it was dark and the lamps of the town were being lighted. The pair passed a rattle watch patrol but, since they weren't drunk or rowdy, they weren't challenged.

As they walked, Sean sought out the darker side streets, in the poorest parts of the town, paying particular attention to the taverns. He listened carefully for a sound that he knew could be found in any seaport in the world -- the sound of Gaelic.

Soon enough, at the head of an unpaved lane, he heard a fiddle and tin whistle playing a reel to the rhythm of clapping hands and chanting voices. "This might be the place, Dick," he said, leading the boy up the alley to the door of an alehouse located in a dank cellar.

"Here?" asked Dick.

"Aye, here," said Sean as he pointed above Dick's head. In the moonlight, a weathered sign above the entry proclaimed the establishment to be the "Harp & Shamrock."

"Stay with me and keep your mouth shut," Sean told Fielding. "Your English accent could be a problem in here."

They descended the steps and sat on a bench alongside the wall in a crowd of rowdy drunkards and slatterns. When a serving girl passed them, Sean grabbed two full tankards of beer from her tray.

She cried, "Hey, what do ye think ye're at," as he handed one to Fielding and quickly turned to the older gentleman seated next to him, toasting the man in Gaelic, "*Sláinte!*" The broad shouldered stranger with a ruddy complexion returned the toast, "*Sláinte duine a ól!*" and they both took healthy swigs of their drinks. The serving girl stood over them, glowering at Sean. "I'll take payment in coin or wampum!" she demanded.

Sean's neighbor reached into his pocket and, taking out a string of beads, threw it on the girl's tray. "Here, Annie," he said in Gaelic. "Take what's due for the three of us out of this."

"Ach, Father Brendan," she said in the same language as she counted off a number of beads, retied the cord and handed it back to him. "Ye're too good. Ye don't know these rascals at all. Do ye? Like as not, they'll slit yer throat for what few beads of wampum ye have there!"

The priest turned, looked Sean in the eye, and said to her, "Nay. I doubt it. He doesn't appear to be the throat-slitting type. You're not, are ye?"

"Nay," Sean replied. "We're just strangers trying to find their way in a strange land. And, I have no idea what 'wampum' might be."

"And how, may I ask, did ye manage to find yourselves in this strange land?"

"Well... Excuse me, but I thought I heard the girl call you, 'father.' Are ye a priest, then?"

"Aye, I am. I'm shepherd to this scandalous flock. And ye, young man? What are ye?"

"Hah! I suppose you'd call me a lost lamb!" Sean said, laughing. Then, quickly deciding that he had to trust someone, and who better than a priest, he whispered, "Actually, father, we just jumped ship!"

"Jumped ship, did ye? What kind of ship?"

"An English frigate, father. We're deserters."

"Deserters? Well, that complicates things," replied the priest, rubbing his chin in thought.

"Can ye see your way clear to help us, father?"

"As I believe that desertion from the English Navy speaks well for your common sense, I believe I can. What kind of help do ye need?"

"We're on the run, father! We'll take any help we can get. And, we don't know if they're searching for us."

"Well, don't worry. You're amongst friends. But tell me, do either of ye know anyone in Manhattan? Do ye have a place to stay?"

"Nay, father. We decided to jump ship here because we thought that the new world would offer opportunities that we might not find elsewhere."

"Aye, that's true enough."

"By the way, father, I'm Sean O'Cathail and my companion is Dick Fielding," said Sean, extending his hand. "Dick is neither Irish nor Catholic but don't hold that against him."

"Brendan, lads, Brendan O'Boyne," said the priest, pumping Sean's hand enthusiastically and then Dick's. "'Tis pleased I am to make your acquaintance."

"First, we need to get ye away from the center of town. Then, we'll have to see about getting ye upriver to Kingston or even Albany. Albany, that's where ye should go. There are lots of opportunities there for clever young men. But first, let's see what we can do about finding ye someplace to stay tonight."

Turning from Sean, the priest gestured for the serving girl, who responded almost immediately.

"Aye, father? Another beer?"

"Nay, Annie. Ye ken that I ne'er take more than one. What I do want, however, is a place where my young friends might hide. Do ye know someone who might have room for them?"

"Do ye really trust them, father? I mean, they don't appear to be terribly respectable."

The priest laughed out loud and, extending his arms to encompass the room, said, "Do any of us, Annie? Look at us. Who are we to judge anyone by appearances? Oh, forgive me!

Ye haven't been properly introduced: Sean O'Cathail, Dick Fielding: Miss Anne O'Shea. Annie: Sean and Dick."

"Milady," Sean responded, miming a bow while Dick blushed.

"Harrumph," replied Annie. Turning to the priest, she said, "Father, if ye trust them, I suppose I should not question ye. Ye ken Megan O'Reilly, father? "

"Aye, of course. She's more likely to take the sacraments than yourself, Miss O'Shea."

"Oh, father...," she said, waving off the implied criticism. "Anyway, Megan is housekeeper to the Viele family. Their house is at the end of King Street. If I remember correctly, there's a barn they could hide in."

"Is that at the corner of Wall Street?"

"Aye, on the left hand side."

Turning to Sean and Dick, the priest said, "Come along, lads. Finish yer beers and we'll be going. We need to get there before Miss O'Reilly goes to bed."

Draining their tankards and bidding farewell to Annie, the trio left the ale house. They walked out of the alleyway, onto a thoroughfare that Father O'Boyne identified as Broad Street, and began walking north.

As they walked, Dick tugged at Sean's sleeve and whispered, "Are ye sure we can trust him?"

Sean replied, "What choice do we have? But, yes, I think we can trust him."

Turning to the priest, Sean asked, "Father, I can see that you're not wearing a cassock. Are Catholics not accepted here in New York?"

"Well, lad, despite the fact that the king, the Duke of York, and the colonial governor are all Catholic, this is still a Protestant colony, and I've found it wise to be inconspicuous."

"What are those beads you used to pay for our drinks?" asked Dick.

"These?" clarified the priest, taking the string from his pocket. "This is wampum. It's what passes for money here in the colony. If you look very closely, you'll see that they're not beads. They're actually seashells. The black ones are called *sewant* and are worth twice as much as the white. Three black or six white are worth an English penny."

"But why use shells instead of coins?" asked Dick.

"Because there's little hard money available in the colony, lad. Originally, the Dutch used wampum when trading for furs because the shells are highly valued by the savages. However, it wasn't long before they started using them to substitute for coins in their own transactions."

Soon, they had reached Wall Street. O'Boyne told Sean and Dick that the street took its name from the palisade that the Dutch had built to protect the town from Indians. The wall, which ran from Hudson's river on the west to the East River, had marked the northern-most limits of the town. Now, it was in disrepair and the town was expanding beyond it.

At the corner, they found themselves in front of an imposing, three-story home. Father O'Boyne led the way around to the rear door. He peered in a window and, satisfied, tapped gently at the glass.

The door opened by a pretty girl, with chestnut hair, hazel eyes and a splash of freckles across her nose, who quietly exclaimed, "Father O'Boyne! What a pleasant surprise!"

"Megan," said the priest, "This is Sean O'Cathail, a fellow countryman of ours, and his friend, Dick Fielding. They're in need of a place to hide for a day or two. Do ye think they could stay in the barn?"

"Well, it's not really a barn; it's more a stable... Although it does have a loft with clean hay."

"That's perfect!"

"But, father, what have they done?"

"They've done nothing terrible. They're deserters, on the run from the English navy."

"Deserters! Oh, father, I don't know..."

"Now, Megan, I've gotten to know the lads and believe that they'll bring no trouble or harm to you or your employer."

"Well, Father, if ye vouch for them, I suppose so. But, only for one or two nights. The Vieles are nice people, but they have their limits."

"Don't worry, lass. They'll only stay until they can catch the packet to Albany. They probably won't be able to leave tomorrow, but there's no reason why they can't leave the day after."

Then, Father O'Boyne said to Sean and Dick, "Well, lads, I'll leave ye in Miss O'Reilly's capable hands. I'll come by tomorrow to see how ye are faring and to let ye know when you'll be leaving."

"Thank ye, father, for all you've done," Sean said.

"Thank ye, sir," said Dick.

"Don't worry," said Sean. "We'll bring no trouble to Miss O'Reilly."

"Good," replied the priest. "Thank you, Megan, I'm sure Sean and Dick will give ye no reason to regret helping them."

With that, the priest started to leave, but Sean stopped him, saying, "Father, I need to make my confession."

"All right, lad, walk with me."

"I'll be right back," Sean said to Megan and Dick.

At the corner, they stopped, and Sean began, "Father, I stabbed a man today..."

"Stabbed! And, I just told Megan that you weren't dangerous! Did ye kill him? Did ye plan to do it?"

"No, father. It was in self-defense. I caught three men robbing the crew's quarters and, when I tried to stop them, they attacked me. In the melee, one was accidentally killed by one of the others. I stabbed one and Dick killed the other. It appears that the one I stabbed got away. I don't know if he's dead or alive. It was them or us. I genuinely didn't want anyone to die. I am so sorry, Father."

"Well, then, as ye truly are repentant, I will absolve ye," said the priest. He murmured the formula, "*Ego te absolvo*," and made the sign of the cross over Sean. "I'll think about a proper penance."

"Thank ye, father," Sean said as the priest turned and walked away.

Sean returned to Megan and Dick who were standing in the dark. "Sit down here on the step," she told them. "I'll bring ye something to eat."

Moments later she returned with plates of cold beef and cooked turnips, brown bread and two tankards of beer. "The Vieles have gone to bed," she said. "So, ye can sit here while ye eat."

"Thank ye, Megan," Sean replied. "We really appreciate all that ye're doing for us."

"Yes, miss, that's the truth," Dick mumbled with his mouth full.

"No need to thank me," she said. "I'm only doing it because Father Brendan asked."

As soon as they finished eating, Megan led them into the barn. "Ye can sleep up there," she said, pointing to the loft. "The straw is clean. Mind now, don't let yourselves be seen."

"Don't worry. We won't," Sean replied as he and Dick climbed up the ladder into the loft. Once there, they covered themselves with straw and were soon sound asleep.

Chapter 2

In the morning, Sean awoke to the sound of someone climbing the ladder to the loft. He drew his knife and moved quickly to the top of the ladder, just as the top of Megan's head appeared.

"Good morning!" she said with a bright smile.

"God, lass, ye scared the life out of me!" Sean said, sheathing the knife. Dick sat up, rubbing the sleep from his eyes, and said, "What's going on?"

"Here, here is your breakfast," Megan said, handing them hard-boiled eggs and slices of soft, white bread, which she called *schoonbrood*. "I'll bring ye some fresh milk as soon as I've milked the cow."

She went back down the ladder and soon returned with two cups of milk, saying, "I've got to make breakfast for the Vieles. I'll come back as soon as I can."

After eating, and still exhausted from the exertion and stress of the previous day, the young men reclined in the straw.

"Sean," said Dick, "how did ye know where to find help?"

"I didn't, but I knew that if I could find some fellow Irishmen, they would help us. We were very lucky to run into Father O'Boyne."

"Do we have to go to Albany?" the younger man asked.

"Why?"

"I was thinking last night. I don't really want to go into the wilderness. I would rather get a berth on a merchant ship. The sea is all I know."

"Well, let's talk about it with Father O'Boyne when we see him again. Perhaps he'll have an idea. But as I told ye yesterday, I want to try something new. Far from the sea! I want to feel solid ground under my feet."

With that, each became lost in his own thoughts with Sean reckoning 'so far, so good. We have a place to hide and Megan is a good cook. She's really a pretty girl, too. And, we have Father O'Boyne to help us. What's next? If I'm able to get out of Manhattan without being caught, and get to Albany, what will happen to me? What kind of work can I find? I have no trade... Although I'm sure I could learn one, but which one? Perhaps Dick is right. Maybe I should go back to sea... No! Never again...'

Shortly, Megan returned to the barn. "Mister and Mistress Viele are both gone, so we have some time to visit. And, I've brought ye some old clothes of Mr. Viele's," she said, handing Sean breeches, woolen stockings, a shirt, coat and boots. "They should fit ye better than those rags you're wearing. Can't let ye walking the streets looking like a beggar now, can we? The English would take ye into custody just because ye look so desperate. Oh! And here's a hat to cover that red hair of yours!"

Turning to Dick, she said, "Here, these should fit ye, Dick. I got them from a maid down the street. The young master of the house had outgrown them. I even managed to find ye some shoes. I hope they fit."

Dick tried the shoes and pronounced them, "Perfect, miss!"

"Thank ye, Megan," said Sean. "Are ye sure your master won't be missing his things?" asked Sean.

"Nay, they're old and, besides, they no longer fit. I've been feeding him too well," she said with a laugh.

After Sean and Dick had changed, Sean and Megan sat and chatted. Megan told him that she came from a small village in County Sligo and that she, like he, was sixteen. She explained that she and her father had sailed to New York after her mother had passed away. The plan was that they both would find work on a farm. But, before they reached America, her father had died.

"After he was gone, I was utterly lost. When we landed, I had no money. We had spent all we had on our passage. I knew that I could sell myself, but my pride just wouldn't let me. So, I started looking for a job as a housekeeper."

"Have ye no other family?" Sean interrupted.

"I have an older brother, Donal. He was transported to Antigua, oh, at least ten years ago. He doesn't know where I am or that our mother and father are dead."

"I'm sorry. Please go on."

"So, I went from house to house in the better neighborhoods inquiring about available positions. I was extraordinarily lucky. Mistress Viele had just dismissed a girl for stealing when I knocked on her door. She gave me a trial and, now, I've been with them for two years. They are good, kind people. They know that I'm Catholic and even allow me to attend Mass on Sundays. Not many would. That's why I don't want to do anything that might upset them."

"Where do ye go to Mass? Is there a Catholic church in the town?"

"There's a chapel at Fort James. But that's only for the governor and other gentlefolk. Father Brendan says Mass in people's homes."

"I take it, then, that Father O'Boyne is not the only priest in the colony."

"Nay. Governor Dongan brought three Jesuits with him, but ye seldom see them outside of Fort James. They are supposed to minister to the savages, but..." she said shrugging.

"To which order does Father O'Boyne belong?" asked Sean.

"He's a Dominican, a Blackfriar. They're required to live amongst the people, so Father

Brendan has a room downtown and, to keep from starving, works as a butcher in the market at Beaver Street."

"He seems to be quite a man," remarked Sean.

"Aye," Megan replied. "That he is."

When Sean asked about her employers, Megan said that Mister Viele was a physician and also handled his father's business interests in New York. The father was a prosperous fur trader in Albany. Mistress Viele, she said, was involved in a variety of charitable works in the town.

"Ye mentioned that Mister Viele's father is a fur trader. Is that a good way to make a living here in the colonies?" he asked.

"I suppose it is. The family, both here and in Albany, lives very well. So, I imagine that he earns a good living. Although I don't know if I would want to spend my days wandering in the wilderness and consorting with red heathens."

Sean was intrigued. Fur trading sounded like an exciting way of life and profitable, as well. It may be just what he was looking for. He resolved to learn more as soon as he arrived in Albany.

"Tell me, Megan, is there some way that Dick and I could repay yer kindness?"

She laughed and said, "A pair of strong lads like yerselves should be able to weed the garden and muck out the cow's stall, don't ye think? That will help me with the chores I've neglected while chatting with ye." With that, she showed them where the tools were kept and went into the house.

Late that afternoon, Father O'Boyne came by.

"Well, lads, I have both good and bad news," he announced. "The bad news is that the county sheriff has issued warrants for the arrest of five thieves who deserted from the *Expeditious* yesterday. Both of you are named and described in those warrants."

"And the good news, father?" asked Sean.

"The good news is that the *Expeditious* will sail on the morning tide tomorrow."

"How is that good news?" asked Dick.

"It's good news because, once the ship sails, the warrants will be put into a drawer and forgotten."

"How can ye be sure?"

"Believe me, that is how things are done in Manhattan. Besides, both of ye will be on your way to Albany by then and, therefore, out of the sheriff's jurisdiction."

"About that, father," said Sean. "Dick would prefer not to go to Albany."

"Is that true, lad? It isn't safe for ye to tarry here," the priest said to Fielding.

"It's true, sir, but, if I may, I wouldn't stay here any longer than it would take to find a berth on a merchantman."

"Perhaps I can help ye with that," said the priest. "I know some of the masters who are now in port. I can ask if they are in need of a good man."

"Thank ye, sir, I would really appreciate anything ye can do."

"Thank ye, father," said Sean.

Just then, Megan joined them.

"Ah, Megan, there ye are. I was just telling Sean that he can leave for Albany tomorrow morning. Sean, the packet will leave from the Mole on the morning tide. So, I will meet ye and Dick there just after dawn. Wait for me next to the chandler's shop. Megan, you'll be sure they're awake and on their way on time?"

"Aye, father, I will."

"Now, Sean, 'tis a four-day trip to Albany. Do ye have money for your passage and for food?"

"Aye, father, I do," said Sean. "I don't know how to thank ye."

"Sean, join me for a moment," said Father O'Boyne, leading Sean away from the others.

"I've decided on your penance."

"Yes, father?" said Sean, his voice trembling with trepidation.

"Ye should live your life as the good and upstanding man I believe ye to be. I want ye to become a success and remember the church when you're rich!"

"I'll do so, gladly," replied Sean.

Then, taking a small gold box from his pocket, Father O'Boyne extracted a wafer of bread, held it up before Sean and made the sign of the cross, muttering, "*Corpus Christi.*"

Sean opened his mouth and extended his tongue. When the priest placed the wafer on his tongue, Sean closed his mouth and swallowed while making the sign of the cross.

"There," said the priest. "You can start your new life in the state of grace."

"Thank ye, father," said Sean.

"'Til tomorrow morning, lad!"

"'Til tomorrow, father."

After the priest had left, Sean and Dick went back to work and, when finished, returned to the barn for the rest of the day. They saw Megan only fleetingly until she brought them dinner after the Vieles had retired for the night.

Megan awakened Sean and Dick at dawn as promised. After they had eaten breakfast, she gave them apples, and some bread and meat wrapped in pieces of linen. Then, she gave Sean directions to the Mole and, going up on her toes, kissed him on the cheek.

"Ye take care of yourself, Sean O'Cathail, and remember to come see me if you're ever again in Manhattan."

"Aye, lass, I will. And, I'll bring ye a fine fur in payment for yer kindness."

"Ach, just bring yerself, in one piece."

Then, she bent and kissed Dick on the cheek.

"Th-th-thank ye, Miss, for everything," he stammered, blushing furiously.

With that, they left.

It was a beautiful, clear autumn day as they walked to Dock Street. Approaching the wharf, they could see that the *Expeditious* was preparing to sail. Telling Dick to stay out of sight, Sean peered around the corner of the chandlery. To his dismay, he saw some of the crew on the dock, loading the last of the provisions for the voyage into a longboat.

"What happens now?" asked Dick, as Father O'Boyne joined them.

"There's a problem, father," said Sean hooking a thumb toward the wharf.

The priest, too, peered around the corner and said, "Now, don't be dismayed. Let's think for a moment."

Just then, a two-wheeled oxcart rumbled onto the wharf. It slowly passed the sailors, who ignored it, proceeding slowly toward a small yacht tied up further down the wharf

"There," said the priest. "There's yer chance. The cart is going to the Albany packet. Just keep it between yourself and those sailors, and ye'll be safe."

"May I have your blessing, father?"

"Aye, of course," said O'Boyne as he etched the sign of the cross over Sean.

Shaking Dick's hand, Sean said, "Dick, good luck. As I said yesterday, I owe ye my life. If ye ever need anything, let me know."

"Good luck to ye, as well," replied the boy

Sean ran to the cart and, keeping it between him and his former shipmates, walked to the packet. He boarded the yacht, unseen by the sailors, while the contents of the cart were being loaded. He paid his fare, settled himself against the rail, and watched as Dick and Father O'Boyne walked quickly away from the wharf and disappeared around a corner.

The sun rose in the sky and, as soon as the tide was in, they set sail and followed the

Expeditious out of the Mole. Then the pilot steered the yacht into the East River, where they turned north.

Tingling with a combination of excitement and apprehension, Sean took note of his fellow passengers. There were only men on board. Besides the crew, there were two soldiers in a uniform Sean didn't recognize and nearly a dozen other men who were all speaking what Sean assumed to be Dutch. After assuring himself that the soldiers had no interest in him, Sean took stock of the others. Five looked to be farmers. Two were well-dressed, prosperous-looking gentlemen. There were also four rough-looking men, with unkempt beards, wearing homespun tunics belted over deerskin leggings and moccasins. Knives and axes hung from their belts, and each carried a musket. Although Sean was tempted to strike up a conversation with someone, he opted for discretion, fearing that his brogue would arouse curiosity.

As he leaned on the rail, taking in the sights, one of the gentlemen, a tall man, taller than Sean's six feet in height but extremely thin, almost cadaverous, with a pinched face, approached and asked Sean something in Dutch. When Sean replied, in English, that he did not understand, the man switched to that language and, with a strong Scots' burr, asked, "Why were ye talking with that papist priest on the wharf?"

"What priest?" said Sean, feigning ignorance.

"Don't pretend that ye don't know he's a Catholic priest! I saw him making his incantations over ye. Don't deny it! I've seen him before, in his Romish robes. Ye're a papist aren't ye!"

Caught off guard, Sean said nothing.

"Where are ye going?" the man persisted.

"If it's any of your business, I'm going to Albany," Sean replied.

"I'm making it my business! We don't like papists! The domine," he said, indicating the other gentleman, a short, plump, dour-looking man in plain, black and gray clothing, "and I have taken note of ye. Be forewarned: we will be watching ye. We won't give ye a chance to spread yer popery!"

With that, he turned on his heel and rejoined his companion.

"So, what did his lordship want with you?" asked a voice in Dutch-accented English.

Turning, Sean came face to face with one of the rough-looking men, "He wanted to be sure that I wasn't going to try to convert anyone to Catholicism."

"Are you?"

"Nay," replied Sean, laughing. "Ye're safe."

Laughing as well, the man asked, "Are you new to the colony?"

"Aye, I'm only recently arrived," Sean replied.

"Where are you bound?" the man asked.

"Albany," Sean replied.

With that, the man introduced himself as Jan Gaw and told Sean that he and his companions were fur traders, also bound for Albany.

"We've been in Manhattan, spending all the wampum we earned this trading season. It's remarkable how quickly a man can drink up his profits," he said laughing.

Sean introduced himself and asked, "Who was that gentleman?"

"That's Squire Livingston," explained Gaw. "He's the manager of Rensselaerwyck, a large patroonship at Albany."

"What's a patroonship?" asked Sean.

"It's similar to an English manor," the man replied. "Livingston is married to the widow van Rensselaer, her former father-in-law is the patroon, the owner. He lives in Holland. Livingston has been negotiating with the governor to have the patroonship recognized as an English manor."

"Is it big?"

"Big? It's huge! It runs from 12 miles above to 12 miles below Albany and extends 24 miles east to west on both sides of Hudson's river."

"Who is the other gentleman? I think Livingston called him 'domine'?"

"That's Domine Schaets. He's the minister of Albany's Dutch Reformed Church."

"So, they're important people?"

"Aye, lad, prominent and powerful. They're what pass for gentry in Albany. Now, can I ask you a question?"

"Of course," said Sean.

"What brings you to New York, if I may ask?"

"Oh, just looking for a new start," Sean replied.

"Well," Gaw said, "you've certainly come to the right place. What's your trade? You don't look like a farmer."

"No, I'm not a farmer and, to tell the truth, I don't really have a trade," Sean replied. "But I was thinking that fur trading might be a good way to make a living."

"Lads!" Gaw called to his companions. "This young man wants to become a fur trader! More competition for us!"

"Poor fool!" cried one as they all crowded around Sean.

"Doesn't he know that there are no more furs in the colony?" said another.

"It would be charitable if we talked him out of such foolishness!" the third added.

Jan Gaw quickly introduced the others as Nanning Visscher, Jan Hendrix de Bruyn and Jochem Ketelhuym.

"And this, gentlemen, is Sean O'Cathail, newly arrived in the colony."

Sean shook hands all around.

"Now, gentlemen," Sean asked. "Why should I not become a fur trader? Are ye truly afraid of more competition?"

"Nay," replied Nanning Visscher, "We're just afraid that you'll starve to death and that we'll have to contribute to your burial!" as all four laughed.

"Why? I thought that there was money to be made in furs."

"Aye, there is," said Visscher. "But not so much nor as easily as in the past. Am I right lads?"

"Aye, Nanning," said Jochem Ketelhuym.

"Why is that?" Sean asked. "Have the animals stopped wearing fur?"

Ignoring Sean's sarcasm, Gaw said, "Nay, lad, but there are not as many beaver as before. In their eagerness to buy our goods, the *wilden* have nearly exterminated all the beaver."

"But, Jan, ye just said that ye had been in Manhattan spending the money ye had made from fur trading."

"Aye lad, 'tis a fact that there are pelts to be had, but the Iroquois don't have as many as in the past. For business to improve, we would need to wrest some of the trade with the Far Indians away from the French," said Gaw.

"And that," observed Visscher, "won't happen until the Five Nations allow the Far Indians safe passage to Albany."

"Wait! Wait!" cried Sean. "Ye talk of '*wilden*,' and 'Iroquois,' and 'Far Indians,' and 'Five Nations.' Help me to understand what ye are talking about!"

"Well, lad," replied Gaw, "'*Wilden*' is the word we Dutch use when referring to the natives of this land. The English call them 'savages' or 'Indians.'"

"And, the 'Iroquois' are the *wilden* whose lands are closest to the colony of New York," said Nanning Visscher. "They call themselves

Haudenosaunee, which means 'People of the Longhouse.' They are also called the Five Nations because they are an alliance of five related tribes -- the Mohawk, who are also called the *Ganienkeh*, the Oneida, Onondaga, Cayuga and Seneca."

"They come to Albany to trade," added Gaw.

"But," continued Visscher, "there are many other tribes living further west who are enemies of the Iroquois. These 'Far Indians' only trade at Montreal, in Canada. We believe that they want to come to Albany because we offer better prices than the French, but the Iroquois won't allow them to cross their land."

"My God!" Sean exclaimed. "There is so much I have to learn!"

"That's why, if you're determined to go into the fur trade," said Jan Hendrix de Bruyn, "you need to first work with an established trader."

Sean told the men that he had heard of a trader named Viele and that he was hoping to meet him.

"Aernout is one of the best in the business. You'd be lucky if he were to agree to take you on. I'd be happy to introduce you," said Gaw.

"I would appreciate it," Sean replied.

As the five men continued to chat, the yacht reached the Haarlem River, where the pilot disembarked and it docked for the night at Niew Haarlem. As there was no inn in the village, the passengers, except Livingston and

Schaets, passed the night on board the yacht. The two gentlemen spent the night in the village with a colleague of the domine.

The next morning, the yacht continued west on the Haarlem River until it met Hudson's river, at a creek called Spuyten Duyvil. When they were at last sailing north on Hudson's river, Sean found himself marveling not only at the breadth and length of the waterway, but at the vast expanse of wilderness on either side, as well. There were trees, thousands upon thousands of trees, for as far as the eye could see. So dense was the forest on both sides of the river that it resembled a great, green canyon.

He also found it a little intimidating. As a fur trader, he thought, I will have to go into that wilderness and, how did Megan put it, consort with red heathens... I don't know the country or the first thing about trading, and I can't speak any of the languages... not Dutch, or French, or any of the Indian tongues. Oh, well... There's no going back now! I'll just have to make the best of it...

When it was almost dark, they made their next stop, at the village of Yonkers, on the east shore of the river. There, two of the farmers disembarked. This time, all of the remaining passengers spent the night in a tavern.

The next morning, they were roused before dawn and, after a breakfast of beer and dark bread, returned to the yacht and were soon on their way north again. There was little enough to see as both banks of Hudson's river were uninhabited between Yonkers and the next stop, a small town on the west bank that Jan Gaw called Esopus, but which was announced by the yacht's captain by its new English name, "Kingston." There, another farmer left the company. As at Yonkers, Sean and his fellow fur traders, for he now counted himself as one of them, and the last two farmers spent the night in a small, common tavern. But Livingston and Domine Schaets again found lodging elsewhere.

The next day, Sean saw his first Indians. Two natives stood on the eastern shore, quietly watching the yacht sail past.

"Look, Jan!" Sean exclaimed excitedly. "Indians! Are they Iroquois?"

"Nay, Sean," he said. "Those are Mohican. They used to live on both sides of the river until the Mohawk forced them east. Their main village, Schodack, is not far from here."

Shortly, Sean noted signs of civilization on both sides of the river. Well-tended farms, in the midst of harvest, became more and more common as they drew closer to Albany. These were tenant farms, he was told, and part of Rensselaerwyck.

It was past noon, but the sun was still fairly high in the sky when Jan Gaw pointed at the western shore and said, "There it is, lad! That's Albany!"

Viewed from the yacht, the town extended from the river, up a long hill, to a log fort at the top. The whole community, except for the side abutting the river, was encircled by a log palisade.

Sean asked if any of his new friends knew a good place to stay.

"Well, lad," replied Gaw, "there are a number of taverns in the town. Some better are than others. But, since you want to meet Aernout Viele, I suggest that you try his tavern."

"He has a tavern? But I thought he was a fur trader."

"Aye, lad, he is. But, like most of us, he has more than one profession. And, when he is out trading, the tavern is run by his wife. That's why I recommend it; she keeps it clean and sets a good table."

Soon, the yacht docked at the town pier and Sean, closely watched by Livingston and the domine, went ashore.

Once ashore, Sean and Jan bade farewell to the other traders, and Jan showed Sean the way to Viele's tavern. "Let me introduce you to Albany," he said as they walked. "Up this passage is Market Street. If you go right, Market Street will take you to the north gate and through that is a road that eventually becomes an Indian trail that leads to Montreal. We'll turn left."

When they reached an intersection dominated by a large, square log building with rifle slits instead of windows, Jan said, "This is the Dutch Reformed Church, Domine Schaets' church. It was designed as a blockhouse to serve as a refuge in the event of attacks by the *wilden*. So far, *God zij dank*, the townspeople have never had to seek refuge in it.

"Now, if you were to go straight, you would be on Court Street. That leads to the south gate. There, on the left side of Court Street, just across that little bridge, you can see the *Stadhuis,* the city hall, where the magistrates meet. We'll turn right here and go up the hill, up Jonkers Street, toward Fort Albany."

Shortly he announced, "Here, at the corner of Pearl Street, is Viele's tavern," as he took Sean up the steps of a handsome, two-story structure.

The front door opened into a large, bright public room furnished with comfortable benches as well as tables and chairs. Although most of the patrons were smoking clay pipes, the room was not terribly smoky, as windows had been opened from the top to clear the air.

Jan guided Sean across the room to a counter which was presided over by a young, brown-haired woman only a little older than Sean.

"Jacomyntie," Jan said, "Is your father about?"

"Nay, Mister Gaw," the woman replied. "He's out a-trading, but we expect him to return in a day or two. Can I help you?"

"Thank you, Jacomyntie. This young man, here, wishes to meet your father. Jacomyntie Viele, this is Sean O'Cathail. Sean, Miss Viele is Aernout's daughter."

"I am very pleased to make your acquaintance, Miss Viele," Sean said.

"And I, yours, Mister O'Cathail," she replied.

"Do you have a bed that Sean can use while he's awaiting your father's return?" asked Gaw.

"We may," she said with obvious hesitation.

"Not to worry, miss," Sean quickly interjected. "I can pay for my lodging."

"Oh!" she said, blushing. "Then I am sure that we can find a place for you!"

Just then, a plump, pleasant-looking woman, who could only have been Jacomyntie's mother, entered the tavern. Gaw introduced Sean to Gerritje Viele and told her that Sean wanted to meet her husband. He then took his leave, telling Sean that he was sure that they would be seeing each other again, around the town.

After Gaw had left, Mistress Viele had Jacomyntie bring Sean food and beer. Later, she, herself, led him upstairs to where he would be sleeping.

Chapter 3

Sean spent the next week exploring Albany, from the warehouses along the river -- empty now that the trading season had ended -- to the fort at the top of the hill, and from the tanneries along Foxes Creek, outside of the north gate, to the public pastures and the ruins of old Fort Orange to the south of the town. Jacomyntie Viele had proudly informed Sean that the town had 500 residents and was one of the major settlements in the English colonies, along with Boston, Manhattan, Philadelphia, and Charles Towne in the Carolinas.

Most of Albany's 150 buildings were located along the river. There were only ten streets. Jonkers Street, which was dominated by the homes and shops of some of the town's wealthier merchants, and four others ran westward, up the hill from the river. Six streets, including Dock, Court, Market and Pearl, ran north and south from Jonkers Street.

The houses of the town were all built in the Dutch manner. Narrow, brick-fronted buildings, standing side-by-side, faced each of the principal and side streets. The main streets were cobbled, while the byways were well-graded.

The palisade that enclosed Albany on three sides was fifteen-feet high with blockhouses located at regular intervals, but Fort Albany was, by far, the town's most prominent feature.

Built by the English only five years earlier, the fort was enclosed by a wooden stockade, separate from the town's palisade. Within the fort were two, two-story buildings. The headquarters building, against the south wall, also served as the governor's residence when he visited Albany. Against the north wall stood a building that contained the barracks for the small garrison, and a kitchen. There were also stables and a stone powder magazine. Atop the four walls of the palisade were firing platforms, and each of the corner bastions contained a cannon.

Sean learned that the fort's garrison was drawn from the two "Duke of York's Companies," which defended the colony. Technically, the twenty-five soldiers who manned the fort belonged to the British army. However, they wore the Duke of York's livery, consisting of a buff-yellow coat with a red lining and cuffs, breeches and stockings. This was the unfamiliar uniform Sean had seen on the boat to Albany.

The fort sat atop the hill in the middle of a broad plain overlooking the town. The land surrounding the fort on all sides had been cleared for an area equal to the distance a musket ball would fly when shot from the walls of the fort. The portion of this area which lay within the palisade served as the town's fur market during high trading season.

Just outside of the west gate were scattered a number of primitive huts that had been built to house Indians who came to Albany for trade or councils. The huts were small, only about ten-feet square, and built of rough, unfinished planks.

Mistress Viele had told Sean that, before the English had conquered New Netherland for the second time in 1673, the natives had been welcomed into the town, then called Beverwyck, or "the beaver trap." They traded furs, drank in the taverns and often slept in the houses of the traders with whom they did business. But, then, the English had come and the huts had been built.

"They said it was to keep the savages from spying on the fortifications," she said, "but we knew that it was a way for the fastidious English to keep drunken, carousing Indians out of the town after dark."

Three streams carried fresh water from the west, under the palisade, then down the hill through the town, emptying into the river.

As Sean wandered around the town, he gradually became aware that he was being followed. At first, he thought it might be a thief with designs on his purse. But he dismissed this idea with a chuckle. Anyone looking at me, he reflected, would certainly know that I have nothing worth stealing.

The next morning, his "shadow," as Sean had begun to think of him, was back. He followed Sean throughout the morning and even ate his mid-day meal in the same tavern as Sean. Leaving the tavern, Sean decided that he was tired of the game and that it was time to confront the man who had been trailing him. He sauntered down the street, then quickly turned a corner and stopped. When the man also turned the corner, he walked right into Sean.

Sean grabbed the man by the collars of his coat with two hands and demanded, "Who are ye and why are ye following me?"

"You'd best unhand me, sir! My name is Pretty, Sheriff Pretty" the man replied imperiously, "I always keep a close watch on newcomers."

Releasing the sheriff, Sean said, "All newcomers? Or, just certain newcomers? Like, this newcomer? Did Squire Livingston tell ye to follow me?"

"You don't need to know that. It suffices that I suspect that you are a loiterer and a vagrant, with no visible means of support, and, therefore, worthy of suspicion."

"Well, let me put your mind at ease. My name is Sean O'Cathail. I just arrived in the colony from Ireland. I am waiting to meet Mister Aernout Viele to secure a position with him. As ye are aware, I am staying at the Viele tavern. I am paying my own way and have sufficient funds to support myself. Oh, by the way, ye can tell

Livingston that, while I am a Catholic, I have no plans to try to convert anyone. So, now, ye know everything about me. Ye can continue to follow me, ye can arrest me, or ye can go chase real criminals!"

"Watch your mouth, lad! If you don't want trouble, you'll keep a civil tongue in your head! I'll be keeping an eye on you!"

"Ye, Domine Schaets, Squire Livingston… Everyone wants to keep an eye on me! I never knew I was so interesting," remarked Sean as he turned and walked away.

That night, as Sean was eating his dinner, he heard Jacomyntie exclaim, "Papa!" and saw her rush into the embrace of a short, sturdy man, dressed in the same manner as Jan Gaw and the other traders he had met on the packet. His skin had been darkened by long days in the sun and his hair and unkempt beard were brown, but even from across the room, Sean could see that his eyes were a brilliant shade of blue.

Soon, Mistress Viele joined her daughter in welcoming her husband home, and it was not long before other members of the family had arrived, as well. In addition to Jacomyntie, the Vieles had two sons, Garret and Philip, 12- and 13-years-old, still living at home. A married daughter, Willemtje Schermerhooren, also lived in Albany. Not in Albany were three more Viele children: the oldest son, in whose stable in Manhattan Sean and Dick Fielding had hidden; and another son and daughter who lived in the village of Schenectady, about 20 miles west of Albany, with their own families.

Sean bided his time, not wanting to interrupt Viele's homecoming. Finishing his meal, he ordered another beer and waited while Viele ate and enjoyed the company of his family.

While waiting, Sean reviewed what he had learned about Aernout Viele since he had arrived in Albany.

Viele had been born and raised in Fort Orange, as Albany was known before it was separated from Rensselaerwyck and became Beverwyck. He was the stepson of a tavern keeper who had been one of the town's first inhabitants. It was as a boy, working in his stepfather's tavern, that Viele had discovered his facility with languages, and he now spoke Dutch and English, Iroquois, French and Algonquin.

Viele was a teenager when he first became involved in the fur trade. Jan Gaw had told Sean that Viele started as a *boschloper*, a "runner in the woods." That is, he was one of a group of young men who would wait in the woods to intercept natives coming to Beverwyck to trade. Using rum or other presents, they would persuade the Indians to sell only to the traders who employed them. Or, they would make quick deals for furs at a favorable price and, since fur trading outside of Albany was illegal, smuggle the furs into town. By the time he was twenty, Viele had earned a reputation as a tenacious and savvy businessman and was soon trading on his own. Now, twenty-five years later, he was one of the most successful traders and merchants in the colony.

As he waited for Viele, Sean considered and then dismissed the idea of telling him that he had jumped ship. He reasoned that, while the information would be of no use to Viele, it would be a hindrance to the understanding he sought with the trader.

As soon as Viele had finished eating, Mistress Viele led him to Sean's table, and introduced the two men, telling her husband that Sean had recently arrived in the colony and interested in learning the fur trade.

"Mistress Viele, bring us two beers, if you please," said Viele. When the drinks arrived, the two men saluted each other's health and Viele said, "I've already heard something of you. According to Sheriff Pretty, Robert Livingston and Domine Schaets think that you're a papist, come to steal Albany for the pope. In addition, they even suspect that you may be a French spy. Are you?"

"Well, I am Catholic, but I am not trying to convert anyone, and I am most certainly not a French spy. I just want to learn the fur trade and to try to make a good living."

"Good! That's just what I wanted to hear."

"But, I wouldn't want to cause ye any trouble with the gentry or the sheriff."

"Don't fret, son. Sheriff Pretty will lose interest soon enough. The domine won't bother you because I am one of the main supporters of the church. And, Livingston and I have never gotten along. Plus, I don't care how you worship God as long as you're a hard worker."

"Thank ye, sir!"

"Now, you say you want to learn the fur trade. You do realize, don't you, that this is not the best time to take up fur trading?"

"Aye, sir, I do," said Sean. "Jan Gaw and other traders I've met have made that abundantly clear. However, they are of the opinion that it is only a matter of time before the Albany traders have access to furs from the Far Indians in the west."

"That's their opinion, eh? Well, far be it from me to question the opinions of other traders, but I don't think that will happen any time soon. The bad blood between the Iroquois and the Far Indians goes back generations. There's a mutual dislike ...nay, a hatred ...that will not disappear overnight. For the foreseeable future, the Iroquois, especially the Seneca, will refuse to allow the *wilden* from the west to cross their lands. And, until the way to Albany is open to them, the Far Indians will continue to take their furs to Montreal.

"That's the reality, lad," continued Viele. "But that does not mean that a man with effort and hard work cannot make a living at trading, even in these hard times. But, why have you come to me?"

"Well, sir, to be truthful, I had heard ye mentioned as being a highly successful trader when I was in Manhattan, and this was confirmed by people here in Albany. I decided that, if I was to learn the trade, it should be from the best.”

“Don’t try to flatter me, lad. There are others in town who are equally or even more successful than I. Johannes Roseboom, for example.”

“Again, to be honest,” said Sean, “since I’ve arrived, I have inquired after other traders. While it is true that many are quite successful, none has the reputation of being as close to the savages or as trusted by them as ye. To my untutored mind, if I am to be a successful fur trader, it seems to make sense to learn as much as possible about the savages from someone who knows them best. That, it appears, would be ye!”

"All right, then. We know what you want from me," said Viele. "Let's talk about what you have to offer me. Can you read or write?"

"Aye, sir, I can. I can read and write English and Latin."

"What languages can you speak?"

"I speak Gaelic, English and Latin."

"English is good, but I fear you'll have little use for Gaelic, here, and even less for Latin.

But... do you have an ear for languages? Are you a quick learner?"

"I believe so, sir. My teachers all praised me for my facility with languages. Indeed, they found me to be quite adept at all my lessons."

"What kind of work have you done?"

"I was born on a farm. My father was a tenant farmer. So, I know a bit about farming..."

"Why did you leave the farm?"

"I was the oldest of eight children. My parents could barely feed all of us and, since there was nothing to inherit but my father's tenancy, I decided that it would be better for everyone if I struck out on my own. So, when I was 12, I left home and went to Galway thinking that I might find a ship and join its crew. As it happened, there was a merchantman in the harbor. I was tall for my age, so it was easy for me to sign on as a common seaman. That's how I came to spend four years at sea," said Sean, bending the truth to hide his service in the navy.

"And, why did you leave the sea?"

"We once made port at Manhattan. I couldn't take my eyes off of the wide expanse of wilderness that stretched beyond the town. It seemed to be a land full of opportunity. I decided that day that I would leave the sea and come back to seek my fortune. And, here I am."

"Have you ever done any trading? Buying? Selling? Been apprenticed to a merchant?"

"Sadly, no. But, as I said earlier, I am a quick learner with a desire to learn all I can about fur trading."

"Well, I'll tell you, it seems that you have made quite a good impression on Mistress Viele in the few days you've been here. And I trust her as a good judge of human nature. The question becomes, what type of arrangement can we make?"

"Mister Viele..."

"Nay, lad, call me Aernout."

"Aernout, then... I have given the issue much thought and I have come to what, I hope, would be an acceptable arrangement for each of us."

"Then, gather your thoughts and I'll bring us another beer."

When Viele returned, he gave Sean his drink and took a long draught of his own. "*Ach, mijn God*, that tastes good! If you do go into trading, lad, you'll find that good beer is one of the things you miss most about civilization when you're out among the *wilden*. Now, where were we? Ah, yes, you were about to give me your thoughts on a potential working relationship..."

"Yes, sir. I would suggest a combination, apprentice-employee arrangement. The way I see it, I would spend one year as your apprentice, working only for my food and board while I learn the trade. Then, the next year, I would work as an employee at a salary ye would determine. At the end of that time, I hope, I will have learned enough to go out on my own."

"It sounds like you've given this considerable thought," said Aernout. After thinking a moment he said, "I would make only one small change... It'll be at least three years before my younger sons, Garret and Philip, will be old enough to join me in the business. So, after a year as an apprentice and then one as an employee, I would like to have you work with me for a final year as a junior partner. We'll share all profits 75-25. That way, you'll have a chance to see if you can actually make a living at the trade. What do you think?"

"Sounds fair to me. When do ye think I can start?"

"Why not tomorrow morning?"

"Tomorrow morning sounds perfect!"

"Excellent. Come to my house on Yonkers Street first thing in the morning. That's where I do business. And, bring your belongings with you. We'll fix you a pallet, and you can sleep there. Since you'll spend your first year working without wages, you won't be able to afford to stay here in the tavern. Now, let's have another beer to toast our new business relationship. Jacomyntie, two more beers, here, please!"

Chapter 4

The following morning, Sean presented himself at the Vieles' front door.   The house, with its high stoop and step-gabled, brick-faced façade, had cost Aernout quite a few beaver pelts the year before, but it had been well worth the expense.   Located halfway between Pearl Street and Fort Albany, it was one of the first buildings the savages passed when entering the town to trade and Viele was in a position to make a first offer on the best peltries coming to Albany.

Like most of the houses in the town, the front room was where Aernout conducted business.   It was undecorated.   Rough wood planks comprised the walls, floor, counter and the shelves on which some trade goods were on display.   There was a large scale for weighing peltries in the right rear corner.   To the left was a small fireplace in which a fire had been laid. Two short stools comprised the remaining furnishings.

Behind the shop was the kitchen, with a fireplace large enough for a man to stand in. Upstairs, the family's sleeping quarters were arranged around a common area that was heated by the chimney from the kitchen. There was a cellar below the kitchen which was reached through a trap door in the floor. While primarily a storage area for trade goods, it could also serve as a hiding place for the women and children of the house in the event that hostile savages breached the town's defenses.

When Sean had knocked, Aernout opened the door, saying, "Welcome, welcome, lad," and ushered him into the room. Aernout had shaved but still wore deerskins and moccasins.

"Where are your things?" asked Viele.

"I'm wearing them," responded Sean.

"Well... harrumph... when you have some belongings, you can put them under the counter. There is a pallet rolled up under there and blankets as well."

Sean looked, again, around the room. He had expected to find piles of furs and stacks of trade goods, like iron pots, tomahawks, muskets, iron ingots for musket balls and kegs of powder or rum. Instead, only cheap trinkets, such as glass beads, small mirrors and pots of vermillion sat on the shelves.

Noticing the look on Sean's face, Aernout said, "What's the problem, lad? Not what you expected?"

"Truth be told, Mister Viele," said Sean, "It's not. I expected to see more trade goods and, perhaps, even some furs."

"Well, sorry to disappoint you, lad, but you're just a few months too late. We Albany traders do the majority of our business during *Handelstijd*, or high trading season, in June and July. Then, in August and September, we ship whatever furs we've bought to Manhattan for transshipment to Holland. So, at the moment, there are no furs and only the few trade goods that were left over from the summer."

"I see," said Sean. "In that case, since there are so few trade goods left, I might assume that you had a good year."

"Yes, you could... But it was middling. This year, the Iroquois, do you know who they are?"

"Yes, sir. They are the five Indian tribes that live directly west of Albany. Because of their proximity to the colony, they are your main source of furs. And, because of their proximity, they also present the greatest hindrance to other tribes who may want to trade at Albany."

"Good, good. You keep your ears open and you listen. Where was I? Oh, yes... This year the Seneca, the Iroquois nation that is furthest west, spent the spring and summer intercepting French traders traveling between Michilimackinac and Montreal. They ambushed French canoes full of furs, stole the furs and brought them here to trade."

"So, you deal in stolen goods?"

"Lad, we don't care how the *wilden* get their furs just as long as they bring them here to trade and not to Montreal. Besides, the French do the same. It's business, Sean, plain and simple. Nothing more, nothing less. If you have a problem with that, tell me now before we both waste our time."

"No, sir. No problem. I just wanted to get it clear in my mind."

"Good! Now, as it's Autumn, there's no trading to be done. This time of year, after they've made sure that their families have enough meat for the winter, the *wilden* raid each other's territory. The raids give their young men the opportunity to prove their bravery.

"In the early winter, the *wilden* seldom venture out except to check their trap lines. Later, after the Winter Solstice, when it's the coldest, they'll seek furs in earnest. Winter pelts are the best and most valuable because they are the thickest. Then, in Spring and early Summer, they start bringing their furs here or to Montreal.

"So, we need to organize your apprenticeship around these realities. Right now, before the snow flies, I'll take you out to familiarize you with the surroundings outside of the palisades. It's information you'll need come spring. I want you to know all the paths that the *wilden* use to reach Albany. Then, once the snow starts to fall and we're trapped inside, you'll start learning Dutch and Iroquois, and perhaps some French, and the business side of the fur trade."Sounds interesting. When do we start?"

"As soon as we get you some clothes that are more suited to the frontier. You need deerskin breeches and moccasins, and a broad-brimmed hat to keep the sun off your head. Also,

you'll need some basic equipment... a musket...
Can you shoot?"

"Aye, both muskets and pistols. Every
sailor needed to shoot in case we had to repel
pirates."

"Good. You'll also need a hand ax, shot,
and a shot bag, as well as powder and powder
horns..."

"That sounds like it will cost a lot of
money..." said Sean, hesitatingly.

"Nay. I have everything you need.
You're now my apprentice, and it's my
responsibility to make sure that you have the
tools needed to do your job. Stay here. I'll be
right back."

Moments later, Viele returned with his
arms full. Behind him came Garret and Philip,
each carrying two pails of water. After putting
the pails down, they were introduced to Sean.
They left and returned with a wooden tub. The
boys emptied the pails of water into the tub and
left.

Holding out a pair of deerskin leggings,
Viele said, "Get undressed."

Sean undressed and took the leggings
from Viele. He no sooner had them on than he
realized that they were too large. "Mister Viele,"
he said, "These don't fit."

"No. They don't. That's what the tub of
water is for. Now, slip on the moccasins and
climb into the tub.

"With the moccasins?"

"Aye. With the moccasins. Now sit there
until the skin is soaked through."

Shortly, Sean said, "I think it's fully soaked."

"Good. Now get out of the tub and stand in front of the fire and keep slowly turning. As the skin dries, you'll feel it shrinking until it feels like a second skin."

As the deerskin dried, Sean noted that it did, indeed, fit much better.

"For the best fit, you'll need to wear them until they are totally dry. Now," said Viele, "you can put your shirt back on. Leave it hanging outside of the breeches. Put this belt around your waist."

A knife in a sheath hung from the belt.

But, Mister Viele, I have my own knife."

"Let me see it."

When Sean held his knife up for inspection, Viele laughed uproariously. "You call that a knife?   It's only good for picking your teeth!"

Hurt, Sean retorted, "It has served me well!"

Viele took the knife from Sean and held it next to the new one. Sean's knife was about half the size of the one Viele had given him.

"In the wilderness, you need a real knife... One that can cut leather, disembowel and butcher a deer, and protect you in a fight at close quarters... You're right-handed, correct?"

"Aye."

Viele hung a shot pouch around Sean's neck so that the strap crossed his chest and hung at his right side. The same was done to a powder horn, except it hung at Sean's left side. A second powder horn was hung to his right side, over the shot pouch.

"Which horn has the fine powder?"

"The one on the right," Viele said. "There's a new flint in the lock. You'll find cotton wadding and more flints in the shot pouch."

Finally, he tucked a hand ax in the belt, set a broad-brimmed hat upon Sean's head and handed him a musket.

Looking Sean up and down, Viele proclaimed, "Now, you look like a real frontiersman!"

With that, Viele led Sean outside, up Jonkers Street and out the gate into the wilderness.

Over the next two months, Sean and Viele spent their daylight hours exploring the territory between Hudson's river and Schenectady.

They rode on what was grandly called the King's Highway, although it was no more than a rutted cart path between the two communities. Because the area was mostly pine barrens, and the ground too sandy to support crops, they passed only a very few farms. Their passing caused clouds of beautiful, bright blue butterflies to rise and scatter. Sean had never seen their like and, when he asked Aernout about them, he admitted that he, too, had only ever seen them here.

They often went off the beaten path, seeking trails used by the Indians. They rode north to the Mohawk River and a waterfall that Aernout said was called *"cohoes"* in Iroquois, meaning "wrecked canoe." The cascade was a quarter-mile wide and the water dropped sixty feet through a slate gorge, so that the river could meet the level of Hudson's river a little further east.

The area to the south of Albany, as far as the river called Norman's Kill, was virtually all farmland. "Although only a few *wilden* travel down Norman's Kill to trade," explained Aernout, "you'll still need to include it in your rounds."

In the beginning, Viele led Sean. Then, as time went on, Aernout would name a landmark and have Sean lead them to it.

"Come Spring, you'll be my agent. You'll be out here with gifts for the *wilden* to induce them to trade only with me. That's why it's so important for you to know the lay of the land," Viele explained.

"You mean, I'll be a *boschloper*?"

"Oh, you know about the *boschlopers*... Aye. You'll be a *boschloper*. But you won't be buying furs to smuggle into Albany. First, it can be expensive if you're caught. Sheriff Pretty earns a good portion of his salary from the fines imposed on smugglers. Second, we have enough excitement dealing with furs smuggled from Schenectady by my stepbrother, Cornelis. Officially, furs can only be traded in Albany, and only those furs can be shipped from Manhattan. Of course, we could sell Cornelis' furs in Boston, but it's too expensive and dangerous to move them overland for such a distance."

While Sean familiarized himself with the surroundings, he and Viele also hunted to fill the larder of the Viele family and their tavern for the winter. Under Viele's tutelage, Sean became a crack shot, able to bring down a deer on the run or a goose in flight. He learned how to trap small game, like rabbits. He also learned how to clean and butcher all manner of wildlife, and enough about herbs and poultices to survive in the wilderness.

Once the temperatures dropped and the snow began to fall, they moved indoors. Sean, Garret and Philip were tutored in Dutch by the boys' mother and Iroquois by their father. Since Sean was only a little older than the boys, he never felt strange or uncomfortable about learning with them. He also met Abel Marrion, a *courier-des-bois* who had left Canada to live with an Oneida woman and who now traded at Albany. Marrion was more than happy to help Sean learn some useful French words.

In addition, Sean worked closely with Aernout learning the trade of fur trading: the value of different trade goods; how to grade the quality of different furs; how to assess the value of a fur, in trade goods or *sewant*; which trade goods were most popular among the *wilden*; which savages could be trusted and which not; which were most likely to bring the best furs to trade; and, how to bargain with them. This last was extremely important, Viele emphasized, "because the *wilden* are crafty and canny businessmen."

Spring came, and each morning before dawn, Sean left the town in search of Indians with furs. Whenever he encountered an Indian with a load of furs, he would practice his slowly-improving Iroquois, offer small presents and tell the man that Viele offered the best trades in Albany and then take him to Viele's house.

Sean noticed that many agents offered rum to the Indians to get them drunk. Aernout refused to use strong drink as an incentive, "I have never had the need to resort to such low tricks. As often as not, the *wilden*, once they're drunk, are robbed of their furs or cheated by the traders. "

Handelstijd arrived with the summer and large groups of Indians began arriving in Albany. They would display their furs on the plain in front of the fort and wait for the traders to come to them. Along with the other traders, Sean and Aernout would inspect the furs and bid on them. It was during this process that Sean had the chance to practice what he had learned about bargaining with the *wilden*. He also learned that the Dutch approached the bidding wars like a game to be played with enthusiasm and enjoyment. As with a game, each day's "winner" was required to stand his opposition to a round of drinks come evening. The furs that Aernout and Sean purchased were inventoried and taken to a warehouse near the town dock, where they were kept under lock and key, and guarded around the clock.

In August, the two men supervised the loading of those furs, plus the furs which Aernout's brother had had smuggled into Albany onto a yacht, and then sailed with them to Manhattan. There, the furs were unloaded into a dockside warehouse leased by Viele and again secured against theft. It was during this trip that Sean met Aernout's oldest son, Cornelis, and his wife, and was able to renew his acquaintance with Megan O'Reilly.

In front of the Vieles, Sean and Megan behaved as if they had never met. But Sean had not forgotten his promise to her. The first time they were alone together he presented her with a prime beaver pelt in appreciation of the kindness she had shown him and Dick Fielding.

During his earlier visit to Manhattan, Sean had only seen the seamier parts of town, and even that was no more than a blur, as he and Dick had run through it. This time, he saw the business district of town and was introduced by Aernout and Cornelis to the international commerce in furs. They went to the Customs House, where the value of the furs to be shipped was declared and the appropriate tax paid to the colonial government. They also visited the City Tavern. The tavern, which had once served as Manhattan's *Stadhuis*, was popular among the city's businessmen; indeed, deals were as often made at its tables as anywhere else in the city. On great boards around the room were posted notices of ships entering or leaving the harbor and information regarding their cargoes. Too, information was available regarding shipmasters who were seeking cargo for transport anywhere in the world.

Upon entering the smoke-filled establishment, Cornelis was greeted warmly by many of the well-dressed patrons.

"'Tis a great many friends ye have, Mr. Viele," remarked Sean.

"Ach, Sean," said Cornelis once all three had their beers in hand, "they're not all friends! No, indeed! Many are competitors and some, I am sure, may even be enemies! But, in the small world of business here in Manhattan, we like to keep up appearances. We smile while we try to cheat each other. The fur trade here in the colonial capital is every bit as ruthless as it is in the wilderness."

Upon their return to Albany, Aernout proclaimed Sean's apprenticeship to have been a success and promoted him to employee.

Chapter 5

Sean's second year with Viele passed pretty much like the first, only now he was earning a wage. The highlight of Sean's year as an employee was a three-month trek with Aernout in Autumn to visit the primary castles of each of the Iroquois nations. "You met most of the sachems during *Handelstijd*, but it's important that you interact with them in their natural environment," the Dutchman said. "The sachems are not only leaders of their castles, but also the primary fur brokers for each of the clans. To earn their positions, they have proven themselves to be good businessmen and are trusted by others to bargain for them. It is also important that they see you and recognize you as my representative. They'll know that if they cheat you, they cheat me!"

Sean realized just how highly regarded Aernout was when, in each castle they visited, they were received as honored guests. Sitting around the cooking fires in the longhouses, he had the opportunity to see Viele at work. Called "Aerie, the Interpreter" by the Iroquois, he was the consummate diplomat and businessman, distributing gifts, speaking respectfully to the sachems, flirting with the clan mothers, discussing frontier politics with all, and generally being outgoing and friendly to everyone. Soon, Sean was practicing his own version of what he had observed and was quickly accepted by the Iroquois and regarded as Aernout's right hand.

While they traveled, Sean learned that the Iroquois were more than warriors, hunters and trappers. "They are also excellent farmers," Viele told him, "perhaps the best among all the different nations I have seen. They specialize in what they call the Three Sisters... corn, beans and squash. Because of this focus on agriculture, they move their castles regularly in search of fertile fields."

On occasion, the sachems of the different clans, Wolf, Bear and Turtle, would argue over whose longhouse the two traders would sleep in. At first, Sean thought it was just diplomacy when they stayed in different longhouses. But he soon realized that Arnout was sleeping with a different woman in each village. Finally, curiosity drove him to ask Aernout about it.

"It's the way of the *wilden*," Aernout explained. "In general, it's about the clan and tribe... keeping them strong. Unlike in our society, there are no proscriptions about consensual sex between unmarried persons, except that it has to be at the discretion of the woman. A single woman can take any man to her bed. Young women take men who can give them sons for the clan and the tribe. Older women, like the ones I stay with, want men to warm their beds of a night."

"But, what about marriage?"

"If you're asking me about me and Gerritje, make no mistake: I love her. She is everything to me. She is my wife, my friend and my partner. An Indian woman is good for keeping you warm at night when you are in the wilderness for months on end, but you need a good Christian woman to give you a home and family. You have no idea how contented a man can be if he finds the right woman. Look at me. Gerritje and I have been married for twenty-four years, we have eight wonderful children, and I forget how many grandchildren, and I am just as happy now as I was the day we were wed.

"However, if you're asking about the *wilden*... They have a different point of view from Christians. Now, there are rules about family and clan relationships, of course, but, generally, when an Iroquois man and woman decide to marry, the man just moves into the longhouse of the woman's family. Any children that they have are cared for communally. When boys are old enough, they are taken by their mothers' brothers to be taught hunting, trapping and war craft. Girls learn their duties from their mothers and other women of the clan. If, at some point, one or the other partner decides to end the relationship, the man just leaves the longhouse and returns to his own family."

"What if one of the partners doesn't want to end the relationship? Can he or she fight against the break-up?"

"Of course. But, the community mediates any disagreements and keeps things from getting out of hand."

Although Sean had not told Aernout, the truth was that he was a virgin and, as a Catholic virgin, he found himself intrigued and more than a little excited by the Iroquois' approach to sex and relationships.

Shortly thereafter, the two men arrived at Onontague, the primary castle of the Onondaga. Aernout explained that, because the Onondaga were located in the middle of Iroquois country, it was here that the Iroquois council fire was kept and where the sachems of the Five Nations would meet to decide matters of importance to the entire confederacy.

This time, both men were invited to stay in the longhouse of the Wolf clan. The longhouse was like the others in which they had stayed during their trip. It was about 25-feet wide and nearly 100-feet long. On either side of a central aisle, with four large cooking fires, were an equal number of sleeping compartments, each of which provided private living space for a family. Privacy was provided by deerskins that could be draped over the fronts of the compartments. Because the Iroquois were a matriarchal society, all of the families living in each longhouse were related through the female line, with the eldest woman acting as longhouse "mother."

That night, after they had shared a meal with the residents of the longhouse, Sean went to the sleeping compartment which had been assigned to him. There, he found a woman waiting. She was wearing a deerskin dress, elaborately decorated with porcupine quills that covered her from neck to mid-calf, but left her arms bare. She smiled at him. He smiled back. She extended her hand to him. Nervously, he took it. Without a word, she led him into the sleeping compartment.

The compartment, like all the others, consisted of a low platform, about six-feet wide, spread with cornhusk mats and covered with furs. Beneath and above it were storage spaces with shelves for extra mats, baskets, herbs and other household and personal items.

Sean and the woman removed their moccasins and knelt on the platform looking at each other. He wasn't sure just how old she was, but he was certain that he was younger than she.

She touched his cheek. "I have never seen any white man as white as you," she said. "Nor have I ever seen anyone with so many spots on their skin."

"Oh, those are called freckles. They are very common among the people of my tribe, the Irish, especially among those who have red hair like mine."

She reached up and touched his hair. She took a lock and rubbed it between her fingers. "So, it is really that color?" she asked.

"Aye, it is. Tell me, what is your name?"

"This woman is called Makkitotosimew. Is your hair, there, the same color?" she asked, pointing generally in the direction of his waist.

"Aye."

"Show me."

Sean undid his belt and pulled his shirt up over his head. Before removing his leggings, he told her, "Ye must undress, as well."

"Wait. After this woman sees you, she will close the drape and undress. You do not want to see an old woman."

"Ye are not an old woman. I want to see all of ye."

Apprehensive, she took off her dress. She wore nothing underneath.

Sean stared at her. She was the first naked woman he had ever seen and she was beautiful! Her skin was smooth and her breasts, although they sagged a little, mesmerized him. He was more excited than ever before in his life.

She put her left hand against his right shoulder and gently pushed him onto his back. She pulled his breeches off and, just before closing the deerskin drape, exclaimed, "Aiyee! It is the same color!"

In the dark, she straddled his body and slowly lowered herself onto him. When she began to move up and down, Sean thought he had died and gone to heaven.

Later, after they had both been satisfied, she lay in his arms, with her head on his left shoulder and her left leg across his middle.

"Was that the first time you have been with a woman?" she asked, looking up at him.

"Aye," he admitted.

"This woman could tell. You were so excited that your hands shook," she said, smiling sweetly.

To change the subject, he asked, "Why does a beautiful woman like yourself not have a man?"

"My man was killed by a Huron devil," she replied in a hard voice.

"I am sorry," he said sincerely. "Do you have children?"

"This woman has no children," she said sadly. "Perhaps this woman will make a baby with you?"

Sean rolled over, facing her, and kissed her softly while caressing her body. Soon, they came together again. This time more slowly and deliberately.

Later, they did it again. Sean could not get enough of Makkitotosimew; nor she of him. "Ah, O-Kahl, I do so like sleeping with a young man!" she exclaimed. "You bring this old woman much pleasure!" she exclaimed.

For the next two nights, Sean slept with Makkitotosimew as she taught him much about how to pleasure a woman.

When it was time to leave, Sean felt a sense of loss. But he was not allowed to show it.

In keeping with Iroquois tradition, Makkitotosimew always ignored him when they were in public. She had told him that, among the Iroquois, when a man and woman wanted each other, they did not look at each other or speak together in the presence of others. If they did, one or both could lose standing before the rest of the village.

The next stop for the two traders was at Gayagaanhe, the primary Cayuga castle. There, Sean became aware that there were a number of women who looked at him in the same way Makkitotosimew had. The pattern was continued at Gandagaro, the eastern-most Seneca castle, and at Chemung, the nation's western-most castle. Sean's knowledge of how to please a woman expanded and his technique was polished with each subsequent encounter with an Iroquois woman.

On the return trek, Sean was looking forward to seeing Makkitotosimew again. But, when they arrived at Onontague, he found that she was now promised to another man. Apparently, the man had wanted her ever since she was widowed, but was only spurred to action when he became jealous of her sleeping with Sean

Part II

June-September 1684

Chapter 6

"Unggh!"

Sean slowly awoke and stretched. Lying there, he thought about how quickly the past three years had passed. He was now nineteen years old, and this was the last trading season that he would work with Aernout Viele. During the time that he'd been with Aernout, as apprentice, employee and, now, partner, Sean had learned enough Dutch to converse with his neighbors, had mastered Iroquois, could understand and speak a little French, and had even picked up a few words in Algonquin. Most importantly, he had become quite adept at trading with the natives.

For the past month, he and Aernout had been on the trail. But, even though it was the trading season, this was not a trading expedition. Rather, they had been hired by agents of William Penn to negotiate the purchase of the Susquehanna River valley from the Iroquois.

Penn wanted to add the valuable land to his colony that lay to the south of New York.

Sean and Viele had traveled 125 miles on foot and by canoe from Albany to Onontague. There, around the Iroquois Council Fire, they had met with sachems of the Mohawk, Oneida, Onondaga and Cayuga nations and put Penn's offer to them. Now, on their way home, Viele and Sean were at the Mohawk village of Caughnawaga, the last stop before civilization.

Sean and Viele had arrived the previous evening and had been invited by Achagari, the Turtle Clan sachem, to stay the night in the clan longhouse. The "mother" of this longhouse was called Nadie.

Sean smiled as the body next to him stirred. There, naked, with her bottom pressed up against him, was Kai, the young Mohawk woman who had invited him to share her bed for the night. She and Sean were not strangers. He had seen her whenever he and Aernout had visited Caughnawaga and he knew that she was Nadie's daughter, but it was not until the previous evening that he had thought of her not as a child, but as an enticing, adult woman.

Kai had long, shining black hair that hung, unbound, to her tiny waist. Her obsidian eyes were bright and almond-shaped. Her skin was soft and silky, and her narrow, straight nose, full lips and high cheekbones gave her face a regal look. She was tall for an Indian woman, with the top of her head just touching Sean's chin. Her full breasts, with their dark areolas and firm nipples, begged to be caressed. Also, she thoroughly enjoyed lovemaking. So Sean had applied all that he had ever learned to satisfying Kai. He found himself wanting to please her more than any other woman with whom he had slept.

Lying there, he remembered how they had exhausted each other the night before. The thought alone was enough to arouse him, but then he felt her hand slide over his hip, caressing him. Her fingers moved through the hair at his lower belly. "Oh-Kahl, this woman finds your red hair to be very attractive."

Sean gasped as she closed her hand around him.

"My God, woman," he whispered in Iroquois. "Ye are going to kill me!"

She giggled playfully as he responded to her ministrations. When he could stand it no longer, he pushed her over and, rolling over her, entered her. Slowly at first, then ever more rapidly, they moved together as they approached their climaxes.

Sean tried to hold back. He didn't want the sensations to stop. But, it was impossible. He began to climax and, just as soon as he started, she did as well. He collapsed on top of her.

For a few minutes, they just lay there in each other's arms catching their breath. "Oh-Kahl, this woman hopes to make a baby with you. A boy baby. I am sure that he will grow up to be handsome and brave and that he will bring honor to the *Ganienkeh*."

Then, as he started to roll off of her, Sean heard Viele call to him.

"Sean, are you awake? Rouse yourself! It's time we were leaving. I want to reach Schenectady before dark."

Sean kissed Kai and began to pull on his leggings.

She got to her knees behind Sean, put her arms around him, and rubbed her breasts against his back. He could feel her hard nipples as she held him.

"Oh-Kahl," she said. "You come back soon to this woman? When you come back, I will let no other woman take you to her sleeping mat."

"Aye, I will come back soon," Sean said, reaching into his pack of trade goods. "Here is a gift -- a pretty brooch for a pretty girl. Wear it so that the other women will see that I am yours."

She squealed with delight and threw her arms around his neck. Laughing and disengaging himself from her embrace, he climbed out of the compartment and joined Viele, who was sitting at one of the fires, sipping a gourd of mint tea.

"Here," Viele said, laughing while gesturing at a second gourd, "I think you could use this. You'll find it to be both invigorating and restorative." Sean could feel his face redden as he took the gourd and sipped the hot liquid.

Just then, Nadie approached them, saying, "Aerie! Take this for your journey," as she gave Aernout a deerskin bag containing ground corn and maple sugar. The mixture could be eaten dry or mixed with water. There was enough for both men.

After Sean had finished his tea, he joined Viele in eating some of the stew that was cooking in a pot over the fire. Day and night, one of the young women of the longhouse tended one of the cooking fires, to keep it from going out, and kept a kettle of corn and beans simmering which could be shared by all.

Finished with their breakfast, Sean and Viele gathered their belongings, expressed their thanks to Nadie and left the longhouse. Outside, Sean saw that Kai was leaving to work in the fields with the other women. As Sean watched her out of the corner of his eye, he thought again that she was the most beautiful woman he had ever seen. Kai was wearing only a long, wrap-around, deerskin skirt decorated with porcupine quills. Like all Iroquois women in the summer, she was naked from the waist up. The sight of her gave Sean pause, making him wish that he did not have to leave.

The two traders left the village and, at the river, loaded their packs and muskets into their elm bark canoe and pushed off. As they began to paddle, Sean turned to watch as Kai and the other women walked in the other direction. When the canoe reached a bend in the river, she was hidden from view.

"Well, Sean, it looks like you've made a conquest! It certainly did not take you long to learn the ways of the *wilden*. I knew you were a quick study the first time I lay eyes on you!" joked Aernout.

Sean, in the front of the canoe, hoped Viele couldn't see him blush with embarrassment.

Viele said, "Come now. Stop dreaming and put your back into your stroke! I want to get back to civilization." And, setting a quick but comfortable rhythm, they paddled down the river.

It was a beautiful summer morning, warm, but not hot, with scarcely a cloud in the sky. The river's current, flowing eastward toward Hudson's river, carried them along and allowed them to maintain a good pace with a minimum amount of effort.

They had been traveling about three hours when, suddenly, "Thunk!" An arrow had struck the side of the canoe. Then, a musket shot rang out, raising a small fountain of water about a yard from the canoe.

"There!" cried Viele. "On the right bank!"

Sean turned and saw a group of six howling savages as a volley of shots rang out. He felt a slight breeze as a musket ball flew past his ear.

"Huron! Hurry, before they get the range!" cried Viele as he turned the canoe toward the far bank. As the canoe started to turn, Sean heard Aernout cry out in pain. Sean looked over his shoulder and saw that an arrow had gone through Aernout's right shoulder.

"I'm all right! Turn around and paddle," Aernout ordered.

More shots rang out and splashes followed the canoe as Sean paddled hard. The Indians ran along the shore, trying to keep pace with the canoe while firing. Eventually, the canoe began to pull away. When they could no longer hear the shouts of the savages, Sean stopped paddling, allowing the canoe to drift, and tried to calm down.

"Aernout, we've got to do something about that arrow!"

"Aye. Just get us to shore and then we can take care of it."

Once they reached the bank, Sean pulled the canoe ashore and helped Aernout get out.

When Aernout was seated comfortably on the grass, Sean built a small fire and gave him a flask of brandy, saying, "Here, take a good healthy drink of this."

After Aernout had drunk, Sean used his knife to score the shaft and carefully broke the arrow just above the point. Going behind Aernout, he grasped the shaft firmly and, holding Aernout's arm still, pulled it back out through the shoulder, eliciting a howl of pain from the older man. After cleaning the wound thoroughly with brandy, Sean heated his knife over the fire until it was red hot and cauterized the wound, eliciting another cry of pain from Aernout. Sean then went into the woods and found some moss, which he applied to both the entry and exit wounds, binding it with a strip of cloth torn from a clean shirt.

Once Sean was done, Aernout said, "Thank you, lad. I don't think the arrow hit anything important."

"No, it seemed to come out cleanly," Sean replied.

"But, that was close! We were lucky that they didn't have canoes. They would have had our hair by now!"

"But what are they doing so deep in Mohawk territory? And, only six of them!" remarked Sean.

"Rest assured, lad, this close to Schenectady, there are more than six of the heathens. But, your question is a good one: What are they doing here? My first thought was that they were part of a larger war party. But, it is too early in the year for a war party. Perhaps, they are scouting for the French in preparation for an attack in the fall…"

"Aernout, do ye think ye can travel?"

"Aye, lad, I can. But I can't paddle."

"Don't worry. I can handle the canoe alone."

With that, they got back into the canoe, this time with Sean in the rear.

They continued downriver, much more alert than they had been. With a minimum of talking and only one, short break for Sean to rest and eat a few handfuls of the ground corn and maple sugar, they reached Schenectady just as the sun was starting to set.

Sean pulled the canoe onto the shore, gathered his and Aernout's belongings and, followed by his friend, entered the stockade and went directly to the tavern owned by Aernout's stepbrother, Cornelis.

The tavern was a simple, two-story structure, built of rough-hewn planks, with a shingle roof. The public space, in the front of the building, consisted of four tables with benches as well as a counter, behind which stood Cornelis surrounded by kegs of beer and casks of rum. As the two men entered, Cornelis greeted them, gesturing for them to sit at one of the tables. He called a servant to carry their muskets and packs upstairs to the loft, and brought three mugs of beer.

It was then that he noticed the blood on Aernout's shirt.

"What happened to you?" he asked.

"I took an arrow when we were attacked by a band of Huron midway between here and Caughnawaga."

"There's no doctor in the village, but maybe one of the old women could take a look at your wound."

"It's not necessary. Sean took good care of it. We'll be back in Albany tomorrow and, if necessary, I'll have Abraham Van Tricht look at it. About the Huron, perhaps you should alert the watch. We saw only six, but I suspect there were more in the vicinity."

Cornelis immediately sent a servant with a message to Sander Glen, Jr., one of the village's magistrates. "Sander will make the necessary arrangements to increase the watch," he said.

"Now, Aernout," Cornelis continued. "Will the *wilden* sell the land to Penn?"

"Aye, they will. But I am concerned that, once Penn gets his hands on the Susquehanna

Valley, his people will set up trading posts and we will see furs going to their colony and not to Albany. That means, of course, that you folks here in Schenectady will not have a chance to try to intercept and buy them before they get to us."

"According to the Cayuga," interjected Sean, "traders from Penn's colony have already traveled up the Susquehanna to trade with them and the Seneca. That means that we must not only stop the sale, but somehow keep other traders from getting to the Iroquois or, eventually, the Far Indians."

"I do not like the sound of that at all," said Cornelis. "What can be done?"

"I really don't know," said Aernout, "but I hope the Indian Commission will have an idea. I plan to find out as soon as we reach Albany."

"Be sure to let me know what you learn. Now, what do you say to some food?

Just then, Aernout's two children who lived in Schenectady, Aernout, Jr. and Mary Vrooman and their families came into the tavern, having heard of their Aernout's arrival. As they entered, Aernout told Sean, "Now, no mention of my being wounded. I don't want to be fussed over by Mary. She'll act like I'm dead and almost buried." He then went upstairs and changed his shirt.

Returning, he exchanged greetings with his family and called out, "Cornelis! Bring us some food and more drink. 'Tis time for a family reunion."

It was quite late that night before Sean and Viele were able to retire. They climbed the

stairs and fell, exhausted, onto the corn husk
mattresses

Chapter 7

"Aernout, how is the shoulder this morning?" asked Sean as he and Aernout ate their breakfast of brown bread and beer.

"It hurts to move the arm but, otherwise, fine," responded Viele.

"Here, let me take a look at it," said Sean as he removed the bandage and moss from Aernout's arm.

"Not bad," he observed as he replaced the bandage. "No oozing, no pus, no inflammation. I guess I would make a pretty good doctor!"

"You haven't gotten me home, yet!" cautioned Aernout.

Shouldering their packs and muskets, they bade farewell to Cornelis and went outside. Waiting there was young Aernout, with two saddled horses.

"As you requested, father, here are two good mounts to hasten your journey home," he said.

"Thank you, son. I'll return them in a few days."

"Please give our love to mother."

"I will. You take good care of my grandchildren!"

Sean and Viele mounted and were quickly through the village gate and riding east toward Albany. Owing to Aernout's wound, they took their time and, at midday, they veered off the trail and rode to the *cohoes* waterfall.

There, they rested and talked while their horses drank.

Viele observed, "Despite what the *wilden* say and what Penn's people believe, the Susquehanna River valley does not belong to the Five Nations."

"But they say that they won the valley when they defeated the Susquehannock," Sean replied.

"That is what they say but, ten years ago, I was the interpreter at councils between the Five Nations and the colonies of Maryland and Virginia. During the negotiations, the sachems thanked those colonies for having defeated the Susquehannock. So, if anything, the land belongs to Maryland or Virginia!"

"In that case, the Iroquois are selling land that does not belong to them!"

Aernout laughed derisively. "Of course they are! That is what the *wilden* have done since the first white man stepped upon these shores! You have to realize that only Europeans think that we can actually own a piece of land. The *wilden* believe that the land belongs to no one person, tribe or people. Rather, they believe that they have been given temporary custody of the land by the Creator. So, when they 'sell' land to us, they think that they are only transferring custody. Thus, it is all right for the Five Nations to sell that land because the English don't really 'own' it either.

"But the ownership issue is not our problem. It's the competition from Penn's people that worries me! It's distressing enough to have the French stealing our furs! We don't need another English colony doing it!"

"But, why would the Seneca and Cayuga go all the way to Penn's colony? Surely, we offer better prices for their furs!"

"Aye, we do." Aernout replied. "But they are closer to the headwaters of the Susquehanna than to Albany. Also, they would avoid paying tribute to the Mohawk for crossing their territory."

"And, what about the traders from Penn's colony who are already visiting the Iroquois? What can be done about them?"

"That, lad, is a much thornier issue. The solution to that problem lies higher up in the colony than you or I, or even the Indian Commission. It's inter-colonial affairs and, I'm sure, will eventually require the governor's involvement."

"So, what will we do?"

"We will do what we were hired to do. We will tell Penn's representatives that the *wilden* are eager to sell. Then, you and I will meet with the Indian Commission and let them know what's afoot. Perhaps they will have some idea of what can be done. Come. It's time that we continue."

Sean and Viele remounted and continued southeast toward Albany, finally reaching the rich, bottom land along Hudson's river that belonged to Rensselaerwyck.

The sun was getting low in the sky when they came in sight of the town. Aernout said, "We'll stop in the fort to report our sighting of the Huron, and to let Penn's representatives know we've returned."

As they approached the fort, Sean and Viele saw some activity around one of the huts outside the gates. At the hut nearest the gate, two native women were roasting corn. From the interior of the hut, a male voice called out, "Aerie the Interpreter, it pleases this man to see you."

Two middle-aged Iroquois, dressed only in breech clouts, in deference to the heat, appeared in the doorway of the hut. "Come, Aerie. Sit and talk with us. We have rum!"

They were both sachems, Adjechne, an Onondaga, and Araquartho, a Cayuga. Both traded regularly with Viele. Adjechne was the taller of the two, almost as tall as Sean's six feet, but with broader shoulders and a regal demeanor. He was exceptionally fit and very much a warrior. Araquartho, on the other hand, was short and stout, with a pot belly hanging over his breech clout. Despite his somewhat comical appearance, Araquartho was a shrewd trader, a sophisticated negotiator, and a fearless fighter. Both men were elaborately tattooed.

Each had his head shaved except for a scalp lock at the back. From their slurred speech and unsteady stances, it was obvious that they had started drinking quite early in the day.

Turning to Sean, Aernout said, "I wondered why they were not at Onontague with the other sachems. Let's find out what they are doing in Albany." Then, as they dismounted, he said loudly, "Of course, my friends, we will join you for talk and a drink."

Both white men had to bend as they entered the low doorway and, inside, only Araquartho could stand up straight. The interior of the hut was cramped, dark and stifling. The smoke from a fire in the middle of the room tried, but didn't always manage, to find its way through the hole in the middle of the roof.

Sean found that he could barely breathe from the combination of the smoke, the heat and the smell of the bear grease with which the Indians had coated their bodies to ward off insects.

After the four men had seated themselves on skins thrown on the ground, Araquartho said, "This man is always happy to see his brother, Aerie." Adjechne grunted in agreement.

"Now we will truly drink," said Araquartho, as he drank and then passed a flask of rum to Viele.

"I, too, am always happy to see my brothers, Araquartho and Adjechne," said Aernout. Taking a deep draught of rum, he said, "Now I have truly drunk," and passed the flask back to Araquartho. "You know my young brother, O'Cathail."

"Oh-Kahl," Araquartho said, "you are Aerie's brother and so you are Araquartho's brother, also."

Araquartho then passed the flask to Adjechne. He saluted Sean with it, took a long drink and said, "The brother of Aerie is Adjechne's brother." He then passed Sean the flask. Sean took a drink, feeling the cheap liquor burn its way down his throat, and said, "Now I have truly drunk! It pleases me to be known as the brother of Araquartho and Adjechne."

After the flask had gone around one more time, Aernout said, "My brothers, why are you here in the heat of summer, and not in your castles?"

"We had come to Orange to trade but, when we were finished, *Quidor* asked us to meet with him," said Araquartho, referring to Albany's mayor, Pieter Schuyler. "He said that he and the other white leaders wanted to talk with us about important things. We have been here seven days. Each day we meet with them, and each day they ask us the same questions, about our earlier wars with the Susquehannock, and how we came to own their lands. They ask us if we would stop coming to Orange with our furs if there were places to trade on the Susquehanna River."

"Did they tell you why they wanted to know these things?" asked Aernout.

"Yes," said Adjechne. "They say it is because the Great English Father across the wide water has given land near the valley to his friend, Penn. Now, they say that this Penn wants to add to his lands by buying the valley from the *Haudenosaunee*."

"And, what do you think?" queried Aernout. "Would this be a good thing?"

The two exchanged a glance, and Araquartho responded, "We do not know this Penn. If he is such a good friend of the Great English Father, it might be wise for the *Haudenosaunee* to sell him the land. Perhaps we can make a Covenant Chain with his people as we have with the other English. If we don't, perhaps Penn's English will make war on us."

"And, what about the idea of going to the Susquehanna to trade your furs instead of coming to Albany?"

"Aerie, you and the other Orange traders are brothers to the Cayuga," replied Araquartho. "You have always given us good trade for our furs. Never have we wanted to bring our furs to the French. But, if there are trading posts on the Susquehanna, it would be much easier for us to go there than to come to Orange. It would be difficult for us to turn our backs on our friends at Orange, but we would have to think about it."

"And ye, Adjachne?" asked Sean. "What do ye say? Where would the Onondaga go?"

"This man must tell the truth. It would depend on the trade goods we could get from Penn's English. It would be no harder for us to go there than to come here."

"Thank you, my friends, for speaking the truth," Aernout said. "O'Cathail and I have just returned from Onontague. There, we met with other sachems of the Five Nations and asked the same questions. We were disappointed that you were not there to meet with us, but we are happy to find you here, and to hear your words that echo those of your brothers. Will you be staying longer in Albany to continue talking with the commissioners?"

"No. *Quidor* has said that we can go home."

"When will you leave?"

"We will leave when the sun rises," answered Adjechne.

"Can you stay one more day? Let me speak to *Quidor*. Perhaps there is something you can do for me. Can you wait?"

Araquartho nodded as Adjechne said, "Of course. We will do as you ask."

"Also," Sean interjected, "Ye must be vigilant as ye return to your castles. We were attacked by Huron warriors between Caughnawaga and Schenectady. There may be more lurking in the woods."

"Do not fear for us, my brother," said Araquartho. "The Huron dog has not yet been born who is a match for a Cayuga woman, let alone a warrior like Araquartho."

"The Huron will foul themselves and run like rabbits when they hear the war cry of Adjechne," that sachem said of himself.

"We know that Araquartho and Adjechne are a match for a hundred Huron," replied Aernout. "But we would not be good friends if we did not warn you. So, let us have one more drink. Then we must go."

After they had drunk, Sean and Viele left the two chiefs and rode through the open gate of the fort. Once inside the fort, they turned left, toward the headquarters building. As important representatives of a sister colony, William Haig and James Graham were staying there.

As they rode up, they found Sergeant Jacob Jones standing in front of the residence. Sergeant Jones had been posted to Albany for nearly ten years. He had married a Dutch woman from the town and was planning to stay once he completed his current term of enlistment.

"Sergeant Jones," said Aernout, "Are Mister Haig and Mister Graham inside? And, if so, would you please inform them that we would like a word with them?"

"Certainly, sir," he said and entered the building.

Sean and Viele tied their horses to a post and, while they waited, Aernout said, "Sean, I think that it would be best for now if we told these gentlemen only some of what we learned over the past few weeks. I don't want them to know that we're worried about any possible trading posts, and it would not be good for them to know what Adjechne and Araquartho have been discussing with the Indian Commission."

"Of course, Aernout," Sean replied.

Just then Sergeant Jones returned and said that the two gentlemen were waiting. "You will find them in the library, upstairs," he said.

"Thank you, Sergeant," said Aernout. "Now will you please tell Captain Sheffield that we saw a party of Huron between Schenectady and Caughnawaga? He may want to notify the guard."

"Aye, sir, I'll do that," said Jones. He then gestured for the two men to enter, saying, "After you, gentlemen."

Inside they found a foyer and a central staircase to the second floor. On the left were offices for the governor's staff, as well as the commander of the garrison. On the right was the governor's office.

Sergeant Jones turned to the left while Sean and Viele proceeded up the stairs and, at the top, found the library. Bookcases lined the east and west walls on either side of the staircase. In the middle of the bookcases on the west wall was a door that, as Sean knew from previous visits, led to the governor's chambers. On the east wall, a second door led to two rooms that were used by visiting dignitaries.

The two gentlemen were seated at a round table in front of a window on the north side of the landing. William Haig, the head of the delegation, was a short, rotund man. He was balding, with gray, thinning hair that hung over his collar. He wore glasses and was smoking a pipe. James Graham was slightly taller, and only a little thinner. He was wearing a powdered periwig. Both men were dressed like successful merchants, with white, linen shirts and woolen waistcoats under long woolen coats, white stockings, knee-britches and buckled shoes.

Graham put down the book that he had been reading as Sean and Viele reached the top of the stairs. After greeting Sean and Viele, Graham offered each a drink, "We have a fine French brandy and, of course, good Jamaican rum."

"Rum, if you please, sir," said Aernout.

"And you, O'Cathail?"

"Rum for me, as well. Thank ye, sir," he replied.

Once all had their drinks in hand, had drunken to the king's health and were sitting at the table, Graham said, "Well, Viele, what have you learned?"

"We will, of course, give you a written report," said Aernout. "But, in summary, I can tell you that the savages say that they are willing to sell the land to your colony."

"You spoke with the sachems of all the Five Nations?"

"All but the Seneca," said Sean.

"Why not the Seneca? They are the largest nation in the confederation. They would have to be included in any negotiations," said Graham.

"According to the sachems, the Seneca had no hand in defeating the Susquehannock, so they have no claim to the territory and need not be included in any negotiations," Aernout replied.

"Well, that simplifies things a little. That's fewer sachems with whom we will need to negotiate," said Graham.

"And fewer gifts that we will have to give," Haig added,

"We must be thankful for that," said Graham, chuckling.

"And, how much do the thieves want for the land?" asked Haig.

"They haven't stated a price," said Aernout. "You know how the *wilden* love to bargain. We proposed that, since the chief sachems of all five nations will come to Albany in four weeks' time to meet with *Corlear*, they could meet with you at that time, as well."

"Good. Very good. The sooner the better," said Haig. "But, who is *Corlear*?

"Oh, sorry. *Corlear* is the name that the Iroquois have given the governor."

"Really? What does it mean?"

"Many years ago, Arendt van Curler was the chief trader at Fort Orange for the Dutch West Indies Company. Later, he was one of the first settlers of Schenectady. The Mohawk came to know and respect him. Because he was honest in all his dealings with them, the *wilden* considered him to be a friend. He negotiated the first treaty between the Dutch and the Mohawk, a treaty that has never been broken. Since then, all of the Iroquois have called the colonial governor *'Corlear'* as a sign of respect."

"Very interesting," said Haig. Then, changing the subject, he said, "Now, when can you give us your written report? I must send it to Mister Penn's factor for his approval before negotiations can begin."

"We can have it for you tomorrow afternoon," said Viele. "Is that satisfactory?"

"That will be fine," said Haig. "Then we can prepare our recommendations and Mister Graham can leave for Philadelphia on the next day."

"Thank you, gentlemen, for your efforts on our behalf," said Graham.

"Of course, sir," said Aernout. "Until tomorrow, then."

Viele and Sean left the governor's residence and retrieved their mounts. Sean asked, "Aernout, when do you plan to talk with Mayor Schuyler and the other Indian commissioners?"

"Tomorrow morning," he replied, "after we have written our report, but before I deliver it to Haig. It is too late to do anything more today."

Riding out of the fort, they headed into the town. Reaching the Viele home, they led their horses around the back of the house, past Mistress Viele's vegetable garden to the stable, and unsaddled them. As they did so, one of Viele's teenaged sons, Gerrit, entered and offered to brush them down and feed them.

"Thank you, Gerrit," Sean said.

"Be sure to do a good job," said his father, "And come into the house as soon as you are finished. We will be eating soon."

Sean and Viele walked back to the front of the house and, upon entering, placed their muskets inside the door.

Aernout called, "Halloo! Is anyone at home?"

Sara, the 10-year-old African house slave Viele leased from Johannes Clute, entered the shop from the kitchen in response to his call.

"Sara, tell your mistress that we have returned and that we need a good Christian meal as soon as we have bathed and changed out of these lice-filled deerskins."

"Yes sir," said Sara, as she ran upstairs in search of her mistress.

Soon the house was filled with a clamor as Jacomyntie, who was now engaged to be wed, and Aernout's other teenaged son, Philip, came to greet their father and Sean. At the same time, Gerritje, carrying baby Susanna, came down the stairs.

"*Welkom huis!*" said Gerritje, 'Tis pleased I am to have you safe at home, Mister Viele. And, you as well, Sean, of course," said Mistress Viele. "Your dinner will be ready as soon as you two are cleaned and changed."

Just then, she noticed that Aernout was favoring his right arm and asked, "Mister Viele, what is wrong with your arm?"

"He took an arrow," said Sean.

"It's nothing," insisted Aernout. "Sean took care of it for me."

She soon had Aernout sitting while she removed the bandage and moss. She inspected the wound, smelled it and pronounced, "It appears to be clean and healing well. You did a good job, Sean!"

"Thank ye, Mistress Viele."

After washing the wound with rum and applying a new poultice and a fresh bandage,

Mistress Viele served a welcome meal of venison, boiled cabbage, white bread and beer. All too soon, it was time for bed and the household settled down to sleep.

Chapter 8

The Viele household was awake and bustling at dawn. After breakfast, Sean and Aernout spent two hours preparing their report for Graham and Haig. Then, knowing that the Indian Commission usually began business at midmorning, they left the Viele home and walked down Jonkers Street.

As they walked, Sean and Aernout greeted everyone they passed, many of whom were other fur traders. Sean made a point to stop and chat with Johannes Roseboom. Roseboom was one of the few Albany Dutch who was no longer content to sit in town and wait for furs to come to him. He was planning a trading expedition to the Ottawa at Michilimackinac, at the juncture of Lake Huron and Lake Superior, on the western edge of French territory. Roseboom told Sean and Viele that the more he heard, the more he was convinced that an expedition to the Ottawa had to be successful.

"I have spoken with a number of French traders. They all say that there are more beaver pelts in the west than we could imagine. Abel Marrion has been telling the Ottawa and other Far Indians who trade at Michilimackinac that we will give more and better goods for their furs than the French. So now, he says, they are eager for us to come to trade."

"When do ye think ye will leave?" asked Sean.

"I want to leave in the fall. That way, we will be in Seneca country when the snow starts and can winter with them. Then we can continue on to Michilimackinac in the early spring, reach there during high trading season and be back here by next fall."

"Do you expect to have trouble with the French?" asked Aernout.

"Nay," said Roseboom. "Abel Marrion believes that we should be able to get into and out of the Ottawa country without being detected. Join me, won't you, Aernout? We can partner with equal shares on costs and profits. We'll both get rich! What do you say?"

"I'll think about it," Aernout replied. "But, with the new baby, I doubt that Gerritje would be too pleased by the prospect of my being away for a year. However, I know that Sean, here, is keen to join you. Isn't that right, Sean?"

"Aye, sir." He replied excitedly. "Mister Roseboom, have ye started to select the traders who will accompany ye?"

"I have some who, like you, have expressed interest. I will certainly keep you in mind."

"Please do, sir. I would appreciate it."

"Not to worry. You'll be on the list, won't he, Johannes?" prodded Viele.

"Aye, Aernout, of course," agreed the other man.

Leaving Roseboom, Sean and Aernout continued down the hill. At the bottom, they turned right onto Court Street. Near the footbridge, crossing a small stream called the Rutterkill, there was a group of women drawing water. Sean immediately noticed a pretty, young Dutch woman whom he didn't know and who seemed to stand out from the others. He excused himself and, leaving Aernout chuckling, approached her.

"Good day, Miss," he said.

"Good day to you, Mr. O'Cathail," she replied, straightening up from her task. She wore a clean, but inexpensive brown wool housedress, with a starched white apron. Her white-blonde hair, covered by a linen cap, was dressed in the Dutch manner with braids wound in spirals over both ears. Her bright blue eyes sparkled with pleasure as she looked at Sean.

"But Miss, ye seem to have the better of me," said Sean. "Ye know who I am, but I have not had the pleasure of making your acquaintance."

"Well, sir, how could I help but know the name of Sean O'Cathail, right-hand man to the esteemed Aernout Viele, who is standing right over there! Indeed, I have it on the very best of sources that you, yourself, are an astute fur trader who someday may be one of the richest men in the colony."

"Bosh! Enough woman! Who are ye?"

"And, sir, why would a fine gentleman such as you want to know a poor servant girl like me?" she flirted.

"Oh, Miss," he replied, employing his Irish charm to its fullest. "I'm no fine gentleman, but ye are as beautiful as Maeve, queen of ancient Ireland. Pray, do not keep your identity a secret from me.   What can I call ye, other than 'beautiful'?"

"Why, sir, how could I possibly reject the request of such a gallant gentleman? My name is Laurentje, Laurentje van Reuyter."

"And," said Sean, "How do ye come to be in Albany, Miss Laurentje van Reuyter, and why haven't I seen ye before?"

"Why, Mr. O'Cathail, I arrived in Albany from Amsterdam only two months ago. I am in service to Major and Mistress Staats," replied the girl. "As to why you have not seen me before, I cannot imagine, because I have certainly seen you. Perhaps you have eyes for someone else."

"Nay, lass, there is no one else and, if there were, she would have been eclipsed!"

"Now, sir," Laurentje continued with a sly smile, "Do you have more questions to ask or can I return to my chores?"

"Just one more question," said Sean. "Would you consent to walk with me some evening after you've finished your work?"

"Well, Mr. O'Cathail, I personally would not say 'No' to a walk with you, but I will have to get permission from Mistress Staats, first. After all, I've only just joined the household."

"Miss van Reuyter... Perhaps I could see ye this evening?"

"Pray, do not be so bold as to assume that I can see you at the drop of a hat, Mister O'Cathail! I will talk with Mistress Staats. It could very well be that she will refuse to allow us to see each other. I will have to wait for the right moment to speak with her. And, you will just have to wait until I tell you that we can go walking. "

"But, Miss, how will ye get word to me?"

"Perhaps, sir, you will see me about here in the town. You will just have to be alert for the next time our paths cross."

"I will, Miss, I promise."

"Now, Mr. O'Cathail, I must bid you good day. It is long past time that I returned home!"

"Good day to ye, Laurentje van Reuyter. I pray it will not be too long before we see each other again!"

Leaving her, Sean rushed to catch up with Aernout who was waiting in front of the *Stadhuis* on the left side of the street.

"Who is the young woman?" asked Aernout.

"Isn't she beautiful?" sighed Sean, watching her walk away.

"Aye, she's a very pretty girl. Now, come on..." Aernout said, taking Sean by the arm and leading him into the *Stadhuis*.

The building was a small structure that looked more like a substantial private residence than a public building. Inside, it consisted of large single rooms on the first and second floors and a jail in the cellar. Both city and county officials had desks on the first floor while the city magistrates and the city and county courts held their sessions on the second floor.

The *Stadhuis* was the first building that one would pass upon entering the town through the south gate. From that gate, the Post Road led south, past the ruins of old Fort Orange and through the Pastures, land held in common for the townsfolk's livestock.   It continued along Hudson's river to the village of Bethlehem, thence to Kingston and, ultimately, to Hoboken, in New Jersey. From there, travelers could take a ferry across the river to Manhattan.

Inside, Sean and Aernout proceeded up the stairs to the council chamber and courtroom. It was in this room that representatives of the colony had held their councils with the Five Nations and other Indian tribes since the earliest days of the colony.

Entering the chamber, they found the city magistrates in earnest discussion. Seated around a long table were the mayor, Pieter Schuyler, Recorder Dirk Wesselse, Treasurer Jan Jansen Bleeker, Sheriff Richard Pretty, two aldermen, Albert Ryckman and Johannes Wendell and, to Sean's irritation, Town Clerk Robert Livingston. Under the colony's laws and by tradition, these seven men also served as the Governor's Indian Commission, with Livingston as Secretary of Indian Affairs. It was their responsibility to treat with the Mohawk and, through them, with the other members of the Five Nations. They were also expected to maintain good relations with the Algonquin tribes and to gather information about the activities of the French and their Indian allies.

As Aernout and Sean took seats near the door, they heard Mayor Schuyler saying, "So, we're all agreed. We will write to Governor Dongan, telling him that, if William Penn buys the Susquehanna River basin, Albany and the entire colony will lose the trade of the most western of the Five Nations; and that only the Mohawk and Oneida will continue to come to Albany. We will emphasize that it is critical - absolutely critical - that he do something to stop Penn from making this purchase."

Robert Livingston rose and said, "I have prepared a draft of just such a missive for your approval. In it, I point out that we are credibly informed of the savages' willingness to sell the Susquehanna to Penn. Then I say, 'They that settle upon said river will be much nearer to the Indians than this place and, consequently, the Indians will be more inclined to go there. Especially since they can get there by water, while they must come here partly by land.'

"I then explain how vital the beaver trade is to the economy of the entire colony, not just Albany, and describe the efforts we have made to verify the savages' position on the matter, including our conversations with the two sachems, Adjechne and Araquartho.

"Following that, I say that it is essential that the governor become involved as only he can deal with Penn on an equal footing, and end with, 'The means for preventing the purchase of the land we leave to your Excellency's discretion.'"

The sound of hands slapping the top of the table, accompanied by cries of "Hear, hear!" and "Well said, Robert!" followed Livingston's presentation.

The mayor asked for a vote approving Livingston's draft and, receiving unanimous approval, said, "Excellent. Robert, if you will, could you have the letter prepared for our signatures tomorrow? And, would you be available to carry the letter to the governor at Fort James in Manhattan and, perhaps, plead our case in person?"

"Of course," said Livingston, "I will do whatever the Commission requires."

Sitting in the back of the room, Sean and Aernout listened to the conversation. Then, Aernout caught the eye of the mayor and cocked his head indicating that they needed to speak with him in private.

Schuyler silently acknowledged the signal and interrupted the discussion saying, "Thank you, Robert. Gentlemen, I propose that we adjourn until the morrow, at which time we will review and sign the letter to the governor."

All agreed and began to file out of the room. Each acknowledged the two traders in passing, but Livingston, after nodding to Aernout, fixed Sean with a cold, hard stare.

Something inside Sean churned as the haughty Scotsman stepped in front of him and said, "Well, O'Cathail, you Papist bogtrotter, what are you doing here?"

"Mister Livingston," said Aernout, stepping between the two men. "My partner and I have business with the mayor, not with you. Now, why don't you just move along and do as the commissioners have instructed you to do."

Aernout grabbed Sean by the elbow, stepped around Livingston, catching the taller man off guard, and walked toward the mayor.

"Pay him no mind," said Aernout quietly. "But you need to be careful around him, Sean."

"I am, Aernout, but he just won't let me be! I've lived in Albany for three years, now, and have never done anything to provoke his ire. He just hates me for my religion and nothing else!"

Just then, Mayor Schuyler spoke, "Mister Viele, Mister O'Cathail, welcome back. I believe that you heard part of our discussion. What news do you have regarding Penn's efforts to purchase the Susquehanna? Are we, indeed 'credibly informed' that the *wilden* intend to sell?"

"Aye, you are," Viele replied. "The *wilden* say that they own the land and have expressed a willingness to sell it to Penn. They want to meet with Penn's people in four weeks' time when they come to Albany for their council with the governor."

"Have you informed Haig and Graham?"

"Aye, we stopped at the fort last evening on our way into town. We are to deliver a written report this morning," said Viele.

"Four weeks is not a lot of time," said the mayor. "I hope that the governor will do something before then."

"Well... on the way into town, we saw Adjechne and Araquartho, and asked them not to leave until after I had spoken with you. Perhaps, we can give the sachems something to think about before they come to Albany," mused Aernout.

"Do you think we could convince them to sell the land to New York? Is that possible?" asked Schuyler.

"I do not believe that the colony could outbid Penn if we went head-to-head with him. Haig and Graham have said that Penn is willing to pay almost any amount for the land. But, there might be a way to get it without paying for it."

"Really? How would that work?"

"I'm not entirely certain as yet, but it may be good to appeal to the Mohawks' self-interest. If the western nations begin to trade with Penn's people, the loss of tribute will hurt the Mohawk financially and damage their standing among the other nations. Also, a few, well-placed 'presents' might help. If you are willing to give us a free hand in this, Sean and I will come up with a way to stop the sale."

"All right, Aernout," the mayor said, "I trust you and Sean to do what is best since what

is best for Albany is also best for you. No offense
intended.”

"None taken,” replied Viele. “But, there’s
another problem.”

"What is that?”

"We were told by the Cayuga, and it was
confirmed by Araquartho, that traders from
Penn’s colony are already coming up the
Susquehanna to trade.”

"*God in hemel!* The thieves!”

"But that’s a problem that I don’t think
we can solve.”

"No, Aernout, you’re right. For that, we
will have to get the governor involved. That is if
we can get his attention long enough to deal with
it. Oh well, we will deal with one problem at a
time. The land first, the traders later. Agreed?”

"Aye, agreed,” said Viele.

"I just wish we had more time.”

"As do I. Oh, by the way, Sean and I ran
into some Huron west of Schenectady. We’ve
notified Sander Glen in Schenectady and
Captain Sheffield at Fort Albany, but I thought
you should know as well.”

"That’s all we need! First, this imbroglio
over the Susquehanna! Now, we have savages
lurking in the woods. But, thank you, Aernout, I
will have Sheriff Pretty alert the rattle watch to
be vigilant.”

At that, Viele said, “Come, Sean, we have
work to do!”

They quickly left the building and hurried
back to Viele’s house. As they walked, Aernout
said, “I will bring the report to Haig and

Graham. I need you to fetch Adjechne and Araquartho and bring them here, to the house.”

Spying Sara sweeping the stoop, Viele said, “Sara, run and tell your mistress that we will have guests for the midday meal.”

“Will the guests be Christians or savages? You know Mistress Viele will want to know,” said Sara.

“Savages,” he said. “Tell her we will need rum, not beer, and that she should prepare boiled beef. It’s a favorite of the *wilden*.”

“Yes sir,” replied Sara as she hurried into the house to find her mistress.

When Aernout had retrieved the report, he and Sean walked up the hill to the fort. There, they separated. Viele went directly to the governor’s residence, and Sean went out through the west gate to find Adjechne and Araquartho.

“Halloo, Oh-Kahl!” cried Araquartho. “Now we will truly drink! Where is our brother, Aerie? He said he would speak with us today.”

“Aernout has sent me to ask you to come to his house to eat and drink. Will you come with me?”

“Of course. We would be pleased to come to Aerie’s house,” said Adjechne.

Sean watched as the two sachems prepared themselves for their visit. Because it was a very hot day, they donned only knee-length kilts over their breech clouts. Each painted his face and fixed a feather in his scalp lock. The addition of a sheathed knife in the belt of each completed the task. While Sean waited, he noted that the two Indian women had already packed most of their belongings onto pack frames in preparation for leaving.

Sean and the two sachems then walked to the town. Viele met them as they passed the gate of the fort.

"Halloo, Aerie," said Adjechne. "We are coming to your house!"

"Aye, and you're welcome," Aernout replied.

Unable to contain his curiosity, Sean asked, "How did it go? Everything went well I assume."

"Aye," Aernout said. "They're eager to get the report to Penn's factor for approval. Even better news is that Haig has decided to accompany Graham to Philadelphia instead of staying here. I was afraid he might discover that we are trying to stop the sale. You know how quickly secrets can become public knowledge in a small town. Anyway, they will leave tomorrow on the afternoon packet to Manhattan."

Just then the quartet reached Viele's home. He led them into the front room, where Mistress Viele had spread a blanket and some furs on the floor. A jug of rum sat in the middle of the blanket.

After they were seated, Aernout lifted the jug and said, "Now we will truly drink!"

They each repeated the phrase and drank as the jug made its way around the circle.

Then, just as they started a second round, Mistress Viele brought in a steaming platter of boiled beef. Sara followed with loaves of dark bread.

As soon as the food was placed in front of them, Aernout said, "Now we will truly eat!" Sean and the two sachems repeated the phrase, and they all began to eat, using their fingers in the Indian manner. Upon finishing, each of the sachems belched in appreciation and Viele again passed the jug of rum.

"Now, my friends, we have truly eaten, and we can talk," he said, turning to Adjechne. "I have a favor to ask of my brother. I would be pleased if you would prepare for an important council when you return to Onontague. In the next few days, the Mohawk will call for a council. You must be prepared to hold the council before the sachems come to Albany to meet with *Corlear*."

Adjechne asked, "Why will the *Ganienkeh* call a council?"

"I cannot say. I can only tell you that they will do so. Your question will be answered when the Mohawk sachems make their propositions. However, it is essential that all of the sachems gather at Onontague as quickly as possible."

"Of course, I will do as you ask."

"Aerie, what would you have me do?" asked Araquartho.

"Araquartho, my brother. I ask that, when the council is called, you listen to the Mohawk propositions with an open mind. Can you do that for me?"

"Of course, Aerie," he replied.

"Good. To express my appreciation for your help, I give you each a bag of shot and a pot of vermillion."

Sean stood and retrieved the items from the shelves behind the counter and handed the gifts to the two sachems.

"Now, let us have another drink," proposed Viele.

The four men drank and then the two Indians left, walking unsteadily up the hill towards the gate.

Aernout then called Sara to come clean up and, turning to Sean, said, "Sean, could you make an inventory of the trade goods we have in stock? I have a feeling that, over the next few weeks, we will be distributing many gifts to our native friends. Meanwhile, Mistress Viele and I must review the accounts for the time you and I were gone. I count myself lucky that I found myself not just a wonderful wife, but a good business partner as well."

Chapter 9

The next morning, Sean and Aernout rode back to Schenectady to meet with Jacques Cornelissen van Slyck. Van Slyck, called 'Aukes' by the Mohawk, was the son of a Dutch father and a Mohawk mother and, as a result, enjoyed the trust of all -- the Iroquois, the Dutch and the English. They needed Aukes' help to convince the Mohawk to stop the sale of the Susquehanna valley.

Upon reaching Schenectady, they went straight to Aukes' home, a log cottage against the west wall of the stockade. There, they found his wife, a plump, red-faced Dutch woman. A little blonde girl, a toddler, clung to her skirts, shyly peeking out at the two men. Mistress Van Slyck told them that her husband was not at home but was working in his wheat field on the other side of the Mohawk River.

Wiping her hands on her apron, she said, "I expect him to return shortly for the midday meal. If you wish, you can wait for him and eat with us."

Sean and Aernout accepted her invitation and sat on a bench in front of the cabin to wait.

They hadn't waited long when Aukes came into sight. He was a tall, barrel-chested man with pale skin, but with the straight, black hair, black eyes and high cheekbones of his mother's people.

"Aernout, Sean," he said, shaking their hands. "What can I do for you?"

"We're here to ask your help," said Sean.

"Your good wife has invited us to share your midday meal," said Aernout. "We can talk as we eat."

As they ate, Sean and Viele explained the situation, and Aernout said, "You and Sean must go to Caughnawaga to speak with Achagari. He has to understand that the Mohawk will lose both tribute and the respect of the other nations if the western tribes start to trade with Penn's people. Then, you have to convince him to seek a council of the Five Nations where he must make the case that selling the Susquehanna valley would be a mistake."

"And, why would Achagari do this?"

"Because we will make it worth his while. We'll give him enough trade goods to make it nigh impossible for him to refuse. And, since Sean will be with you, he will know that this is important to me and that, if he refuses, it could affect our future trading relationship."

"But why me? Why not go yourself?"

"Because you are one of them and they trust you. They know me, but I am still a white man. Besides, I do not want Achagari to see me as a supplicant. It could affect our future dealings."

"And Sean, what is your role in this?"

"Not to brag, but I think that I have come up with a way to thwart Penn. For it to be successful, however, the Mohawk must request a council at which they will remind the other nations that the Iroquois gave the valley to the English when Governor Andros was in office."

"Did they? I don't remember that!"

"No, they did not, but the important thing is to convince them that they did." Sean continued, "I think we can do this. But we need Achagari, and we need the help of the mother of the Turtle Clan, Nadie. She is the key to winning the support of the clan mothers and other old women. With a few presents, I'm sure we can convince her to take a leading role in our little ruse."

Aukes considered this and asked, "So, why should I do this?"

"Because it is worth your while, as well!" said Aernout. "As we all know, you often find yourself in possession of furs that, by law, should be traded in Albany. Now, if the Susquehanna is sold to Penn, your trading opportunities will be reduced to the few Mohawk and Oneida who might still come through Schenectady. If we can stop the sale, then you will continue to be as prosperous as you are now!"

"All right, you've convinced me. When do we to leave?"

"As soon as possible," said Sean. "Can ye leave the day after tomorrow? Aernout and I will go back to Albany to gather the gifts. I'll return tomorrow evening, and we can start out early the following morning."

"Good," said Aukes. "But we will need gifts for all the old women and the sachems of the other clans, as well. Achagari and Nadie will need the support of the entire castle if they are to accomplish what you want."

"That's a very good point," Sean said. "We'll be sure to have enough, won't we Aernout?"

"Aye, that we will!"

When Mistress van Slyck came to clear away the remains of the meal, Sean and Viele expressed their thanks, said goodbye to Aukes, and walked back to young Aernout's house. There, they acquired two fresh mounts and, by dusk, were back in Albany. Together with Mistress Viele, they spent the evening assembling a suitable selection of gifts for Achagari and the other sachems, as well as Nadie and the old women.

Early the next morning, after a good night's sleep, Sean was ready to go. With the help of Garret and Philip, he packed the trade goods on one of young Aernout's horses and, mounting the other, rode back to Schenectady. He spent that night at Cornelis Viele's tavern where, at dawn the next morning, he was met by Aukes.

The two men carried the trade goods to Aukes' canoe. After loading, Sean climbed into the bow while Aukes pushed it off and climbed into the rear. Then, they started the hard paddle up the Mohawk River to Caughnawaga. Aukes steered the canoe into the slipstream, using the ebb flow to avoid paddling against the current. Even so, they would be unable to complete the trip before dark. They would have to spend the night somewhere along the banks of the river.

The sun was high in the sky when they reached Caughnawaga the next day. They quickly unloaded the trade goods from the canoe and stored them with Aukes' mother in the Wolf Clan longhouse. Then, they selected two of the more impressive items and went to see Achagari.

"Hello, uncle," said Aukes. "I see that you are well."

"Hello, nephew," replied Achagari. "Yes, this man is well. The Great Spirit, Orenda, has smiled on me."

Turning to Sean, he said, "Welcome, Oh-Kahl, this old man is pleased to see you, as well. Is Aerie the Interpreter with you?"

"Hello, uncle," Sean responded. "It is good to see ye. No, Aernout is not with us.

"Uncle," said Aukes, "Oh-Kahl and I have come to speak with you on a matter of great importance."

"But first, I have gifts for ye," said Sean, presenting the sachem with a bolt of duffel cloth and a bag of gunpowder.

"Such fine gifts, this must be a matter of truly great importance."

"It is, uncle," said Aukes. "It is a matter of importance to the *Ganienkeh* and to the Dutch at Orange."

"Then come, let us sit and talk," Achagari said as he led Aukes and Sean into the Turtle Clan longhouse.

They arranged themselves on the floor around the cooking fire as one of the women filled bowls with stew for them. As she did so, Sean looked around the lodge, but did not see Kai. "Now we will truly eat," pronounced Achagari.

When they were finished eating, Aukes explained the situation to Achagari, emphasizing the problems that the Mohawk would face if the Susquehanna was to be sold, and then told him that it was essential that he arrange a meeting of all the Iroquois to try to stop the sale.

Achagari listened intently and then said, "Nephew, as much this man wants to help, this is not a decision I can make alone. This man will have to seek the advice of the other sachems and the elders of the village. Luckily, nearly everyone is here. Any who are not here will agree with whatever the majority decides. We will gather tonight, and this man will talk with them. Have you brought gifts for all the sachems and old women?"

"Aye, uncle, we have," responded Aukes. "Oh-Kahl has brought many gifts for you and the others as a sign of his appreciation for your help."

"Good," Achagari said, and he called Nadie to join them. After Sean had explained his plan, the three Mohawk began to plan their strategy for the night's council. Since Sean had nothing further to add, he went in search of Kai. He found her, working in the village cornfield. Sean nonchalantly walked past the group, without looking at Kai, and into the woods.

Moments later, Kai excused herself from the group, saying, "I am sorry, my sisters, but this woman must relieve herself." She walked toward the trees into which Sean had disappeared as the other women looked at each other knowingly and giggled behind their hands.

When Kai entered the forest, Sean was hiding behind a tree, and she did not see him. As she passed, he came up behind her and took her into his arms. She squealed and pretended to struggle but soon, smiling broadly, turned fully toward him and pressed her body against him.

"Oh-Kahl, you have returned to Kai," she said in Iroquois. "Did you miss this woman?"

"Aye, woman," he growled from deep in his throat and, grabbing her hand, pulled her deeper into the woods.

As soon as they were out of the sight and hearing of the other women, Sean embraced Kai again and kissed her deeply. She responded with a sharp intake of breath and pushed up against him. Breaking the kiss, Sean stepped away from her, drinking in her beauty. His attention was immediately drawn to her firm, proud breasts, with their hard nipples pointing up at him.

As Sean raised his hands to Kai's breasts, her hands were busy at the crotch of his leggings. She soon had him free. Moaning, they sought each other's lips. Kai pulled away and, by just pulling the drawstring at her waist, was soon naked. She fell to her hands and knees and looked over her shoulder at Sean with desire in her eyes. He went to his knees behind her and exulted at the sensations as he entered her. They were soon lost in their need for each other.

By the time they were satisfied and had returned to the castle, it was almost dark. A large pile of wood, taller than a man, had been laid in the huge fire pit that stood in the middle of the village. As night fell, the bonfire was lighted, and the villagers began to gather for the council.

They arranged themselves around the fire by clan; Turtle, Wolf and Bear. In the front row of each sat the clan sachems. Next to them were seated the clan mothers and the other old women. They were accorded places of honor in village councils because it was the old women who would have the final say in whatever their clans decided. Behind them sat the younger women and, in the rear, stood the men of each clan.

Achagari rose and addressed the gathering. "My sisters and brothers, let us give thanks to Orenda for our good fortune. Our women are fertile; our warriors strong and brave. The three sisters, corn, beans and squash, grow well in our fields, and our hunters are finding much game. We enjoy peace as our enemies are weak."

At this, he threw a handful of tobacco on the bonfire and took a lighted pipe from a shaman. Putting the pipe to his lips, he drew in and then released a mouthful of tobacco smoke. As the shaman chanted, Achagari raised the pipe above his head. Turning, he offered the pipe to each of the four winds. The pipe was then passed to each of the other clan sachems in a counter-clockwise fashion. They, in turn, repeated Achagari's actions. Once the pipe had been returned to the shaman, Achagari began to speak again.

"My sisters and brothers, we all know the story of how warriors of the *Ganienkeh* joined with our brothers, the Onondaga, and our nephews, the Cayuga, to take the warpath against the Susquehannock. We know of how our warriors defeated them and drove them from their lands.

"We know that, because we were victorious, our nephews, the Cayuga, built castles along the river that runs through the valley. So, the land of the Susquehannock became the land of the *Haudenosaunee*."

As Achagari made each point, the crowd howled and keened until the noise shook the very stakes of the palisade. He waited until calm was restored and then continued.

"Recently, our brother, Aerie the Interpreter, came to tell us that some new English, led by a man named Penn, want to buy our land. At first, we thought this would be a good thing. New trading posts in the valley would bring us many trade goods and the promise of peace by extending the Covenant Chain to these new English. And so we, with our brothers, the Onondaga, and our nephews, the Oneida and Cayuga, told Aerie that we would sell the land to Penn's English.

"Now, however, this man says that this would not be a good thing for the *Ganienkeh*. If these new English come to the valley, we will become the poor nephews of the *Haudenosaunee*. Our brothers, the Seneca and Onondaga, and our nephews, the Cayuga and Oneida, will no longer travel through our lands to trade with the Dutch at Orange. Instead, they will go south to these new English. They will no longer pay tribute to us and no longer respect us as Keepers of the Eastern Door of the Longhouse and the first friends of the Dutch."

Achagari paused as angry murmuring in the crowd became louder and louder.

"My sisters and brothers, this man tells you that we do not want this thing to happen!"

Shouts of "NO!" and "Do not sell our land!" came from the crowd.

"But," Achagari continued, "This man is afraid that, if we do not sell the land, these new English will make war upon us and try to take the land from us. They might even convince the English of Maryland and Virginia to break the Covenant Chain and join them. Perhaps, they may even persuade our old enemies, the Susquehannock, and their protectors, the Lene Lenape, to join them. And, this we do not want to happen, either!"

More cries of "NO!" but, this time, they were mixed with few war cries from the men in the rear.

"My sisters and brothers, Achagari does not doubt the bravery of the warriors of the *Haudenosaunee*, but this man fears that we would not be able to withstand such an alliance of enemies. Too, once our other enemies, the Huron in the north, the Mahican and Abenaki in the east, and the Ottawa, Erie, Illini and others in the west, learn that our eyes are looking to the south, they will not hesitate to attack, as well.

"We know that the French do not hesitate to attack the *Haudenosaunee* when they think that we are weak. Not long ago, they even attacked the *Ganienkeh*! It was only because Orenda was watching over us and led us to the Dutch at Schenectady that we were saved. If we have problems with Penn's English, we can be sure that the French will go out among our enemies and encourage them to attack us. Even now we hear that there are Huron in our hunting grounds. The French will not only encourage them, but also they will give them guns, powder and shot, and may even join them on the warpath!

"My sisters and brothers, we have enemies to the north, east and west. We cannot look for more enemies to the south. Only a few years ago, we extended the Covenant Chain to the English of Maryland and Virginia to avoid such a circumstance. I ask you, my sisters and brothers, how can we stop the sale of this land to Penn's English and keep from putting ourselves at the mercy of our enemies. I ask you to give me your advice and guidance."

At that, Achagari sat, and the old women began talking among themselves.

After a few moments, Nadie stood and said, "My sisters, it is time that we withdraw and discuss what Achagari has said. This woman invites you to join me in the Turtle lodge where we will consider what might be done."

All of the old women arose and left the fire. With them went a few of the younger women, including Kai.

Sean turned to Aukes and asked, "Why are some of the young women joining them?"

"They are the ones who will become clan mothers. They must observe and learn the customs and manners of the women's councils," Aukes replied.

As Sean watched Kai follow the other women, he admired her dignified, almost regal bearing as if she were already a clan leader. Then, he was distracted by the way that her erect posture and sensuous stride made her bottom undulate under her skirt as she walked.

He shook his head, to clear it of the thoughts that had him wanting her again. Sean turned back to the fire and found that Aukes was now talking with Achagari. He joined them and asked, "What will happen now?"

Aukes replied, "Nadie will try to lead the discussion in the way we planned this afternoon. Hopefully, she will convince the women that the direction we want them to take is their own idea."

"Do not worry, nephew," said Achagari to Aukes. "Nadie is highly skilled in the art of persuasion. They will come back with the results we want!"

As they waited, all of the men and the remaining women stayed near the fire, talking quietly. No one left.

Then, the deerskin that covered the entrance of the Turtle Clan longhouse was pushed aside and the women came out, rejoining their clans around the fire.

Nadie was the last to leave the longhouse and, as she approached, she nodded almost imperceptibly to Achagari.

As the people settled back into their places, Nadie began to speak, "My sisters and brothers, the women have agreed upon the course of action which we believe must be taken.

"First, we must ask that the Onondaga, Keepers of the Council Fire, call a council of the *Haudenosaunee*. At that council, the *Ganienkeh* will propose that the issue of the sale of the Susquehanna be revisited. Then, if the council decides that the land is not to be sold to Penn, we will propose that we ask *Corlear* to protect the *Haudenosaunee* from Penn's wrath."

"But, why would *Corlear* turn against another English to protect the *Haudenosaunee*? Surely, he would side with his white brother," said Odegorrassee, sachem of the Wolf Clan.

With a sly smile, Nadie called out, "Tell all the people, Onata, what you just told the women."

At that, a wizened little old woman, barely five feet tall and bent by years of work, rose and stood in front of the Bear Clan. Sean immediately recognized the necklace she was wearing as one that had been included in the trade goods that he had brought.

As she opened her toothless mouth, Sean thought he saw a mischievous look cross her face. She looked almost like a little girl as she began to speak.

"My sisters and brothers, *Corlear* will take the side of the *Haudenosaunee* because he owns the land!"

At that, pandemonium erupted.

It took a while for Achagari and Nadie to restore order to the meeting. When it became quiet again, Nadie said, "Onata, tell the people how it came to be that *Corlear* owns the Susquehanna."

The little old lady, thoroughly enjoying herself in the pivotal role she was playing, said, "Ten winters ago, the *Haudenosaunee* gave the Susquehannock lands to the English who was *Corlear* at that time. It was a gift to bind him closely to us and to ensure that he accepted the Covenant Chain from our hands."

The sachem of the Bear Clan, Odegorrassee, asked, "But why didn't you say anything before, when we told Aerie the Interpreter we would sell the land?"

Onata, glancing at Nadie for an indication that she should proceed, responded, "I was not at Onontague with you. Besides, I am an old woman. My memory is not as good as it once was. It was so long ago that it happened. And, it was just one of many gifts that were given to *Corlear* at that time. I had forgotten about it

134

until all this talk about the Susquehannock lands made me remember."

Achagari rose and said, "Based on what Onata has told us, we will ask the Onondaga to call a council. This should be done as soon as possible. It is essential that all the nations be of one mind regarding the course of action to be taken."

Achagari looked around the fire as the sachems and clan mothers nodded and grunted their agreement with this proposal.

"Then it is agreed," he said. "Tomorrow I will send runners. As soon as the Onondaga sachems select a day for the council, they can send word to all the castles of the *Haudenosaunee*."

The meeting quickly broke up as the villagers sought the comfort of their sleeping robes.

Aukes, smiling broadly, put his hand on Sean's shoulder and said, "Well, Sean, you will have good news to take back to Albany. I am sure that the Indian Commission and the Albany traders will be pleasantly surprised."

"Aye. Of that, I have no doubt."

Just then, Kai appeared at Sean's side and softly touched his hand. Then, she turned and walked toward the Turtle Clan's longhouse. Taking his leave of Aukes, Sean followed her.

As he did so, he noticed a young warrior who closely watched Kai as she passed and then fixed Sean with a glare.

Inside the longhouse, Sean said, "Did you see the young warrior who stared at you?"

"Many young men stare at this woman," she replied. "But, yes, I did see him. It was Nahohidaye. We were good friends when we were children. Many people thought that we would marry. I think he still hopes that we will. However, because I will become a clan mother, neither he nor his family can afford the bride price my mother would set for me."

"Would he cause trouble for you?"

"No. No. He is harmless."

"He didn't look harmless. He looked aggrieved."

"Do not concern yourself, O-Kahl. There is nothing to worry about."

When they were in their sleeping compartment and getting undressed, Sean told her how surprised he had been by Onata's story, and asked her what had occurred in the women's meeting.

Smiling enigmatically, Kai got down on her knees and, looking up at him as she took him in her hand, said, "No man can know what happens in the women's council just as no man can know what is in a woman's mind." Lying back, she drew him to her. Sean eagerly entered her, and they quickly climaxed together. She then wrapped her body around his, and they fell asleep.

Chapter 10

Two weeks later, Aernout stood before the Indian commissioners and reported, "The Onondaga have agreed to hold a council and have sent runners to all the castles of the Five Nations. The council will be held in one week's time. Then, we will have our answer. As of now, though, the issue is still undecided."

"Surely, you must have some idea of how they will decide," said Mayor Schuyler.

"No, I really don't," replied Viele. "If the land is sold, the other nations will benefit while the Mohawk will lose. While we are further ahead than we were before, there is still a chance that things could go against us. It all depends on how persuasive the Mohawk can be."

The commissioners looked at each other, resignation etched in their faces. Then, Mayor Schuyler looked at Robert Livingston and asked,

"Robert, what of the governor? Has he responded to our letter?"

"Nay," replied Livingston, rising from his place at the opposite end of the table. "As you know, I delivered our letter and tried to get an audience with him, but he was not at Fort James. His secretary assured me that he would be given the letter. But, as of today…"

"We do know, of course, that he will be here in Albany at the end of this month," observed Dirk Wesselse.

"Aye," noted Livingston. "But he will be accompanied by the governor of Virginia, Lord Howard of Effingham. An opportunity to raise this problem may not present itself while the governor is hosting Lord Howard."

"Well, gentlemen," the mayor said, "There is nothing we can do to influence whatever decision the Five Nations may make, but I am of the mind that we must get the governor's attention before he and Lord Howard meet with the sachems, especially since we know that Mr. Penn's representatives will have returned to Albany by then to begin their negotiations. We have to convince the governor to intervene. We must, again, express our position in the most urgent terms possible."

"If you please, gentlemen," said Livingston, "anticipating your desires, I have, again, taken the liberty of preparing what may be a suitable text."

"Thank you, Robert, let us hear it," said Schuyler.

"I start by relating, once again, what we have learned from Mister Viele, Mister Penn's agents, and from the savages themselves. Then, I say, 'If William Penn buys the valley, it will destroy the beaver trade at Albany. The Indians themselves recognize this fact. While, for many years, the French have endeavored to usurp our trade in a piecemeal fashion, this would cut it off all at once. We shall try to delay any meetings between the savages and Mister Penn's agents until we have received your Honor's commands.'

"At the end, I inform him that we have been told that there are already traders from Penn's colony among the Iroquois. I point out that, obviously, people from Penn's colony are behaving as though the Susquehanna was already theirs. I close by, again, humbly requesting his direction in the matter."

"Very good, Robert, what do you gentlemen think?"

The commissioners chorused their approval of Livingston's suggestions, and Dirk Wesselse said, "I trust, Robert that we can impose on you once again, to carry our message to the governor?"

"I would be pleased to do so," he replied.

"Perhaps there is something else we should do," mused Viele.

"What is it, Aernout? Speak up, we need to do everything we can," said Schuyler.

"While Mister Livingston's letter is excellent, and I know that he would be a strong advocate on your behalf, I think that it is essential that we build a stronger case regarding the economic impact of the situation. I think that we would be remiss if we did not send a trader to speak with Governor Dongan."

"But on whom could we impose to leave his business at the height of the trading season and spend who knows how many days waiting for an audience with the governor? Not you, surely," said Schuyler.

"No, not me, I have already spent much time on this matter. However, as you know, my eldest son, Cornelis, represents my interests in Manhattan. I think you would agree that he would ably represent the interests of both the traders here in Albany and the merchants who ship our furs from Manhattan to England or the home country.

"Also, my associate, Sean O'Cathail, whom you all know and who is intimately acquainted with all aspects of our situation, can travel to Manhattan with Mister Livingston and apprise Cornelis of what needs to be done."

"Excellent idea," said the mayor. "Robert, how soon can you leave?"

"I can have the letter prepared for your signatures today. So, I can leave on tomorrow's packet. But, I don't see why we need O'Cathail to travel to Manhattan. He is not an experienced trader. He has only this year become Mister Viele's partner. And, he is certainly not a gentleman. I doubt that the governor would deign to recognize him, let alone actually converse with him."

"My dear Mister Livingston," said Viele. "If I had any qualms about Sean's ability to represent the traders of Albany, I would not have proposed his participation in the first place. Also, it may help that, like the governor, he is Irish and Catholic. Perhaps a common background could foster a common understanding. Besides, what does it matter if he's not a gentleman? Few men in this town and even in this room would pretend to be such."

As the other men around the table laughed at this last remark, Mayor Schuyler said, "I agree with Mister Viele. There can be no harm and, perhaps, some help from Mister O'Cathail, especially since Cornelis Viele will be there, as well.

"So, Mister O'Cathail? Can you also leave tomorrow?"

Rising from his seat against the wall in the back of the room, Sean said, "I am at your Honors' service."

After all of the commissioners had signed the letter to the governor, the meeting broke up. Standing on the steps of the *Stadhuis*, talking with Aernout and the commissioners, Sean spied Laurentje van Reuyter driving two cows through the south gate from the Pastures.

Sean quickly excused himself, again accepting the thanks of the commissioners for his efforts with the Mohawk and their best wishes for success with the governor, and hurried to intercept her.

"Laurentje! Here, let me help ye," he said.

"Why Mister O'Cathail! I thought you had quite forgotten about me," she said haughtily while brushing him aside.

"Laurentje!   Please wait," he said, catching her arm.

"Don't you touch me Mister O'Cathail!" she insisted, swiping at Sean with her switch. "I'll lose control of the cows. I know that you were out among the *wilden*. But you've been home for days and haven't come looking for me! I thought you wanted to see me. What were you doing? Have you been consorting with one of their women? Is she prettier than I? Has she made you forget me?

"Laurentje. It's not that way at all," Sean stammered. "Since my return, I have been very busy dealing with the Indians who have come to town to trade their furs." As he spoke, he tried to take the switch from her. But she pulled away and swiped at him again.

"Keep your hands to yourself, sir!"

"Laurentje, Laurentje. Here, give me the switch and I'll explain as we walk."

Feigning reluctance, she surrendered the switch. As they walked together, Sean told her about his trip to Caughnawaga. He avoided any mention of Kai, but told her how Achagari and Nadie had bent the will of the council in the way that would most benefit the Mohawk and the traders at Albany. And, he told her of the mission he would be undertaking the next day, to Manhattan. All too soon, they were at the Staats' home on the river side of Market Street but, by then, Sean had learned that Mistress Staats had given Laurentje permission to see Sean. However, she had insisted on meeting him first.

"So, if you would like to see me this evening…"

"Oh, yes! I do!" said Sean.

"Then present yourself at the kitchen door after the evening meal. I will tell Mistress Staats that I am expecting you."

At the appointed hour, Sean arrived at the Staat's back door. He was wearing his best clothes, including a cravat, woolen coat and waistcoat, and was perspiring profusely from the heat and nervousness.

Laurentje appeared at the door, flushed with the heat of the evening and of the kitchen.

"Oh, Mister O'Cathail! Just a moment while I get Mistress Staats. She has said we can go walking this evening, but she wants to take a look at you first. Do you mind?"

"Not at all, Laurentje," he replied, and she hurried into the interior of the house.

Standing at the back door, Sean ran his finger under his stock as it was sticking to his neck, and turned to gaze out over the river in the moonlight.

"Well, turn around and let me look at you!"

Caught unawares, Sean almost jumped, but managed to turn and stammer, "Good evening, ma'am. My name is Sean O'Cathail, and I'm asking your permission to take Laurentje van Reuyter walking on this fine summer's evening."

"Harrumph," said the tall, thin, gray-haired woman. She looked him over and said, "So you're the Irishman who has my girl mooning around the house and forgetting half of her chores! You're not my type. But... I can see where a young girl might find you attractive. Say, I know you. You work for Aernout Viele, don't you?"

"Actually, ma'am, I'm now his partner."

"Well, I suppose there are worse things you could be doing. Did you know that my husband, the major, was once a fur trader?"

"Why, no, Ma'am, I did not know that!"

"Aye, that's right. He was quite a successful fur trader before he bought a yacht and began sailing up and down Hudson's river. Now, tell me, what are your plans for my Laurentje?"

"Well, ma'am, 'tis such a beautiful, warm evening, I thought we would just take a stroll along the riverfront."

"A stroll, eh? Harrumph! Well, she can go with you on these conditions: first, you are not to take her beyond the stockade or into a tavern. Is that understood?"

"Yes, Mistress Staats."

"Second, you will have her back here safely by the time the rattle watch starts patrolling. The church bell rings when they close the gates, so you'll have plenty of time to get back. And, three, do not, I repeat, do not bring her back to me pregnant! She has more than four years remaining on her indenture, and I'll not be having a bastard running around my house because some fur trader has befuddled her with his smooth talk. Am I understood?"

"Perfectly, ma'am."

"All right, then." Turning, she called out, "Come on, Laurentje. I know you're just there behind the door. Come along. Your young man is getting impatient and doesn't want to talk anymore with an old woman like me."

Laurentje came rushing out. She had changed her dress, put on a clean apron and loosened and brushed her hair. She looked so beautiful that Sean's breath caught in his throat.

They said farewell to Mistress Staats; Laurentje took his arm, and they started walking. The two young people took a path that led to the river and strolled along the bank as the shadows lengthened in the growing dusk. There was no sound except for the croaking of frogs, an occasional "Hoot!" of an owl, and the gentle lapping of water on the shore. After a while, they came to a large rock. Sean laid his coat on the rock and lifted Laurentje up to sit on it.

"Thank you, Mister O'Cathail," she said as she settled herself on the rock.

"Please, Laurentje, call me Sean," he insisted.

"All right then, thank you, Sean," she replied.

"That's better," he said. "Now, tell me, how did ye come to be indentured to Mistress Staats?"

"It's not a very pretty story," she said.

"But I want to know everything about ye."

"Well, all right, then. My mother and father died of the fever when I was only a baby. I had no other relatives, so I was placed in an orphan's home until I was old enough to go to the workhouse in Amsterdam and begin to earn my keep. The orphan's home was not too bad. The women who cared for us did their best, although I remember always being hungry. But the workhouse was a nightmare. I arrived there when I was seven. At first, I did laundry for the gentry. We younger girls washed and ironed from dawn until dark. When I got older, I was put to work making lace. We were only given two meals a day. Breakfast was gruel and a cup of hot water. At night before going to bed, we got a thin stew, a crust of hard bread and a cup of tea. If you were extraordinarily lucky, your bowl of stew would contain a piece of meat or a potato."

She looked so sad while telling her story that Sean could not help but put his arm around her shoulders and hold her close. After a few minutes, he coaxed her to continue.

"They always gave us more work than we could finish in a day. Anyone who did not achieve the minimum would be punished. They would take the offenders to the woman who supervised the workhouse. There, one by one, we would be made to lean over a chair. Our skirts would be lifted over our heads, and we would be whipped with a switch. Ten stripes. And, if you moved, you would get ten more. It was awful. Not so much the pain. I could deal with the pain, but the shame... It was mortifying!

"Then, one day, a man came to the workhouse. He said he wanted to give twenty-five girls the opportunity to come to the Americas and seek their fortunes. You can believe that I was one of the first in line! He had a paper that we had to put our marks on. He told us it was just a formality. None of us could read or write, of course, and no one told us what it was. The matron witnessed our marks, so everything was legal. It was not until we were on the ship and at sea that we learned the truth. The man had purchased us from the workhouse! We had signed our indenture contracts, and we had been indentured for five years to pay off the cost of our transport."

"My God, Laurentje," said Sean. "I am so sorry. Surely, there must be some way for you to get out of the contract since you were tricked into accepting it! Isn't there?"

"No, I'm afraid there isn't. But I have been uncommonly lucky. Things have turned out well for me. When we reached Manhattan, we were put up for auction. Major Staats bought my bond and brought me here, to Albany. Mistress Staats is a good woman and treats me well. She is fair and doesn't beat me or work me to death. Also, she is teaching me to read and write.

"Barring illness or some other catastrophe, I should be able to complete the indenture in just a little more than four years. In fact, Mistress Staats has often hinted that, once the contract is satisfied, I could stay on as a paid servant if I wanted. Besides, I am here in the Americas... which is better than where I was... and soon I'll be free to seek my fortune."

As Sean listened, he found himself becoming more and more impressed with this girl, her strength and common sense, as well as the fact that they seemed to have much in common.

"Ach," she said. "Enough about me. Tell me about yourself, Sean O'Cathail. How did you come to find yourself here in Albany?"

"Well, I've not had it as hard as you. But, nevertheless... I left home at the age of 12. I thought that the life of a sailor would be exciting. So I found an English frigate and enlisted as a common seaman. That's how I came to spend four years in the English navy. Because I was bright and clever, I was able to avoid many of the pitfalls that come with being a young lad at sea. All of us younger lads, especially the powder monkeys, had to work hard to avoid the quirts of the officers and the bosun's mate, and we had to be constantly alert to the unnatural interests of some of the crew."

"Surely, though, it must have been an exciting life! Did you see much of the world?"

"Aye, it was exciting enough. We made port in many exotic places, the Portuguese Faro Islands, Rio de Janeiro in Brazil, and the West Indies. Once, we were caught in a hurricane off the coast of the Carolinas, and we fought pirates in the Dry Tortugas."

"So, why did you leave the navy?"

After thinking for a moment, Sean decided to be forthcoming with Laurentje, "I didn't so much leave as desert."

"Desert? Why on earth..."

"This is where my story becomes ugly," he said.

"We were anchored in Manhattan Harbor. I was part of a skeleton crew, left to watch the ship while the rest of the crew took shore leave. One of my mates and I caught three men robbing the crew's quarters. A fight ensued, and two of the thieves were killed. The third was injured, but escaped. One of the dead men was a ship's officer, so we knew that, no matter what excuse we had, we would hang! That's when the two of us jumped ship."

"And then?"

"Well, I didn't stay long in Manhattan. I met some people who suggested that it would be wise for me to come to Albany. When I arrived here, I asked around town and learned that Mister Viele was not only one of the best fur traders in the colony but that he was a fair man, as well. So, I contrived to meet him, talked him into teaching me the fur trade and, now, three years later, here I am, sharing this rock with a beautiful Dutch maiden."

"But, Sean, that means that you're a wanted man!"

"Aye, I suppose it does. But no one seems to be looking for me. At first, I lived in constant fear that my secret would be revealed. But, it has been three years, and I have even been back to Manhattan on occasion... At the time, a friend told me that it was likely to be forgotten and so it appears to have been."

"But, Sean..."

"Hush, now, Laurentje, let us enjoy what's left of the evening!"

As Sean said this, he gathered Laurentje into his arms and tried to kiss her. She twisted away, giggling, "Ach, now, remember Mistress Staats' conditions, you're not to try to seduce me with your sweet talk and beguiling ways!"

She sprang away and, just as Sean was about to pursue her, the church bell began to peal.

Laurentje stopped running and turned to say, "It looks as though our lovely evening is over, Sean. And, none too soon, I imagine. Now, walk me home so that we don't incur the wrath of my mistress."

When they reached Staats' door, they could see Mistress Staats in the kitchen, knitting and patiently awaiting their return.

"Come, Sean, kiss me quick! I must go in!"

Sean pulled her close and kissed her with all the passion that was in his heart. She returned the kiss with an equal amount of ardor, and they were both breathing heavily when she pulled away.

"Laurentje, when I return from Manhattan, can I see you again? I want to see you again!" he said.

"Aye, Sean, you can. I want to see you again, as well," and she rushed inside.

As Sean walked back to the Viele residence, he felt that, this night, he was happier than he had ever been in his life.

Chapter 11

Standing on the deck of the packet to Manhattan, Sean could feel the morning sun burning through the haze, and through his woolen coat to his shirt. It was a typical summer day in the colony of New York -- hazy, hot and unbearably humid.

As he had for his evening with Laurentje, Sean was wearing his best clothes. He wanted to remove his coat or at least loosen his cravat but, at the same time, he felt that he had to maintain the appearance of a gentleman, no matter how hot and uncomfortable he might be. Especially since Robert Livingston had made a point of his station in life.

Sean looked up at the mast and saw that what little breeze there was hardly ruffled the canvas of the sail. Luckily, they were sailing with the current, so the yacht would still make good time on the trip down the river.

He then looked across the deck at Robert Livingston. Livingston was dressed as warmly as Sean but looked comfortable despite the heat. There was no way Sean could let himself be perceived as less of a gentleman than Livingston.

When they had boarded the yacht at dawn, Livingston had barely acknowledged Sean's existence. Looking down his long, patrician nose, Livingston examined Sean much the same way he would an insect that had crossed his path.

Sean, as was his wont, had greeted the man with a lively, "Good morning, Squire Livingston!"

But, in return, he received a curt and arrogant reply, "O'Cathail, you and I are tenuously connected by the business we need to conduct in Manhattan. No more. And I would prefer to keep it that way."

"As Yer Worship desires, so it shall be," Sean responded with as much sarcasm as he could muster, sweeping his hat from his head and bowing deeply. "Far be it from me to impose meself where I'm not wanted."

And so the two men ignored each other for the remainder of the trip.

The voyage required two days. They would sail past Norman's Kill at Bethlehem and Kinderhook, the spit of land jutting into the river which Hudson was said to have named for the Indian children he had seen swimming there. In the evening, the yacht would make a stop at Kingston. There, they would spend the night, continuing to Manhattan the following morning,

Sean spent the day reviewing the points that he and Viele felt needed to be made to the governor. He hoped that he would be able to explain the situation clearly to Cornelis Viele.

"You needn't to worry about speaking to the governor yourself," Viele had told him. "Cornelis is a born politician. I am sure that he will take matters in hand and make an air-tight case for us before the governor. Just be sure that he has all the facts he needs."

Of course, Sean also reflected on his evening with Laurentje. He thought about how beautiful and desirable she was, and how much he wanted to make her his own. But he also considered her intelligence and how she would make a wonderful partner in life. He truly believed that, with effort and the support of a good woman like Laurentje, he could achieve great things.

The next morning, the yacht entered the Spuyten Duyvil and sailed down the Haarlem Kill into the East River. Finally, at mid-afternoon, the captain turned the packet into the protection of the Mole and tied up at the Town Dock.

Disembarking, Sean watched as Livingston headed across town in the direction of Fort James. Sean assumed that Livingston would find lodgings in one of the inns along Whitehall Street near the city's *Stadhuis*. Sean turned in the opposite direction, walked across Dock Street and continued west along Broad Street.

Having the rest of the day to himself, Sean decided to stroll about the city. As he walked, Sean recalled that he had been told that Broad Street had once been a canal that the Dutch had built to remind themselves of Amsterdam. By 1675, the canal had become stagnant, and the repulsive odor caused the first English governor, Edmund Andros, to order the residents to fill it in. The canal was raised to the level of the surrounding streets, pitched to promote drainage and then paved with stones. As soon as that was completed, the governor built a mercantile exchange and the town's first covered market at Beaver Street. Sean stopped at the market for a snack of cheese, bread and fresh milk. Nearby, he noticed a millinery shop where, after eating, he purchased a selection of ribbons as a gift for Laurentje.

Some of the streets crossing Broad Street, especially Beaver, Market and Mill, were home to many of the city's poor. Along the byways, Sean could see numerous disreputable taverns, with dangerous-looking men standing about and whores plying their trade. Despite his familiarity with the city's poorer quarters, Sean still felt less at ease here than he had ever felt in the wilderness. When one of the many street urchins bumped into him, Sean felt the lad grab for his purse, but Sean was able to grab him by the wrist before he could get away.

Sean retrieved his purse and, holding the boy tightly by the wrist, began dragging him toward the *Stadhuis* where he hoped to find the sheriff. By twisting and squirming like an eel, however, the urchin managed to pull away from Sean and ran down Mill Street. Sean began to give chase, shouting "Stop! Thief!"

But, the further he ran, the more alone Sean began to feel. Getting dark looks from some of the loiterers and rapidly losing ground to the would-be thief, Sean soon gave up the chase. Followed by the laughter and catcalls of the strumpets and their pimps, Sean started to walk back to Broad Street.

Suddenly, he felt a heavy hand clamp down on his right shoulder and, at the same time, felt the point of a dagger in his back.

"Just keep walking, O'Cathail," said a voice that sounded somewhat familiar to Sean. "Nay, nay, don't turn around. Just keep walking and turn into the alley just up there on the right."

As soon as Sean stepped into the alley, he was swung around and pushed against a wall. Holding him against the wall with his forearm pressed against Sean's throat was a slovenly dressed man with a scruffy beard and an eye patch over his left eye. Searching his memory, Sean tried to match the face with a name. Suddenly, he had it! It was Cox. Sean was sure of it; even though the past three years had not been kind to the former sailor.

Cackling, Cox said, "Ah, so ye recognize yer old shipmate, do ye? Do ye kenn that ye owe me something? Ah, ye be asking yerself what ye could owe me, ain't ye? Well, let me help ye. Ye be owing me an eye, ye bogtrotter! And, as the Bible says, an eye for an eye!"

Cox brought his dagger up to Sean's face, moved it back and forth before Sean's startled eyes and, then, pointed the tip directly at Sean's left eye.

Sean tried to twist out of Cox's grasp, but the man only pressed that much harder against his throat. "Don't squirm around so much," Cox said. "Accept yer punishment like a man!"

Just then a fist came out of nowhere and struck Cox on the temple, knocking him to the ground. Cox got up roaring and started toward the unknown assailant but seemed to think better of it and said, "So, not today, O'Cathail, but someday soon... when ye least expect it." Then, he turned and ran off down the alley.

It was then that Sean got his second shock of the day. His rescuer was none other than Father O'Boyne, dressed in the mantle of a Black friar. "Thank ye, father. It seems that ye must rescue me every time we meet!"

"I know ye, don't I?" asked the priest.

"Aye, father, I'm Sean O'Cathail. Ye and Megan Reilly helped me and a friend escape a bit of trouble about three years ago."

"Ah, yes, I remember. But that thief knew ye, as well."

"That was no thief, father," replied Sean. "That was the man I stabbed when I jumped ship. It appears he survived, albeit with just one eye."

As he said this, he noticed a movement behind the priest. "Grab him father! That rascal tried to steal my purse!"

Grabbing the urchin before he could scamper away, the priest said, "Kevin, Kevin, Kevin, how often have I told ye that ye make a terrible thief and should find another way to make a living!"

"Hold him, Father!" said Sean. "I was taking him to the sheriff when he got away from me."

"Now, Sean, don't ye think that, in repayment of the help I have given ye, now and in the past, ye could find it in yer heart to forgive young Kevin, here."

"But, he's a thief, father! He must be punished!"

"Nay. First, he's a terrible thief, and I think he is finally realizing it himself. Second, the penance I will give him will be punishment enough for this infraction. And, third, a little Christian charity on your part would go far toward redeeming the lad."

"All right, father. I suppose that I owe ye that, if not more..." said Sean.

"That's a good lad! Now, Kevin," said O'Boyne, grabbing the boy by both shoulders, "I will come to your lodgings this evening. I want your mother there! We will discuss your penance at that time. Now, apologize to the gentleman!"

"Sorry, sir!"

"Good!" said the priest, "Now, off ye go!"

As the boy ran off, Father O'Boyne turned to Sean and said, "Well, now, Sean O'Cathail, how are ye? Are ye rich yet?"

"Rich? Not yet, but I hope that I will soon be able to make my own way."

"What are you doing in Manhattan?"

"I'm here to meet with Governor Dongan on behalf of the traders in Albany. In fact, I'm just on my way to see Megan Reilly's employer. His father is my partner in Albany."

"Well, why don't we walk together for a while and you can tell me how you've fared since last we met."

As the two men walked, Sean told the priest about the past three years — his arrangement with Aernout Viele, his experiences among the savages and his encounters with the French Jesuit missionaries who worked among the Iroquois.

"Be careful of the Jesuits, Sean," warned the priest. "They become easily confused about what their ministry entails. They often forget that they work for God and not for King Louis the Fourteenth!"

"Aye, father, I've learned to be wary of them. All of us who deal with the savages consider them to be spies for the French and working to win the natives over to the French side."

"I can certainly see that happening. But you do take the sacraments from them, don't you?"

"Yes, father, don't worry. I do so whenever I get the chance. Even though I live in a nest of Calvinists, I am still a practicing Catholic. But, don't tell my neighbors that! "

Laughing, Father O'Boyne said, "Well, here is where we must part. Don't forget, you're to remember the church when you become rich!"

"I haven't forgotten, father. May I have your blessing?"

"*In nomine Patre...*" he intoned while making the sign of the cross.

Then, Sean said, "Oh, father, I wanted to ask: Whatever happened to Dick Fielding?"

"Ah, yes, your young English friend. As I remember, I found him a berth on a Dutch merchantman. He sailed shortly after you went to Albany. But I've heard nothing more of him."

Shaking hands, the two men parted. Sean continued walking, much more alert to his surroundings after his encounter with Cox, and was soon at the Viele home.

Megan Reilly answered his knock at the door.

"Good evening, Megan," Sean said, removing his hat and mopping the sweat from his brow. "I hope I find ye well this evening?"

"Ach, Sean O'Cathail! As I live and breathe! Come in, come in," she said. "What brings ye to Manhattan on such a hot day as this?"

"Well, actually, I've come in search of yer master on a matter of great importance."

"Mister Viele has spent the day at the docks supervising the loading of a shipment of furs to Amsterdam. But we expect him to return for the evening meal. My mistress is not at home at the moment, either. However, I am sure that I can offer ye the hospitality of the house, if only the kitchen, until they return. Would ye like something to drink?"

"Aye, Megan, thank ye."

"Just you sit down here, at the table, and I'll get ye a beer. We can talk while I prepare dinner."

She went down into the cellar, emerging moments later with a foaming tankard of beer.

"*Sláinte!*" said Sean, as he took a good, healthy swallow. "Ah, that tastes wonderful!" he said.

"It keeps quite cool in the cellar," said Megan. "It should be truly refreshing on a hot day like today. Now, tell me Sean, how have ye been?   Have ye been after having more adventures among the heathen savages?"

Not needing much encouragement, and feeling quite full of himself because of all he had experienced in the past few weeks, Sean began to talk. After noting that he had run into Father O'Boyne that very day, but avoiding any mention of his run-in with Cox, he told Megan about his recent travels among the Iroquois, and of the intrigue surrounding the possible sale of the Susquehanna valley to Penn's colony,

As he spoke, Megan stopped working to listen and soon sat down on the bench, next to him. She looked at him with adoring eyes and kept prompting him to continue, asking, "What happened next?"

He described how he and Aernout had come under fire from hostile Huron and how they had escaped although Aernout had been injured, eliciting "Ooohs" and "Aaahs" from the girl. She moved closer to him and soon her hip was pressing against his.

He then told her about his visit to the Mohawk with Aukes, and all that had transpired during the council.

"And now, ye're in Manhattan, sitting here and regaling me with all yer tales! What important errand brings ye here?"

"I've come to ask your master to argue the case of the fur traders to the governor. The traders and the Indian commissioners are hopeful that Governor Dongan will take their side against William Penn."

"Ach, Sean, 'tis an exciting life ye lead. Traveling hither and thither, and living amongst the savages. And, now, ye may even get to meet the governor!"

"Now, Meg..."

"Tell me, Sean," she asked still pressing against him, and then placing her hand on his thigh, "Have ye never felt the need of a woman in your life?"

Sean turned toward her and found her looking deeply into his eyes. "Aye, there are times when I've felt the need for someone special in my life. In fact, not too long ago, Mister Viele was extolling the benefits of marriage to me.

"I think," he continued, chuckling, "that he was hinting that I should do something about finding a wife. Maybe he's tired of me sleeping on the floor of his kitchen. But, until I can make more money, there is no point in even thinking about marriage," he said, taking another sip of his beer and gazing off into space.

"But, if ye were in the market for a wife," Megan asked, "what kind of woman would ye want, Sean?   Do you think she could be a poor servant girl, like me?”

“Aye, Meg,” said Sean, thinking immediately of Laurentje van Reuyter. “I do believe that would be very possible.”

Suddenly, to Sean’s surprise, Megan threw her arms around his neck and kissed him forcefully on the lips.

As she continued to kiss him, Sean tried to extricate himself from her grasp. Finally breaking the kiss, Megan exclaimed, “Oh, Sean, this is wonderful! I’ve been dreaming of this for, oh, so long! I just never believed that ye could feel the same way about me! Oh, Sean, I love ye!”

“Megan...,” Sean started to respond, but she placed two fingers on his lips to silence him.

“Hush, Sean, don’t say anything.”

“But, Meg...”

“Quiet!   Words would only spoil the moment.”

Just then, they heard the front door open. Megan jumped up and started rushing around the kitchen.

“Megan!” called Mistress Viele, “Megan! Come girl! Mister Viele will be home soon, and he’ll be hungry after his long day at the docks.

“Oh,” she said as she swept into the kitchen and Sean rose to greet her. “Mister O’Cathail! We didn’t expect you. Or, did my husband know you were coming and forget to tell me?”

“No, ma’am, no one here knew that I was coming. It was only decided yesterday. I’m here with messages for your husband from his father and the Indian Commission."

"Then, of course, you'll stay for dinner and even spend the night," she said.

"Oh, no, ma'am, I couldn't impose on ye," I said. "I can find suitable lodgings in a tavern."

"Lodgings? In a tavern? In Manhattan? Never! I would feel as though I was making you sleep in a sty with the pigs! Never! Neither my husband nor my father-in-law would ever tolerate such a thing. You'll stay here and there'll be no arguing. Megan! Get a move on girl, go make up a bed for Mister O'Cathail! He'll stay in the room across from yours. Hurry! And I'll finish preparing dinner."

"Yes, Ma'am," said Megan, as she hurried upstairs.

"Now, you, Mister O'Cathail, you go out back and wash yourself. You must be terribly uncomfortable with this heat." And, with her hand on his back, she gently guided Sean out the kitchen door.

On the back wall of the house, Sean found a shelf on which sat a basin and pitcher of water. While he washed, Sean thought about what had just transpired with Megan. Although he genuinely liked the girl, and found her to be pleasant company, he didn't love her. He decided that he had to clear things up with her and the sooner the better.

When he finished washing and had dried himself with the cloth he found hanging from a nail, he went back into the house. As he came in the back door, Cornelis Viele was just coming in the front.

"Good evening, Mister Viele," said Megan, as she came down the stairs to take his hat and walking stick. "Ye have a visitor," she said. "Mister O'Cathail has come down from Albany to see ye."

"He has, has he? Sean! Oh, there you are! What brings you to Manhattan on the hottest day of the year?"

"Good evening, Mister Viele," said Sean, shaking the merchant's hand. Cornelis Viele was a softer version of his father, and looked like the successful businessman he was. While Aernout Viele preferred buckskin to wool, Cornelis looked as if he would have been at home in a London coffee house, with his fashionable brown coat, fawn waistcoat and red silk cravat.

"I've come on an errand from the Indian Commission. It's an extremely long story, I'm afraid."

"Then, come, we'll eat while you tell us. Mistress Viele, is dinner ready? I'm starving, and I'm sure our young friend is as well!"

"Yes, Mister Viele, dinner is ready," she replied. "Megan, please begin serving."

They then sat down to a meal unlike any Sean had seen in Albany. First, there were oysters brought fresh that morning from Long Island. The main course was roasted shoulder of mutton with thyme, fresh vegetables, and crisp, fresh white bread to sop up the gravy. This was topped off with cheesecake and coffee. As directed, Sean talked while they ate. He told the whole story once again, emphasizing, this time, the concerns and needs of the Indian Commission. The meal was over, and Megan had cleared the dishes by the time he had finished.

Later, as Cornelis and Sean sat sipping claret and enjoying an after-dinner pipe, Cornelis said, "So, my father thinks it would be helpful if I could plead the case for the traders before Governor Dongan?"

"Aye, sir. Your father doesn't want the governor to think that this is just another example of the Albany Dutch being greedy. He wants the governor to realize that there is a real threat of economic disaster for the entire colony."

"Humm," said Cornelis, "I must say that I agree with him. First thing in the morning, we'll go to Fort James to seek an audience with the governor. He and I have met and we are on exceptionally good terms. I am sure we will be able to get in to see him, even without an appointment."

Carrying a candle, Megan led Sean up to the garret under the roof where he was to sleep.

The room was small and bare, with just a narrow bed with cornhusk mattress, a small nightstand on which stood a candle and, under the bed, a ceramic bowl for his night soil. Megan lit the candle with hers. Earlier, she had opened the small dormer window and its shutters so that the heat that had been trapped beneath the roof during the day could escape.

"Megan," Sean said, "We need to talk."

"Now, ye must be patient. We'll have many opportunities to say all the things we need to say to each other." Squeezing his hand, she went up on tiptoe and kissed his cheek tenderly. Then, she quickly left the room.

Sighing at the lost opportunity and feeling guilty that he was somehow leading the girl on, Sean undressed and, naked, crawled between the crisp, cool sheets.

He was just on the edge of sleep when the door creaked, and a figure entered the room. In the moonlight, Sean could see that it was Megan and that she wore only a nightdress. Her long, auburn hair was hanging loose, covering her shoulders.

"Megan," said Sean, sitting upright in alarm. "What are ye doing?"

"Shhh," she said as she approached the bed. "Be quiet! The Vieles might hear ye!"

"But Megan, ye shouldn't be in here!" he insisted, wrapping the blanket around himself while climbing out of bed.

"Hush, Sean O'Cathail! I know this is sudden for ye, but I've been dreaming of it since the first day we met. I love ye Sean, and I want to be yours."

"Megan? We can't do this. I don't love ye."

"Ach, Sean, will ye please hush your blather!"

"Megan, listen to me," he almost growled while grasping her shoulders and looking her in the eyes. He said, very slowly and clearly, "I... don't... love you. I love someone else... a woman in Albany."

Suddenly, understanding dawned in Megan's eyes. "Oh, my God!" she exclaimed, "What have I done? What ye must think of me!"

Then, bursting into tears, she ran from the room. Sean ran after her, but she had run into her room and barred the door.

"Megan," he whispered through the door, "Megan, speak to me. I'm sorry to have disappointed ye. I wouldn't hurt ye for the world. It's just that I don't feel the same way as ye do."

Still sobbing, Megan replied. "Go away, Sean. Please, just go to bed and leave me alone."

"Megan..."

"Go away!"

So, he did.

Chapter 12

When Sean awoke the next morning, his first thought was of Megan. 'What can I possibly say to her? She's a wonderful girl, pretty and easy to talk to, but I don't want to marry her. How can I make her see that, although I do not love her, I appreciate her as a friend and don't want to lose that friendship?'

When he went downstairs, Sean tried to get Megan alone to speak with her, but she made sure that she was too busy to talk. Finally, after breakfast, he was able to confront her in the kitchen.

"Megan, about last night," he began.

"Forget about last night," she insisted while washing dishes and avoiding his eyes. "It never happened."

"But, Megan, it did happen, and we have to talk about it."

"Not if I don't want to! Oh, God! I was such a fool! Ye must be laughing at me."

"Megan! Megan!" Sean exclaimed. "Listen! I am honored to know that ye love me, and I am so terribly sorry that I do not feel the same way. You are a wonderful woman…"

"Harrumph! Not wonderful enough to love!"

"…A wonderful woman whom I am proud to call my friend."

"Don't say another word, Sean O'Cathail! It was my mistake entirely. Now, go! Ye have a busy day ahead of ye."

"But, Megan!"

"No! Go and find Mister Viele, and go about yer important business. Then, ye can go back to yer woman in Albany! Don't worry about me. I'll be fine!"

She pushed him out of the kitchen just as Cornelis came looking for him.

"Well, Sean, we should get started. If we are too late getting to Fort James, we will not get to see the governor. There is always a crowd of supplicants demanding his time."

Soon, they were out the door and on their way west along Wall Street to The Broadway and then south to the fort.

While they walked, Cornelis questioned Sean further about what he had seen and heard at Caughnawaga. So, Sean again described what had happened when old Onata had suddenly remembered that the Five Nations had given the Susquehanna Valley to Governor Andros. Preoccupied with the conversation, Sean was unable to dwell on the situation with Megan.

"That just may be the bait we need to get the governor to bite," Cornelis said. "Dongan is only the acting governor of the colony. He is not in a position to challenge a colonial proprietor like William Penn. Even though Penn is a Quaker, he still wields considerable influence at court. But, if Dongan thinks the Susquehanna valley truly belongs to New York, he will be reluctant to let it go without a fight! The Duke of York would never forgive him if he did!"

"But, sir," Sean responded, "we do not know yet if all Five Nations will accept the old woman's story. The Mohawk have, yes, but the others may still want to try to sell the land."

"No matter," Cornelis said with confidence. "Our job today is to plant a seed. We can suggest that his clerks search the archives for the transcript of the council in which the Five Nations gave the land to Andros. By the time they are able to report that no such evidence exists, the Five Nations will have decided what they will do. If they decide to follow the Mohawk, then there is no problem. The governor will readily agree with them that New York owns the land. However, if they decide to sell, he will either get the Duke of York to fight Penn, or he will shrug his shoulders and leave Albany to its fate."

Just then, they arrived at the gates of Fort James. Entering the main gate, the two men crossed the parade ground, passing the old Dutch Reformed Church, and entered the governor's residence where they joined a large crowd of men, including Robert Livingston.

Cornelis Viele walked up to Livingston, who was talking with some other men, and clapped his hand on Livingston's shoulder. "Robert, how are you? It's been a while since I last saw you!"

"Why, Cornelis, it is good to see you. I hope that you and Mistress Viele are well."

"We are both exceedingly well, Robert. Thank you for asking. And, Mistress Livingston is well, I trust?

"She, too, is well, thank you," replied Livingston.

"Now tell me," asked Cornelis, "How are things in Albany?"

"Not good. But, I see you have met up with O'Cathail. I trust that he has acquainted you with our problem. I tell you, Cornelis, it is imperative that we get the governor to take a stand. Otherwise, we are lost!"

"I am quite sure that we can do something about that," said Cornelis. "Have you spoken to the governor's secretary about an appointment today?"

"No, not yet. He is only just entering the room," Livingston replied, gesturing at a bookish-looking, little man with spectacles perched on the end of his nose who was just settling himself at a desk in front of the door to the governor's office. Men from the crowd had already started jostling for positions in line in front of the desk. Each wanted to be the first to make his case for an audience with Governor Dongan.

"Come," said Cornelis to the others, "Let us not stand on ceremony, or we will be left standing." Raising his silver-headed walking stick upright, Cornelis began striding toward the head of the line with Livingston and Sean trailing in his wake.

"Excuse me, excuse me," he muttered as he pushed his way past merchants and burghers, military officers and common folk alike.

"Mister Greavey!" Cornelis exclaimed when he finally reached the desk. "Mister Greavey, it is imperative that I see his Excellency at once. It is a matter of grave concern to the colony as a whole and cannot wait another minute!"

"Mister Viele," said Greavey, the governor's secretary raising his eyes from the journal in which he would assign appointments to the waiting throng. "What could possibly be so urgent?"

"Why, it's the very existence of the colony that's threatened!"

"Are the Dutch planning to attack us again? Or have the French loosed their heathen dogs?" asked Greavey.

"Nay," exclaimed Cornelis. "'Tis far more perilous than a mere military threat. This is a grave economic threat! One that could ruin the colony!" As he spoke, Cornelis became more and more animated. He waved his arms in the air and, then, brought his walking stick down hard on the secretary's desk.

Startled, Greavey looked up at the wild man before him. Cornelis' face was so red that it looked as though he would become apoplectic. He kept waving his cane to emphasize his agitation as bystanders ducked and backed away.

"Hurry. Greavey, it is imperative! Imperative, I tell you!" Cornelis cried as he gave Livingston and Sean a wink.

Greavey jumped up, knocking his chair over backward, and scurried through the door into the governor's office.

When he reappeared, he gestured to Cornelis, saying, "Mister Viele, His Excellency, the Governor, will see you now."

"You see, gentlemen," said Cornelis, turning and speaking to the crowd with a smile, "Sometimes you just have to convince people of the seriousness of your problem."

Motioning for Livingston and Sean to follow, Cornelis strode imperiously past the cringing secretary and into the governor's office.

When they had entered, and Greavey had closed the door behind them, Colonel Thomas Dongan, lieutenant governor of the Colony of New York, rose and walked around his desk to greet Cornelis.

"Mister Viele, 'tis a pleasure to see ye again. However, I must say I am a little confused. Greavey told me that there was a madman demanding to see me and ranting about some threat to the colony. Could it have been ye that he was talking about?"

"Yes, Your Excellency, it was me. I apologize. I tend to become agitated when I think about someone trying to steal furs from the colony."

"Well, I suppose that I should hear ye out, ranting or no. But, first... Mister Livingston! I have not seen ye since I was last in Albany. I hope that ye are well!"

"Very well, Your Excellency!"

"Good, good. Ah, Mister Livingston, I know that I have received a letter from ye and your colleagues. I am sorry, but I just have not had the opportunity to respond," said the Governor, gesturing at the piles of papers on his desk.

"Entirely understandable, Your Excellency. We can only imagine how pressing the affairs of a colony can be," replied Livingston.

"True, all too true. Now," said Dongan, turning toward Sean. "I do not believe that I have had the pleasure of meeting your companion."

"Your Excellency, replied Cornelis. "I have the privilege to present to you Mister Sean O'Cathail, a fellow countryman of yours and a fur trader at Albany."

Dongan shook Sean's hand with a strong grasp. Sean noted that the governor, who had served as a colonel in command of the *Régiment d'Irlandais* while waiting for the Catholic Stuarts to regain the English throne, was the perfect picture of a military man. He was taller than Sean, and his shoulders were broader. His erect posture, despite a thickening waistline, added to his imposing presence. He looked like someone who was decidedly in control of himself and any situation that might arise.

"Mister O'Cathail," said the governor, turning to Sean, "'Tis always good to meet a fellow Celt. Where were ye born?"

"In Munster, Your Honor," said Sean.

"Munster, beautiful country. I'm a Kildareman, myself. Have ye been a soldier, perhaps, Mister O'Cathail?"

"No, Your Honor, unfortunately not," replied Sean.

"A pity," said the governor, quickly losing interest in Sean. "Well, then, gentlemen, what is this emergency that demands my immediate attention?"

"If it pleases Your Excellency," Cornelis began, "We regret to report that agents of William Penn are negotiating with the Five Nations to purchase land along the Susquehanna River."

"Also, Your Excellency," interjected Livingston handing an envelope containing the Indian Commission's latest missive to Dongan, "we are credibly informed that the savages are willing to sell the land to Penn and are predisposed, eventually, to take their fur trade to his colony."

"Not only that," added Cornelis. "But traders from Penn's colony are already among the Seneca and Cayuga trading for furs that rightfully belong to New York.

"As you are aware," he continued. "Furs are the economic lifeline of the colony. Cut it off and the colony will wither and die. That is why it is imperative that we act to stop the sale.""Now, gentlemen," said Dongan. "You must realize that I cannot prevent a colonial proprietor from buying whatever he wants to buy from the savages. In fact, his representatives met with me here, at Fort James, before going to Albany. They seemed quite determined to affect the sale."

"True, Your Excellency," said Cornelis. "But you could stop him from buying land that actually belongs to New York! We have been told that, ten years ago, during a council with Governor Andros, the Five Nations gave him a gift of the land in appreciation for his having completed the Covenant Chain with them. You should be able to find evidence of that fact in the transcripts of that council."

"Well, gentlemen, if that is true, then it changes things considerably. I am quite sure that his highness, the Duke of York, would look poorly on any transaction that severed lands from this Colony. I will have my clerks look into this. You say that the council was held in 1674?" asked Dongan, making a note of the date.

"Yes, Your Excellency. My father was an interpreter for the council and remembers the occasion quite clearly," said Cornelis, lying deftly.

"Good," the governor said. "Now, how soon do we need to act? How long do we have before the sale becomes final?"

"Well, Your Excellency, Penn's agents are expected to return to Albany soon with final approval to buy the land. We believe that they will be given a free hand to buy the land at any price they can negotiate with the savages," said Livingston.

"The only thing standing in the way of the sale," said Sean, "is the fact that the sachems with whom they must meet are currently at Onontague for a council. After that is finished, they will come to Albany for their meeting with you and Lord Howard. They will probably start negotiating with Penn's agents at that time."

"The truth of the matter, Your Excellency," said Cornelis "is that we simply do not have time to waste. Penn's agents could be back in Albany at any time. And, the savages will likely complete their discussions and start traveling to Albany within a fortnight."

"Damn it all!" cursed Dongan. "First, I have Lord Howard complaining that the savages are raiding Virginia, and wanting to punish them. Then, I have *Monsieur* La Barre, the governor of New France, complaining that the Seneca are stealing from the *couriers-des-bois*, and demanding that I do something about it! Now, this! I swear! These savages are more trouble than they are worth!"

"You have had complaints from La Barre!" exclaimed Livingston. "How dare he complain about our savages, when his are wandering all through the colony making all manner of mischief?"

"Be that as it may, he has complained, and I have to respond," said Dongan. "Remember, gentlemen, England is currently at peace with France. Now, where is that letter?" he muttered to himself

"Greavey!" the governor called. "Where is that letter we received from Governor La Barre?"

"One moment, Your Excellency," said Greavey, running into the room and searching through the piles of paper on the governor's desk.

"Here it is!"

"Ah, yes. Listen to this, gentlemen, the man bemoans the outrageous conduct of the Seneca," said Dongan as he began to read. "He says that the savages 'pillaged seven hundred canoes belonging to Frenchmen and...' Huh! Seven hundred canoes. That's astounding! I hope that all those furs found their way to Albany!

"Anyway, he then says that the Seneca '...afterwards attacked Fort Saint Louis on the Illinois River where,' ahem, 'Chevalier de Bougy gallantly defended himself.' If the man is still alive, I imagine he did! Then he complains that the savages have introduced English traders into waters sacred to the French. I suppose he means the Great Lakes. My God, how I wish that were true!"

"How will you reply, Your Excellency?" queried Livingston.

"I plan to reply that I have no control over the savages. That they will attack whomever they want to attack, with or without my permission or support. At the same time, however, I will remind him that any attack on the Seneca would be an invasion of English territory. I will also tell him that, to my knowledge, no Englishman is currently trading in the Great Lakes and that, if he would be so kind as to forbid his traders from this side of Lake Ontario, I would be happy to forbid

Englishmen from trading on the other side of the lake."

"That should quiet him," said Livingston.

"Let us hope so, but it means that after Lord Howard is finished disciplining the savages, I will have to do so, as well! But, of course we have to be careful how we do it. God forbid that we should offend them! I have asked Lord Howard not to be too hard on them. They are all that stands between us and the French. And, if they believe that we have insulted them, they may just go over to the French. But, that is my problem, gentlemen, not yours."

"Greavey! Greavey!" he called. "Bring my calendar!"

The secretary again scurried into the room, this time carrying the ledger into which he had been entering appointments.

"Let us see, Lord Howard and I are due to arrive in Albany in two weeks. How long do you gentlemen think this affair will last? Two, three weeks?"

"Three weeks should be sufficient, Your Excellency," said Livingston.

"Aye," agreed Sean. "Three weeks is about right. The savages do love their ceremonies."

"So, there you have it Greavey," said Dongan, "I will leave for Albany in two weeks and will be there for at least three weeks. Also... gentlemen, please give Mister Greavey the information he will need to find the transcript of the council we were discussing.

"Oh, and one more thing... as this will be my first meeting with the savages, I will need as much background information as possible. Mister Livingston, can you accompany me on the journey up to Albany? I know that this will require that you return to Manhattan in two weeks. I hope that it will not be too great an imposition..."

"Not at all, Your Excellency. I am in Manhattan regularly on business for Rennselaerwyck Manor," replied Livingston.

"Oh. That reminds me. The manor... That is an issue we need to discuss. We should have an opportunity to do so on the trip up the river. Most importantly, I will need you to share with me your knowledge of the savages and their customs so that I will be adequately prepared for any eventuality."

"Governor," said Cornelis, "May I suggest that Mister O'Cathail join you, as well?"

"That will not be necessary," interjected Livingston quickly. "As Secretary for Indian Affairs, I am in a position to provide any information the governor might need."

"I'm sorry, Robert, but I must disagree," replied Cornelis. "Mister O'Cathail has recently been among the Iroquois and can provide the governor with the most current intelligence regarding the savages."

"I am sure that Mister O'Cathail can provide us with important information," said Dongan. Turning to Sean, he continued, "If possible, sir, you should make yourself available to join us, as well."

"As Your Excellency wishes," said Sean, bowing slightly.

"Then, is everything settled? Gentlemen, thank you for bringing this issue to my attention. Mister Viele, you were correct - this is of immense importance to the colony."

"Thank you, your Excellency," chorused the three men as they followed the secretary from the chamber.

After providing Greavey with information about the purported gift of the Susquehanna to Governor Andros, the three men left the governor's residence and parted, with Livingston going to the Rensselaerwyck warehouse to check on a shipment of household goods that his wife had been expecting from Amsterdam. Cornelis walked Sean to the Town Wharf where he would catch the next packet to Albany. It would be leaving at three in the afternoon for the journey back up the river.

"Sean, I appreciate the fact that you are willing to join the governor and Livingston on the trip up to Albany. I don't trust Livingston at all. He is a schemer, and I don't think that he would have any trouble using Albany's problems to his own benefit. Perhaps your presence will keep him from being too blatantly greedy. Or, barring that, you will, at least, be privy to any questionable dealings that Livingston and the governor might contrive."

Then, as the two men shook hands, Cornelis said, "Farewell, Sean. Greetings to my father and mother!"

"Farewell, Cornelis. I will see you in two weeks."

Once on the Albany-bound packet, Sean again reflected on what had happened with Megan. Finally, he decided that there was nothing he could do until he returned in two weeks. The next time he saw her, he thought, he would straighten it all out. He would make her understand that, even though he didn't love her, she was still very special, even dear to him. After all, she was the one who put the idea of fur trading in his head.

Chapter 13

The days before Sean's return to Manhattan were exceptionally busy. Aernout wanted to take advantage of Sean's return downriver to assemble a shipment of beaver pelts for Cornelis to ship to Amsterdam. So, many days were spent gathering and loading the peltries onto a yacht.

Despite the time spent in these activities, Sean still managed to make time to see Laurentje. Usually, they were able to steal a few moments together in the evening after they had both completed their work.

Once the furs were loaded, Sean left for Manhattan. When he arrived, Cornelis joined him with a group of workers to unload the pelts. Watching the process with Sean, Cornelis observed, "This is a superior load of pelts! It should bring quite a profit! Luckily, I have already been able to consign the shipment to a vessel leaving in just ten days. Another fur merchant had to cancel a shipment, and I heard of it in time."

After the furs were safely stored in the Vieles' warehouse space, Cornelis said, "There, that's done. Now, what do you say to a drink?"

"That would be most welcome. Thank ye, sir!" said Sean.

Once they were seated in the City Tavern, Cornelis asked, "Now that you've completed your arrangement with my father, Sean, what are your plans?" he asked.

"I will join Johannes Roseboom on an expedition to the Ottawa in the fall. If things go well, I should make enough money to set myself up in business."

"Good lad! I have no doubt that you will be successful! And, when you start trading on your own, come and see me. I would be honored to represent you here in Manhattan."

"Why thank ye, sir, the honor would be mine."

"Good. Finished with your beer? We should be leaving. I am certain that Mistress Viele is holding supper for us. By the way, I know that you and our former maid, Megan, were friendly. So, I was wondering if..."

"Your *former* maid, sir? What do you mean?"

"She's gone! Just up and left us! Came to Mistress Viele with all her belongings wrapped up in a bundle and said she was quitting. Immediately! Mistress Viele tried to question her, but she wouldn't explain. Only said that she was sorry that she couldn't give notice but she had to leave immediately. Put us in quite a spot! Mistress Viele was none too happy. She said she would not have another independent servant in the house. So, I have spent the past week attending indenture auctions instead of taking care of business. I think I found what she wanted. At least the girl seems promising enough. In fact, tonight's supper, if I'm not mistaken, will be prepared by this new girl. I hope that she is as good a cook as she says she is. Damn Megan! She was a good cook!"

"But, why would Megan leave you? She seemed to be quite happy with her situation."

"We don't know! In fact, I was hoping that you might be able to shed some light on the mystery."

"No, I'm sorry, sir, I can't," Sean replied, fearing that he might be the reason for Megan's abrupt departure. "Megan never said a word to me about leaving."

Exiting the tavern, Sean and Cornelis headed toward the Viele home. As they walked, Cornelis talked, pointing out people and places of interest, and telling the stories behind them. But Sean barely heard him. Sean was preoccupied, keeping an eye out for Cox and turning the news about Megan over and over in his mind.

They were met at the door by Mistress Viele. "Mister Viele, finally! You know how much stress I have been under these past days and, yet, you insist on being late for dinner!"

"Sorry, my dear. But Sean and I stopped at the City Tavern. We found ourselves quite parched."

"Oh, hello, Mister O'Cathail! Please forgive me! I've not been myself since Megan left. Did Mister Viele tell you?"

"Only that she left without warning, Ma'am," said Sean.

"Do you have any idea why she would have done such a thing?"

"No, Ma'am," he said. "As I told Mister Viele, I had thought that she was quite happy here."

"So did we! She had been with us for almost five years, and we thought of her almost as family. Am I not correct, Mister Viele?"

"Yes, of course, my dear," Cornelis responded.

"But, apparently she wasn't as happy as we thought she was! Although I am convinced that we did everything we could to make sure she was. Oh, and Mister Viele, I have learned something of interest concerning the matter."

"Really, dear? What is that?" Cornelis asked.

"Well, the new girl -- Sean, her name is Margaretha, by the way -- was speaking with Mistress Wantenaar's girl and learned that, the day before Megan left, there was a stranger hanging about the street. The girl told Margaretha that she had assumed that he may have been newly arrived and taking in the sites of the town, so she just put him out of her mind."

"Interesting, very interesting," said Cornelis. "Sean, what do you make of it?"

"I really cannot say, sir," Sean replied. "It may have just been a coincidence. Do either of you think that something untoward may have happened to Megan?"

"Oh, dear! I hope not!" said Mistress Viele. "I've been so busy thinking about my own problems that it never occurred to me that Megan could be in trouble or even in some sort of danger. Well! Both of you go get cleaned up for dinner. We can speak more of this later."

After dinner, which Sean thought was delicious but was deemed, "Not bad..." by Mister Viele, Mistress Viele joined the men while they enjoyed their pipes and claret.

"Mister O'Cathail," she said, once she was settled next to her husband, "All through dinner, I was worrying that something might have happened to Megan. And...well, I was hoping that, since you were friendly with Megan, you might want to help us find her."

"Find her!" exclaimed Cornelis. "Why would we want to find her? I've just spent an entire week finding her replacement!"

"But, Mister Viele," said his wife, "Do you not want to learn what happened to her? Are you not the least bit curious to know if she is safe?"

"Harrumph! When you put it that way... I suppose that I would like to know why she left and if she is safe."

"So, Mister O'Cathail," Mistress Viele continued, "Do you think you could try to learn what has become of the girl?"

"Now, my dear," Cornelis interjected. "Sean has much more important things to do in the coming days!"

"Well, that's not entirely true," said Sean. "Although I cannot do anything immediately... I have to travel with the governor to Albany tomorrow, and I may have to stay in Albany for the councils. But, I should be able to come back and do as you request. Be assured, I am as concerned as you are, Mistress Viele, and will make time to find her."

"Thank you, Mister O'Cathail," said Mistress Viele. "Now, Margaretha has already prepared your room. You can find your way? I believe that you will find a lighted candle at the foot of the stairs."

"Yes, I can. Thank you," replied Sean.

"Then, we will bid you good night. And, again, thank you for agreeing to look for Megan."

"No thanks necessary. I only hope that her trail has not gone cold by the time I return. Good night."

As he lay in bed, waiting for sleep to come, Sean found himself thinking of Megan. Why would she have left without notice?

Early the next morning, Sean was at the Mole to catch the governor's official sloop. Although he had been careful while walking through the town, he failed to notice that he had been followed and that, while he boarded the sloop with all the other passengers, he had been observed by Cox who, after ascertaining the owner of the vessel and its destination, headed back downtown.

Also traveling that morning with Sean, the governor and Robert Livingston were the governor of Virginia, Lord Howard of Effingham, members of both governors' staffs and sundry hangers-on. On board as well was Stephanus Cortlandt, a member of the governor's Advisory Council, who would represent the colony of Massachusetts in the council with the Iroquois.

With no specific duties except to answer the governor's questions, if he had any, and to keep an eye on Robert Livingston, Sean passed the time observing the other passengers who were all trying to curry favor with one or both of the governors.

"Quite entertaining, isn't it?" asked a well-dressed man of military bearing, interrupting Sean's musings. "Although I cannot determine why ye are here. Ye do not look like a sycophant."

"Excuse me, sir," said Sean. "I do not believe I have had the honor."

"Pardon me," the man replied. "I am Major Patrick MacGregory, former soldier of fortune, newcomer to America and, unlike ye, a sycophant!"

"My name is O'Cathail, Sean O'Cathail, and it's pleased I am to make your acquaintance, Major MacGregory. Although I must say that ye do not seem to be fawning quite as strenuously as our fellow passengers."

The two men were soon chatting like old friends. MacGregory, after serving in France in a Scots Catholic regiment loyal to James Stuart, had returned to England where he tried a variety of occupations, without much success. Seeking his fortune in the New World, he led a band of settlers to Catholic Maryland. However, not finding the colony to his liking, he traveled north to New York.

He had purchased some land in the highlands along Hudson's river not far from Manhattan and was seeking a patent for an estate. He had hoped that Dongan, a fellow Catholic, would look kindly upon his application. But, while Dongan had been welcoming, MacGregory was still awaiting his patent.

As he and MacGregory talked, Sean found that his new friend was extremely interested in the fur trade and eager to hear all that Sean could tell him. Sean, of course, was flattered by the older man's attention and pleased to share his knowledge. In fact, Sean became even closer to MacGregory when he realized that the major had a rather low opinion of Robert Livingston.

"Ach," observed MacGregory, "I've been watching him. He's a flatlander from Edinburgh and does not have the sensibilities of a Highlander or even an Irishman such as yourself.

"Right now," he continued, "I'm convinced that he is scheming to make the governor beholden to him in some way or another so that he can profit from their association. Just as I am sure that Dongan wants something from Livingston."

"Well," replied Sean, "Livingston is one of the richest men in Albany. He's a successful merchant and politician, and he's married to a rich widow with a huge estate. So, I can see why the governor might want to befriend him. But, he also has the reputation of being the stingiest man alive! So, our governor would have to work extremely hard to get something from him. I've got it! Livingston wants the governor to recognize the Rensselaer estate as an English manor. And..."

"And," interjected MacGregory, "Dongan needs money! That's the obvious *quid pro quo*. But, if you truly want to know what is going on, you need to get closer to them. Join their conversations. Perhaps one or the other will let his guard down and then you'll learn something useful."

On the fourth and final day of the voyage, Dongan and Livingston were standing by the rail enjoying the scenery. Sean joined them just as the governor said, "Ach, Robert, is it not beautiful?"

"Ah, Your Excellency, but no less dangerous for all its beauty," responded Livingston.

"Aye, but only dangerous to those who are blind to its dangers, or who do not respect them," interjected Sean.

"Why, what do you mean, Mister O'Cathail?" asked Dongan, as Livingston turned a cold eye on Sean for intruding.

"Why, Your Excellency," said Sean. "If one recognizes the dangers of the wilderness, respects them for the threat they pose and acts in a way to protect himself, the frontier need be no more dangerous than a walk through any large city in the world. For example, I imagine that there are areas in London that can be much more dangerous to life and limb than the forests of New York."

"Aye," responded Dongan, "I've had the misfortune to find myself in some of those neighborhoods. Your point is well-taken."

Just then, a sailor approached. Saluting the governor, he said, "The captain's compliments, sir, he wants you to know that we will be arriving at Albany in about two hours' time."

"Good. Good. Thank you," replied Dongan, returning the salute.

"Now, Robert," he said, turning to Livingston, "As we will soon arrive at Albany. I think it best that I prepare myself with details about the town. First..."

"Do you wish to know some of its history?" asked Livingston.

"No. What I want to know is something of the town as it is today. Now, tell me," he said. "Are these Dutchmen as ignorant as they seem to be? I have observed that many of them not only cannot speak the king's English but also do not even try to learn it."

"Well, Your Excellency, they are not ignorant. I would say, rather, that they are crafty," replied Livingston. "More of them can speak English than let on. I have been living among them for nigh onto ten years, and I have found them to be very astute businessmen, if a little too set in their ways. Under Dutch rule and even under yer predecessor, Governor Andros, the traders and merchants at Albany were left to their own devices. So long as they produced profits for the colony, no one bothered them. As a result, they became quite independent. For example, until yer arrival, Albany enjoyed an official monopoly in the fur trade of the colony. The traders and merchants have been hoping that ye would reaffirm that arrangement. I imagine that, when ye meet with the magistrates, they will be anticipating such an action on yer part."

"My God, Robert! I know they want a monopoly. It's all I have heard from them since I arrived on these shores. But, why would they need me to proclaim a monopoly? The savages already come to Albany to trade!"

"More than anything," replied Livingston, "They need to be legally protected from traders who live elsewhere in the colony, especially in Schenectady. You see, Schenectady was originally settled by Albany traders who wanted to divert furs from their brethren. And, to this day, there are those who take part in the illegal trade in furs that occurs in Schenectady, and in the woods outside of the palisades of Albany. It is a way for unscrupulous traders, called *boschlopers,* to intercept the Indians and buy their furs at prices that are lower than those offered at Albany. Most often, these furs are then smuggled into Albany and shipped to Manhattan for legal shipment to Amsterdam. However, the *boschlopers* have been known to smuggle the furs to Boston, as well, where they are sold to merchants who can ship them to London without paying taxes to the Duke of York.

"So, a monopoly protects the colony's and the Duke's interests. Requiring that all furs be traded within the palisade at Albany ensures that they will be properly taxed. When Governor Andros granted Albany its monopoly, he did so to protect the colony's revenue. He did not care about the Albany traders and merchants. In fact, he was so eager to restrict trading to Albany where it could be controlled that he made the county sheriff's salary contingent upon the fines he could levy against smugglers. Anyone who is caught smuggling by the *Schout*, as the Dutch call him, can be fined as much as half of the value of his furs."

"As you can imagine, Your Excellency," interjected Sean with a laugh, "Sheriff Pretty is the most active and vigilant *Schout* in all the Americas!"

"I am sure that you, O'Cathail, could enlighten the governor better than I on the practices of the *boschlopers*," said Livingston scornfully.

"And, what do ye mean by that remark," retorted Sean.

"Only that you and your partner and his brother, the tavern keeper in Schenectady, are known to have..."

"Watch your tongue, Livingston," threatened Sean, "Or, I'll make ye eat yer words!"

"Gentlemen! Gentlemen!" said Dongan, stepping between the two men. "That's enough from both of ye! I want to hear facts, not slander!"

Sean and Livingston begrudgingly allowed the governor to separate them.

"All right," the governor continued. "So, the Albany traders want a monopoly. But why do they sit there in Albany instead of going out among the savages, as the French do?"

"Well, at least until recently, they have had no trouble getting the savages to bring their furs to Albany," said Livingston.

"But, what about the tribes further west who do all their trading with the French?" asked Dongan. "What have the Dutch done to attract them to Albany? I'll tell you: nothing! Hundreds of tons of peltries in thousands of canoes find their way to Montreal each summer. Why haven't the Dutch gone after this trade?"

"Your Excellency," interjected Sean, "There is no way, currently, for the Far Indians to come to Albany. The Five Nations would never grant them safe passage along the Iroquois trail. They have been at war for as long as anyone can remember and there is much bad blood between them. Too, the Dutch have always been merchants, not adventurers. However, there are those of us who want to trade among the Far Indians. In fact, if I'm not mistaken, one trader, Johannes Roseboom, will seek an audience with you while you are in Albany. He'll want to discuss his plans to trade among the Ottawa."

"Why, Your Excellency," said Livingston conspiratorially, "I've just had a thought... As governor of the colony, it is within your authority to issue licenses for almost any purpose. Why not issue licenses for fur trading? Then, you could insist that the savages only deal with licensed traders. If you only grant licenses to Albany traders, it might assuage their demands for a monopoly. In addition, the granting of licenses would address the concerns of the Albany traders regarding the interlopers from Penn's colony.

"And, another thing," said Livingston, excited by the notion that had just come to him and forgetting for the moment that Sean was present, "this is one way to solve that money problem of yours that we've been discussing... This could be a way for you realize income that could go far toward relieving the financial strain under which your paltry salary has placed you.

"The granting of licenses would, of course, involve a fee, which could even include a percentage of the value of the furs delivered to Albany. These charges, unlike the taxes imposed on the furs, need not be reported to the Duke of York, and would nicely supplement Your Excellency's income. I would, of course, be honored to serve as your licensing agent in Albany. For a small consideration, of course!"

"Hummm," pondered Dongan. "Indeed, Robert, I like your thinking. We must discuss this in greater detail. But, first, let us return to the topic at hand. How do we get furs from the Far Indians to Albany?"

"Well, Your Excellency, let us look at this logically," said Livingston. "In order for the Ottawa, for example, to come to Albany," he continued, "each of the Five Nations would have to agree to provide safe passage. Even if such an arrangement could be made, it would first require peace between the Iroquois and the Ottawa, and someone, either the Indian Commission or you, yourself, to establish a reasonable levy for the Iroquois to charge for passage through their territory."

"On the other hand," said Sean, "if our traders go to the Ottawa, you simplify the whole process!"

"But, wouldn't our traders, this Roseboom, for example, have to pay some sort of toll to the Five Nations?" queried Dongan.

"No," said Sean. "They would have to give gifts at any villages in which they stopped, but that isn't anything they don't already do as a matter of course, and the value would be far less than any toll the Ottawa might pay."

"That does make sense. I will have to think on it," said Dongan. "Now, let us turn to the Iroquois. Are they truly as ferocious as I've been told?"

"They are, indeed, Your Excellency." said Sean. Having captured the governor's attention, he was unwilling to relinquish it. "They are fearless and fearsome warriors. Their goal is to conquer or subjugate all the tribes with which

they come in contact. In battle, they do not
surrender. They may run away, but only in the
face of vastly superior numbers. They nearly
wiped out the Huron about forty years ago."

"What do they fight over? Land?" asked
Dongan.

"Sometimes they will fight over hunting
grounds or to annex new lands to their own," said
Sean. "But, usually, they fight for pride and to
avenge real and perceived wrongs, and... to
replenish their numbers."

"That's interesting," said Dongan. "Do
you mean that captured warriors join the
Iroquois?"

"Nay, captured warriors are usually
tortured to death by the women of a village.
They call it, 'caressing.' The purpose is to test
the bravery of the captive. If he dies screaming,
he is considered unworthy. However, if he dies
bravely, while singing his death chant, the
Iroquois will honor him by eating his heart."

"Are they cannibals, then?"

"Not really. They only eat the hearts of
brave men in order to ingest their bravery."

"So, how do they add new members to the
tribe if they kill their captives?"

"They only kill captive warriors. Women
and children are adopted into the tribe to replace
a son or husband killed in battle, or a wife or
daughter who has died. Since the Five Nations
were almost totally decimated by smallpox fifty
years ago, this is how they manage to survive.
They are very susceptible to our diseases.

Catarrh is often fatal, and smallpox can wipe out entire villages in a matter of weeks."

"Interesting, very interesting," said Dongan. "Now, how do these Five Nations relate to each other? How are they organized?"

"Well, Your Excellency," said Livingston, seizing the floor from Sean. "The Iroquois were first united many years ago by a warrior named Hiawatha, with the goal of preserving peace between them while presenting a united front against their enemies.

"The Mohawk are one of the larger nations. Because they were the first to meet the Dutch, they consider themselves to be spokesmen for all the Iroquois at Albany; and they also control the fur trade at Albany by charging tolls, even for other Iroquois.

"Moving west, the next is the Oneida, one of the smallest nations. Then, there are the Onondaga, in the middle of Iroquois country. They are called 'Keepers of the Flame' because the Iroquois council fire burns at their main castle.

"Further west is another minor tribe, the Cayuga. And, finally, there are the Seneca. They are the largest of the Iroquois nations, and the most warlike. By custom, when the Iroquois meet in council, the Oneida and Cayuga are considered 'little brothers' of the Mohawk, Onondaga and Seneca. They have fewer representatives and, therefore, a smaller voice in decision making."

"I am sorry, Robert, but you speak of larger and smaller. How many Iroquois are there?"

"No one actually knows an exact number. But you can be certain that they number far more than the 3,500 Christians who live in the colony," said Livingston.

"I can provide some idea of their numbers," interjected Sean. "My partner, who is familiar with all the tribes, estimates that the Mohawk can field about 1,000 warriors; the Oneida, 250; the Onondaga, another 250; the Cayuga, nearly 500; and, the Seneca have nearly 1,500. Thus, the Five Nations together total more than 3,000 warriors. If we assume one woman and two children for each warrior, then there are more than 12,000 Iroquois."

"And your partner is Mr. Viele's father, correct?"

"Yes, Your Excellency,"

"And," continued Dongan, "does he speak the languages of the natives?"

"Aye, Your Excellency. He speaks Iroquois, as well as Algonquin," said Sean. "Oh, and French, of course, from his dealings with French traders who come to Albany."

"Mister Viele often acts as interpreter for the Indian Commission," added Livingston. "He can be trusted to give a good accounting of what is said in a council."

"Excellent, excellent," said Dongan. "Perhaps we can make use of his talents while we are in Albany. Would he be willing to interpret our discussions with the savages?"

"Undoubtedly," said Sean. "The Iroquois sachems know him and trust that he will correctly interpret their words, as well as those of Lord Howard and yourself."

"Good, good," said Dongan. "Now. We are currently at peace with the Five Nations. Is that not correct?"

"Yes, Your Excellency, we are and have been for many years," responded Livingston. "And how faithful have the savages been in keeping this peace?"

"The peace has never been broken by the Five Nations. The Iroquois speak of peace as a chain. They say that when the Dutch arrived, they 'attached their ship to a tree with a rope.' Then, when the peace was reaffirmed with the English in 1674, the rope became a 'chain of silver.'"

"However, Your Excellency, one cannot take the peace for granted," said Sean. "The French have done everything in their power not only to intimidate the Five Nations by force, but to win their allegiance by sending missionaries among them. In my travels among the Iroquois, I have seen evidence of intrigue by French Jesuits among the savages. They have built churches in some of the villages and have even encouraged some baptized Mohawks to move to New France and live in Christian villages there. Of all the nations, only the Seneca have never allowed a priest to live among them."

"Aye, Your Excellency," said Livingston, "O'Cathail makes a good point. Officially, the Five Nations are also at peace with the French.

Almost thirty years ago, an Onondaga sachem negotiated a treaty with the French and was even baptized. It was he who first allowed the Jesuits to establish missions among the Onondaga. Now, the French priests act both as spies and as *agents provocateurs*, trying to turn the Five Nations against us. Luckily, they have not had much success. Since the Iroquois are also friendly with us, the French do not trust the Iroquois; and because the French are allied with all their enemies, the Iroquois do not trust the French."

"And with good reason," said Sean. "When pressured, the French have always taken the side of their allies over the Iroquois. To counter this, the Iroquois target French traders bringing weapons and ammunition to the Far Indians. This has made the French traders afraid to travel near Iroquois territory and has even caused the Far Indians to question the strength of the French, since the French seem unable to protect them from the Iroquois."

"Well, gentlemen, ye've given me much to think about. Is there anything else I need to know?"

"Mayor Schuyler has asked me to offer the hospitality of his home while you are in Albany," said Livingston.

"I thought that I would be staying at the fort," said Dongan.

"William Penn's agents are currently staying at the fort," noted Sean. "Until we know for certain what the Iroquois will do, it might be well for you to maintain your distance."

"Perhaps, Your Excellency, it would be better if you stayed with the Schuylers. I would invite you to stay with me, but that could cause problems with the Dutch. It may be best if you stay with one of their own."

"Your points are well taken, both of you, I will do as you suggest," said Dongan. "But, what of Lord Howard? Or, Cortlandt? Where will they stay?"

"I have offered the hospitality of my home to Lord Howard," replied Livingston. "And, Mister Cortlandt has family in Albany with whom, I assume, he will stay."

"Good. Good. Now then, is there anything else?"

"Well, Your Excellency," said Livingston. "Each of the magistrates, myself included, is appointed. We hold our current appointments from Governor Andros. As you can expect, we would be extremely grateful to be re-appointed by your Excellency."

"Grateful, you say, Robert?" queried Dongan.

"Aye, Your Excellency, *extremely* grateful," responded Livingston.

"I will keep that in mind. But, while we still have some time to talk, what of the town's inhabitants? Are they loyal?"

"Well," said Livingston, "Loyalty is relative. They are loyal to the beaver trade, and they can be loyal to a government that protects and promotes the trade. But, as I said earlier, they are highly independent and will complain loudly if they feel that the colonial government is interfering in local affairs. Luckily, you were able to silence most of those complaints when you established the General Assembly for the colony…”

Just then they were interrupted by the sound of cannon from Fort Albany, booming a salute of welcome to the governor.

“Well, gentlemen, it appears we have arrived,” said Dongan, as sailors began to take in the sails. “Mr. Greavey! Please advise Lord Howard that we have arrived!”

Looking toward the shore, Sean saw that the whole town had turned out to greet the governors. Although he could not distinguish individuals from such a distance, he strained his eyes nonetheless to see if he could find Laurentje in the crowd.

Chapter 14

The guns of Fort Albany continued to resound as the governor's sloop was tied up at the town dock. As soon as the gangplank was run out by the crew, the welcoming crowd, led by the town magistrates, pressed forward.

When the governor and Lord Howard stepped onto the dock together, Mayor Schuyler approached. Sweeping his hat from his head and bowing, Schuyler said, "Your Excellencies, it is my honor to welcome you to Albany, the westernmost point in all of His Majesty's colonies in America, and England's first line of defense against the French and their heathen allies. Please do us the honor of accepting our hospitality, and please do me the personal honor of allowing me to serve as your host during your visit."

"Thank you, Mayor Schuyler, on behalf of Lord Howard and myself, I assure you that the honor is all ours," replied Dongan.

Schuyler then introduced the other town magistrates, emphasizing that, as members of the Indian Commission, they stood ready to provide any needed assistance in the upcoming councils with the Iroquois.

Dongan and Lord Howard acknowledged each gentleman in turn, and then Schuyler began introducing some of the town's leading citizens who were gathered on the dock. Among these were Domine Schaets and Domine Gofredius Dellius, his assistant. Although they were uncomfortable welcoming a Catholic to their Calvinist community, Dongan was quite charming, even enquiring about the size and health of their congregation.

Next, Schuyler introduced some of the merchants and traders of the town, including Aernout Viele and Johannes Roseboom, who were both accompanied by their wives.

Dongan took a moment to study each of these men. "Yer young colleague, Mister O'Cathail, has spoken highly of both of ye. Also, Mister Viele, I am acquainted with yer son, Cornelis, and must say that he is a credit to ye, sir, and his good mother," he said, smiling pleasantly at Mistress Viele.

"Why, thank you, Your Excellency, I am very pleased to hear that you hold him in such high esteem," Aernout replied.

"Now, Mister Viele," the governor continued, "I am given to understand that ye are an accomplished interpreter of the heathen languages. I would appreciate it if ye would serve in that capacity for Lord Howard and me during the upcoming councils."

"Of course, Your Excellency," replied Viele. "It would be my honor."

"Good, I believe Lord Howard is to meet first with the savages, on the morrow?" he said, turning to Mayor Schuyler for confirmation.

"I am sorry to report, Your Excellency, that the councils will not begin for at least a fortnight, or perhaps longer," replied Schuyler.

"What! What the devil do you mean, sir?"

"Your Excellency, the fact of the matter is that the savages have not yet arrived. In truth, the majority of the sachems are still at Onontague. Apparently there is some matter that they have been unable to settle. They have promised to send runners as soon as they are finished and have started the journey to Albany."

"The devil take the savages!" said Dongan. "I suppose that we are expected to sit here and wait for them!"

"I am quite sure that we can find ways to entertain you and Lord Howard, governor," said Livingston.

"There is much to see, and the hunting is excellent," said Schuyler.

"And, I am sure that the ladies of the town would welcome some evenings of diversion from the norm," said Livingston.

"Well, since there is nothing to be done..." said Dongan.

"In that case, Mister Viele," he continued turning to Aernout, "would we still be able to avail ourselves of your services? Will you still be available in two weeks' time?"

"I would make myself available of course, Your Excellency," said Viele.

"Then, sir, could ye possibly meet with Lord Howard and me beforehand so that we can familiarize ourselves with how ye will work?"

"Of course, Your Excellency. We would need but a few minutes."

"Excellent! Excellent!"

"And you, Mister Roseboom," said Dongan, turning to that gentleman. "It is a pleasure to meet ye, as well. I understand that ye are planning a trading venture to the Ottawa?"

"Yes, Your Excellency, I am," he said, surprised that the governor knew of his plans.

"Then, Mister Roseboom, would ye be kind enough to speak with my secretary and make an appointment for us to meet while I am here in Albany?"

"Of course!" he replied.

Dongan motioned for Greavey to step forward. "Mister Greavey," he said, "Be sure to give me at least two hours to meet with Mr. Roseboom. We have much to discuss." As Greavey and Roseboom set an appointment, Dongan and Lord Howard turned to be introduced to others in the crowd.

Meanwhile, Sean had been standing on the gangway, scanning the assembly on the dock. It was not until the governors and magistrates began to make their way toward the *Stadhuis* that the crowd thinned enough for him to catch sight of Laurentje. She was standing just behind Major and Mistress Staats.

His heart leapt as he saw her smiling up at him. She waved, and he returned the gesture as he jumped from the gangplank to the dock, nudging several people aside as he pushed his way forward.

As he reached the trio, Mistress Staats smiled kindly at him and said, "Why, it's Mister O'Cathail! And, here I thought Laurentje came to see Governor Dongan and Lord Howard! Major Staats, did you know that Laurentje wanted to come to greet her young man?"

"Young man? Young man?" queried Major Staats. "Why, my dear Mistress Staats, whatever are you talking about? What young man?"

"Why, *this* young man. The one standing right in front of you! I swear I don't know how you can see to pilot your yacht up and down Hudson's river! It's a wonder that you don't run aground. This is Laurentje's young man, Mister O'Cathail, the one I told you about."

"Ah, yes, Mister O'Cathail. You work with Aernout Viele. Is that correct?"

"Aye, sir, I do," said Sean, as politely as possible although he would much rather have been talking with Laurentje.

"Good man, Viele, knows his business," said the major. "It's a pleasure to make your acquaintance, young man," he said, shaking Sean's hand.

"All right, Major Staats," said Mistress Staats. "Let us repair to the *Stadhuis* before all the good spots are taken. We will leave these young people alone. Laurentje, don't forget that you have work to do at home…"

"No, ma'am, I won't," she replied.

As the older couple departed, Sean made to gather Laurentje into his arms, but she held him off, saying quietly, "No Sean, not here, or the whole town will be gossiping."

Though disappointed, Sean took a deep breath and whispered, "Laurentje, I have missed ye so much. After the welcoming ceremonies are completed, I will have to report to Aernout but, later this evening, I want to see ye!"

"Of course, Sean, I want to see you, too!" she replied. "I will speak to Mistress Staats. I am sure she will let me see you later. But now, I must rush home. There is a reception, this evening, in honor of the governors. The Major and Mistress Staats will be attending and I must make sure that all is in readiness so they can dress and leave as quickly as possible."

Just then, Major MacGregory approached the couple and, removing his hat, said, "Sean! You have to introduce me to this lovely maiden."

"Laurentje van Reuyter… Major Patrick MacGregory," said Sean.

"I am pleased to make your acquaintance, major," said Laurentje with a slight curtsey.

"Not half as pleased as I am to make yours, beautiful lady," said MacGregory, taking Laurentje's right hand and, with a bow, kissing it.

"Why, major," stammered Laurentje, abashed by the gesture.

"Patrick," Sean, becoming red in the face, interrupted. "Did I fail to mention that Laurentje is the woman I plan to marry?"

"Why, Mister O'Cathail," said Laurentje, indignantly, "whatever do you mean? I don't remember you asking me to marry you!"

"Why Sean," noted MacGregory, "it appears that the young lady disagrees with you. She may even be available to go walking with me. Would you care to walk with me this evening, my dear?"

"I am sorry, major, but I already have a prior engagement for this evening."

"Do not leave me hanging! Just name a day and time, lovely lady!"

"But... Laurentje!" exclaimed Sean.

"I am afraid, sir, that I am a bond servant and, therefore, bound by my mistress' desires. If you want to go walking with me, you must obtain permission from my mistress first. If you are serious, perhaps you could call on Mistress Staats and make your proposition to her?"

"But, Laurentje!" Sean insisted.

"I will do so, indeed, my dear, at the earliest possible moment!"

Turning to Sean, MacGregory said, "Sean, I will see you about the town, I am sure!" Then, bowing once again to Laurentje, he said, "Until I again have the pleasure of your company, Miss van Reuyter!" With that, he turned and followed the crowd toward the *Stadhuis*.

"Laurentje!" protested Sean. "Ye can't be serious about seeing him! I thought ye... me... we..."

"Mister O'Cathail, I am not bound to anyone but Mistress Staats. I can go walking with whomever my mistress approves. At the moment, I have her permission to see you. Perhaps, if the major can make a good case for himself, I will have permission to see him, as well. Only time will tell. Now, I must get home. Will I see you this evening?"

"If ye still want to see…"

"Of course, I want to see you. But do not make any assumptions regarding our relationship. We will have to see what happens as we become better acquainted." With that, she left Sean standing on the dock.

Shaking his head in confusion, Sean made his way to the *Stadhuis*. By the time he had pushed his way up the stairs and into the council chamber, Mayor Schuyler had completed his formal welcome and Governor Dongan had started to speak.

"Mayor Schuyler, members of the Indian Commission, burghers of Albany, ladies and gentlemen… I bring ye greetings from our liege lord, His Majesty, King Charles, and our proprietor, His Grace, James Stuart, Duke of York.

"It is my distinct pleasure to visit yer fine community. Albany, as Mayor Schuyler said earlier, serves a vital role in the protection all of His Majesty's American colonies. Only ye stand between us and the heathen savages and their French masters. His Grace, the Duke of York, asked that I assure ye that we are cognizant of and appreciate the hardships and dangers with which ye live on a daily basis.

"At the same time, Albany is far more than a frontier community; it is an integral part of England's commerce. The furs ye purchase from the savages sustain the colony, as well as production and marketing enterprises in England. The wheat and other grains that are grown here in Rensselaerwyck and its environs provide sustenance to His Majesty's island colonies in the Caribbean, the Mediterranean and the South Seas. And, the timber that is harvested from yer forests provides the masts and spars of the ships of the Royal Navy that protect the empire.

"All these things, and the knowledge that yer king, Charles, and proprietor, James, have yer loyalty and support, makes ye precious to them and to me.

"Now, I have the distinct honor to introduce Lord Howard of Effingham, governor of the colony of Virginia."

Lord Howard stepped forward and said, "Governor Dongan, Mayor Schuyler, members of the Indian Commission, ladies and gentlemen, thank you for your warm welcome. I bring you greetings from your compatriots in Virginia, and am pleased to thank you, on their behalf, for the services you render in your dealings with the savages who comprise the Five Nations. As you are no doubt aware, these same savages have had the audacity to conduct raids into our environs, harassing our savages and even threatening our settlers. I have come here to discourage them from their nefarious activities, and I trust that I will have your support in this endeavor."

At this, Robert Livingston stepped forward and said, "My lord, as Secretary of Indian Affairs for the Colony of New York, I assure you that it will be our privilege to assist you in dissuading the Iroquois from further harassing the people of Virginia."

At this, there was polite applause from the assembled citizenry. As the crowd quieted, mugs of rum and glasses of brandy and punch were distributed. Once all and sundry had been provided with beverages, Governor Dongan raised his glass of brandy and concluded the ceremonies, saying, "Again, I am well pleased to be here among ye and to serve ye and his Grace, the Duke of York, as his lieutenant and governor of the colony of New York. May God bless His Majesty, King Charles the Second, ruler of England, Scotland, Wales and Ireland!"

"The king!" echoed the crowd.

With the ceremony concluded, Aernout Viele and Johannes Roseboom approached Sean.

Roseboom shook Sean's hand and said, "I assume it was you who told the governor about my plans. I can't thank you enough. I already have an appointment to meet with him. I truly believe that, finally, we have a governor who understands what the colony needs by way of commercial ventures."

"Aye, that was a good move, lad," echoed Viele. "Now, we need to sit down and plan how we can make the most of this opportunity. Johannes, you will join us?”

“Of course, thank you, Aernout,” Roseboom replied.

As the three men left the *Stadhuis*, Sean noticed Patrick MacGregory chatting with Major Staats. He stopped, ready to interrupt the conversation but, fearful of creating a scene and upsetting Laurentje, he joined Viele and Roseboom as they walked to Aernout’s home. Once there, they seated themselves around the kitchen table with mugs of beer.

“So, Sean, what did you learn while traveling with the governor?” asked Viele.

“Well, sir,” replied Sean, “The governor is in dire need of money. Apparently, his expenses exceed his income. As we already knew, Livingston and he are trying to reach an understanding regarding the recognition of Rensselaerwyck as a manor. But, more importantly for us, Livingston has suggested to Governor Dongan that he could improve his finances by selling licenses to fur traders.”

“Licenses! Humph! A fat lot of good that will do him when all a man needs to do is walk into the woods to make a trade. How will he enforce it?” asked Roseboom.

“It will only work if he can get the *wilden* to agree to limit their trades to only those traders who hold licenses,” observed Sean.

“And, that will only happen if he can get us, the Albany traders that is, to agree,” added Viele. “The question becomes, is this something we want? And, how do we ensure that the form it takes is best for our business?"

"I have a thought," said Roseboom. "You know how the Iroquois are always complaining that we have never done enough to protect them from the French? What if Governor Dongan offered them the protection they have always wanted? If he did that, he could probably get them to agree to anything."

"Livingston also told the governor that licenses could take the place of an official Albany monopoly," said Sean.

"That's it!" exclaimed Roseboom excitedly. "Licenses would only be granted to Albany traders. Or, at most, only to traders approved by us. That would eliminate the threat posed by Penn's settlers."

"But," asked Sean, "how would that keep anyone who wanted to from trading with the Far Indians? What could Dongan offer the Ottawa to get them to agree to limit the trade to license holders?"

"It would not be necessary to offer them anything!" said Roseboom. "Any traders going to the Far Indians would have to travel through Iroquois territory. The governor could require that the Iroquois demand to see any traders' licenses before they are allowed to continue unmolested."

"All right," said Viele. "So, Johannes, it will be your responsibility to convince Dongan that Livingston is right and that licensing the best way to go. Now, since we know as well that Dongan cannot afford to support your expedition, it looks like we, that is, you, me and a select few other traders and merchants, will have to do it."

"Not to be presumptuous, sir," said Sean to Roseboom, "but do not forget that I would like to join you as a trader on this expedition."

"I have not forgotten, lad," said Roseboom. "But, can you afford the trade goods you will need?"

"Well, sir, I have some money put aside, and I was hoping that Mr. Viele might loan me whatever else I might need to secure the necessary trade goods."

"You realize, of course, Sean," said Roseboom, bantering, "that your partner will charge an unreasonably exorbitant amount of interest on any loan he makes!"

"Pay him no mind, lad," said Viele, laughing. "You know that I will treat you more than fairly. Especially since you will be accompanying this *boschloper* and so can ensure that my portion of any profits does not go missing!"

"So, Aernout," said Roseboom, no longer joking, "are you saying that I can count on you to back me in this endeavor?"

"Aye, you can. I have spoken with Abel Marrion. He makes an exceptionally strong argument for your expedition. He has convinced me that it would be foolish to miss such an opportunity."

"Now," Aernout continued, "Who else can we approach? To make this expedition a success, you will need a large stock of trade goods."

"Well, my father has already agreed to back me," said Roseboom.

"What about Livingston?" asked Sean. "I can't stand him, but his money is as good as anyone else's."

"No!" exclaimed Roseboom. "I will not be beholden to him or his wife. The van Rennselaers have always behaved as though they were better than my family, just because my father came as a settler and not as a landowner. And Livingston, that pompous ass, is worse!"

"But, what if he hears that you are offering shares and wants to participate? You really cannot deny him the opportunity to invest," observed Viele.

"Well, if he wanted to invest... That would be a different situation entirely. He would be coming to me, not the other way 'round," said Roseboom.

"I understand. So, who else is there? The Mayor?"

"Aye. Put Schuyler on the list. If we can say we have him, it will be easier to get others."

"There's Myndertse, the cobbler," said Roseboom. "He is always looking to invest his money in a profitable scheme."

"And Fredericksee, the blacksmith," said Viele.

"Aye, but we don't want his money. We want him to buy his shares with bars of lead," countered Roseboom. "And, we want Groesbeck the carpenter. We should have plenty of musket stocks in our inventory."

"What about Pieter Winne, who owns the mills on Norman's Kill? He has backed some expeditions in the past, am I correct?" Sean asked Viele.

"Aye, son, he has." said Viele. "He should be on the list, as well. So, Johannes, what do we have so far?"

"Counting you, me, my father and young Sean, here, that's ten."

"That's a good start. Perhaps some of them could suggest others," said Viele.

"Now, I must take my leave," said Roseboom. "I will speak with my father again this evening and tomorrow I'll start talking with the others. And, of course, Mistress Roseboom is terribly excited about attending the reception for the governor and Lord Howard."

"Aye. Mistress Viele is as well. Johannes, if you need any help enlisting investors, let me know," said Aernout.

"Aye, I will. I will probably want you to accompany me when I speak to the mayor. And, of course, you are welcome to join me when I meet with the governor."

"I will go with you to speak to Schuyler, but it would probably be best for you to meet with the governor alone. That way you will have his full attention. I will see him often enough during the council, and will drop hints about the value of your proposal."

After Roseboom had left, Viele turned to Sean and asked, "Well, son, are you off to see that young lady of yours? I saw her at the dock today when the packet docked this afternoon."

"Yes, I am to see her this evening. Oh, I almost forget. Cornelis has asked me to return to Manhattan as soon as possible," said Sean. "Their maid has disappeared. Cornelis and his wife have asked me to try to find her."

"Harrumph!" exclaimed Aernout. "Why all this dither over a runaway maid? Do you genuinely want to do this, Sean?"

"Yes, sir! Ye see, she's a friend. What she has done is totally out of character for her. I am afraid that something untoward may have happened to her."

"Well, it looks like the council won't start for at least a fortnight. And, there'll be no trading until the council is completed. So you are free to search for your friend. When will you return to Manhattan? Tomorrow?"

"Aye, if ye have no need of me, I will."

"Well, then, it's even more important that you see that young woman of yours this evening. You'd better get ready."

"I will. But, first, I had a thought... should I mention the expedition to Mistress Staats or the major? Perhaps he would be interested in investing."

"Perhaps he would at that. But, you may not want to tell them that this is how you plan to earn enough money to marry the girl. They may not want to lose her."

"Yes. You're right. That could be a problem. I will leave it to Mister Roseboom to talk with the major. Now, if you will excuse me, I'll go get cleaned up."

"Of course, of course," said Viele.

Chapter 15

It was just past the dinner hour when Sean knocked on the Staats' rear door. It was opened immediately by Laurentje.

"Oh, Sean," she exclaimed throwing herself into his arms. "I am so glad that you came. I was afraid that I might have hurt your feelings this afternoon."

"Nay, lass," he responded, holding her tightly. "I understand why ye are afraid of any public display of affection. Small towns are full of small minds and large mouths. It's the same everywhere."

"No, not that! I meant the situation with Major MacGregory."

"Well, lass, I kenn that ye are not mine and that I have no claim on ye..."

Just then, Mistress Staats bustled into the kitchen, and the young lovers reluctantly broke their embrace.

"Aha," she said, teasingly. "Who have we here? Well! If it isn't Mister O'Cathail! I see that you are now a close friend of some great personages! Why, it's rumored that you can count the governor himself as one of your boon companions! It won't be long now before you will be too high and mighty to bother with us common folk!"

"Oh, Mistress Staats," countered Laurentje, "you don't honestly believe that do you? Sean is not the kind of man who would do that!"

"Pshaw, girl," she responded, "I was just teasing and trying to get a rise out of your young man. It's one of the few entertainments an old woman has!"

Turning to Sean, she said, "Well, Mister O'Cathail, I can't say that I am displeased to see you again. I have inquired about you and have gotten positive reports from all who know you. With the exception of Robert Livingston and Domine Schaets, who think you are a Papist spy! You're not, are you?"

"Nay, Mistress Staats," insisted Sean.

"Why, Mistress Staats, how could you say such a thing?" said Laurentje.

"Don't worry, you two. I didn't believe it for a moment. I just want you both to be aware that there are rumors about Sean which some folk have no trouble embellishing and promulgating. Now, to my eyes, Mister O'Cathail, you appear to be a hard-working young man with a good future ahead of you. You should be pleased to know that Mistress Viele speaks of you as though you were one of her own children."

"It pleases me very much to know that Mistress Viele holds me in such high esteem," said Sean. "I can only hope that I can continue to be worthy of her praise."

"You two children go on now. It's a beautiful evening for courting. Look, there's a full moon," said Mistress Staats. "And, you, Mister O'Cathail, do you remember my rules?"

"Yes, ma'am," he replied as he and Laurentje left the house. Sean took Laurentje's hand and again, led her down the path toward the river.

"Sean," said Laurentje, as they walked, "can Mister Livingston, or Domine Schaets cause trouble for you?"

"Well, I've been here for three years and, other than annoying me, Livingston has left me alone. Domine Schaets has never actually given me any trouble at all. Of course, I've had few occasions to even speak with the man. Now, I have a question for ye..."

"Yes, Sean?"

"Are ye serious about seeing Patrick MacGregory?"

"Well, I may have no choice. You see, he has already spoken with Major and Mistress Staats and has their permission to see me. Of course, it helps that he's handsome and charming and quite the gentleman..."

"Aye! He's all the things I'm not!" said Sean, sullenly.

"Now, Sean, don't be like that! I never said that! You have to remember, I have no experience with men. You are the first with whom I have kept company..."

"And, I had hoped that I would be the only one..."

"Sean! That wouldn't be fair. What if we did marry without me ever walking with another man? What would it be like if I began wondering if there could have been someone else for me?"

"But, if we love each other, neither of us should need anyone else!" argued Sean, ignoring the fact that he also had Kai in his life.

"But how do we know that?" she insisted. "I think that we should, of course, continue to see each other, but each of us should feel free to see others, as well. At least, until we do decide that we want to spend the rest of our lives together. And, I'm not convinced that I am there yet."

"All right, Laurentje. I am willing to do it your way. Just as long as I can continue to see you."

"Ummm. That's good to hear. I wouldn't have it any other way. Now, I have another question..."

"Aye, what is it?

"Is there really a future for you in the fur trade? I have heard Major Staats say that the fur business is almost finished. Can you truly build a future on a business that depends on animals being in plentiful supply, and on the whims of savages?"

"There is reason to believe that the future of the fur trade is bright," Sean replied. "There are millions of beaver in the west. We only need to go buy the pelts. Johannes Roseboom is planning a trading expedition for the fall. He expects to return with hundreds, if not thousands, of peltries. In fact, he has agreed that I can accompany him. Upon our return, I should realize a substantial profit."

"But, Sean, can you afford to join the expedition?"

"Aye, I can. I have some money of my own saved, and Aernout has agreed to lend me whatever other funds I need to purchase trade goods. When I return I will have enough furs to repay Aernout and make a tidy profit with which I can buy or build a home and start to think about getting married."

While Sean spoke, the couple had reached "their" rock, and he again laid his coat on it for Laurentje to sit on. Going to pick her up, he took the opportunity to hold her closely to him, relishing the sensation of her breasts pressed against his chest. As she settled onto the rock, Sean leaned forward in an attempt to kiss her. This time, she allowed his kiss and returned it, sliding her arms around his neck. They kissed long and hard and, as they stopped to catch their breath, Sean noticed that, even in the half-light of the moon, her face appeared to be flushed with excitement.

"It will be better if we talk," she said, putting her hands against his chest as he leaned forward to kiss her again.

Reluctantly, Sean yielded and, although he loosened his hold on her, he still kept one arm around her shoulders.

"But Sean, is it not a dangerous way to make a living? You go out among the *wilden,* not knowing when they might turn on you and slay you in your sleep! Just to steal your furs or trade goods. Or, you could be captured by the French, or tortured and killed by their savages."

"Aye, all that is true. But, farming is just as dangerous. Think of all the farmers who have been slain in their fields or captured by roving bands of savages. Even their women and children are not safe! Those who are not killed outright are taken captive and never heard of again. So, fur trading is no less dangerous, and it is work that I enjoy. And, really, the business of fur trading is no more uncertain than farming. A farmer has to worry about whether there will be enough rain, or too much rain; whether his seed will take root or be eaten by birds; or, any of a hundred other things that could go wrong. No, I would rather be a fur trader. And, it's a trade in which a man can make a good living. Look at Mr. Viele and Mr. Roseboom, or any of the other successful traders here in town. Aernout owns property in Albany and Schenectady and has given his family a comfortable life with what he has earned from furs!"

"Oh, yes, Mr. Viele is a perfect example," she said sarcastically. "He's gone for weeks and months at a time! Leaving his poor wife at home alone to run his businesses and raise his children! And, as for your Mr. Roseboom! I have heard Major Staats speaking of his plans. His trip to Michilimackinac will take the better part of a year! And, you're going with him! And, what am I to do, while you're off having your adventures, living with the *wilden* and, perhaps, getting yourself killed!"

"Laurentje, perhaps you should speak with the women in town, Mistress Viele or Mistress Roseboom, or even Mistress Staats. Remember, the major was once a trader. Perhaps they can put your mind at ease.

"Laurentje, *chuisle mo chroí*, enough of such serious talk. Come, kiss me again. I love the taste of your lips on mine. Just one more kiss."

They kissed again. This time, Sean opened his mouth a little and used his tongue to caress her lips. Soon, her lips, too, parted and their tongues touched and twined about each other. Breathing heavily and feeling a persistent longing below his belly, Sean pulled her closer. He moved his right hand down her back until it reached her bottom and he began to caress its fullness. At the same time, he moved his left hand to her bosom, and he could feel her nipple hardening through the fabric of her bodice.

Again, she planted her hands against his chest and pushed. "Enough!" she cried, gasping for breath. "Sean, I am only human! I want it as much as you, but I am not going to suffer the shame of becoming pregnant out of wedlock!" She hopped down off the rock and brushed her skirts.

"Laurentje," said Sean, "I love ye. I want ye. Come here. Ye want it too, ye just said so."

"Aye, I want it, but not this way! I have seen too many girls in my position who have had to raise children on their own while all the 'good' people of the town treated them like dirt! No, that's not the life I want for myself or any child I might have."

"Then, I promise that I will marry ye!"

"Aye, that's what you say now, Sean O'Cathail! And, what will you say after I have given myself to you? Or, after I am big with child and an embarrassment to you?"

"What do ye want of me, Laurentje?"

"What I want, Sean O'Cathail, is for you to respect me. This is exactly why it is good for us to see others. If we only see each other, we will be tempted to do things that may come to haunt us. And, now, I think you had better be bringing me home."

Listening to the sounds of conversation and laughter emanating from the reception at the *Stadhuis*, they walked along the shore arm in arm. As they walked, Sean said, "Laurentje, I am sorry to say that I have to return to Manhattan, tomorrow."

"Oh, Sean! Why? You only just returned! I just know that, once the councils are over, you will be off into the wilderness again!"

"Now, lass, we will have ample time to be together. I just have to go to Manhattan on some business for Cornelis Viele."

"Why? What does he want you to do?"

"It appears that his maid disappeared, and he and his wife are worried about what may have become of her."

"But, I don't understand. How can you help?"

"Well, the maid, Megan is her name, is Irish, and I said that I would ask around among the Irish of the town to learn if anyone knows what has become of her. Mister Viele knows that I have friends there and have their confidence. He believes that I can get information more easily than he. Besides, I shouldn't be there longer than two or three days. So, with the trips to and from the city, I should be back in town in about ten days. Mayor Schuyler doesn't think the savages will arrive for two weeks or more. So, we'll have almost a week before the councils and, then, however long the councils will take. We'll have plenty of chances to be together!"

"I hope so!" Laurentje replied. "However will we get to know each other if we never see each other?"

Just then, the bell sounded the curfew. When they reached the Staats' door, Sean said, "Good night, Laurentje. Sleep well."

"Good night, Sean. Be careful in Manhattan, and come home quickly and safely."

"I promise that I will be careful and that I will return as soon as possible."

Sean watched her enter the house and latch the door behind her. Turning, he started for home, wondering at the power this woman had over him, and how she could get him to agree to just about anything just to please her.

        ###

Three evenings later, Sean was back in
Manhattan and having dinner with the Vieles
when he asked, "So, you've heard nothing further
about Megan?"

"No. Nothing," replied Mistress Viele.
"I've even had Margaretha ask the other
servants in the neighborhood but, other than the
stranger who was seen the day before Megan
disappeared, no one has seen or heard anything."

"What will you do, Sean?" asked Cornelis.
"Do you have a plan of action?"

"Not really, sir. I will start by making
inquiries among people who know her. As that
will require a lot of walking around the island, I
think I will retire now."

"Of course, lad! Get some rest!" exhorted
Cornelis. "Mistress Viele, I trust that we have a
bed for our young friend?"

"Of course, Mister Viele," she replied.
"Mister O'Cathail, you have the same room as
before. I've had Margaretha prepare it for you.
You will, of course, continue to stay with us as
long as you are in Manhattan..."

"If I may...," said Sean.

"Can we also expect you to dine with us
each evening?" she asked.

"Thank you, but I cannot say how late I
will return each day. It would probably be best if
you did not expect me. I have no doubt that I
will be able to find sufficient victuals in my
wanderings."

"Then, we will leave the kitchen door
unlatched each evening."

232

"Thank you. Now, if you'll excuse me, I will bid you both a good night."

"Good night, Sean. Rest well!" chorused Mr. and Mrs. Viele.

Sean climbed the stairs to the garret room. Suddenly, all the questions and concerns he had been ignoring all day came rushing back. Laying in the dark and recalling what happened with Megan, he thought, 'how could I have avoided hurting her? Why didn't I tell her about Laurentje when we were still downstairs in the kitchen? Why did I hesitate to tell her that I didn't love her? God, if something has happened to Megan, I'll never forgive myself!'

Then, he thought about Laurentje, and the threat he feared Patrick MacGregory posed for him. And, of course, he thought about Kai, and how selfish it was for him to have her but to deny Laurentje the same freedom.

Sean's thoughts would not let him rest. He tossed and turned, reviewing the should-haves, could-haves and would-haves until exhaustion finally took him. Even then, he was awake before dawn.

After hurriedly bolting, but hardly tasting, his breakfast, Sean left the Viele home to make his way down The Broad Way to the center of the city.

His first stop was to be the "Harp and Shamrock." He hoped to find Annie O'Shea at the dram shop or, at least, someone who knew her or Megan. He realized that much had probably changed over the past three years, but he didn't know where else to start.

Finding the place was not easy. His first and only visit had been at night. In the daylight, the establishment, if it could be called that, looked even more squalid and dirty than he remembered.

He descended the steps and, once his eyes had become accustomed to the dim light that came through the grimy windows, he saw that even at this early hour the tavern had customers. Four men in varying degrees of inebriation were seated on the benches that lined the damp, stone walls. Three paid Sean no attention at all, but the fourth, the one closest to the entrance, extended his hand, cupped palm up, and begged with a thick Irish accent, "Wampum, sir, a shell for a crust o' bread. I haven't eaten today. Please, sir, just a shell..."

"Shut yer gob, Seamus! Leave the gentleman alone, or I'll split yer skull and toss yer worthless body into the street!" shouted a giant of a man who stood behind a bar consisting of a plank resting on two barrels. He was holding a stout oak club in his right hand and slapping it against the palm of his left.

"I meant no harm, Paddy! Just thought the gentleman would be willing to spare a shell for some food," pleaded Seamus.

"Food, me arse!" said the bartender. "Ye want wampum 'cause I'll not give ye any more credit. Ye want more rum, not food! Ye know it's the truth. Don't try to deny it!

"My apologies, young sir. Pray, pay him no mind," said the man, addressing Sean. "Now, what would be yer pleasure? Beer? Rum?

Whiskey? Ah, wait… Is it a doxy ye're craving? I'm sure I could find something that will tempt ye."

Speaking in Gaelic, Sean said, "Information. All I seek is information."

"Well, sir, information is a very valuable commodity if ye get my meaning," replied the bartender in the same language.

"I'll pay, but only for quality information," said Sean.

"Fair enough!" said the bartender. "What do ye want to know?"

"First, the girl, Annie O'Shea, does she still work here?"

"I know Annie!" shouted Seamus. "What'll ye pay?"

"For the last time, ye sot, shut up! The gentleman and I are conversing. I swear I'll break yer skull if I hear another peep out of ye!" the barman threatened.

"The answer to that question will cost ye five *stuivers*," he said, turning back to Sean.

"Two," replied Sean.

"Three," the other retorted.

"All right, three," said Sean.

"Annie quit almost six months ago. That priest, O'Boyne, found her work as a maid somewhere uptown.   Sorry I was to lose her. She was a hard worker and honest. She didn't try to steal from me, not like most o' the whores in this town."

He immediately put out his hand, palm up. Sean took a string of wampum from his pocket and counted out nine black shells. But he hesitated before handing them over.

"Now, do ye know where she's working?" asked Sean.

"That'll cost ye another two *stuivers*," the bartender argued.

"No," said Sean. "And, if ye keep arguing, ye won't get these three."

"All right. All right. No. I don't know where she's working. Ye'll have to ask O'Boyne," said the bartender bobbing his hand up and down.

As Sean dropped the beads into his hand, he asked, "Where can I find Father O'Boyne?"

"I don't know. And, it's a good thing that I don't, or I'd commit the mortal sin o' sacrilege by hitting a priest! He's always coming in here, bothering me customers. He wants 'em to stop drinking and fucking. Trying to ruin me business! All I know is that I'm glad he's not here right now!"

"Thank ye for yer help," said Sean. He turned to go and walked over to Seamus. "Here, old man," he said, holding out three white shells. "These are yours if you can tell me where to find Father O'Boyne."

"I know o' nowhere in particular. Most days he just walks about the city. 'Seeking his flock,' he calls it. Sorry I can't tell ye more. I could certainly use the wampum."

"Here, they're yours," said Sean, dropping the shells into the drunk's hand. "For food, mind ye, only for food."

"Aye, young sir, food it is, I swear!" he responded licking his lips in anticipation of his next drink.

As Sean emerged back on the street, he was almost blinded by the bright sunshine. Looking around, he saw that the city was coming to life. Peddlers were pushing barrows full of merchandise and hawking their wares at the tops of their voices. Sean bought an apple from one and inquired if he knew Father O'Boyne. The peddler responded angrily in Dutch, demanding to know why the gentleman would think he would know a papist priest. Sean apologized and moved quickly on.

The rest of the day was spent in much the same fashion. Although the street urchins were out in force, none would help Sean in his quest. Even those of Irish ancestry refused to answer Sean's questions, obviously trying to protect the priest.

It was growing dark, and the streets were being occupied by the denizens of the night -- whores, their prospective customers and the nefarious characters who preyed on both -- when Sean decided to call it a day.

As he started walking back uptown, he was accosted by a brazen, blonde doxy. "Are ye looking for a bit of company, love?" she asked in a lilting Irish accent while cupping and lifting her breasts so that her nipples peeked out above the bodice of her dress. "I could make ye very happy." In the light of a streetlamp, Sean saw that, while she looked much older, she couldn't have been more than sixteen years old.

"No," Sean replied, "Thank ye, but no. However," he said, hesitating before her, "I will pay for some information..."

Just then, something hit Sean on the back of his head. Things went black, and he collapsed to the ground.

As he started to come around, he heard a woman say, "Thanks be to God! Ye're alive! Ah, love, ye're much too beautiful to be dying in the middle of the street!"

Sean leveraged himself to his knees but quickly sat back down on the ground. When he put his hands to the back of his head, the pain was almost unbearable. "Ugh, what happened?" he asked while shaking his head to remove the cobwebs but, instead, felt his brain sliding around inside his skull. He looked at his hands and saw that they were covered in blood.

"A fookin' coward came up behind ye and smacked ye with a barrel stave!" the woman said.

As Sean's eyes focused, he realized that it was the doxy with whom he had been speaking when he was hit. He grabbed her wrist, saying, "Ye're his partner, aren't ye? What happened? Couldn't get away fast enough?"

"Nay, love, nay. It's not like that! I don't know the scoundrel! I may be a whore, but I'm no thief! Please sir, don't call the rattle watch on me. I'm only trying to earn a living! "

"Then how do ye explain the way he came up on me while ye distracted me? It looks to me like a well-rehearsed plan! Who is he? Yer pimp? I want his name!"

"I've never seen him before! He clubbed ye and took out a knife... Then, I started screaming. He threatened to come at me so I screamed even louder and people began to yell from the houses 'round about. Someone threw open their shutters, and he was caught in the light! That's when he ran off!"

"Did ye see his face?"

"Aye, sir, I did. He had an eye patch, he did! I thought it was passing strange that he didn't try to find yer purse. I swear, sir, I don't know him! Can't you see? I only stayed to make sure that ye were all right. Please, sir, don't punish me for being concerned about ye."

As Sean's head cleared, he could see that the woman was truly frightened and that she was being truthful. He released her wrist and struggled to his feet. He was dizzy and lightheaded, and was surprised when she helped him steady himself instead of running away.

Sean responded, "Thank ye, miss....."

"Ye can call me Lizzie."

"Thank ye, Lizzie; I apologize for what I said. I truly appreciate the fact that ye stayed with me. If not, who knows? I would be dead if ye had abandoned me."

"Pish-tosh," she said. "'Twas only what anyone would do. Are ye feeling better, then?"

"Aye, I am."

"So, what were ye going to ask me when we were so rudely interrupted?"

"I was going to ask if you knew Father O'Boyne, the Catholic priest, and, if so, where he could be found."

"Ach! That I'll tell ye for free! I do know the good father, and where you might find him. Weekdays, he works at the City Market."

"At the market?"

"Aye. He has to eat. He's not one of those pompous Jesuits as came over with Governor Dongan. So, he works. Ye'll find him at one of the butchers' stalls."

"That's right! I was once told that he worked as a butcher! Lizzie, here, here are 30 *sewant*," said Sean as he counted out the black shells.

"No, love! No! I can't accept that much. That's worth a pound sterling!" she exclaimed.

"Please, Lizzie, please take it. The information and the way you stayed with me are worth far more to me," said Sean.

"Far more, eh? Perhaps I should set my price a little higher?" she replied laughing. "No, I'm only teasing. I'll take the *sewant*, though, with thanks.

"Now," she continued, "Ye'd better get yourself home. Do ye have a home or a place to stay in the city?

"Aye, I do."

"And probably a pretty wife and a house full of wee ones, unless I miss my guess. Well? Be off with ye! And be careful! Someone in this town means to harm ye!"

"So it would seem! Again, many thanks, Lizzie!"

They parted, and Sean slowly and carefully made his way to The Broad Way where he could walk a little more safely. As he did so, he reflected on who, in Manhattan, would want to harm him. It had to be Cox! He's the only person with a reason to hate Sean enough to harm him.

It was terribly late when he reached the Vieles' home, so he went around to the rear of the house and entered as quietly as possible through the kitchen door. He hoped that he would not disturb the Vieles but, as he crossed the kitchen in the dark, he accidentally brushed against a pewter pitcher that sat at the edge of the table and knocked it to the floor. It clattered and, by the time Sean had retrieved it, Margaretha was in the kitchen.

Margaretha was a large woman and, in her nightdress and wielding a broom, she was quite formidable. Not being able to see Sean in the dark room, she demanded, "Who's there!"

"Margaretha! It's me, Sean O'Cathail," he said in a whisper. "Please keep yer voice down! I don't want to wake the Vieles!"

"Oh! Mister O'Cathail! You scared me out of my wits!" said the maid, lighting a taper from the embers in the fireplace and using it to light a candle. As the candlelight grew, she exclaimed, "*God in de Hemel*! What happened to you?"

And, before Sean could stop her, she ran out of the kitchen crying, "*Meesteres Viele, komm! Komm snel!* Mister O'Cathail is dying!"

Soon both Mister and Mistress Viele were in the kitchen, and more candles were lit so that Mistress Viele could examine the back of Sean's head.

"Well, it looks much worse than it is," she determined after she had examined the wound. "There appears to be a lot of blood, but not much damage."

"'Tis lucky, I am, that I am a hard-headed Irishman," joked Sean.

"How ever did this happen, my boy?" queried Cornelis.

"I was in an area of town where it is not good to drop your guard," said Sean. "I was lucky, though. My attacker was scared off before he could do worse."

"Aye, you were indeed lucky," replied Cornelis.

The two ladies soon had Sean's wound cleaned and bandaged, and he was helped upstairs and put to bed.

Before she closed the door, Mistress Viele said, "Rest. I don't want to see you up too early in the morning. But, if you feel anything unusual -- dizzy or sick to your stomach -- call out. Margaretha is just across the hall. Understand?"

"Yes, ma'am," murmured Sean, as he began to fall asleep.

Chapter 16

The sun was quite high in the sky by the time Sean awoke. He roused himself and carefully got out of bed. He stood and tested his balance. There seemed to be no residual effects of his injury. He dressed and went downstairs to the kitchen, where he found Margaretha.

"Ach, Mister O'Cathail!" she exclaimed. "How are you feeling? How is your poor head?"

"I'm much better, Margaretha. Thank ye. And thank ye for your help last night."

"Ach, there is no reason to thank me, Mister O'Cathail. It was Mistress Viele who saved your life! *Godzijdank,* you are well!"

"Nonetheless, I am truly glad that ye woke Mistress Viele. And, please, Margaretha, call me Sean, not Mister O'Cathail!"

"I will try, Mister... I mean Sean!" she replied and giggled coquettishly. "Now, are you hungry? What would you like for breakfast?"

"Oh, please, do not trouble yourself. I can find something on my way downtown," he replied.

"You will eat breakfast, Mister O'Cathail," ordered Mistress Viele in a stern voice as she entered the kitchen. "Margaretha, make Mister O'Cathail some eggs. And, give him some of the fresh bread and butter. And, a cup of hot tea."

"Yes, ma'am," responded the maid.

"Now, Mister O'Cathail, sit down and let me take a look at your wound," said Mistress Viele.

Sean sat as ordered and allowed her to unwrap the bandage. She inspected the wound, making him wince with pain on occasion, and then rewrapped it, saying, "Well, it looks and smells clean. I see no pus or putrefaction. I think it will be all right. But, you must be more careful! Another blow like that one could do permanent damage, or even kill you."

"Yes, ma'am," said Sean as he began to eat.

"Were you able at least to learn something about Megan?"

"Well, at least I now know where to find someone who knows someone who may know where Megan is. It isn't much, but it is more than I had yesterday."

"Good!" replied Mistress Viele. "Perhaps today will be a better day for you!"

"I certainly hope so!" said Sean.

After eating, Sean left and headed, more slowly and cautiously than the day before, to the City Market in search of Father O'Boyne.

When Sean entered the covered market, he realized that he had forgotten how large it was. And, noisy! Even though it was open on all four sides, the buzz of the shoppers, mingled with the shouts of the vendors and the noise of animals made for a thunderous din. It was almost too much for Sean, with his injured head, to bear.

He made his way past the fruit and vegetable stands, the handicraft and clothing vendors, the flower sellers, the baked goods, fish and seafood vendors, the animal pens and chicken coops and, finally, reached the butchers' area. At first, Sean didn't see the priest. But, soon, he saw him enter a booth. Father O'Boyne was wearing a leather apron with a leather cape over his shoulders and was carrying a side of lamb. He was besmeared with blood. He dropped his load onto the marble butcher's block and was beginning to cut the meat when Sean approached him.

"Father O'Boyne? Can I speak with you a moment?" asked Sean in Gaelic.

"Yes, what is it?" demanded the priest, concentrating on his work and annoyed by the interruption.

"I'm sorry to disturb ye," said Sean, "but I need to ask ye a question."

"Well?"

"Can ye tell me where I might find Megan Reilly or Annie O'Shea?"

"Who wants to know?" demanded the priest, finally looking up at Sean. "Oh, it's you, O'Cathail," said O'Boyne, wiping his hands on a rag and reaching out to shake hands with Sean. "Just a minute and we'll go outside where it's quieter and more private."

"Frem!" he called to a colleague, "I'll be back soon. I just need a breath of fresh air." The other nodded, and O'Boyne led Sean outside to a quiet corner where he immediately asked, "What happened to your head?"

"I had the misfortune to run afoul of the man who threatened me the last time we met. He hit me from behind with a barrel stave but, before he could do worse, he was scared off."

"Thank God, he didn't do worse!" said the priest. "I'll keep ye in my prayers."

"Thank ye, Father; I can use all the prayers I can get. There's no doubt that he means to do me harm. But, more importantly, I need your help in another matter. I need to find Megan Reilly."

"Why? Is something wrong? Come to think of it, I haven't seen her at Mass in quite a while."

"I believe that there is something terribly wrong. She's no longer working for the Vieles. She left them without notice and without telling them why or where she was going. Over the past three years, we had become friends and, since she never said anything to me about leaving the Vieles, I am quite worried about her. The Vieles are, as well. I had hoped that Annie O'Shea might know, but I can't find her either. I stopped at the 'Harp & Shamrock,' but could only learn that she was working as a maid and that ye might know how to contact her."

"Ah, ye must have spoken to that reprobate, O'Shaughnessy! I'm surprised he told you even that much!"

"Well, I did have to pay for the information," said Sean.

"I don't doubt it. He'd sell his own sainted mother given half a chance."

"But... about Annie, Father?"

"Oh, yes, of course. Annie is working as a maid in the home of Isaac Graevenraet."

"Where might that be, Father?"

"Oh, it's easy enough to find. It's one of the largest dwellings on The Broad Way. Mister Graevenraet is a highly successful businessman. The house is in the middle of the block below Church St."

"And, you're certain that she is there?"

"Oh, yes, I spoke to her after Mass on Sunday. She's still there."

"Thank ye, Father. Ye've been a great help. Can I give ye something for your trouble?"

"No trouble, lad, no trouble at all. Although I would not say 'No' to a contribution to the church."

"Of course, Father," said Sean, pulling his string of wampum from his pocket. "Here. Here are 10 *stuivers* in *sewant*. Perhaps ye could say a prayer that I will find Megan and that she will be safe?"

"Of course, my son. That goes without saying."

"Could I have your blessing, Father?"

"Of course," said the priest, and made the sign of the cross over Sean.

Sean left the market and made his way to The Broad Way. Soon, he was standing in front of a large private residence. Following directions from a gardener, he found his way around to the rear entrance.

His knock was answered by a muscular, baldheaded man in full livery. The man looked down his nose at Sean and asked, "Can I help you?"

"Yes," replied Sean. "I would like to speak to Annie O'Shea on a personal matter if she's available."

"We do *not* provide aid to the lovelorn!" the man stated imperiously as he tried to close the door on Sean.

But Sean, moving quickly, put his foot in the door to prevent its closing. "I only said it was a *personal* matter, I did *not* say I was a suitor!" He said through clenched teeth. "It is vital that I speak with Miss O'Shea. I will only need a few minutes of her time and then she can go back to her duties. Can ye please tell her that I am here?"

"What is your name?"

"Sean O'Cathail."

"Wait here. I will see if she is available."

"Thank ye."

Sean was left to cool his heels for almost fifteen minutes before the man returned and said, "Annie will be able to speak with you shortly. But she can only spare a few minutes. I will not allow you to disrupt this household in its duties."

He left Sean alone again and, a short time later, Annie appeared at the door. Sean had no trouble recognizing her although she was in a maid's uniform and had put on weight. Obviously, Sean reflected, steady work agrees with her.

"Yes? What can I do for ye?"

"Annie, you may not remember me but, three years ago, ye suggested to Father O'Boyne that Megan Reilly might be able to put me up for a night in the stable at her employers' home. My name, although it will probably mean little to ye after all this time, is Sean O'Cathail."

Annie's expression quickly transitioned from inquisitiveness to anger as she said, "Oh, I remember ye, all right, Mister O'Cathail! You're the fur trader from Albany that Megan loved! What did you do to her? The last time I saw her she was distraught. There was no consoling her. Did ye rape her? That's it! Of course! There is no excuse for what ye did to that poor girl! Ye should be ashamed of yerself. Go on, go away! I've nothing to discuss with the likes of ye!"

"Annie! That's not what happened at all," said Sean as he tried to interrupt her stream of invective.

"Mister Barrows!" Annie cried, turning toward the interior of the house. "Mister Barrows, come help me!"

Just then the butler reappeared.

"Mister Barrows, please show this 'gentleman' from the property.

"What has he done, Annie? Did he hurt you?"

"No. No. Just be sure he leaves."

"Annie, please!" cried Sean as he grappled with the butler. "Just a moment! I never harmed Megan! I could never harm her! I only want to know what happened to her! Where is she? How is she? Do ye know? I'm worried about her!" said Sean as the butler grabbed his coat collar to drag him away. "Please Annie! The Vieles are worried, as well. We only want to be sure that she is all right."

"Wait a moment, Mister Barrows. I'll tell ye where she's gone. Her brother escaped from Antigua. He went to Maryland and sent word for her to join him. She couldn't stay here any longer! Said she couldn't face ye again! She didn't tell the Vieles because she was afraid that they would inform the authorities. So, that's where she is, in Baltimore Town and, I hope, happier than she would have been here!"

"Come on, move along, lad," said the man tugging at Sean's collar.

"Wait! Wait a moment! Annie, please listen to me!"

"All right, Mister Barrows," Annie acquiesced, "let me hear what he has to say."

"Make it quick!" growled Barrows.

"Annie, please believe me. It was all a terrible misunderstanding. I never knew how Megan felt about me. I thought we were just friends. I never tried to lead her on. I can't help that she fell in love with me. Do you understand? Please tell me you understand."

"Mister Barrows," she said turning to go into the house, "he had better leave."

At that, Barrows renewed his hold on Sean's collar, pulled Sean's arm behind his back and forced Sean around the house to the street, where he unceremoniously shoved Sean into the gutter.

Sean picked himself up, dusted himself off and reflected that he had been spending a lot of his time lying in the street.

"Which is probably no less than I deserve," he said to himself.

Not knowing where else to turn, he went back to the market in search of Father O'Boyne. Although the priest was willing to talk with Sean and was glad to hear that Megan was safe, he had no more information about Megan or her acquaintances to share.

Upon returning to the Viele home that evening, he sadly reported his findings to Megan's former employers.

"That's it, then," said Cornelis. "Although we do not know why she wouldn't trust us, at least we know where she has gone, and that she should be safe. Thank you, Sean, for your efforts."

"Yes, Mister O'Cathail, thank you," echoed Mistress Viele.

"Tomorrow, I will return to Albany," Sean said. "Please promise that ye will get word to me if ye ever hear from Megan."

"Of course, we will," said Mistress Viele.

The next morning, as Sean walked toward Dock Street to catch the packet to Albany, he was once again accosted by Cox.

"Well, O'Cathail today seems to be yer lucky day!" he said, opening his coat and showing a dagger stuck in his belt.

"Cox! Ye've become braver! Are ye going to attack me here, on a main thoroughfare in broad daylight? I didn't think ye had it in ye!"

"I said this was yer lucky day, didn't I?" Cox rejoined. "I've decided to let ye keep yer eye and yer life. It seems that ye're more valuable to me alive and whole!"

"What are ye talking about, Cox? Get to the point."

"I see that ye travel in exalted company, Sean, me' lad. And, I've learned that ye've become a successful fur trader."

"So? Come to the point! I have a packet to catch!"

"Well, ye see? That is the point. We're going to take that packet together. And, when we get to Albany, ye're goin' to pay me to keep quiet about yer past."

"Extortion, Cox?" Why would ye think I'd allow ye to get away with that?"

"Because ye have a future and ye want to protect it. Remember, there's a warrant out for ye for desertion."

"How much will it cost me?"

"Just 500 guineas and I get out of yer life."

"I don't have that kind of money. 100 guineas."

"400! And not a penny less!"

"I told ye that I don't have that much money. 250 guineas is as high as I can go."

"I'll take it. Now, let's take a wee boat ride together."

"Ye don't have to go with me. Ye're right. I have no choice. I'll get the money and come back to Manhattan to give it to ye."

"Nay, lad. No way ye'll be out of my sight until I have the money in me hand. Then, ye'll never see me again.   Ye see, it's become imperative that I leave the colony."

Reluctantly, Sean agreed that Cox would accompany him to Albany. Four days later, Sean and Cox, who apparently didn't sleep during the entire journey up the river, arrived at Albany.

Going to the Viele home, they went to the rear yard where, under Cox's watchful eye, Sean retrieved the money from its hiding place in a hollow stump. Being sure that Cox saw that there was no more money hidden in the stump, Sean gave him five fathoms of black *sewant,* ten fathoms of white, and 275 shillings in coin.

"There! There's yer 250 guineas. Now, get on the next packet and out of my life!"

"Why, thank ye, Sean. Ye'll not regret the investment you made this day. I give ye me word, ye'll hear no more from Jeremy Cox."

Sean made sure that Cox got on the next packet down river. At once pleased with himself for thinking ahead and splitting his savings among a number of hiding places, he was also extremely humbled by the experience. Never had he thought that he would find himself in such a predicament. All he could hope was that Cox would keep his word. He didn't genuinely believe he would. However, he did say that he was leaving the country. At issue now were: how long before Cox came back looking for more money; and, what would he do about it?

When he returned home, Aernout was waiting. "Ah, Sean, you're just in time for the start of the council," he said. "The majority of the sachems have arrived, and the opening session will start tomorrow. Oh, by the way, I've asked Aukes' sister, Hilletje van Olinda, to assist me in interpreting the proceedings."

"What can I do?" asked Sean.

"I'll need you to keep an informal, written record of the translations to which Hilletje and I can refer as needed. Will you do that, lad?"

"Aye, Aernout, of course," he responded immediately. Pushing the episode with Cox from his mind, Sean became quite excited about having a front row seat at one of the biggest events in Albany's short history.

Chapter 17

Hilletje van Olinda arrived at the Viele's door early the next morning, just as Sean was stowing his pallet. She had actually arrived in Albany the previous day but had spent the night with the Iroquois outside of town.

"Sean! Aernout!" She said excitedly. "I have never seen so many *Haudenosaunee* in one place in my whole life! There are seventeen sachems, and each has brought about fifty warriors, as well as hundreds of clanswomen and children. There are thousands here. And, that is without the Seneca, who have not yet arrived."

"Harrumph!" grumbled Aernout. "I hope that the rattle watch will be able to control them. Garret! Philip! Do you know if the town has curtailed the sale of strong drink to the *wilden*?"

"Not that I know of," Garret replied.

"Nor I," said Philip.

"God help us all if they haven't," mused Viele. He then called his wife to join them.

As Garritje entered the room, she said, "Oh, Hilletje! I did not know that you were here. Forgive me for not welcoming you earlier."

"Mistress Viele," asked Aernout. "Have the magistrates enacted any ordinances regarding strong drink during the council?"

"Yes, they did. But they are extraordinarily weak due to pressure from some of the other tavern keepers. Under the new rules, each tavern keeper can sell only one quart of spirits per day to each savage. Man, woman or child. So, a warrior and his family can go into one tavern, and each buy a quart of rum. Then, they can all go to the next tavern and buy another. And so on, as long as their furs or wampum last."

"Harrumph!" said Viele. "That is as useless as having no law at all! Come, Sean and Hilletje! We must go to meet with the governors."

With that, they left the house and walked up to the fort. There, they learned that the sachems would not be ready until midday. Mr. Greavey said that the governors, too, were otherwise occupied and that they should come back shortly before noon.

So, they returned to the Viele home where, while Hilletje visited with Mistress Viele, Sean and Aernout began discussing the trade goods Sean would need to join the Roseboom party.

Aernout estimated that, based on what he had paid for his property two years before, Sean would need between 100 and 150 beaver pelts to buy a house.

"And, if you want to get married, there is the matter of your girl's bond," he noted. "I do not know what Major Staats paid for her services, but I think you can expect to pay at least 300 shillings to buy her freedom. So, I think that you would need to return to Albany with no less than 250 beavers. Of course, more would be better."

He continued, saying, "As you know, one prime beaver pelt is currently valued at 12 shillings. If the *wilden* were to come to Albany, we would pay about four shillings in trade goods for a prime pelt. I would not pay the Ottawa more than that."

Together, the two men then reviewed the current trading rate at Albany. One choice beaver pelt was worth four pounds of powder, six quarts of rum, three iron ax heads, or four knives. An iron cooking pot was worth one and one-half beavers and a bolt of duffel cloth, two beavers. A musket would cost ten pelts.

"You should take no more than a dozen muskets. Use them only in trade for the highest quality furs," said Viele. "The bulk of your inventory should consist of duffel cloth because it is popular among the *wilden*, easy to pack and won't be ruined by water; also gunpowder, still in kegs, that you can put in one-pound bags as you trade it; and ax heads and knives, because they are easy to handle. Don't take rum or brandy. The other traders will have plenty of strong drink, and it causes more trouble than it is worth. Don't bring cooking pots, either, because they're too heavy and cumbersome.

"I think that, with a minimum of 12 muskets, 25 bolts of duffel, 80 pounds of gunpowder, 60 axe heads and 60 knives, you will have no problem buying 250 pelts. Also, you will need vermillion, buttons, beads, ribbons, mirrors and other trinkets as gifts for the *wilden*. Altogether that will cost close to 1,800 shillings. How much do you have?"

"I have 1,000 shillings in coin, five fathoms of black *sewant* and another 10 fathoms of white," said Sean, wishing that he still had the 500 shillings he had given to Cox.

"Ummm. That comes to about 1,250 shillings."

"Yes. It appears that I still need at least 600 shillings," said Sean.

"I would gladly loan you that amount," said Viele. "Since 250 pelts are worth 3,000 shillings, you should have no trouble repaying me."

"Yes. And, after that, I will still have more than 2,000 shillings. That is enough for me to buy Laurentje's indenture from Major Staats, to build or buy a house, and still have funds for next year's trading. How can I ever thank you enough, Aernout?" said Sean.

"You can thank me by returning with even more pelts than we expect," said Aernout, as the two men shook hands.

Just then, Sara came in saying, "Excuse me, Mister Viele, but there's a soldier at the door asking for you."

"Thank you, Sara," said Viele, as he went to the door. "Would you please get Mistress van Olinda? I believe she's with Mistress Viele."

At the door, he found Sergeant Jones. "Well, Jacob, are the *wilden* finally ready to start?"

"Aye, sir, they are. The governors have requested your presence. You should know that, because of the large number of savages, colonial officials and others who will be attending the council, the Indian Commission has decided that it should be held on the parade ground of the fort instead of in the *Stadhuis*."

"It doesn't surprise me," said Aernout. "Albany hasn't had so much excitement in a very long time. The townspeople are ripe for some entertainment!"

"One more thing," said Sergeant Jones, "the Seneca still have not yet arrived. It appears that they are still a few days' distant."

"Yes, I had heard. Have the governors been told?"

"Aye. They are discussing the merits of waiting for them to come."

"Personally, I think that we should start without them. What do you think, Hilletje?" asked Aernout.

"I agree, Aernout."

"Come along, then, Sean, Hilletje! Mistress Viele, we are off to the fort!"

They accompanied Sergeant Jones to the governor's office, where they were met by Mister Greavey. "Come in, gentlemen... and lady," he said.

As Governor Dongan, Lord Howard and Colonel Cortland rose to greet them, Viele introduced Hilletje, saying, "With Your Worships' permission, I have asked Hilletje van Olinda, a native Mohawk, who is also adept at interpreting, to assist me. I will call upon her should I need to rest. Does that meet with your approval?"

"Of course, Mister Viele," said Lord Howard.

"It goes without saying," said Governor Dongan.

"Then, Your Lordship, your Honors," Viele said, "I propose that, during the proceedings, I will provide a running account of what each side says. I will do my best to be as accurate as possible. However, you must realize that interpretation is an inexact science, especially when dealing with primitive languages."

"We trust that you will be as accurate as possible," said Lord Howard.

"While I am translating, my associate, Mister O'Cathail, will take rough notes to which I can refer as needed. For example, if you should need me to repeat anything, or if there is some interruption in the proposals by either side. You realize, of course," he continued, "that Mister Livingston, as Secretary of Indian Affairs, is responsible for making the official transcript of the council and will be providing each of you with a copy."

"Of course," said Dongan.

"So, Your Lordship, Your Honors, do you have any questions?"

"I don't believe I have any," said Lord Howard. "Do you, Thomas?"

"No, Your Lordship," said Dongan. "Thank you, Mister Viele, for providing this service to us. Oh, one more thing. You and your associates will be remunerated for your services at whatever is the accepted rate. The colonial treasurer will deal with you separately on that matter."

"Thank you, Your Excellency," responded Viele. "I am sure we will be able to reach a fair and amicable agreement with him. Now, I understand that you all are aware that the Seneca sachems have not yet arrived. They are expected within a matter of days, but I suggest that we start without them. If we wait, the other sachems will entertain themselves in Albany's taverns and be unable to conduct business when the time comes."

"We will be guided by your experience," said Lord Howard.

"Fine, then. Shall we start?" asked Aernout, who opened the door and then, with Hilletje and Sean, followed the three officials out onto the parade ground.

At the far end of the parade ground, in front of the west wall of the fort, stood a table with three chairs. Behind these was the Union Flag along with the colonial flags of New York, Virginia and Massachusetts. The flags drooped in the hot humid air as Governor Dongan, Lord Howard and Colonel Cortlandt approached the table and took their seats.

Along the north side of the parade ground, the Albany magistrates in their role as Indian commissioners were seated in two rows. Robert Livingston sat in front of the first row, behind a small writing desk with bottles of ink, a selection of quill pens and a ream of paper.

On the south side, at a table in front of the governor's residence, sat Viele, Sean and Hilletje. Sean, like Livingston, had ink, pens and paper assembled in front of him. Arrayed behind them were trade goods that would be given as gifts to the sachems at appropriate times during the proceedings.

The sachems, eight Mohawk, three Oneida, three Onondaga and three Cayuga, sat on blankets in the middle of the parade ground, in front of the governors. Immediately behind them were clan mothers who had accompanied them to provide advice and guidance.

Behind them, three score or more townspeople, fur traders and merchants, as well as the governors' staff and hangers-on, were seated on rows of benches. William Penn's agents, Haig and Graham, were there as well. These two had already cornered Sean and Aernout, demanding to know when they would be able to meet with the Iroquois sachems. They were told that protocol required that the Indians finish their work with the governors first.

The hundreds of warriors who had come to Albany with the sachems stood around the perimeter of the parade ground while members of the fort's garrison stood at intervals on the firing platforms of the palisade, overlooking the assembly.

Everyone, white man and savage, governor and burgher, man and woman, wore his or her finest clothing. The governors and Colonel Cortlandt were dressed in brocade and lace as for a day at court. The sachems were freshly painted, and they and the clan mothers wore kilts and dresses of soft doeskin embroidered with porcupine quills. The townspeople were dressed in their Sunday finest, while the soldiers wore their best uniforms.

Sean scanned the crowd. He saw Nadie, who had accompanied Achagari from Canaughwaga, but did not see Kai, or any other young women for that matter. Although somewhat disappointed, Sean was also a little relieved. He certainly did not want Kai and Laurentje anywhere near each other.

After waiting a moment for everyone to become situated, Governor Dongan stood. At the same time, Viele stood and moved to stand in front of the platform facing the sachems. Governor Dongan began his welcoming speech and Aernout began to interpret:

"I am pleased that my brothers have journeyed so far to meet with me and Lord Howard, the governor of Virginia, whom you call *Assarigoa*, and Colonel Cortlandt who speaks for Massachusetts.

"Our father, Charles, great sachem of all the English, has asked that I open my arms to you in welcome. He has said that he wants to be a father to the People of the Longhouse and that it would make him very happy if the People of the Longhouse were brothers with the English and turned their backs on the French in Canada. He has said that he would welcome you as his children and has asked me to give each of you a new musket as a token of his love for you."

At this, Sean and Hilletje got up from the table and distributed the muskets to the sachems. They were certainly the prettiest muskets Sean had ever seen. Each featured brass fittings and decorations on the stock and the barrels were elaborately engraved.

When Governor Dongan had finished his greeting, Lord Howard rose and began to speak:

"Brothers, almost seven years ago, you came into Virginia, where you committed many murders and robberies and carried away our Christian women and children as prisoners to your castles. We wanted to take revenge on you but, at the request of Sir Edmond Andros, who was then governor of this colony, we did not destroy you. Instead, we agreed to bury the injuries you had committed in the pit of oblivion.

"Since then, however, you have continued to break the Covenant Chain with Maryland and Virginia. Each year, your young men come into our country to fight with our Indians. Those Indians are our friends and neighbors. You not only killed or took many of them prisoner, you also killed our Christian people; destroyed our corn and tobacco; and, killed our horses, hogs and cattle, not to eat, but to leave laying in the woods to stink. This you did even though we had never refused anything you had asked of us!

"Because of the many injuries that you have done to us, I have raised an army to protect our lands and to defend our people. I came to New York to ask Colonel Thomas Dongan, your governor, to join me in warring against you, to avenge the Christian blood you have shed, and to force you to give satisfaction for all the goods you have destroyed.

"Instead, at his request, I have come here to speak with you. I want to know why you have broken the Covenant Chain, not only with us but with Maryland and our neighbor Indians."

As Lord Howard spoke, the sachems became more and more agitated, and they began arguing amongst themselves. Meanwhile, the warriors who were ranged around the perimeter of the crowd had begun muttering and making threatening gestures. However, as long as their sachems remained seated, the warriors kept themselves under control. Lord Howard, however, ignored them all and continued to speak

"Now I tell you that, despite what you have done, I am willing, at the intercession of your governor, to make a new Chain with you for Virginia and Maryland, and our Indians. This new Chain should be stronger and longer lasting, even to the end of the world so that we may all be brothers and children of the great King Charles.

"I propose to you, first, that you call home all of your young men who are now in Virginia and Maryland.

"Second, that you do not molest our Indians when they are hunting in our mountains. These mountains have always been their country, and not yours. They never go into your country to disturb you!

"Third, though the damages you have done demand a great deal of satisfaction, I will pass it by and forgive you. I do so only by the persuasion of your governor. You should never forget what he has done for you.

"However, my forgiveness hangs upon this condition, that your people never again attack our Christians or the Indians living in Virginia or Maryland.

"To confirm this and to ensure that the peace may last, I propose that we bury two hatchets. One hatchet is for us and our Indians and the other for all your nations together that ever warred against us, our Indian friends or Maryland.

"And finally, I propose that some of our Indian sachems come to this place next summer, when you can speak together as friends and ratify this Covenant.

"To keep this Covenant, remember: When you travel southward, keep to the feet of the mountains, and do not come near the heads of our rivers as there is no beaver hunting there.

"Also, be aware that, because you have so often deceived us, we will never again trust you, even if you lay down your arms as friends."

At this, Lord Howard sat down. For a few minutes, the Iroquois sachems argued with each other. Then, Odianne, the primary Mohawk sachem, stood, and Aernout moved to stand next to him.

Odianne acknowledged Aernout's presence with a curt nod of his head and said, "We have heard the great sachem of Virginia. But we are surprised and hurt by his words. We must speak among ourselves to determine if any of us have been guilty of such nefarious deeds."

When Viele had finished translating, the sachems rose as one and, followed by their people, filed out of the fort and out of the town. The remainder of the crowd began to disperse while the two governors and Colonel Cortlandt, accompanied by Viele, Sean, Hilletje van Olinda and Robert Livingston, went to the governor's office.

"Well, Thomas, what do you think? Did I set the proper tone? I think I was fair-handed in my approach, don't you?" asked Lord Howard.

"Aye, Your Lordship," replied Dongan. "I believe you were. You clearly demanded that they reform, but you ordered no reparations and imposed no sanctions. What did you think, Mister Viele?"

"I agree, Your Excellency," replied Aernout. "You scolded them and then you forgave them."

"I, for one, was quite impressed, Your Lordship," interjected Livingston. "They should be grateful for your patience and mercy!"

"What they should be and what they will be are two different things," said Sean. "Hilletje, what do you think they're doing right now?"

"Right now, I think they're all pointing fingers and trying to assess blame. I don't think any of them were prepared for this, although they certainly should have expected it. Why else would Lord Howard have wanted to meet with them?"

"Well, gentlemen and lady," said Lord Howard, "We will see what happens tomorrow. I am extremely interested to see how they respond. So, until then, I am sure each of us has other duties to attend to. Thank you for your efforts today. We will see you all on the morrow."

Sean, Aernout and Hilletje left the fort and walked down the hill. Sean left them at the Viele house, where Hilletje would spend the night, and continued to the Staats' home to see Laurentje.

Along the way, he caught up with Major Staats who was returning home from the council. "By Jove, lad," exclaimed the major. "Lord Howard really gave the *wilden* what for today!"

"Aye sir, that he did. Of course, now we must wait and see how the sachems respond."

"Aye, one can never predict how the *wilden* will act. Their thought processes are just incomprehensible to the Christian mind."

Upon reaching the Staats' home, Sean said, "Excuse me, major, but do you think I could see Laurentje?"

"Are you expected?"

"No sir. I came by on a whim. I was hoping to tell her of today's events."

"Let me see, lad, perhaps Mistress Staats can release her from her duties for a few minutes. Wait here."

Moments later, Laurentje came rushing out. Her hair was disheveled with strands hanging in her face, which was covered with flour, and she was wiping her hands on her apron.

"Oh, Laurentje, you look beautiful," exclaimed Sean when he saw her.

"Oh, hush, Sean O'Cathail," she replied. "You don't fool me with your empty compliments!"

"A compliment, aye, but not empty!" said Sean, laughing. "I am telling you the truth, you do look beautiful!"

"Ach, I am baking bread, and I know very well how I look. And 'beautiful' is not the word I would use to describe it," she responded.

"Well," he said, "that's how I think you look and nothing you say will change my mind. Anyway, I have important news for you."

"Tell me Sean, quickly, I'm afraid the bread will burn!"

"Well, Aernout and I met this morning to discuss my participation in Mister Roseboom's expedition. We determined that, with the money and wampum I already have, and the money Aernout will lend me, I will be able to buy enough trade goods to trade for about 250 beaver pelts. When I sell those pelts here in Albany, I will realize enough profit to repay him, to pay off your bond, and still have enough to buy or build a house!"

"Oh, Sean, that's wonderful! Thank you for coming by to tell me." Laurentje gave Sean a lingering kiss, but broke free of his embrace, and turned to go into the house, "Now, I must get back to my baking."

"Laurentje, wait! When can I see you again?"

"I will have to ask Mistress Staats. Oh, I suppose that you should know that I was walking with Major MacGregory while you were in Manhattan."

"Laurentje! I don't know what to say!

"Don't say anything, Sean. Please just be as happy to spend time with me as I am to spend time with you. Just don't think about Patrick and me being together."

"Oh, so now it's 'Patrick'!"

"Sean! Stop it! Jealousy is not attractive! You don't hear me getting upset when you go off among the *wilden*."

"There's nothing for you to get upset about!" exclaimed Sean, realizing, to his shame, that he was lying.

"Oh, Sean. I know what goes on among the Iroquois. Do you think that we women don't talk with each other? We know that the Indian women will give themselves to men whom they think will give them babies. I just hope that there isn't one special woman. Is there?"

"I don't want to talk about it anymore! Please ask Mistress Staats if we can see each other tomorrow evening."

"I will. Perhaps you can come by after dinner. Then, you can tell me all about the council with the savages."

"Of course, my dearest, I will see you tomorrow evening."

Chapter 18

Again, it was not until midday that the savages finally gathered before the governors. Odianne, the Mohawk sachem, rose and, through Viele, addressed Lord Howard, saying, "We must, first, rebuke the other nations for not keeping the Covenant. We desire that you, great sachem of Virginia, and you, *Corlear*, and all people here present listen, for we will not conceal the evil they have done."

He then turned to face the sachems of the other three nations and said, "You heard what *Assarigoa* said yesterday. For our part, we Mohawk are free of any blame for the mischief done in Virginia and Maryland. But you! You are stupid, brutish and have no understanding. We Mohawk have always been obedient to *Corlear* and have kept our Covenant with Virginia, Maryland and Boston. Therefore, we must stamp understanding into you. Let the Covenant we make here be carefully kept for the future. This we earnestly recommend to you. We are so ashamed of you that we are ready to cry. Do not shame us further. Be obedient. Take this belt of wampum to keep what we say in your memory.

"Hear me now! Now is the time to listen. The Covenant Chain had very nearly slipped. You did not observe the Covenant. Observe it now, when all former evil is buried in the pit.

"You, Oneidas, I speak to you as children so that you may understand me!

"You, Onondagas, our brothers, you are like deaf people that cannot hear, your senses are covered with dirt and filth!

"You, Cayugas, do not return into your former ways.

"There are three things we must all observe:

"First, the Covenant with *Corlear*. Second, the Covenant with Virginia and Maryland. Third, the Covenant with Boston. If we have to, we will stamp understanding into you. You must be obedient. Take this belt of wampum to help you remember."

Odianne turned to face Lord Howard and said, "We are very grateful to you, great sachem of Virginia, that you have been persuaded by *Corlear* to forgive all previous faults. We are very glad to see your heart softened. Take these three beavers as a token of our gratitude.

"We thank the great sachem of Virginia for saying that the ax shall be thrown into the pit. Take these two beavers as a token of our joy and thankfulness.

"We are pleased that *Assarigoa* will bury in the pit what is past, and stamp on it. May a strong stream run under the pit to wash the evil away. Take these two beavers as a token.

"My Lord, you are a man of great knowledge and understanding, to give us the opportunity to renew the Covenant Chain, to make it bright as silver, and to make it stronger."

Odianne then pointed at the other three nations and said:

"But they are Covenant breakers. I lay down two beavers and a raccoon as tokens that we Mohawk have kept the Covenant.

"The Covenant must be kept. This Covenant House must be kept clean. I give two beavers as tokens.

"We now plant a tree of peace, whose tops will reach the sun and its branches spread far abroad so that it shall be seen from far away. We shall shelter ourselves under it and live in peace, without molestation. I give two beavers as tokens."

Sean turned to Hilletje and whispered, "Tree? What does he mean?"

"It's a symbol, Sean," she responded. "When the *Haudenosaunee* speak of peace, they always describe it as a tree that protects those who are under it."

Odianne continued, "You proposed yesterday that, if we desired to see the Indians of Virginia, you would send their sachems to this place. This proposal pleases us very much. The sooner they come, the better so that we may speak with them as friends. I now give two wampum belts to confirm it.

"You have now heard what we have said to the other three nations. We have taken the hatchet out of their hands. We now, therefore, pray that your hatchet may likewise be buried in the pit. I give two beaver as tokens.

"My Lord, be aware that some Mohawk are out against our enemies that live far off. When our young men come near your lands, they will do you no harm. Nor will they plunder as these others have done. Be kind to them, if they shall happen to come to any of your plantations. Give them some tobacco and some food. They will neither rob nor steal, as the Oneidas, Onondagas and Cayugas have done.

"We again thank Your Lordship that the Covenant Chain is renewed. Let it be kept clean and bright, and held fast. Let not anyone pull his arm from it. We include all four Nations in giving this belt of wampum to remember the Covenant."

At this point Tekanista, the chief Oneida sachem, rose and said, "Oh, great sachem of Virginia, we Oneida pray Your Lordship will speak to Lord Baltimore of Maryland and intercede with him on our behalf. We give twenty beavers as satisfaction for the harm we have caused his people with the request that he find it in his heart to throw the ax into the pit as you have done."

Lord Howard stood and told the sachems that he would do his best to persuade Lord Baltimore to forgive the Oneidas.

Then, the sachems asked that the hole be dug to bury five axes: one on behalf of Virginia and its Indians; one for Maryland and its Indians; and, one each for the Oneidas, Onondagas and Cayugas. Odianne reiterated that the Mohawk had not broken the Covenant Chain, so there was no need for them to bury an axe.

Thanohjanihta, the chief Onondaga sachem, speaking for the other three nations, said, "We thank the great sachem of Virginia that he has so readily forgiven and forgotten the evil that has been done. We will catch at and grasp the Chain."

The sachems of the Oneida, Onondaga and Cayuga each presented Lord Howard with a hatchet to be buried, and each gave a belt of wampum to commemorate their promise to respect the Covenant Chain.

Thanohjanihta continued, "We will open the path for the Indians under your Lordship's protection to come safely and freely to this place, in order to confirm this peace. I give one fathom of wampum as a token."

Then with much pomp and ceremony, the two governors, the members of the Indian Commission and the seventeen sachems proceeded to the southeast corner of the parade ground where a hole had already been dug. The five hatchets were thrown into the pit, and the sachems threw dirt over them.

When the hatchets were buried, and all had returned to their original places, Lord

Howard said, "Now, a firm peace has been concluded. We shall hereafter remain friends."

Lord Howard then asked Sean and Hilletje to distribute gifts of beads and mirrors and pots of vermillion to the assembled sachems.

When this was done, all the sachems stood and began chanting their peace song while their followers whooped and yelled with joy.

Finally, Thanohjanihta, again speaking for all three nations, thanked Governor Dongan for interceding on their behalf with Lord Howard.

By this time, the sun was getting low in the western sky, so Governor Dongan decreed that the day's meeting was completed.

The savages left the fort, chanting and singing, while the governors again repaired to Governor Dongan's office. There, over glasses of fine French brandy, they discussed the day's events.

"Well, Mister Viele, I think we did very well today," said Lord Howard. "Odianne certainly said everything we wanted to hear."

"Aye. And he certainly reprimanded the other tribes," said Governor Dongan.

"Aye, Your Worships," said Viele. "He did do all that. But I, for one, would not claim this as a great victory. You have to remember that Odianne and Tekanista were the only sachems who admitted any wrongdoing. And, Odianne made sure you knew that it was the other nations, not the Mohawk, who were to blame."

"That's right," said Hilletje. "Also, you needed to listen carefully to how Thanohjanihta phrased his response. All he did was thank you for burying the hatchet. And, the Cayuga sachem never said a word all afternoon. Sean, do you have the passage from Thanohkanihta's speech that I marked in your notes?"

"Aye, Hilletje, here it is."

"Ah, so. He said, 'We thank the great sachem of Virginia that he has so readily forgiven and forgotten the evil that was done.' Nothing more. He did not commit the Onondaga or the other tribes to anything."

"Hah!" added Sean, "Odianne was even more clever than that! He candidly admitted that there were Mohawk in Virginia and Maryland. But he was careful to say that they would not 'rob nor steal as the others have done.' As if he had any control over what his young men are doing right now, hundreds of miles away."

"True, true," said Lord Howard. "But they did agree to meet with our Indians, and include them in the Covenant."

"Aye," said Hilletje. "But, again, there is more meaning in what was not said than what was said. The *Haudenosaunee* have made a habit of forcing other tribes to become tributaries to them. The Esopus, the Nevesink, the Mahican and others have all been frightened into submission. The Susquehannock avoided that fate by going to live among the Lene Lenape. The *Haudenosaunee* have been attacking the Virginia and Maryland tribes in order to make them subject to the Longhouse. Now, they have your commitment to make your tribes come here, to their territory, to make peace. This puts your

Indians in the position of being supplicants to them.

"Aye," said Aernout. "It looks as though the big winners here have been the Five Nations!"

"As I told you, Governor," said Sean. "They are shrewd negotiators."

"So I am quickly learning," said Dongan.

"So, do you, gentlemen and lady, believe that this has all been a colossal waste of time?" asked Lord Howard.

"No," said Livingston. "If nothing else, you have made them aware that you will hold them accountable for any mischief. And that you will continue to call them to account if they do not change their ways."

"Aye," said Aernout. "And the last thing an Iroquois wants is to be reprimanded by a white man."

"So, what is on the agenda for tomorrow? Is there any news of the Seneca?" asked Dongan.

"My brother has sent word that the Seneca have arrived at Caughnawaga," said Hilletje. "They will probably be in Schenectady by the day after tomorrow and here, in Orange, by the day after that."

"Good. I am glad to hear that they are nearly here," said Dongan. "So, what must we do tomorrow?"

"Your Excellency," said Livingston, "a meeting between the sachems and Colonel Cortlandt has been scheduled for tomorrow morning. And, the sachems of each of the four nations have asked for some time with you, alone, tomorrow."

"I am supposed to confirm Boston's Covenant with them tomorrow," said Colonel Cortlandt. "That should not take long. I just want them to acknowledge that the Covenant will continue and that they will stay on this side of Hudson's river. Then, I will give them some small presents."

"Well, it certainly looks as you will have the easier time, tomorrow, Stephanus," said Dongan. "Mister Viele? Will you assist him? And, Robert, will you make a record for the government in Boston?"

"Aye, Your Excellency," chorused both men.

"Sean," said Aernout, "will you please go to the heathen encampment and tell Odianne that the sachems cannot be late meeting with Colonel Cortlandt. Tell him that they have to start early in the morning in order to conclude their meeting by midday so that they will have time individually to meet with *Corlaer*. Tell him that if they don't, *Corlaer* won't be able to meet with them."

"Aye, Aernout," said Sean.

"Upon my soul!" exclaimed Dongan, slamming his fist on the desk. "I never thought that I would be hoping that the savages would be late for a meeting. Each of them will come looking for favors and making demands! And, then they'll get together and compare what each got from me. Then, they will come back asking for more! I will have to be on my guard, not to give one more than another. At least you are well out of it, Your Lordship!"

"I don't envy you at all, Thomas," said Lord Howard, with a wry smile on his face.

"Mister Viele, I will certainly need your services. We cannot afford any misinterpretation of what either side says in any of these meetings. I am sure that the savages will take any misunderstanding and use it to pester me. Can you make yourself available?

"Aye, Your Excellency, I can and will. Although I think, since the meetings will be one on one, we won't need Mistress van Olinda's services?"

"Yes, I agree. Mistress van Olinda, thank you for your assistance and sage advice over the past two days. I hope that you will be available, again, when the Seneca arrive."

"It would be an honor to continue to be of service, Your Excellency," said Hilletje.

"And I, Your Excellency?" asked Livingston. "Will you want an official transcript of these meetings?"

"No, Robert. I prefer that these meetings be private. I may have to make some promises that I will not want on the record. Thank you anyway.

"So, Your Lordship, Mistress van Olinda, Mister O'Cathail, it appears that you all will get some rest while Stephanus, Mister Livingston, Mister Viele and I soldier on. As always, thank you for your help!"

Leaving the fort, Sean went to the Iroquois camp where, in addition to the huts which had been appropriated by the chief sachems, the Indian women had constructed hundreds of wigwams of spruce saplings and birch bark. There, he delivered Viele's message to Odianne. On his way back to town, he encountered Nadie, who told him that Kai had remained at Caughnawaga. Nadie said that she had to stay at home because, as the next Turtle Clan mother, she needed to learn responsibility and the importance of putting the clan before oneself.

Reflecting on his good fortune that Kai had not come to Albany, Sean left Nadie and hurried to the Staats' house with the hope of walking with Laurentje that evening.

"I'm sorry, Mister O'Cathail," said Mistress Staats when Sean appeared at her door. "Laurentje cannot see you. I have given permission to Major MacGregory to see her this evening. Perhaps, you could stop by tomorrow evening. I don't think there will be any problem then."

Looking behind her, Sean saw MacGregory sitting in the kitchen with a smug look on his face. Not wanting to upset Mistress Staats, Sean refrained from reacting, saying only, "Thank you, ma'am. I will return tomorrow evening at this same time. Please tell Laurentje that I stopped by and that I hope to see her then."

"I will," she replied. "Have a good evening."

Disappointed and more than a little jealous, Sean made his way back up the hill to the Viele home where, nonetheless, he had an enjoyable evening visiting with the Viele family and Hilletje van Olinda.

The next afternoon, after the sachems had completed their council with Colonel Cortlandt and had renewed the Convent Chain with Massachusetts, Aernout took Sean aside and asked if he could go to Schenectady to check on the progress of the Seneca towards Albany.

"As I feared, the sachems who are already here are getting a little too much rum and, as time goes on, they will have a harder time conducting business," explained Viele. "While this might normally work in our favor, I'm afraid that while under the influence of rum, they might begin to complain about the treatment they received from Lord Howard. We can't have them becoming angry and breaking off the council. We need to have the Seneca here as soon as possible so that we can conclude the proceedings before someone does something everyone will live to regret.

"See Aukes. Or, Cornelis. One of them should have news of the Seneca. It will be evening when you arrive there, so I won't expect you to return until tomorrow. But at least then we will know how much longer the Seneca will keep us waiting."

Sean found both Gerrit and Philip working in the barn. While Gerrit saddled a horse for him, Sean asked Philip, "Philip, could you take a message for me to the Staats' house? You know where it is? Good. Ask to speak with their servant, Laurentje van Reuyter. Please tell her that I am sorry, but I won't be able to see her this evening. Tell her that I must go to Schenectady on an important errand. Will you do that for me?"

"Aye, Sean, I would be happy to do so."

It was dusk by the time Sean came in sight of the village. Immediately, he could see that the Seneca had arrived and were camped outside of the stockade. He could also see that the town gate was open, with both savages and townspeople wandering in and out. Most of the Seneca and more than a few white men were noisily drunk. Sean rode through the gate and went straight to the Viele tavern, where he found Cornelis and young Aernout, together, serving rum to a mob of demanding savages.

"Halloo, Cornelis! Aernout!" called Sean over the din. Looking up, Cornelis acknowledged his call with a wave of his free hand.

"Sean! We can use your help! Come here and help us pour!"

When things had quieted somewhat, Sean asked, "What is going on? "What's the cause of this bedlam?"

"Ach, Sean," said Cornelis, "the Seneca arrived this afternoon, and brought with them hundreds of peltries which we, of course, offered to buy. We explained to them that, since they had carried the furs for so many days, they should not have to carry them another twenty miles to Albany. Of course, we gave them good prices, and now they have much wampum to spend with us."

"How much longer will this continue?"

"Not much longer. The curfew bell will sound soon, and the rattle watch will herd any stragglers out of town and close the gate."

True enough, for the bell sounded shortly thereafter and, although the sounds of drunken carousing continued to be heard from the Seneca camp, the town itself became quiet.

"So, tell us Sean, what brings you to Schenectady this evening?" asked young Aernout, once the tavern was empty. "Surely with all the tribes in Albany to meet with the governor, you must be busy."

"Very busy. The governor asked your father to serve as official interpreter. Hilletje van Olinda and I have been assisting him. But, today, I came in search of the Seneca. We were afraid that the council would degenerate into a drunken melee before they arrived."

"Well, as you can see, the Seneca are here," said Cornelis. "But, I doubt if they will get to Albany before the day after tomorrow. They will all be ill tomorrow and, given the size of the group, it will surely take them a whole day to get there.

"Did you ride? Here, let's have your horse taken care of. Then, Mistress Viele will bring you some food and arrange a bed for you."

Cornelis sent a servant to take care of Sean's horse while his wife served him supper and had a servant prepare a bed for him. After eating, Sean went straight to bed and fell asleep immediately.

Chapter 19

Up at dawn, Sean ate breakfast, took leave of the Vieles and began the journey back to Albany. As he rode past the Seneca camp, he saw that there was no activity, except for some dogs scavenging for food around the lodges.

Keeping his horse fresh by alternating between a walk and a trot, Sean arrived back in Albany just past noon. As he passed the nearly empty Indian encampment, he could tell that the day's council had already begun. He went straight to the Viele home, where he left his horse in Garrit's care.

"Garrit," he asked, "Is your father at the fort?"

"Aye. But I think he left word for you with mother."

Sean went into the kitchen where he found Mistress Viele and Sara working.

"Why, Sean," said Gerritje Viele, "I don't believe that Aernout expected you to return so soon. Here, let me get some food for you..."

"Thank you, Mistress Viele, but no," replied Sean. "I should go to the fort immediately."

"Well, here, wait a moment. You need something in your stomach. You must be starving. Sara, get some apples from the cellar for Sean."

"Thank you," said Sean, accepting two apples from Sara.

Arriving at the fort, Sean slipped into his seat at the table with Hilletje, just as Thanohjanihta, the Onondaga sachem, began to speak, "Brother *Corlaer*, your sachem is a great sachem, and we are but a small people. But, when the English first came to this country, they were a small people, and we were great. Then, because we found you to be good people, we treated you civilly and gave you land. We hope, therefore, now that you are great and we small, you will protect us from the French. If you do not, we shall lose all our hunting and our beavers. The French will get all the beaver. The French are already angry with us because we carry our beaver to our brethren here at Orange.

"We have put our lands and ourselves under the protection of the Duke of York, the brother of your great sachem, who is likewise a great sachem.

"We have given the Susquehanna River, which we won in battle, to this government, and we desire that it may be a branch of the great tree of peace that grows in this place, the top of which reaches the sun, and which shelters us from the French and all other nations. We desire that it may always be so."

At this, Sean quickly scanned the crowd of onlookers, searching for Haig and Graham, but he could not see Penn's agents.

"Where are Penn's people?" Sean asked Hilletje.

"They left on the morning packet," she whispered. "The sachems told them last night that the land was no longer for sale. But Aernout can tell you more."

Meanwhile, Thanohjanihta had continued, "We have put ourselves under the great sachem, Charles, who lives on the other side of the great lake. We give you these two white, dressed deerskins to send to him that he may write on them, and put a great red seal to them to confirm what we do now. We put the Susquehanna River above the falls and all the rest of our land under the great Duke of York and give that land to nobody else. His people have been like fathers to our wives and children, and have given us bread when we were in need of it. We will never join ourselves or our land to any other government but this. We desire that *Corlear*, our governor, send this Proposition to the great sachem, Charles, with this belt of wampum, and this other smaller belt to the Duke of York, his brother. We give you, *Corlear*, this beaver, to send over this Proposition."

Then, Thanohjanihta spoke directly to Lord Howard, "You, great man of Virginia, we tell you that the great Penn, through his agents, spoke to us here in *Corlear's* house. He desired to buy the Susquehanna River from us, but we would not sell it, for we had given it to this government. Tell your friend, the great sachem who lives on the other side of the great lake, that we are a free people, though joined to the English and that we may give our lands, and be joined to the sachem we like best. We give this beaver to remember what we say."

Then, as all the sachems rose and made their way out of the fort, Aernout walked over to Sean and Hilletje.

"Ah, lad, you've returned," he said. "What news of the Seneca?"

"They're at Schenectady, but I don't think they'll be here for another day or two. They've sold all their beaver and have been drinking up their profits. From what I saw, it will take them a full day and night to get sober, and then only if they no longer have access to spirits."

"Well, at least we know now that they are close. We can't complain. Yesterday and today have been exceptionally good days," said Viele.

"You must tell me what happened! Hilletje said that you could tell me."

"Ach, it's a long tale, lad. Best told over a beer. Let me go speak with the governors. You and Hilletje can go to my house. I'll be along shortly, and then I'll describe all the happenings to you."

Later, Sean, Aernout and Hilletje sat at the Viele's table with mugs of beer, a pot of boiled beef and vegetables, and a loaf of freshly baked bread.

The aroma of the food reminded Sean that he was famished and that the apples he had eaten had done little to relieve his hunger. He began to eat quickly, much to the amusement of Aernout and Hilletje, and the pleasure of Gerritje, who said, "I told the lad he needed to eat but, no, he had to go directly to the fort. Thought he would miss something!"

Finally sated, Sean sat back, sighed contentedly, sipped some beer and said, "Now Aernout, tell me, please, what did I miss?"

"Yesterday's meetings started out pretty much as expected," Viele began. "The Mohawk, first, and then the others each met separately with the governor. They repeated much of what had been said before about Virginia and Maryland. The Mohawk blamed the other three nations. Each of those blamed the other two, and so on. I'm sure you can imagine what went on. The only difference was that each of them went to considerable pains to show their esteem for Governor Dongan. They thanked him effusively for interceding with Lord Howard; told him how he had won their affections by the way he had treated them; and, then, each nation made him a present of 20 beaver pelts.

"You know, it was quite strange listening to them. Even the governor recognized that their presentations had been carefully planned and rehearsed. 'My God, Viele,' he said later, 'I thought I was attending a theatrical production, instead of sitting in the middle of the wilderness listening to some savages!'"

Aernout's attempt to mimic the governor's brogue had them all laughing.

Catching his breath Aernout continued, "The Cayuga were the last to meet with him and, as soon as they were done, he invited all the sachems to speak with him together. That's when they began to wheedle for protection against the French.

"They requested cannon! And, of course, powder and cannonballs. Do you believe it? Oh, and men to teach them how to use them! Dongan was aghast! He actually was at a loss for words for a moment. Then, by God, the man had a stroke of genius! He told them that he only had eight cannon in the whole colony, four here at Albany and four in New York. He said that, because cannon are so valuable, the Duke of York keeps a precise count of them and would punish him severely if he let even one go! Then, he told them that he had something better than cannon! He told them that he would give them copies of the Duke of York's Arms engraved on brass to put on the gates of their castles. He said that the French would quail in fear at the sight of the Duke of York's Arms and wouldn't dare to attack.

"Well, as you can imagine, some of the sachems were not too sure about this, but enough of them were convinced — the man has a golden tongue, I tell you — that they were begging him to give them the shields!

"Then, he told them how upset he was that they had allowed the French Jesuits to come into their castles. He said that he was distressed for the families and friends of those who had become Christian and had gone to live among the French. He said that King Charles wanted all his children to return to the land of the Five Nations and that he, Dongan, wanted the sachems to call their brethren home. He said he would arrange for English priests to come and serve them.

"They told him that they would be extremely happy if he could get English priests to come to their castles because they preferred the English over the French. But, they told him, they knew that he and Governor Le Barre were in communication and that he should try to convince Le Barre to send the Christian Indians home to their own country. Then, they gave him a beaver as a token of their gratitude."

"This is all very interesting, Aernout," said Sean. "But what of the Susquehanna, how was that achieved? Obviously the other tribes decided to follow the Mohawks and not sell the land to Penn!"

"Governor Dongan himself raised the issue of the Susquehanna. He told them that he had been informed that the Five Nations had given the land to Andros, but that he had been unable to find any record of the gift. He asked them if they could confirm that the land had been given to Andros."

"The four chief sachems, led by Odianne, agreed that, indeed, the land had been given to Andros.

"He then asked them if they would confirm it during today's council so that he could make an official record of it, and send Penn's agents away. Of course, they agreed. And that's what led up to Thanohjanihta's speech, today."

"Who told Penn's people? How did they react?" asked Sean.

"As soon as the sachems had left, Governor Dongan invited Haig and Graham to his office. Then, he informed them that he had confirmed the land had been given to Governor Andros and, so, was part of the colony of New York and not for sale," said Viele.

"How did they take it?" asked Sean.

"Not well. They cursed the savages for having wasted their time and for trying to sell them land that belonged to New York. Then, they thanked - yes, thanked - the governor for keeping them from falling prey to the conniving *wilden*. He, of course, was appropriately humble, tut-tutting and telling them that it was the least he could do for Mr. Penn."

"Well, at least we no longer have to worry about trading posts on the Susquehanna," said Sean. "Did I miss anything else important?"

"No. After the sachems left, he and I met privately. That was when he asked me to serve as a special envoy to the Five Nations. I told him that I would be interested in the job but that I would not do it unless I was allowed to work directly for him and without any interference from the Indian Commission. He agreed, and said that he would deal with the commissioners. I told him I would sleep on it. And, after today's council, I accepted the position."

"That's quite an honor, Aernout! Congratulations!" said Sean.

"Yes, Aernout, congratulations!" echoed Hilletje.

"Of course," said Viele. "It means that my life will change, at least for the foreseeable future. But Gerritje and I discussed it last night. There is no reason why the business cannot continue. Although I will be representing the government as I travel among the *wilden*, I will still be able to arrange trades on the side. Gerritje will run things here in Albany. God knows she's had enough experience over the years while I've been off a-trading. Young Aernout will continue to make trades in Schenectady and assist his mother as needed. They will have both Gerrit and Philip to assist them. The boys are now old enough to learn the business. And, of course, young Cornelis will continue to run my affairs in New York City.

"I have never been a politician, and have never been involved in government but, as I am getting older, the idea of steady employment with a salary, and a generous one at that, looks better and better.

"Oh, and Hilletje, the governor wants to know if you would be interested in serving as the official interpreter for the Indian Commission? He is certain that there will be more councils in the future and that I may not always be available to do it.”

“I would be very interested,” said Hilletje. “When do you start your new duties? And, what exactly are they?”

“I am to start immediately. My first task will be to accompany the sachems back to their castles and mount the Duke’s arms on their castles. Other than that, it appears that the job will be what I make of it. You know, I have always had opinions about our relations with the *wilden*. Now I can see if I can make a difference. I believe that it will be both a challenge and an opportunity.”

“I certainly wish you all the best,” said Sean.

“And I, as well,” said Hilletje. “And, thank you for recommending me as interpreter to the governor...”

“Why, who said I did...”

“I know you, Aernout. Thank you.” With that, Hilletje left to go to the Iroquois encampment, leaving Aernout and Sean alone.

“Sean...”

“Yes, Aernout?”

“There is something else. The governor actually wants two envoys. He asked me to ask you. He seems to have a great deal of confidence in you. He said that he has found you to be particularly astute and that he values your views and opinions. Unfortunately, however, if you take the job, it means that you will be unable to go to Michilimackinac this year.

"I told the governor something of your plans, and that you might refuse his offer. In response, he said that he was prepared to give you a grant of land near Schaghticoke to join me. I know the area, Sean, and it's very valuable land. Whether you keep the land or sell it later, it would be worth much more than the pelts you might bring back from the Ottawa.

"Now, before you decide, I must tell you that there is more to the job than I alluded to in front of Hilletje. It is true that we will mount the Duke's Arms on the Iroquois castles but, over the long term, we are to determine the threat presented by the French and their Jesuits. That is, we are to be attentive to any French traders or priests who are living among the *wilden*. We are to hinder any efforts to woo the savages, and to try to neutralize the priests' influence on them. We are also to monitor any French presence on Lake Ontario and, at some point, identify a suitable location on the south shore where the governor could build a fort.

"As you can imagine, the position is not without its dangers, and I would fully understand if you were to reject the governor's offer. On the other hand, I can think of no one else better suited for the job. Well, Sean, what do you think?"

"I must say, Aernout, ye and the governor have managed to surprise me. It is certainly a tempting offer. However, at the moment, I don't know what to think! I would appreciate the opportunity to think it over. And, I would want to discuss it with Laurentje. It could affect her future as well."

"Of course, lad, of course! It goes without saying. But I would ask two things. First, that you tell no one, not even Laurentje, what we really will be doing. If word gets out, our entire mission will be compromised. That's why I waited for Hilletje to leave before getting into details."

"But, of course, Aernout. I will tell no one. And, your second request?"

"The governor wants your answer as soon as possible. We would have to leave as soon as the council is concluded."

"I hope to see Laurentje tonight," said Sean. "If I have the opportunity to speak with her, I should have a final answer for ye in the morning. Will that suffice?"

"Aye, lad, I can ask no more. Now go and see that girl of yours."

At that, Sean headed to the Staats' home to see if he would be able to see Laurentje. When he reached their kitchen door, he found Laurentje waiting for him.

"Laurentje," he said, "I apologize for not coming last night. I hope you got my message."

"Yes, Sean, I did. Philip Viele was a trustworthy messenger. But, what happened? He didn't tell me why you were unable to come."

"Oh, I'm sorry. Forgive me. I was in such a hurry, and I only wanted to make sure that I did not leave you waiting." He then proceeded to tell her about his trip to Schenectady. He also summarized the events of the last two days, especially what had happened regarding the Susquehanna valley.

"Well, I must say that you have been terribly busy. You must be exhausted."

"I am. But I genuinely wanted to see ye. Are ye free to walk for a while?"

"Not really, but we have a few moments before I have to go back in."

"So, how was your evening with Patrick MacGregory?"

"Sean, you can forget about Major MacGregory."

"Why? What do ye mean? Did he hurt ye? I swear that, if he hurt ye, I'll..."

"Sean! Please let it go! Let's just say that the major and I had different ideas about what our relationship could or should be. It's past and done with! Let us, please, move on and try to forget it ever happened."

"Are ye sure?"

"Yes, my love, I am quite sure."

At that, Sean took her into his arms and held her, gently but firmly. "Oh, Laurentje, I'm so glad that is over. I love ye, ye know and, as soon as I am in a position to support a wife, I will ask ye to marry me."

"I am looking forward to that day," she replied, earnestly. "By the bye, I happened to mention to Mistress Staats that Mister Roseboom is seeking investors for his trading expedition to the Far Indians."

"Really? What did she say?"

"She said that she believed that Major Staats would be very interested in investing in

Mister Roseboom's project and that Mister Roseboom should make it a point to discuss his plans with him."

"Why thank you, Laurentje! That was very kind of ye. I will tell Johannes to speak with the major."

"Also, I told her that you would be going with him. And I mentioned how concerned I was for your safety."

"About that," he said. "There is something very important that we need to discuss."

"What is it, Sean?" she asked.

"I might not be going with Johannes."

"Really! Why not? Did something happen?"

"The governor has asked me and Aernout to be his special envoys to the Five Nations. He has offered me a grant of land if I take the position. Aernout says that he knows the land and that it should be worth more than the money I would make from trading among the Ottawa."

"What did you say?"

"I haven't said anything, yet. I wanted to talk with you first. What do you think?"

"I think... I think... that you should take the position! Just imagine what you could do with a grant of land!"

"But, Laurentje, I have no desire to be a farmer! I want to be a fur trader!"

"I know, darling, but you can be a trader and still own property! Look at Mister Viele and the other successful traders. They all own land!

"And, another thing... Even though you'll be out among the savages, and I will still worry about you... Somehow, it doesn't seem nearly as frightening for me as it would if you were going to Michilimackinac! As I started to tell you, I told Mistress Staats how concerned I was about your safety..."

"And? What did she say?"

"She said that she always worries when Major Staats is away, even though she knows that it's pointless. She told me that it is women's burden to stay behind and worry. But she also said that she believed you to be intelligent and an expert woodsman, having been under Mister Viele's tutelage, and that I needn't worry that you would do anything that might cause you harm."

"She's right, ye know," he responded. "Perhaps, before, I might have taken foolish chances, but not since you've entered my life. I have too much to live for now!"

With that Sean gathered Laurentje in his arms and kissed her. As they kissed, he held her more and more tightly.

Breaking the kiss, she said breathlessly, "Sean, I have to go in. What will you be doing tomorrow?"

"We assume that the Seneca will arrive tomorrow, so I will be at the council. Do ye really have to go in now?"

"Yes, Sean. Although I would much prefer to stay here with you!"

Sean kissed her once more. She returned the kiss and then pushed away, saying, "That's

enough before we both lose control. Go home,
Sean.   Get some sleep so that you can ably
perform your duties tomorrow.”

“Good night, Laurentje, sleep well. I love
ye.”

“I love you, too, Sean.”

Chapter 20

The next morning, while waiting for the sachems to arrive at the fort, Hilletje told Sean and Aernout that the Seneca had been told how the two governors had severely reprimanded the others for invading the Virginia territory. She said that their sachems, at first, were dismissive, claiming that they had not been responsible for any problems in Virginia. They also boasted that neither *Corlear* nor *Assarigoa* would dare to make war on the Seneca. They said that the English needed the Seneca to protect them from the French and their Indian allies.

"Eventually, however," she said, "the other sachems, particularly those from the smaller nations, prevailed on them to, at least, pretend to be contrite."

"Takanista, the Oneida sachem, was particularly persuasive," she said. "He pointed out that, with only 250 warriors, the Oneida would have no chance of surviving an attack by the combined militias of Virginia, Maryland and New York. His war chief, Achinnara, demanded to know how quickly the Oneida could expect the Seneca to respond to a call for help.

"The Seneca sachems never gave Achinnara a clear answer, but agreed that, in today's council, they would be appropriately humble."

As she was speaking, the sachems arrived, and the day's council began with the usual welcoming addresses by the two governors. Colonel Cortlandt, having concluded his business on behalf of Massachusetts, had already left Albany to return to Manhattan. The sachems, who now numbered thirty-four, each responded in turn to the governors.

Finally, Adissas, the chief Seneca sachem, rose to address Lord Howard and Governor Dongan, saying:

"We have heard about the mischief that was done in Virginia. We have it as perfect as if it were upon our fingers' ends. Oh, *Corlaer*! We thank you for having been our intercessor so that the ax did not fall on us.

"And you, *Assarigoa*, great sachem of Virginia, we thank you for burying all evil in the pit. We were told that the *Ganienkeh*, Oneida, Onondaga and Cayuga have buried the ax already. Now we, who live the farthest away, have come to do the same. We desire, therefore that an ax, on our part, may be buried with one of yours.

"Oh, *Corlaer*! *Corlaer*! We thank you for holding one end of the ax. And we thank you, great governor of Virginia, for putting all evil from your heart. Now we have a new Chain, a strong and a straight Chain that cannot be broken. The tree of peace is planted so firmly that it cannot be moved. Let both sides hold the Chain fast.

"You tell us, *Assarigoa,* that your friend Indians will come here to strengthen the Chain. Let them not make any excuse, that they are old and feeble, or that their feet are sore. If the old sachems cannot come, let the young men come. We shall not fail to come to meet them, though we live the farthest off, and then the new Chain will be stronger and brighter.

"We understand that because of the mischief which has been done to the people and cattle of Virginia and Maryland, we must not come near the heads of your rivers or near your plantations, but keep at the foot of the mountains. We understand that, though we lay down our arms as friends, we shall not be trusted, but looked upon as robbers. We agree to stay away from Virginia. We do this in gratitude to *Corlaer,* who has been at so great pains to persuade you, great governor of Virginia, to forget what is past. We commend you for listening to *Corlaer's* good advice.

"We are now done speaking to *Assarigoa.* Let the Chain be forever kept clean and bright, and we shall do the same.

"Oh, *Corlear,* we understand that the other nations have delivered up the Susquehanna River, and all that country, to your government. We confirm what they have done, by giving this belt of wampum. Ten beavers are at the Onondaga's castle and on their way hither; five of them are for *Corlaer*, and the other five for the sachem of Virginia."

With that, the sachems and the governors proceeded to the spot where hatchets had already been buried and, digging another hole, buried the hatchet of the Seneca as a symbol of their sincere desire to have peace with Maryland and Virginia.

Once this had been done, all the sachems and their followers left the fort. Aernout, Sean, Hilletje and Robert Livingston repaired, with the governors, to Dongan's office to review the day's events. As they were talking, Sergeant Jones knocked and, entering, announced the arrival of a messenger from Canada.

The messenger was *Sieur* Pierre de Salvaye, the personal ambassador of Governor La Barre to Governor Dongan. Salvaye was an officer of the *Compagnies franches de la Marine*, a unit of professional soldiers raised by the French navy to protect France's colonies. Normally, he would wear the unit's distinctive grey-white uniform with blue cuffs and brass buttons but, when he entered and saluted Governor Dongan, he was dressed as a fur trader in deerskin leggings and a belted, linen shirt. Reaching into his dispatch case, Salvaye brought out a letter bearing La Barre's official seal and handed it to the governor.

After opening and glancing over the document, Governor Dongan addressed Salvaye in French, saying, "I will respond to this, but not today. Can you stay and await my response?"

"*Mais, naturellement, monsieur le gouverneur!*" responded Salvaye, who then switched to English, saying, "I have instructions to speak with you alone, Your Excellency, after you have read the letter."

"All right. But, as I said, it will not be today," replied Dongan.

"I am at your service, your Excellency," said Salvaye. Then, turning to Aernout, he said, "Ah, Monsieur Viele, we must speak on a matter of business."

"Of course," said Aernout. "We can talk as soon as I am finished here."

"*Merci, beaucoup!*" said Salvaye.

Dongan then instructed Sergeant Jones to find the Frenchman some food and a place to rest. "But, he is not to be left alone. Please ask Captain Sheffield to assign two men to keep our guest company. You understand, of course, Salvaye, don't you?"

"But, of course, *monsieur le gouverneur!* We would do the same with any messenger who came from you!"

"With the governor's permission," said Aernout, "I will offer *Sieur* de Salvaye the hospitality of my own home."

"Why, of course, Viele," said Dongan. "That is very generous of you."

Viele then addressed Salvaye, asking, "Do you have any companions with you?"

"*Mais oui*," responded Salvaye. "I have ten Christian Mohawk with me. But they can fend for themselves among their brethren whom, I see, are gathered here."

"Good," said Aernout. "Sergeant Jones, would you be so kind as to have some men accompany *Sieur* de Salvaye to my home? And, please inform Mistress Viele that I will be along shortly."

"Aye, sir," said Jones, who saluted and led Salvaye from the room.

Once the door was closed, Lord Howard said, "I say, Viele, what business do you have with that Frenchman?"

"Just fur trading, Your Lordship," replied Aernout. "We offer better prices for furs than are offered in Montreal. If I am not mistaken, some, if not all, of the furs he has brought actually belong to Governor La Barre."

"Why, that's astounding!" said Lord Howard.

"Not really, milord," said Robert Livingston. "During the last war with France, a brisk traffic in furs between here and Montreal continued unabated."

"Well, I am glad that I do not have to offer him the hospitality of the fort," said Dongan.

"I thought that you would not want him in the fort, spying." said Viele. "I may do business with him, but I do not trust him."

"So, Thomas," said Lord Howard, "What does our French friend have to say?"

"Only the same things he's been saying for months!" replied Dongan, reading La Barre's letter.

"Oh? What is the problem?" asked Lord Howard.

"Oh, the perfidiousness of the savages. Last spring, the Seneca and Cayuga attacked a French fort, then waylaid seven canoes full of trade goods, stole the goods and took fourteen Frenchmen captive for ten days. This is the second time he's written. This time, he adds that his demands for reparations have gone unheeded."

"Well, what does he expect you to do?"

"It isn't so much what he expects me to do but, rather, what he plans to do."

"And, what is that, pray tell?"

"He says he plans to attack the Seneca and Cayuga!"

"He what? He actually says this?"

"Aye. He says that because our two nations are now at peace, he is advising me of his plans to show that he has no designs on English territory, only to attack the Seneca and Cayuga. He also says that he does not intend to attack the other three nations as they have done nothing to provoke his anger. Oh, and he asks that I order the Albany traders to stop selling muskets, powder and lead to the Iroquois.

"He also suggests that I advise him of any complaints I may have against the savages. He believes that the savages will be intimidated if they see that we Christians, both French and English, are united against them. He thinks they would be more respectful."

"And," said Lord Howard, "what do you think?"

"After what we have observed these past days, I think he is a fool to believe that!"

"Do you plan to tell him that?"

"No. I know very well that the Seneca hate the French because of their alliances with the Far Indians. I also know that, because of this, the Seneca are our strongest allies. We need them to keep the other nations in line."

"So, what will you do?"

"Well, first I plan to speak with our savage friends. I suppose, Lord Howard, that it is now my turn to chastise them. But, I must be careful. I have to try to maintain their allegiance while doing so. Then, I will determine how to respond to La Barre.

"Well My Lord, gentlemen and lady, it continues to be an exceptionally interesting council. Heaven knows what surprises tomorrow will bring. But, for now, I wish you each a good evening."

The company parted, with Sean and Aernout going directly to the Viele home to see Salvaye, while Hilletje went to the Iroquois encampment.

When Sean and Aernout arrived home, they found soldiers on guard at the front and rear doors, and could hear Gerritje and Jacomyntie in the kitchen, laughing and giggling like young girls. Upon entering the kitchen, they saw that it was Salvaye who was the source of all the mirth.

"Oh, Aernout, finally you've come to deliver us from this man!" Gerritje exclaimed while gasping for breath. "He is absolutely incorrigible!"

"Oh, father," said Jacomyntie, "Don't listen to mother. *Sieur* de Salvaye is very charming."

"*Monsieur* Viele, how I envy you!" said Salvaye. "To be surrounded by such lovely ladies."

"You see, Aernout? The man is incorrigible!" said Gerritje.

"I am very sorry, my dears," said Aernout, "but Sean and I must steal *Sieur* de Salvaye away from you. We have business to discuss."

Aernout, Sean and Salvaye, accompanied by the guards, went across the back garden to a smaller house facing the next street, which Viele also owned. It was here that Salvaye would spend the night.

Seated around a table, they began to deal. Salvaye said that he had 100 prime beaver pelts for sale. He noted that the furs were not his and that the person he represented would accept no less than twenty shillings per pelt. Viele laughed and responded with an offer of five shillings per beaver. Hours later, after much back and forth, frequent quaffs of beer and an evaluation of sample furs, Viele proposed ten shillings and Salvaye accepted. This was a favorable price for both men. In Montreal, Salvaye would have only gotten eight shillings per pelt while Viele paid two shillings less per fur than he would have normally paid.

Their business concluded, Sean and Aernout left Salvaye under the watchful eyes of his guards and returned to the main house.

Once they were alone, Sean said, "Aernout, I spoke with Laurentje about the governor's offer and I have decided to accept. Please tell him that I am extremely grateful for the opportunity to serve him and the colony."

"That is excellent, lad! I will tell him. I am sure that you will not regret your decision. Now, let us get some sleep! Tomorrow will be a difficult but, no doubt, interesting day."

Early the next morning, Governor Dongan sent for *Sieur* de Salvaye. Sean and Aernout accompanied him to the governor's residence. There, they were met by Mr. Greavey.

The secretary conducted Solvaye into the governor's quarters where Dongan and Lord Howard were waiting. A few moments later, Greavey beckoned Sean and Aernout to join them.

When Sean and Aernout entered, Dongan said, "Come in, gentlemen, come in. I was just explaining to *Sieur* de Salvaye that, as you are my representatives to the Iroquois, you should hear what his master has to say. Please, be seated. Now, Salvaye, what is it that *Monsieur* de La Barre wanted you to tell me that is not contained in his letter?"

"Your Excellencies, gentlemen," began Salvaye in English, "*Sieur* de La Barre wanted me to emphasize how angry he is with the Seneca and Cayuga, both with respect to their theft of goods from French traders as well as to their unwarranted attack on Fort Saint Louis.

"He directed that I clarify that the pillaging of the canoes took place in what has always been French territory and that Fort Saint Louis, of course, is more than 400 leagues to the southwest from Montreal, and in an area that has been occupied by the French for more than twenty-five years.

"He said that you must understand that these attacks did not take place in the country of the Iroquois, nor along the eastern shores of Lake Erie. They took place far west of there.

"He wants you to know that these attacks took place even though he had but recently negotiated a peace with the Seneca, and that he has taken steps in response to the attacks. First, he has detained their ambassador, the sachem Tegaucout, and will keep him hostage until reparations are made. Second, because he can no longer tolerate such treachery, he has decided to go to war.

"He has said that he has no choice and that he does not believe that you, sir, would interfere in any way. His troops have been assembled and are now on the march toward the Seneca territory. He cannot and will not postpone his attack.

"Finally, he said that he has been advised by King Louis, his master, that you were directed by the king of England to maintain a good understanding with the government of New France. Therefore, he does not believe that you would ignore the treachery and injustice that the murderous savages have committed upon Frenchmen.

"I am to wait for your response. I am not to leave Albany without one. So, I await Your Excellency's pleasure," concluded Salvaye with a slight bow.

"Well! Well!" exclaimed Dongan. "*Sieur* de La Barre has certainly been quite clear about what *he* wants! Salvaye, as you are aware, the sachems of the Five Nations, including the Seneca and Cayuga, are here to meet with me. During today's council, I will tell them of the complaints your master has made of them. After that, I will respond to *Sieur* de La Barre. If you will, please return to Mr. Viele's home. We will speak, again, later."

"I am your servant," responded Salvaye.

"Harrumph!" exclaimed Dongan after the Frenchman had left. "If La Barre thinks he can dictate to a representative of His Majesty's government, he is sadly mistaken!

"And he claims that he had negotiated a peace treaty with the Seneca! That is totally inappropriate. We can't have our supposed allies making treaties without our say-so.

"Come, gentlemen, let us see what our savage friends have to say about all of this."

Upon reaching the parade ground, they found the sachems assembled and waiting. As soon as the opening formalities were concluded, Dongan told them of the complaints that the French governor had made.

"My brothers," he began, "the governor of Canada, whom you call *Yonnondio*, has told me that warriors of the Seneca and Cayuga attacked one of the French forts in the west and, later, stole seven canoes full of trade goods and took fourteen Frenchmen captive for ten days. *Yonnondio* said that he had asked you to pay for the stolen goods but that you have ignored his requests.

"Now, he has asked me to join him in reprimanding the Five Nations. He says that, if you do not pay for the stolen goods, he will attack you and he asks me to join him in this venture. He says that, if he and I stand together, the People of the Longhouse will do as he demands.

"My brothers, my sachem, Charles, who lives across the big lake, is at peace with the French sachem. Therefore, I must heed the words of *Monsieur* de La Barre. He has said that you have stolen French goods and refused to pay for them. Because the English and French peoples are at peace, I must ask that you pay *Monsieur* de La Barre for the goods you have stolen. What else can I do? I do not want to attack my brothers, the Seneca and Cayuga. What shall I tell him? What do you say to the things that he has told me?"

Adissas, chief sachem of the Seneca rose and said, "We were sent for, and have come, and have heard what you have said. *Corlaer* has heard great complaints about us, both from Virginia and Canada. What they complain of from Canada may possibly be true, that our young people have taken some of their goods. But *Yonnondio* is the cause of it. He not only permits his people to carry ammunition, guns, powder, lead and axes to the Far Indians, our enemies, but sends them there on purpose. These guns knock our beaver hunters on the head, and our enemies carry the beavers to Canada. These are beavers that we would have brought here to our English brothers. Our beaver hunters are warriors and could bear this no longer. They met with some French on their way to our enemies, carrying ammunition, which our men took from them. This is appropriate under our customs of war, and we, therefore, openly admit to it.

"When the governor of Canada speaks to us of the Chain, he calls us children and says, 'I am your father, you must hold fast the Chain, and I will do the same. I will protect you as a Father does his children.' Is this protection, to say this and, at the same time, to knock us on the head by giving ammunition to our enemies?

"He always says, 'I am your father, and you are my children' and yet he is angry with his children for taking these goods. But, Oh *Corlaer*! We must complain to you. You, *Corlaer*, tell us. Is it proper that our father is going to attack us over these things? We rejoiced when the previous French governor left and went over the great lake, because he had given our enemies ammunition. But our hopes for change have been smashed. Our enemies are still supplied with guns and ammunition. We ask you: is this fair? *Yonnondio* forbids us to make war on any of the nations with whom he trades but, at the same time, furnishes them with all sorts of weapons so that they can destroy us.

"*Corlaer* has said that satisfaction must be made to the French for the mischief we have done them. He said this before he heard our answer. Now let *Corlaer* judge and determine. If you say it must be paid, we shall pay it, but we cannot live without free beaver hunting.

"*Corlaer*, hear what we say. We thank you for the Duke's Arms, which you gave us to put on our castles. You command us. Have we wandered out of the way as the governor of Canada says? We do not threaten him with war as he threatens us. What shall we do? Shall we run away, or shall we sit still in our houses? What shall we do? We speak to him that governs and commands us.

"Now *Corlaer* and *Assarigoa* and all people here present remember that we have answered the complaints of the governor of Canada.

"In remembrance of this we give this belt of wampum and will send five more beavers to *Corlear*."

With that, Adissas sat, as the other sachems murmured their approval of what he had said.

Hilletje turned to Sean and whispered, "The governor must be careful in how he responds. He can't be seen as aligning himself with La Barre. The sachems will see it as weakness."

Governor Dongan stood and said, "My brothers. I have heard your words. I agree with you when you say that what the governor of Canada demands is not just. By taking the

Frenchmen's trade goods, you are protecting yourselves from your enemies. But we are now in a terribly difficult position. *Yonnondio* has said that he will attack you. He has asked me to join him but, even without my help, he will still attack you. I will try to persuade him that to do so would be foolish and not end well for him or you. But, I fear, he is bound to this course of action. I fear that my words will fall on deaf ears.

"But, my brothers, do you understand why you find yourselves in this predicament? It is because you have tried to make peace with the French, whom you cannot trust. Why do you communicate with the French at all? Why have you tried to extend the Chain of friendship to those who support your enemies? Haven't I told you that you should not council with the French? They are not to be trusted. They smile and grasp your hand while knocking you on your heads. You must understand that the English are your only true friends. We will never knock you on your heads so long as you hold the Chain. This is why I have given you the Duke's Arms to place on your castles so that *Yonnondio* will know that you are children of the great English sachem, Charles, and are under his protection.

"When this council is over, and you go back to your castles, you must avoid all commerce with the French. Do not receive their emissaries at your council fires. Tell the French fathers who live in your castles to go home. I will find English priests who will come and serve your people, and who will not try to entice them to leave your castles as the French fathers do.

"As a gesture of my paternal devotion to you, I have asked Aernout the Interpreter, who is well known to you, to return to your castles with you, to help you mount the Duke's Arms on your palisades, and to assist you in ridding yourselves of the insidious influence of the French governor, his emissaries and his priests."

"Oh, *Corlear*," responded Adissas. "We have heard your words, and we are shamed that we were so foolish as to try to treat with *Yonnondio*. For many years, the Seneca have resisted the blandishments of the French. We knew that they were the friends of our enemies and not to be trusted. However, our brothers, the Onondaga, who are under the influence of the French priests, told us that it would be best for all the *Haudenosaunee* that we make peace with the French. Now, we know that they were wrong, and we were right to watch the French as a deer watches a rattlesnake.

"You see, you foolish men?" he exclaimed, turning and addressing the other sachems. "The French are *not* our friends, not now and not ever! We should never again try to forge a Covenant with the French!

"But, oh, *Corlear*, what are we to do?" he continued, turning back to Dongan, "You say that the French will attack us. Shall we fight them, or shall we run and hide in the woods? What say you?"

Dongan responded, "My brothers, the Seneca will not have to fight the French. Once the French come in sight of your castles, they will see the Duke's Arms mounted on your palisades and know that the Seneca are under the protection of the Duke of York. Because the English sachem, Charles, is at peace with the French sachem, the French will turn away from your castles and return to their homes. However, I am afraid that you will have to give *Yonnondio* satisfaction for the goods you have stolen. Only then will you be able to live without fear."

"*Corlear*, we hear you, and we heed your words. We thank you for giving us the talisman of your Duke, the brother of your sachem, to hang on our walls. This talisman must have tremendous power to turn away the French. We also thank you for sending Aerie the Interpreter to represent you in our councils and to help rid us of the French fathers. We will attempt to provide satisfaction for the goods we took from the French. And, we promise you, we will never again seek to treat with the French. You have opened our eyes to their treachery. To remember our words, we give five beaver."

"Thank you, my brothers," said Dongan. "I thank you for coming so far to meet with me and *Assarigoa*. I thank you for hearing our words and heeding them. It is well that we have buried our axes and planted the tree of peace. I thank you for being good brothers to the English. I am well pleased with this council. We have renewed the Covenant Chain between your peoples and the peoples of the English sachem, Charles, who lives across the wide lake. Never again will either of our peoples have reason to worry about the relationship between us. It is as strong as a Chain.

"Now, return to your castles. Put the Arms of my master, the Duke of York, upon your castles. Welcome our friend, Aernout the Interpreter, into your councils. Open your ears, hear what he tells you as though it comes from my own mouth. Never question his advice, just as you would never question mine. I give you these belts to remember.

"I declare this council to be concluded!"

Then, as the natives left to return to their encampment, where they would soon begin an all-night celebration of a successful council, Dongan turned to Aernout and Sean, and said, "Now, let us deal with our friend, Salvaye."

Chapter 21

When Salvaye was brought to the governor's chambers, Dongan told him, "I am prepared to reply to *Sieur* de La Barre, and I want you to hear what I have to say so that you can report that these are my words. Mr. Greavey, please take a letter.   Sir," he began as Greavey wrote. "I do not intend to justify the wrongs the Indians have done to the French so far to the southwest of Montreal. Although, in all probability, if we were to dispute these regions, they would be more likely to be ours than yours since they are much closer to the English colonies than to New France.

"The pretenses that you make to that country by sending Jesuits among the Indians are very slender. Although it is charitable of you to bring the faith to the heathens, it gives you neither right nor title over the territory.

"I also wonder, sir, why you would need to make a peace treaty with any Indians who belong under this government. This government is at peace with the government of Canada. If we are at peace with you, so then are our Indians.

"As for the injuries, affronts, insolences or robberies committed by these Indians upon the French, I have earnestly pressed them to make satisfaction. However, out of a concern for the miseries that may arise from making war on the savages, I wish that you had given me notice of your intended hostility sooner, before you had detained Tagaucout, their ambassador, or marched to war. Perhaps I could have taken measures to prevent a war that may be destructive to both parties. It distresses me to hear that your troops have already begun their advance on the Seneca territory.

"Those Indians are under this government, and I assure you that they have voluntarily given themselves and their lands to it. In addition, they have agreed that, if they have done anything amiss, they will readily give reasonable satisfaction.

"Sir, I would be extremely sorry to hear that you invaded the Duke's territories, even after I have promised that the Indians will punctually give satisfaction for all the injuries you claim they have committed.

"I do not doubt that, if you please, this affair can be quietly reconciled between you and the Indians. If not, we have masters in Europe to whom we should properly refer the matter.

"I have sent the bearer with this letter, in order to prevent, as much as I can, any inconveniences that may occur. Additionally, please be advised that I have ordered the coats of arms of His Royal Highness, the Duke of York, to be put up on the Indian castles as tangible evidence that the Iroquois are under the protection of this government. I hope that this may dissuade you from acting in any way that may create a misunderstanding between us.

"I assure you, sir, that no one has a greater desire for continued friendship between the subjects of this government and yours than I.

"Sir, I am with all respect, your most humble and affectionate servant, etcetera, etcetera."

"Mr. Greavey, please prepare two copies, one for *Sieur* de La Barre, and another for our records.

"*Sieur* de Salvaye, I trust that this will answer all of your master's questions and address all of his concerns. I truly hope that he will refrain from invading this colony. With England and France currently at peace, such an action could only be construed as a grievous affront to His Majesty's government.

"Please take a seat in the hall. Mr. Greavey will provide you with the original as soon as I have signed it, as well as a safe conduct pass for your return to Montreal. Then, you and the Christian Mohawk who accompanied you are free to go. I assume you have concluded your business with Mr. Viele?"

"*Oui, monsieur le gouverneur*, I have."

"Then, I will bid you *adieu!*"

"*Merci!   Au   revoir,   monsieur   le gouverneur*," said Salvaye, saluting. He then turned and, taking Aernout's hand, said, "*Merci, Monsieur* Viele, both for your hospitality and for the good trade we made. Please also express my appreciation to the lovely *Madame* Viele."

"I will," said Aernout.

"*Monsieur* O'Cathail, *au revoir,*" said Salvaye, shaking Sean's hand.

"*Au revoir, monsieur,*" Sean responded.

After Salvaye had left, Dongan turned to Aernout and Sean, saying, "Well, gentlemen, there you have it! On one hand, we have the French who want to steal our furs, our land and our Indians. On the other hand, we have savages we cannot trust, who would just as easily ally themselves with our enemies as with ourselves.

"Therefore, as you travel among the Iroquois on my behalf, it is essential that you undertake to dissuade them from entering into any treaties with the French. The Seneca can make amends, if they so choose, in order to avoid a confrontation. But, under no circumstances are the Iroquois to treat with La Barre."

"I seriously doubt that the Seneca will treat with the French," said Aernout. "They hate them for arming the Far Indians."

"And, the Mohawk are also unlikely to do so," added Sean. "They have neither forgotten nor forgiven the French for De Tracy's invasion twenty years ago."

"Aye, but the others... I don't know which way they might bend," said Aernout. "The Onondaga are quite close to the French. Of all the Iroquois, they are most under the influence of the French priests. And, because the Oneida and Cayuga are small tribes, they are the most likely to try to sue for peace.”

“Yes, yes,” said Dongan. “I understand all that. But, be that as it may, I order you to prevent *any* of the tribes from consorting with the French! If one goes, they will all go! Am I understood?”

“Yes, Your Excellency!” chorused Sean and Aernout.

“Now, gentlemen,” said Dongan, “I must prepare for my return to Manhattan. Please remember, at all times, that you are our eyes and ears on the frontier! I will need you to keep me fully apprised of what you see and hear.”

“We will do so, Your Honor,” promised Aernout.

“I assume that you will be leaving with the natives?”

“Yes, Your Excellency,” said Aernout. “But, first, I want to speak with some of the sachems to learn what they plan to do about La Barre. If they plan to meet with him before he attacks to try to make satisfaction, I will be sure to be there. If I am there, they might not try to treat with him.”

“Good, good,” replied the Governor, his mind already on other matters. As Sean and Aernout made to leave, Dongan said, “Again, Mr. Viele, Mr. O’Cathail, thank you for agreeing to undertake this task,” said Dongan, shaking their hands in turn. “Good bye for now, gentlemen, and Godspeed!”

"Thank you, Your Excellency!" both men said as they left.

Leaving the fort, Sean and Aernout went first to the Iroquois encampment. They found it in complete chaos. Drunken Indians, male and female alike, staggered about drinking rum, cavorting in unrestrained debauchery or lying prone in drunken stupors.

Reaching the area occupied by the Mohawk, they looked for Achagari. They finally found him and Nadie observing their brethren with looks of disdain. As they approached, Achagari rose to his feet and said, "Ah, Aerie, my brother, it shames this man that you should see our people like this."

"Achagari, my brother," replied Aernout. "You have no need to be ashamed. Your people have had a good council with *Corlear* and *Assarigoa*, axes have been buried, the People of the Longhouse are now under the protection of the Duke of York, and many of them have made excellent trades with the Dutch of Albany. They have reason to celebrate!"

"That is so," replied the sachem. "But I wish that our people could practice moderation when drinking rum. I don't know why it affects the *Haudenosaunee* so badly."

"Unfortunately, strong drink affects most *wilden*, and even some white men, in just the same way," replied Viele. "It steals their reason and leaves only senselessness. The difference between Indians and white people, I believe, is just that your people are unused to strong drink and, therefore, are not wary of its effects."

"Perhaps, you are right. But, my friend, why did you seek me out today?

"I came to ask if you knew if the Seneca plan to make reparations to the French."

"Yes, they do," Achagari replied. "Although Adissas will not meet with *Yonnondio*, he has asked the Onondaga sachems to make whatever arrangements are necessary to avoid a war. And, I believe that at least one or more sachems from the Oneida and Cayuga will do so, as well.

"But, you should also know that they are fearful of *Yonnondio*," he continued. "They are afraid that even if the Seneca make restitution, the French and their allies among the Far Indians will still declare war on the *Haudenosaunee*. They want to treat with him despite the warnings of *Corlaer* and Adissas. It has already been agreed that, when we leave here, all of the sachems will proceed to Onontague for a council. There, we will decide if we will seek a treaty with *Yonnondio*. Whatever we will do, we have already decided that we must do it together. We cannot let *Yonnondio* divide us."

"While I am happy to hear that you will act as one, Achagari," said Aernout, "I would be happier still if your people were not to treat with *Yonnondio* at all! If you disobey *Corlaer* in this matter, he will no longer look upon the Iroquois as his brothers. And, I am afraid that he will no longer hold you under his protection. He has made this abundantly clear to me."

"I understand, my friend. The *Ganienkeh* agree with the Seneca and *Corlaer* that *Yonnondio* is not a friend. His interests lie in the west, where there are more beaver. Therefore, he will always look upon the Far Indians are his favorite children, not the *Haudenosaunee.*

"But you must understand, as well, that our younger brothers, the Oneida and Cayuga, will follow the lead of the Onondaga because they, too, are under the influence of the French fathers."

"I understand, my friend. That is why I will join you when you meet at Onontague. I will represent *Corlaer* in your council."

"It is well, Aerie, that you will be there. Your presence will remind the others of the words of *Corlaer.*"

"When will the sachems be leaving?" Sean asked.

"We will all leave together, in the morning. We will be on the trail long before the rest of our people are ready to go. We must get to Onontague and council as quickly as possible so that we will have a plan before *Yonnondio* can attack us."

"It is well," replied Aernout. "Oh-Kahl and I will be ready and will leave with you. Until morning, my friend."

"Until morning," said Achagari.

As Sean and Aernout proceeded to the Seneca area of the encampment, Sean said, "It does not look good, Aernout. I'm afraid that the Onondaga will go over to the French."

"I agree," said Aernout. "That is why I have to go to Onontague with the sachems. You will have to go to the Seneca castles to post the Duke's Arms before La Barre can get there."

"Since Adissas agrees with us that the French cannot be trusted, perhaps he can help us somehow," said Sean.

"Aye, and we will ask him for a warrior to show you the fastest route to their castles."

After greeting Adissas, Aernout said, "I understand that you and other sachems will meet at Onontague to decide how to keep *Yonnondio* from attacking your people."

"Yes," replied Adissas. "Although I am fearful that some of the sachems will defy *Corlaer* and try to treat with *Yonnondio*. I have heard that the Onondaga sachem, Garangula, has received many presents from *Yonnondio* and, therefore, he is likely to encourage the others to make peace with the French."

"Would it cause you discomfort if I were to join the sachems at Onontague?"

"No, my friend," the sachem replied. "I would welcome you. *Corlear* said that you are now his eyes, ears and mouth among the Iroquois. Perhaps you can keep the Onondaga, Oneida and Cayuga sachems from doing something we will all come to regret. We must convince all of the sachems that it is in the best interests of our people to listen to *Corlaer*. I believe that your presence will only help our cause."

"Good. Then I will be there."

"Will you travel with us?"

"Yes, I will. But Oh-Kahl must go to your castles at Gandagaro and Chemung to mount the Duke's Arms that *Corlaer* has given you in case *Yonnondio* attacks before you can meet with him. But, to ensure that he will be able to do so as quickly as possible, I ask that you select a warrior to show him the fastest path to the lands of the Seneca. Can you do that?"

"Of course, my brother," said Adissas. "I will select two of my most trusted warriors to accompany Oh-Kahl."

"Thank you," said Aernout. "We will see you in the morning."

Leaving the Indian encampment behind, Aernout and Sean walked back to Arnout's house. When they arrived, they found the Viele family, at least those living in Albany, waiting for them. Because Mistress Viele knew that it was to be the last time the whole family would be together before her husband left, she and Sarah had spent the entire day preparing a lavish feast.

"Ach, Mistress Viele, you should not have gone to so much trouble," said Aernout. "Although I greatly appreciate your efforts."

"Aye, ma'am, as do I!" added Sean.

After all had eaten, Sean took his leave, saying, "I am going to the Staats' house to see Laurentje. I truly hope that Mistress Staats will allow us to have some time together. This will be my last chance to see her before we leave."

"Just explain the situation to Mistress Staats, Sean," said Gerritje. "I know her to be a fair and reasonable person. I am sure that she will let you visit with your young lady."

With that, Sean hurried from the house and down the hill to the Staats' residence. There, Laurentje answered his knock at the kitchen door.

"Oh, Sean, I did not expect to see you this evening," she said while wiping her hands on her apron.

"I'm sorry, Laurentje, but the governor has ordered Aernout and me to leave tomorrow with the Iroquois! This will be the last chance I will have to see you for many weeks! Please... ask Mistress Staats if you can walk with me for a little while."

"Since I've finished my chores, I am sure that Mistress Staats will allow me to go out with you. Just wait here and I will go ask her."

A few moments later, Laurentje returned with Mistress Staats.

"So, young man," said the older woman. "I hear that you and Mr. Viele are off into the wilderness at the behest of Governor Dongan."

"Aye, ma'am, we are," replied Sean. "We are now the governor's ambassadors to the savages, and he wants us to leave with them tomorrow. Please, Mistress Staats, can Laurentje come walking with me for a while this evening."

"Of course, young man!" she said. "Laurentje has finished her chores and is free to go with you. Just mind that you do not keep her out too late!"

"No, ma'am, I won't! I promise!" said Sean.

"Then, be off, the two of you!" ordered Mistress Staats. "Go walking! Oh, how I envy you your youth!"

"Thank you, Mistress Staats!" said Sean, taking Laurentje by the elbow and leading her toward their spot near the river. Once they reached the large rock on the river bank, Sean took Laurentje into his arms as if to lift her up. But, instead, he pulled her close and gently turned her face up toward his so that their lips met in a deep and lingering kiss. As they kissed, Sean let his tongue lightly brush her lips. Soon, Laurentje opened her lips slightly to allow Sean's tongue to penetrate her mouth.

As they kissed, their passion became more intense, and they were soon pressing their bodies against each other. Sean could feel Laurentje's hardened nipples through her bodice pressing against his chest while she could feel the evidence of his desire pressing against her belly.

"Oh, Sean!" Laurentje breathlessly cried upon breaking the kiss. "This becomes more difficult each time we meet! I want you so badly and I know that you want me, too! In fact, knowing of your desire makes me want you even more! Oh, how I wish we were married!"

"Laurentje, Laurentje!" exclaimed Sean pressing his advantage. "I don't know if I can wait any longer!"

He again pulled her into his arms, pressing his lips against hers as he gently lowered her to the ground. There, they lay, Sean on top, squeezing Laurentje ever more tightly and insinuating his leg between hers.

He began to fumble with her bodice but, trembling with desire as he was, he could not will his fingers to work properly to unlace her.

"Wait, wait, Sean!" she said while placing both hands on his chest to push him away.

"Sean!" she said, sitting up. "We must control ourselves, or we will succumb to our desires and, I am afraid that once that happens, you will lose interest in me."

"Nay, my love, never!" Sean proclaimed.

"Well, be that as it may," she replied. "I still must demand that we wait until we are married to consummate our love."

"Laurentje! I am only human!" he insisted as he renewed his attempts to open her bodice.

"Sean, soon you will return from your adventure and, with the land grant you will have from Governor Dongan, we will be in a position to marry. Then, we can let our desires run wild. Because, my dear, I want you every bit as much as you want me. I feel my resistance weakening each time we are together. And I know that I must be strong if we are to have the future that we both want."

Then, as if pre-ordained, the curfew bell began to toll.

Sean rose and straightened his clothing. Taking Laurentje's hand, he helped her to rise, as well. As she stood, she brushed leaves, grass and dirt from her skirts. They then walked arm in arm to the Staats' kitchen door. There, they again melted into each other's arms and kissed.

"I will miss you, Laurentje!" said Sean.

"I will miss you, too! I love you, Sean. Do not let anything happen to you. Tell Mister Viele that I will hold him personally responsible if you do not come back to me!"

They kissed, and Sean reluctantly walked back to the Viele's home.

Chapter 22

When Sean awoke the next morning, he found that Gerritje had already prepared his and Aernout's packs with clean shirts, socks and linens. "There is some food for your first day as well," she said. "I prepared only a small repast, as I know you will be spending the night at Schenectady where, I hope, one of our children will feed you!"

The two men bade her farewell, shouldered their packs, blanket rolls and muskets, and walked out of the town to the Iroquois encampment. There, they found the women dismantling the wigwams and arranging the components into packs that they could carry on their backs. Baskets of food for the journey were also ready to go.

When Sean and Aernout found Adissas, he introduced them to two young warriors, Gaghqua and Hanadodon. To Sean's eyes, they could have been twins. Both were taller than

Aernout, yet not as tall as Sean, with broad shoulders and muscular arms and legs. They were dressed similarly, in breech clouts and moccasins. Each had a knife and ax in his belt and a powder horn and shot bag slung over his shoulder. They both carried trade muskets and wore scalp locks with a single feather. They exhibited the proud, arrogant demeanor that was common to Seneca warriors.

Adissas said, "This man is pleased to tell you, Oh-Kahl, that both of these men can speak in the tongues of the English and the French. They have been tested in battle, and each has the heart of a panther. Both have been told to help you as they would help me."

"Thank you, Adissas," Sean replied. "I am honored to have such warriors accompany me."

Adissas then addressed the warriors in their own language, telling them that, when they reached the Seneca castles, they were to tell the people to hide all the grain and to abandon the castles before *Yonnondio* attacked.

"The women, children and old men are to go as far from the castles as possible," he said. "Sentries must be posted to watch for the French. Once they are seen, our warriors should hide themselves along the paths that the French will follow and ambush them, if possible. If the French are too many, the warriors, too, should melt into the forest."

The two Seneca grunted that they understood.

While the main body of natives was still assembling, the sachems and their wives along with Sean and Aernout began the trek westward.

"How long do you think it will take to reach Onontague?" asked Sean.

"I doubt that the sachems will lose any time getting there. After all, it's in their best interest to reach a decision as soon as possible and to intercept La Barre before he has a chance to strike."

Although the group moved quickly, it still took the whole day for them to reach Schenectady. The sachems' wives made camp outside of the town while Sean and Aernout were treated to a hearty meal prepared by Aernout's daughter. Later, Sean and Aernout went to Cornelis' tavern where they spent the night.

Early the next morning, Cornelis and young Aernout accompanied them to the banks of the Mohawk River, where they found Gaghqua and Hanadodon waiting. The two Seneca had already selected what they thought was the best canoe from those that were lined up on the shore. After loading his belongings and supplies into the canoe, Sean said goodbye.

"As I am going directly to Onontague, it will be up to you to post the Duke's Arms on the Mohawk and Oneida castles you pass as well as on those of the Seneca," Aernout told Sean.

"Don't worry, I'll take care of it," said Sean, adding the copper plates to his luggage. "But, what about the Cayuga castles?"

"Enlist a Seneca warrior to take the Duke's Arms to the Cayuga. Be sure he understands that they are to post them immediately. Oh, and don't forget that the governor is looking for sites on Lake Ontario where he might build a fort."

"No, I won't," replied Sean. "I will see you at Onontague as soon as I can get back. That is, of course, unless Le Barre has already attacked the Seneca."

"I don't think he'll reach the Seneca territory before you," said Aernout. "You three should certainly be able to travel more quickly than an army!"

At that, Gaghqua climbed into the bow of the canoe, followed by Sean, while Hanadodon took the stern seat. Keeping close to the shore, where they could avoid the stronger current in the middle of the river, they began paddling upriver.

The first day's travel was uneventful and, with the three men paddling, they had no trouble reaching Caughnawaga before nightfall. As they pulled their canoe onto shore, they were surrounded by jabbering children. Soon, Kai, accompanied by a crowd of villagers, came out to greet them.

In her role as acting Turtle Clan mother, Kai formally welcomed them and said, "Oh-Kahl, we are pleased to see you! Unfortunately, our sachems and clan mothers are not here to greet you. They are still at the great council with *Corlaer*."

"Actually, they are returning," Sean informed her. "The council has concluded. They should be here in just a matter of days."

"That is good to hear," said Kai. "But, where are my manners! It is unthinkable for this woman not to offer you and your companions some refreshment. Please come with me to the longhouse of the Turtle Clan and we will truly eat!"

Just then, an old man, a former sachem who was now too old to have made the trip to Albany for the council, approached them.

"Oh-Kahl, it does this old man's heart good to see his nephew!" he said.

"Cahaiadoirs! I am pleased to see you, as well!"

"Oh-Kahl, my niece has neglected to tell you that we have recently had visitors with very disturbing news!"

"Uncle, what kind of news could be so disturbing that it would trouble the heart of a brave warrior?"

"Three days ago, two Christian Mohawk came to Caughnawaga. They said that *Yonnondio* had sent them to carry wampum to Odianne. They said that they were told to tell him that the French were going to make war on the Seneca and the Cayuga because they had stolen from the French. *Yonnondio* told them to tell Odianne that the French wanted to keep the peace with the *Ganienkeh* and that the French wanted to live as friends with us, but that this could only happen if the *Ganienkeh* did not interfere in the war against the Seneca and Cayuga!"

"But Odianne was not at his castle!" said Sean.

"No, he was not. So the two Christians left the wampum with the French father who was visiting the castle and asked him to tell Odianne what *Yonnondio* had said. Then, they told us that *Yonnondio* had sent messengers with wampum to the Oneida and Onondaga, as well. Tell us, Oh-Kahl, what do you make of this?"

Speaking to the surrounding crowd as much as to Kai and Cahaiadoirs, Sean said, "I fear that the Christian Mohawk told you the truth. *Yonnondio* will make war on the Seneca and Cayuga. He sent a message to *Corlaer* telling him of his plans and asked *Corlear* to join him."

The crowd began to mutter and talk among themselves, but obeyed when Cahaiadoirs gestured for quiet and asked, "What did *Corlaer* say?"

"*Corlaer* told *Yonnondio* that the *Haudenosaunee* are children of the great English sachem across the big lake. He said that their lands are under his protection and that the French should not invade Seneca territory because it would be the same as invading English territory and attacking Englishmen."

"Thank you, Oh-Kahl, for telling us what you know of this. It is not good for *Yonnondio* to attack the Seneca and Cayuga. No matter what he says about wanting peace with the *Ganienkeh*, we would have to stand with our brothers against him. And, *Corlaer*, will he stand with us? Will the English stand with us against the French?"

"The English sachem and the French sachem are at peace with each other. I do not believe that they want war between their peoples. Even so, *Corlaer* has sent me to put a talisman on every *Haudenosaunee* castle so that *Yonnondio* will know that they are under the protection of the great English warrior, the Duke of York."

While he was speaking, Sean reached into his pack and took out one of the engraved copper plates. He showed the plate to the crowd of Indians and then walked to the palisade where, with a hammer and iron spikes, he nailed it to the post nearest the main gate.

Then, he continued, "My brothers and sisters, *Corlaer* says that when *Yonnondio* sees this talisman, he will go back to Montreal without attacking. That is why I can only visit with you for this one night. I must hasten to put the talismans on other castles before *Yonnondio* can attack."

"Also, you should know that *Corlaer* has sent Aerie the Interpreter to join your sachems in a council at Onontague. There, they will determine the best way to avoid war."

"That is a good thing," said Cahaiadoirs. "Thank you, Oh-Kahl, for sharing this information with us. Thank you for your words that comfort this old man's heart."

While Kai led Sean to the Turtle Clan longhouse, Gaghqua and Hanadodon, who were both members of the Wolf Clan, had been met by members of that clan and taken to another longhouse where they would eat and spend the night.

After they had eaten, Kai took Sean's hand and led him to her family's sleeping compartment.

"Oh, Oh-Kahl, I had hoped you would return soon. It has been so long since we have been together," she said as she helped him get undressed. With just a pull at the wrap around her waist, he quickly had her naked, as well. They fell into each other's arms and soon were lost in each other.

Afterwards, while they were lying quietly together, Sean said, "You understand, Kai, I must leave in the morning. I must reach the Seneca lands as soon as possible."

"I know. But, Oh-Kahl, this woman wants to come with you. I want to see what lies beyond the palisades of this castle."

"No, Kai, you can't come with us! This is no trip for a woman!"

"But you need a woman with you!" she insisted.

"No, Kai, you can't come with us! One woman and three men! It wouldn't be right!" At that, Sean climbed out of the sleeping compartment while pulling on his leggings. Kai followed, not bothering with her clothes, and stood her ground right in front of him.

Naked, with her hands on her hips, she demanded, "Not right? Not right for whom? Not right for a white woman perhaps, but very fitting for a woman of the *Ganienkeh*! Do not offend me by judging me as you would a white woman!

"I would be your woman on the trail. No other man would dare to touch me. I am strong; I can paddle a canoe and carry my share of supplies. You are my man. I am your woman. You must let me come with you!"

"But, Kai..."

"No, Oh-Kahl, listen to this woman! I am a woman of the *Ganienkeh*! I am not like the soft white women whom Oh-Kahl has known. This woman is strong and brave. I fear no Huron or Frenchman. Besides, you will need me. Who will build your lodge each night? Who will carry your fire and prepare your food? Certainly not the two Seneca warriors who are traveling with you!"

"But, what will your mother say when she learns that you went with me?"

"She will say nothing! I am a woman. I have a man. I have chosen to travel with that man. She will say nothing!"

"But, you will slow us down! You will be a distraction! If we run into trouble, you will expect me to think of you first, possibly placing our companions in grave danger!"

"No, Oh-Kahl! You are wrong!" demanded Kai. "You will see! This woman will move as fast as the rest of you! I will carry as much as the rest of you! I can fight using a knife or ax! I have a bow and can shoot an arrow as straight as any man. And, I will awaken before the rest of you to make your breakfast and to prepare for the day's journey! I am a woman of the *Ganienkeh*! I have no equal! There is no one better than this woman!"

The two lovers continued argue but soon, Sean realized that, just by sheer force of will, Kai would prevail.

And, eventually, she did. Sean capitulated and agreed that she could come with them, even though he was not entirely convinced that it was the right thing to do.

"But, if I think things are too dangerous, you must promise to do as I say," said Sean. "No arguments."

"Yes, Oh-Kahl, this woman promises. When you say things are dangerous, she will not argue."

With that, they climbed back into the sleeping compartment. After they had gotten comfortable, she snuggled up to him and said, "Do not worry Oh-Kahl, all will be well. You will not be sorry that this woman is with you."

"I hope so, woman, I hope so," he replied as he drifted off to sleep.

Starting early the next morning, the little party, with the addition of Kai, continued traveling up the Mohawk River. Throughout the day, Kai kept her word and willingly paddled in rhythm with the men. As a result, they made even better time than they had on the first day. By late afternoon, they had stopped and posted the Duke's Arms on two, small Mohawk castles, Canagora and Canajorha, and had arrived at Tionondogen.

There, after Sean had mounted the Duke's Arms on the palisade, he met with the French Jesuit, Father De Lamberville, who had received the French governor's request to stop the Mohawk from joining the Seneca against the French.

Sean, who knew the priest from prior visits, told him that he was acting as the representative of Governor Dongan and that he had been sent to put the Arms of the Duke of York on the castles of the Iroquois. He told him that La Barre had advised Dongan of his plans to attack the Seneca and that Dongan was greatly opposed to any such action.

Dongan, Sean told him, had advised La Barre that all the Iroquois, including the Seneca, were under the protection of the English and that he, Dongan, would consider an attack on them as an attack on the English. Further, he told him that they were hopeful that La Barre would accept restitution from the Seneca and, thus, avoid throwing the entire country into turmoil.

The priest dismissed this, saying, "The Seneca have refused to accept priests in their castles or to be baptized, so they deserve whatever punishment God might inflict on them. I must say that I am astounded that a Catholic, such as your Governor Dongan, would take the side of the savages against another Catholic nation."

"You've got to understand, father," Sean emphasized, "if the French attack the Seneca, the other Iroquois nations will stand with the Seneca. The confederacy is grounded in support for each of the nations by the others."

"I have been assured," Father De Lamberville told Sean, "that Garangula, the

Onondaga sachem, will make peace with Governor De La Barre. In fact, I have been told that he has promised that the Oneida and Cayuga would, as well. I am convinced that, once those three nations treat with the governor, even the Mohawk will fall in line."

"Remember, father," Sean said, "Garangula is the chief sachem of the Onondaga, but he is not the only sachem. He has others he must persuade, not only among the Onondaga but among the other nations, as well. It is not at all as simple as he would make it seem."

But Sean's arguments fell on deaf ears. The priest insisted that, even if all the Iroquois stood together, they would be unable to withstand the combined forces of French soldiers, Canadian militia and their Indian allies.

Finally, Sean tried to appeal to the priest as a fellow Catholic. He told him that, as a Christian, he should be prepared to forgive the Indians for things they did in savage ignorance.

But, no matter what Sean said, the priest refused to listen. Instead, he inveighed against the treachery and savagery of the Seneca, and insisted that the other tribes would abandon them. Finally, Sean gave up, convinced that the priest couldn't see beyond his own desire to remake the savages in his own image.

The next morning, he went looking for the priest to try, again, to enlist his aid in preventing the war, but the Jesuit was nowhere to be found.

"He left very early, even before dawn," one of the Christian women told Kai. "He said that he had to go to Onontague as quickly as possible."

When Kai told Sean, he said, "I am not surprised. Without doubt, he will try to use his influence to persuade the sachems to negotiate with the French. Oh well, he's Aernout's problem, now."

After Sean had enlisted a Mohawk warrior to carry the Duke's Arms to the two Oneida castles, the four travelers again took to the Mohawk River and paddled to its end, where they made a portage, carrying their baggage and the canoe a short way across country to Wood Creek. Embarking again, they paddled down the swiftly flowing creek, which proved to be much more challenging than the slow-moving Mohawk River. There were many rapids that had to be negotiated. But Hanadodon took charge and steered them safely past the boulders and deadwood that continually threatened to gouge or overturn the canoe.

Upon reaching Oneida Lake, Gaghqua and Hanadodon conferred and announced that they should camp for the night. At this point, Kai truly began to demonstrate her value to the group. While the three men went in search of game, Kai gathered saplings and built the framework for their wigwam. Then, using rolls of birch bark that she had brought with her, she quickly covered the dome-like frame and stitched the pieces together with thin, pliable willow branches. She also gathered fir branches and spread them over the ground inside the structure so that they could sleep in comfort.

That done, she gathered wood and started the fire. When the men returned with two partridges, she deftly plucked the birds and soon had them roasting over the fire.

As soon as they were finished eating, the men decided the order in which they would do sentry duty. Gaghqua, Hanadodon and Sean would each take a three-hour shift, in that order. Then, they would switch over the ensuing nights, with the last going first and so on.

Sean and Kai entered the wigwam first, followed by Hanadodon. Using his pack as a pillow, Sean lay on his back and covered himself with his blanket. Immediately, Kai snuggled up to him, laying her head on his chest and putting her right leg over his torso.

She hugged him and whispered, "Are you not pleased that this woman has come with you? I have prepared your wigwam, cooked your food and, now, will keep you warm in the night. Tell this woman that you are pleased."

"Aye, woman, I am pleased," whispered Sean.

"Tell this woman that you are sorry that you doubted her."

"Aye, woman, I am sorry."

"Good. Then, this woman will have sex with you," she said as she put her hand into his leggings and began to caress him.

"Kai!" Sean whispered urgently, "what are you doing? What about Hanadodon? He will hear us."

"He will sleep soon," she replied. "We will not disturb him."

Moments later, Hanadodon began snoring, and Kai made Sean even more pleased that she had come with them.

When Hanadodon woke Sean for his watch, Sean had some difficulty untangling himself from Kai. He could not help but wake her. Kai, realizing how close it was to dawn, got up, as well. While Sean stood his watch, Kai gathered more wood for the fire, built it up again, and began preparing breakfast.

As soon as the others were awake and eating, Kai dismantled the wigwam. She rolled and tied the bark into a compact package and put it into the canoe. The quartet then continued their journey, paddling the length of the lake to where it flowed into the Oneida River. The Oneida, like Wood Creek, was quick-flowing and filled with rapids. In fact, they were no more than halfway down the river when they could hear the roaring of a waterfall.

Hanadodon directed them to the shore where all but he got out of the canoe. Gaghqua explained, "We do not need to portage here. The falls are not very high, and Hanadodon can ride the canoe over them. He will meet us at the bottom."

With that, Gaghqua pushed the canoe away from the shore. Hanadodon carefully guided it to the center of the river where it was caught by the current, and the others watched as the Seneca warrior and the canoe disappeared over the edge of the falls.

Sean, Arnout, Kai and Gaghqua hurried around the falls and, at the bottom, they found

Hanadodon waiting for them. They all climbed back into the canoe and were soon again on their way. From the falls, it was but one more day's travel to Lake Ontario.

Upon reaching the lake, they paddled to a small beach and pulled the canoe out of the water. As Sean looked around he realized that this was the largest expanse of water he had seen since he had jumped ship nearly four years earlier. The far shore of the lake could not be seen.

Kai exclaimed, "Are we at the end of the world?"

Chuckling, Sean assured her, saying, "Nay, woman, there is land on the other side. You just can't see it because the shore is beyond the horizon. This is but a puddle compared to the big salt water lake that I had to cross when I left my homeland."

Then he began walking up and down the shoreline, looking up at the steep hill that led up from the beach.

"Kai," he said. "Take your bow and arrows and come with me. I want to see what's up there."

Sean and Kai started up the hill, while Gaghqua and Hanadodon went hunting. At the top of the hill, they found that they were on a broad, flat plain.

Turning in a circle to look in all directions, Sean thought to himself that this may be just the place for Governor Dongan's fort. According to Gaghqua and Hanadodon, they were about in the middle of the south shore of the lake. A fort located here would command a good portion of the lake. It would be an ideal spot for a trading post, as well, readily accessible for Indians following the water route through the Great Lakes from the West.

Its location is exceptionally favorable, he ruminated. It's protected on the east side by the river; and, on the lake side, the slope of the hill would make a frontal assault suicidal. And, since the area is so flat, the defenders would have plenty of warning if someone tried to attack overland. Most importantly, the depth of the ground water here should be such that it would not be too difficult to site and dig a well. This should be an acceptable spot for a fort and trading post.

Aloud, he said, "Kai, count the number of paces to that line of deadfall to the west, and I'll pace off the distance from the river to that pine grove there to the south. After you do that, come and join me. I want to see if there's sufficient timber in that grove for a blockhouse and stockade."

It only took a few minutes for Sean to reach the grove and, while waiting for Kai, he heard rustling in the undergrowth. Looking in the direction of the sound, he spied a catamount feeding on a freshly killed doe. Fearful of disturbing the animal, Sean tried to quietly back out of the trees. Unfortunately, as he was backing up, he stepped on a fallen branch with a resounding "Crack!"

At the noise, the big cat looked up and, seeing Sean, hissed. It then began moving slowly toward Sean. Fearing for his life, Sean raised his musket and fired. But, just as he pulled the trigger, the animal turned to its left, and the musket ball hit its shoulder instead of its head. Wounded, the beast bellowed and attacked. Sean turned to flee. Running wildly, he failed to see a root jutting out in his path. He tripped and fell just as the catamount leapt toward him.

Suddenly, the cat fell, dead, on top of Sean. Sean saw that an arrow had punctured the animal's heart. Looking up, he saw Kai notching another arrow in her bow, approaching carefully, not taking her eyes off the cat. When she reached Sean and saw that the cat was truly dead, she removed the arrow from the bow.

Seeing that Sean was covered in blood, Kai dropped to one knee and asked, "Are you all right, Oh-Kahl?"

"Aye, woman. This all appears to be blood from the catamount. And, nothing seems to be broken. 'Tis lucky I am that you were nearby! Thank ye."

"Do not thank me," she replied. "Your life is precious to this woman. Although, it is unfortunate that it was a catamount. Catamounts are poor eating."

"But, Kai, it had just killed a deer. Perhaps it's not too mangled to eat. Let's look."

They walked over to where the doe's body lay, but found that the catamount had been feeding for too long. The body was in shreds.

"So much for that," said Sean. Then, looking around, he quickly assessed the timber growth in the grove. He could see that the pines were tall enough for a palisade and plentiful enough for a strong blockhouse.

Together, they started back to camp. Along the way, they met Gaghqua and Hanadodon, who had killed a turkey. As they walked, Sean told the two Seneca of his run-in with the catamount and how Kai had saved his life. "Kai was like lightning. She raised her bow and shot! As fast as this!" he said, clapping his hands.

When they reached the campsite, Kai quickly erected the wigwam and started the fire. She then plucked, cleaned and roasted the turkey.

The next morning, they broke camp, loaded the canoe and continued westward on Lake Ontario. As they paddled, a gale started to blow. Rain came at them in sheets. Soon they were soaked through. Day after day, they paddled into the teeth of the wind. Although Kai constructed a wigwam each night, they were so wet and the ground so soggy that they slept poorly. Their progress was so slow that Sean began to worry that they would be unable to reach the Seneca castles before the French.

Then, one day, Gaghqua, who was in the bow of the canoe, became very excited and began pointing ahead. Through the heavy mist, Sean could see canoes ahead of them, also going west.

He said aloud, "It must be the rear of the French army."

But Gaghqua said, "No, Oh-Kahl, there are no bateaux, only canoes. They must be scouts for the French. They outnumber us. We cannot let them see us!"

He quickly turned their canoe toward shore, and they paddled until they were hidden under some overhanging trees.

As they sat watching until the canoes were completely out of sight, Sean said, "So, *Yonnondio* has sent his devils to prepare the way for his invasion. He cannot be far behind! We have very little time left. We must get to the Seneca castles before them. Is there a quick, overland route to the castle at Gandagaro from here?" asked Sean.

The two Seneca discussed the issue for a moment, and Gaghqua said, "There is a path to Gandagaro, but we will have to move very quickly through the forest. We can have nothing to slow us down. The woman must stay behind."

Hearing this, Kai exclaimed, "No! I will not stay behind! I can move as fast as any of you!"

"No, Kai," said Sean. "Gaghqua is right. You must stay behind."

"But, Oh-Kahl, you said that this woman could travel with you!"

"Aye, and you said that, when I said it was dangerous, you would abide by my decisions."

"Yes, Oh-Kahl, this woman did say that. Although I disagree with you, I will stay here."

They paddled to a small bay, called Sodus by the Seneca, with sandy beach and pulled the canoe out of the water. Concealing it behind some bushes, they turned it over to provide shelter for Kai.

Sean and Kai walked a little away from the two Seneca and Sean said, "I will be back soon."

"I know," said Kai. "Please be careful. This woman didn't save you from the catamount only to have a Huron take your scalp!"

"I promise," said Sean, as they embraced and kissed.

Then, taking only their weapons, pouches of corn with maple sugar and the pack with the Duke's Arms, the three men started to jog westward. Running in single file, with Sean in the middle, they moved efficiently. They ran fast enough to cover ground but not so fast that they would tire too quickly.

Chapter 23

For three days, the men kept up a steady pace through the forest. Although Sean was not as fast as the two Seneca, the two warriors adjusted their speed without complaint. Each night they stopped to sleep as soon as it became too dark to keep running safely, and they were up and going again as soon as it became light enough to see.

On the fourth day, they passed the ruins of a castle which had been destroyed by fire. Only pieces of the palisade and remnants of longhouses remained where there once had been a thriving village. The fire had burned a wide swath around the castle and, now, a few bushes and saplings were struggling to grow within and around the palisade.

"It was the spotted sickness. Almost everyone in the castle was killed. Those who survived burned the castle and cursed the land. It is a haunted place. No one can live here anymore," said Hanadodon.

Smallpox, thought Sean. It is astounding how much our diseases have impacted these people.

Finally, at sunrise on the fifth day, they found themselves at the edge of a clearing, looking across at the palisade of Gandagaro, the largest of all the Iroquois castles. Sean was amazed at its size. Gaghqua told him that it contained more than 150 longhouses with more than 2,000 residents.

"What do you think?" asked Sean. "It seems peaceful enough."

It was true, not a sound other than an occasional dog barking could be heard from within the palisade. Although they stood across from the main gate, they could not see in. Hanadodon explained that the palisade was actually two concentric circles. Each had its own gate, and the gates did not open on to each other.

"But, we should first look to see if the enemy scouting party is already here and watching," said Sean.

"There is a small gate in the back that is used by the women to go to the fields," suggested Hanadodon.

"Good," said Sean. "Gaghqua and I will circle around to the left of the castle. Hanadodon, you go right. We'll meet in the rear. Be careful."

As quietly as possible, the men separated. Moving through the trees and watching for enemy warriors, Sean and Gaghqua made their way around the castle. Eventually, they reached the opposite side of the stockade. There was a large cornfield between them and the castle. Gaghqua pointed to a small gate in the palisade.

Soon, they were joined by Hanadodon.

"I saw and heard nothing," reported Hanadodon.

"Neither did we," responded Sean. "Shall we go to the gate?"

Gaghqua nodded an assent and led the way through the cornfield. They were about halfway to the gate when they heard the sound of voices belonging to some young women coming to work in the field.

Seeing the men in the cornfield, the women squealed with fright and began running back toward the gate until Hanadodon called, "Aiyana!" At the sound of her name, one of the women turned and cried out, "Hanadodon!"

"She is my woman," he explained to Sean.

By the time men had reached the gate, many men and women were gathered around them. One of the men, who had the look of a person in charge, approached Hanadodon and grasped his shoulders.

"Little brother! It is well that you are safely home!" he said.

"Kaghnawias! It is good to be home! But, I fear that I come with grave news," said Hanadodon.

"What is wrong, brother?"

"I will tell all. But, first, come, meet my English friend."

At that, Hanadodon introduced Sean. Kaghnawias, Hanadodon told Sean, was his older brother and a war chief of the Seneca. "He is in command of the castle while the sachems are at Orange," Hanadodon said proudly.

Then, turning to Kaghnawias, he said, "My brother, please have all the people gather at the fire pit. Then I will explain what has happened."

While Kaghnawias sent word for all the villagers to gather, Sean, accompanied by a crowd of children, walked around to the main gate and nailed the Duke's Arms to one of the timbers of the palisade nearest the gate. Once that had been done, they all went inside to the fire pit to await the rest of the villagers.

When Kaghnawias was sure that everyone was present, he had Hanadodon speak to the people.

"My brothers and sisters," the warrior proclaimed, "while we were at Orange, we learned that *Yonnondio* is extremely angry with the Seneca. *Yonnondio* told *Corlear* that he that he will make war upon the Seneca because some of our warriors attacked French canoes. Even now, his army is on the march! His allies, the accursed Huron, are already lurking in our forests between here and Lake Ontario, making a path for the French."

Hanadodon was interrupted by shouts of anger from the warriors and cries of dismay from the women.

"We are Seneca, and we fear nothing!" shouted Kaghnawias.

"Nothing! We fear nothing!" cried the warriors.

"My brothers and sisters," continued Hanadodon, "we have nothing to fear because Seneca warriors are the bravest of all the warriors of the *Haudenosaunee*! And because *Corlear* has given us a special talisman to protect our castles from *Yonnondio*."

This last was greeted with some disbelief by the crowd, and even Kaghnawias felt the need to question his brother, "A talisman? What kind of talisman can protect us from *Yonnondio*?"

At this, Sean stepped forward and announced, "My Seneca brothers and sisters, by the order of *Corlaer*, I have fixed the talisman of our sachem, the great Duke of York, to your gate. This talisman will protect you from the French. *Corlaer* told me to tell you that your castle is now as safe from attack by *Yonnondio* as an English village."

The Indians continued murmuring among themselves. Hanadodon held up both his hands for quiet and said, "My brothers, it is true. *Corlaer* has given this talisman to the *Haudenosaunee* to put on all our castles! He says that, because the English and French sachems who live across the great lake are at peace, *Yonnondio* will not dare to attack.

"But, if he does attack," said Hanadodon, "Our sachem, Adissas, has ordered that the Seneca be prepared to answer this threat!"

"My brother," he said, turning to Kaghnawias, "Adissas wants all of the food hidden from the French. He wants all of the women, children and old men to leave Gandagaro and to hide in the forests. Finally, he asked that you and your warriors stand guard against the French. You should hide in the woods and ambush them as they approach Gandagaro."

"This we will do," said Kaghnawias, turning to the crowd. "We will kill the French! Never will Gandagaro yield to *Yonnondio*!" he exclaimed as his warriors whooped loudly.

"My brother," interrupted Hanadodon, "Adissas also said that we must be realistic. The French are as numerous as the leaves on the trees. Not only do the Huron march with them, but many of our enemies from the west may be coming, as well. Adissas fears that the warriors of Gandagaro may not be able to stop the French. If the French capture and burn Gandagaro, you are to melt into the forest and continue to harass them if they march toward the castle at Chemung. Do you understand?"

"Yes, brother, I understand. If, as Orenda wills, the French capture Gandagaro, we will make them pay with their blood."

"Good!" said Hanadodon, "Now, everyone should prepare to leave before the sun is any higher in the sky. Our enemies are very close. But there is one more thing, my brother. Adissas asked that you send a trusted warrior to Chemung. They, too, must be warned of this threat and told what to do. This warrior must also attach the talisman of the Duke of York to the gate of Chemung, as was done here. Can you do that?"

"Of course, my brother!" At that, Kaghnawias beckoned a warrior and explained what was expected of him. Sean gave the warrior one of the copper plates and some iron spikes, and he left at a run.

"We must also warn the Cayuga," interjected Sean. "*Yonnondio* has said that he will attack them, as well."

"I will send a runner to the Cayuga," volunteered Kaghnawias, gesturing to another warrior, who came forward.

"Thank you," said Sean, handing the man two copper plates and some spikes. This man, too, left at a run.

Meanwhile, the other warriors ran to get their weapons and then, with Kaghnawias leading them, went into the forest to take up defensive positions.

At the same time, under the direction of the clan mothers, the young women gathered all the grain in the castle and any ripe vegetables from the garden into baskets, and began carrying them into the woods to be hidden. While this was being done, the older women, children and old men began to leave. They understood that they would have to go quite far before they would be safe.

Before she left with the others, Hanadodon's woman, Aiyana, brought food for the three men to eat then and gave them corn with maple sugar for their return journey.

By the time they had finished eating, the castle was empty, except for a few stray dogs.

With one last look, Sean and the two Seneca warriors began to retrace their steps. Again, they ran in a single file. It was not long before they passed the last of the Seneca warriors hiding in the forest. Immediately, they began to jog a little more slowly and much more cautiously.

On the second day, just as they were passing the ruined castle. Hanadodon suddenly turned and sprinted into the remains of the palisade. Without question, Sean and Gaghqua followed, hot on his heels. Once behind one of the larger sections of the wall, all three threw themselves to the ground and lay there, scarcely daring to breathe.

Moments later, through a gap in the palisade, Sean saw a warrior appear from amongst the trees and look over the area. He was soon joined by a dozen more warriors and two white men. One white man was dressed in the uniform of the *Compagnies franches de la Marine* and carrying an officer's sword. The second, dressed in deerskin leggings, a belted, linen shirt and a woolen cap, was clearly a *courier-de-bois*. At first, they conferred quietly but, soon, there was an argument. Sean could hear the officer, in French, loudly order the Indians to go search the ruins. When the *courier-de-bois* had translated, the warriors refused. When the officer gestured dismissively that they should do as he ordered, the warriors became more and more agitated. Finally, at the urging of the *courier-de-bois*, the officer capitulated and ordered his French companion to search the ruins. As the *courier-de-bois* slowly made his way to the castle, Sean and his companions quietly crawled further into the village, finally hiding behind the remains of a longhouse.

Watching, they saw the Frenchman cautiously enter the perimeter of the palisade. Clearly uncomfortable, he made only a cursory inspection of the castle before announcing to the others that it was empty and that they should move on.

He quickly rejoined the others. Then, moving slowly and in single file with the two Frenchmen in the middle, the scouting party made a wide detour around the village and continued in the direction of Gandagaro.

To Sean, laying there with his hand on the hilt of his hatchet, it seemed to take forever for the enemy party to reach the trees beyond the village. When they did, Hanadodon rose to a crouch, looking around and listening intently. Then, gesturing to the others to follow, he moved quickly through the palisade and into the forest. He crouched behind a tree and watched until Sean and Gaghqua had safely joined him. "Huh," he commented, "Huron."

Then, they all began to run. Now, much more quickly than before.

Soon, they reached the lake. A little searching soon revealed where the scouting party had hidden its five canoes. Using their hatchets, they stove in the bottoms of all of the canoes except one.

"Good!" grunted Gaghqua. "The Huron devils now have no way to escape the wrath of the Seneca!"

They climbed into the remaining canoe and set off toward where they had left Kai and their own canoe.

As soon as they were in sight of Sodus Bay, Sean had a feeling that something was wrong. Quietly, he urged the others to pick up the pace. When they had landed, they saw immediately that someone had chopped holes in their canoe. Anything of value was gone while the rest had been scattered around. Sean went in search of Kai as Hanadodon and Gaghqua began looking for clues.

The first thing Sean noticed was the remains of a fire. He thought to himself that Kai would not have built a fire. She would not have wanted to call attention to herself.

At a call from Gaghqua, Sean ran to a spot about 1,000 yards down the shoreline. There, it was obvious that a canoe had been pulled onto the shore. Pointing at the footprints in the mud, Gaghqua said, "These tracks were made by Huron moccasins. Four men came here, and the same four left. But, the prints of one man were deeper when leaving than coming. He must have been carrying something."

Returning to the campsite, Sean showed the Seneca the remains of the fire. Squatting closely, Gaghqua examined the ashes and then announced that they were about two days old. He agreed with Sean that the woman would not have made the fire.

Splitting up, the three men continued searching the area. Hanadodon found signs on the bark of a nearby tree that someone had been tied there, and had scraped the bark from the tree by straining at his or her bonds. Pointing to the ground, he indicated traces of blood on the grass.

"Oh-Kahl," said Hanadodon, "your woman has been captured by the Huron."

"No!" cried Sean. "Kai would never have let them catch her! She would have let them kill her first!"

"Why?" asked Gaghqua. "It is the nature of things. Women are captured and taken home. Every nation does it. Your woman knows this. As long as she doesn't fight, she will live. "

"We must follow them. We have to get her back!"

"Where, Oh-Kahl? How will we follow them? Canoes do not leave tracks upon the water," commented Hanadodon.

"But, I can't just leave it like this!"

"You must, Oh-Kahl. You, too, must accept the nature of things," said Gaghqua.

"Come, Oh-Kahl," said Hanadodon. "We must leave this place. Adissas needs to know that our people have been warned. We must go."

Despite Sean's misgivings, they were soon in the canoe and headed back toward the Oswego River. Sean found some solace in the rhythm of paddling, but he could not help but keep thinking of Kai and what had happened. What would he do if he ever lost Laurentje? He now knew that the thought was too terrible to consider. He decided that, as soon as he returned to Albany, he would ask her to marry him. He believed that if he did so, he could protect her.

When they reached the Oswego River, they found Adekodara, a Mohawk warrior from Tionondogen, waiting for them. After greeting them, he said, "O-Kahl, Aerie the Interpreter has sent this man to meet you."

"Why? What is wrong?"

"This man knows only that Aerie wants you to go to La Famine. The sachems of the Oneida, Onondaga and Oswego have gone there to meet with *Yonnondio*. Aerie said that it was important that you go there, too."

"But, where is Aerie? Isn't he with the sachems?"

"Aerie went to Orange to see *Corlear*. He said that you should go to La Famine as soon as possible."

Overhearing the exchange, Hanadodon asked, "What of this man and Gaghqua? Are we to go to La Famine as well?"

"No. Adissas wants you to join him at Onontague. This man will go to La Famine with O-Kahl."

Leaving the two Seneca to find their way to Onontague on foot, Sean and Adekodara took the canoe and began paddling eastward along the lake's coastline until they reached the small cove, called La Famine. Entering the cove, Sean was amazed at the mass of tents housing the French army.

The two men beached their canoe and made their way to the Iroquois encampment. There they found Aernout waiting for them.

"Welcome back, lad," said Aernout, grasping Sean's hand. "Were you successful? Are the Duke's Arms on the castles?

"Aye, I suppose ye could say we were successful," answered Sean. "We did everything that we set out to do. But, we lost Kai in doing it."

"What do you mean, you 'lost Kai,'" demanded Aernout. "The girl was with you?"

"Aye," said Sean. "It was my fault. Kai wanted to come with us. At first I refused but, eventually, she wore me down and I agreed. Everything was fine until we were almost to Gandagaro. We saw canoes ahead of us that were moving more slowly than we. To avoid them, we decided to go ashore and proceed on foot. We thought it would be quicker if Kai stayed behind. Then, on our way back, we found that she had been captured by some Huron who must have come upon her by chance. I have no idea where they could have taken her."

"I'm sorry to hear that," said Aernout, putting his arm around Sean's shoulder. "I liked the girl. She had spirit. But, I hope you don't blame yourself for what happened. It sounds to me that she was where she wanted to be."

"Aye," said Sean. "She was. But, how will I ever face Nadie, now that her daughter is a prisoner?"

"You have to," said Aernout. "But Nadie knows how her daughter felt about you. It would be best, both for you and Nadie, if the news came from you."

"But, tell me Aernout, why did ye want me to come here? Adekodara said that ye had gone to Albany to meet with the governor!"

"Aye, I did. But, let me start from the beginning. It has been a busy two weeks! Come, we'll get you some food, then we'll talk."

After they had eaten and were sitting with Adjechne, Aernout said, "Well, let's see. When we got to Onontague, the French priest, De Lamberville, was waiting. He said he had met you at Tionondogen."

"Aye, he did," said Sean. "I assumed that he had gone to Onontague to persuade the Iroquois to treat with La Barre."

"Aye, exactly so," said Aernout. "I joined them in a council with him. First, he told them what La Barre planned, and gave them the wampum that La Barre had sent. The *wilden* told him how much it grieved them to take up arms against the French. They said that the Seneca are proud and insolent because they have so many warriors but, if La Barre genuinely wants peace, the others would convince the Seneca to make reparations. However, if La Barre wants war, then he should worry about how much the French will suffer. They told him that, if La Barre attacks the Seneca, the warriors of the other Iroquois nations will prowl throughout Canada, killing Frenchmen and burning their crops and homes.

"Adissas told him that the French seem to have a desire to be stripped, roasted and eaten. He even went so far as to wonder, aloud, if the salt the French like to eat would affect their taste. One of the other sachems said that he didn't think that the French would taste as good as the other enemies they had eaten.

"Hannatakta, a Cayuga sachem, and others even told De Lamberville that they pitied La Barre," he continued. "They told the priest to beg the governor not to make war because the Five Nations would unite against him. They told him that the war would be disastrous for the French. They said that the French army could not overcome the *Haudenosaunee* because the French only know how to fight against towns, not in the forest."

"What did De Lamberville say to that?"

"Nothing. But I know that he sent his brother, another priest, to plead with La Barre to avoid war because the Iroquois would unite against the French."

"So, what did the sachems decide?" asked Sean.

"Well, at first," Aernout continued, "the Seneca held their ground, saying that they were willing to go to war, and would accept no presents from the other nations or from the French. In fact, they even returned belts that De Lamberville had given them on behalf of La Barre."

"And then?" asked Sean.

"Well, by then, La Barre and his army had landed here, at La Famine. He sent one of his lieutenants, a man named Le Moyne, to help the priest encourage the Iroquois to meet with him. Le Moyne told them that La Barre only wanted them to help him decide what reparations the Seneca should make and that La Barre had no quarrels with any of the other nations.

"Hearing this, Garangula and the other Onondaga sachems were almost able to convince the other nations to join them in meeting with La Barre," continued Aernout. "They claimed that they would not ask for a peace treaty. They said that they would only meet to decide on reparations.

"I forbade them to do this. I told them that Governor Dongan did not want them to meet with La Barre for any purpose without his permission. I reminded them that they had agreed to be subject to the king of England and the Duke of York and that the governor had absolutely forbidden them to meet with the French. Then, I gave them two fathoms of wampum to mark my words."

"That should have stopped them," said Sean.

"Well, it slowed them down a little. The sachems asked Le Moyne to go to La Barre and ask him for some time while they sought Dongan's permission to speak with him. That's when I went back to Albany. Unfortunately, Dongan had already left for Manhattan. Knowing that I didn't have time to go to Manhattan and back, I returned and told the sachems that they did not have the governor's permission to meet with La Barre.

"There ensued more councils and arguments between the different sides. Ultimately, I convinced Adissas and Achigari and the other Seneca and Mohawk sachems to stay away from the French. However...."

"However?"

"However, Garangula became belligerent. I think he wanted to look good in front of De Lamberville and Le Moyne, who had returned from La Famine. What do you think, Adjechne?"

"You are right, my brother," the Onondaga sachem replied. "There is good reason why the French call Garangula '*La Grande Gueule*'"

At that, Sean laughed out loud. "They do?"

"Aye," laughed Aernout. "*La Grande Gueule*, Big Mouth! And, he certainly is that."

"What did he say?"

"I will let Adjechne tell you, I get too angry when I talk about it!"

Adjechne began, "Garangula said that *Yonnondio* had invited all of the nations to speak with him in friendship and that he had sent five great belts of wampum to persuade us to meet with him. Not just two fathoms as Aerie had brought!

"Garangula asked Aerie why the *Haudenosaunee* should not go to La Famine to see *Yonnondio* after he had made so many requests, had come so far, and was so near. He said that he was afraid that, if we did not meet with *Yonnondio*, we would provoke his wrath.

"Saying that Aerie had said that the *Haudenosaunee* are subjects of the King of England and the Duke of York, Garangula proclaimed that we are not subjects, but brothers! We *Haudenosaunee* must take care of ourselves, he said, the talismans fixed upon the Iroquois castles will not protect us from the army of *Yonnondio*!

"Garangula said that he wished that *Corlaer* was here but since he was not, he would have to speak to Aerie as he would to *Corlear*. He said that *Corlear* should not be dissatisfied. Why should the *Haudenosaunee* not embrace peace instead of war? To achieve this, the Onondaga would take the evildoers, the Seneca, by the hand, and *Yonnondio* as well, and throw their ax and his sword into deep water."

When Adjechne had finished, Sean asked, "So, they have come to meet with La Barre?"

"Aye," said Aernout. "Garangula and Adjechne along with the sachems of the Oneida and Cayuga and about thirty warriors came here with Le Moyne and the priest. Since I was not invited, I waited a few hours before following. Officially, you and I are not here."

"Oh. I should mention one other thing: when the sachems left Onontague, Garangula was wearing the coat of a French officer with a very large medal on it. He seemed to be quite proud of the coat, so I asked Adjechne about it."

"And, Adjechne, what did the coat mean?" pressed Sean.

"The coat was a present to Garangula from *Yonnondio*," replied the sachem. "*Yonnondio* gave the coat to Garangula because he was such a close friend to the French and had allowed the French fathers to teach the Onondaga about their god."

"So, Garangula was ready to sell out the Five Nations for the coat of a French officer!" muttered Sean.

"Well," said Aernout, "perhaps not sell out. But he appears to have been willing to aid and abet the French in stealing the allegiance of the Five Nations. And, in any event, he's no longer wearing the coat."

"Really! Why?" asked Sean.

"While we were on the trail to La Famine," said Adjechne, "we learned that *Yonnondio* had come prepared for war, not for talk! We were met by some Christian Mohawk who lives on the French side of Lake Cadaraqui. They warned us that *Yonnondio* had gathered an army of more than a thousand Frenchmen, and Huron and Abenaki warriors at Fort Cadaraqui, and had brought them with him to La Famine. We also were told that he had ordered the French at Michilimackinac to meet him at Irondequoit Bay with another 600 Frenchmen and Far Indians. There, the two armies would meet and invade the Seneca territory. That was when Garangula took the coat off and has not worn it since."

"So, have the sachems met with La Barre?" asked Sean.

"No. Not yet," said Aernout. "It's as though La Barre is trying to humiliate them. They have been waiting two days."

"I have been told," interjected Adjechne, "that *Yonnondio* will meet with us tomorrow. Although we do not yet know when."

"What we do know is that all of the Frenchmen, militia and regulars, are sick with fever." Aernout revealed. "They are almost out of provisions and, in any event, can barely feed themselves."

"Yes," Adjechne agreed. "Our brothers who live near Fort Cadaraqui told us of the sickness that had infected the French army, and we knew that we need not fear *Yonnondio's* army. And the Abenaki and Huron dogs that run with the French are disgusted. They complain that the French are too weak to war against women, let alone the mighty Seneca."

"Well," said Aernout, stretching, "I, for one, am ready to sleep. I am sure, Sean, that you are tired, as well. Let us wait and see what the morrow brings."

The next morning, while the sachems waited for word on when La Barre would meet with them, Sean told Aernout that he wanted to go to the Huron camp to see if he could find Kai. Aernout insisted that he accompany him, saying, "I may have traded with some of them, so they know me. Also, there is safety in numbers."

They skirted the French and Abenaki encampments and soon were surrounded by grumbling and threatening Huron. "My friends," pronounced Aernout in Huron. "I am Aerie the Interpreter, a friend to the Huron. My brother, here, is O-Kahl, who is also a friend to the Huron. We are seeking a *Ganienkeh* woman who was taken by Huron warriors from a camp at Sodus Bay on Lake Cadaraqui. We will trade for the woman. We will exchange a musket, a keg of rum and a bolt of duffle cloth for the woman."

At first the Huron were stunned by the generosity of the offer. Then, a warrior said to Aernout, "Aerie, I am called Sandegho. I know you. I have traded at Orange. So, I must ask, why do you offer such a valuable trade for a woman? Is she a witch? Does she have strong powers?"

"Yes, Sandegho, I know you and so I will speak the truth. She is not a witch. She is just a woman. But she belongs to O-Kahl and he wants her back."

Another warrior spoke up, saying, "I have seen the *Ganienkeh* woman. She was with four warriors. They are not here. They stopped only to get provisions and then left."

"How long have they been gone?" asked Aernout.

"Five days, maybe more," said the warrior.

"Which way did they go?" asked Sean.

"That, I do not know," said the warrior. "I did not watch them leave."

"Thank you, my friend," said Aernout. "If you ever come to Orange to trade, come to see me. I will give you good value for your furs."

As they left the Huron, Sean asked, "Can we go after them?"

"Nay, lad, they're too far ahead of us. There's no way we could catch them, and we don't know where they're going. No, we won't go after them. You have to resign yourself, Sean, Kai is gone."

Just as they returned to the Iroquois camp, at midday, one of La Barre's officers called the sachems together and told them, "*Monsieur le Gouverneur* orders that you come to his tent immediately!"

The sachems, insulted that they had been ordered and not invited, refused to go.

The officer said, "*Monsieur le Gouverneur* has told me to tell you that, if you do not do as he says, you will regret it!"

"My brothers," said Garangula. "Since we have come so far to meet with *Yonnondio*, we should do so!"

And so, with Sean and Aernout trailing behind, the group made its way to the center of the French camp. The French officer who had summoned the sachems tried to stop Sean and Aernout, saying, "Englishmen are not welcome here!"

"That's fine, then, isn't it, lad," said Sean, "seein' as how we are not English. He is Dutch and I am Irish. At the same time, however, we are here to look out for the best interests of the savages who have sworn allegiance to His Majesty's government."

"But, but," stuttered the Frenchman.

"That's all right, lad, we won't tell anyone if ye won't!"

Just then, La Barre emerged from his tent and sat on a camp stool in front of the council fire with his officers standing around him. There was no place for the sachems to sit -- no blankets, no furs. They were forced to stand while La

Barre sat and began speaking without the customary words of welcome.

With Le Moyne translating, La Barre said, "I have informed the King of France, my master, that the Iroquois have often broken the peace. So, he ordered me to come here with an army, and to require that the Onondaga bring all of the chief sachems of the Iroquois to my camp. The king wants us to smoke the calumet of peace together, but only if you promise me, in the names of the Seneca, Cayuga, Onondaga, Oneida and Mohawk, to give full satisfaction and reparations to his subjects and to never molest them again.

"'The Iroquois have robbed and abused French traders who were going to the Illinois, Miami and other Indian nations, who are the children of my king. In doing so, you have acted contrary to the peace treaty you had made with the previous governor of Canada. My king has ordered me to demand satisfaction, and to tell you that, if you refuse or if you plunder us anymore, I have his express orders to declare war on you. Take this belt to confirm my words." La Barre continued, saying, 'The warriors of the Iroquois have brought the English into the lakes which belong to my king, and have also brought the English among the Indian nations, which are the children of my king. You have done this in order to destroy my king's fur trade and to steal those nations away from him.

"Your warriors have carried the English there, even though you were forbidden to do so. I am willing to forget these things, but if they ever happen again in the future, I have my king's express orders to declare war on you! This belt confirms my words."

Then, La Barre said, "Your warriors have made several barbarous attacks on the Illinois and Miami. They have massacred men, women and children, who thought themselves safe in their villages. They have made prisoners of many people from these nations. These people, who are my king's children, cannot be your slaves. You must send them back to their own country. If you refuse to do this, I have my king's express orders to declare war on you. This belt confirms my words."

La Barre directed his final comments to Garangula, "This is the declaration that the king, my master, has commanded me to make to the Seneca, Cayuga, Onondaga, Oneida and Mohawk. He does not wish you to force him to send a great army to begin a war which must be fatal to you. He would be sorry if Fort Cadaraqui, which was the work of peace, became a prison for your warriors. We must endeavor, together, to prevent such misfortunes. We French, who are brothers and friends of the Iroquois, will not trouble them, provided that the satisfaction, which I demand, is given, and that the treaties of peace be hereafter observed. I shall be extremely grieved if my words do not produce the effect which I expect. For then I shall be obliged to join with the governor of New York, who is commanded by his master to assist me, and *burn the castles of the Five Nations, and destroy you!* This belt confirms my words!"

There was utter silence. For a few moments, the sachems appeared shocked. Garangula, himself, kept his eyes downcast, fixed on his pipe as he walked five or six times around the council fire.

When he had returned to his place, Garangula raised his head, looked directly at La Barre and said, "*Yonnondio*, I honor you, and the warriors who are with me likewise honor you. Your interpreter has finished your speech; now I begin mine. Listen to my words.

"*Yonnondio*, when you left Quebec, you must have believed that the sun had burnt up all the forests which make our country inaccessible to the French, or that the lakes had overflowed their banks and surrounded our castles so that it was impossible for us to get out of them. Yes, *Yonnondio*, surely you must have thought so, and the curiosity of seeing so great a country burnt up, or under water, has brought you so far. Now you are undeceived since I and my warriors are here to assure you that the Seneca, Cayuga, Onondaga, Oneida and Mohawk are all alive.

"Hear, *Yonnondio*, I have my eyes open, and this man sees a great captain at the head of a company of soldiers, who speaks as if he were dreaming. He says that he only came to the lake to smoke the pipe of peace with the Onondagas. But Garangula says that he sees the opposite. I see that you came to knock us on the head. I see that you would have done so if sickness had not weakened your army.

"This man sees *Yonnondio* raving in a camp of sick men, men whose lives the Great

Spirit has saved by inflicting this sickness on them.

"Hear *Yonnondio*, we did not plunder any French traders except those who carried guns, powder and ball to the Miami and Illinois. We did this because those arms might have cost us our lives. Our warriors do not have enough beaver to pay for all the arms that they have taken. But, we are not afraid of war! This belt preserves my words!

"We carried the English into *our* lakes, to trade there with the Ottawa, as the Algonquin brought the French to our castles to carry on a trade which the English say is theirs.

"The Iroquois are born free. We depend on neither *Yonnondio* nor *Corlaer*.

We may go where we please, and carry with us whom we please, and buy and sell what we please. If your Indian allies are your slaves, use them as such. You can command them to receive no other, but your people. But, do *not* attempt to command us! This belt preserves my words!

"We knocked the Miami and the Illinois on the head because they hunted beaver on our lands. We knocked them on the head because they acted contrary to the custom of all Indians by killing both male and female beaver. We knocked them on the head because they hated us so much that they brought the Shawnee into their country and gave them muskets. But, in doing so, we have done less than either the English or the French that have stolen the lands of so many Indian nations, and chased them from their own countries. This belt preserves my words!

"Hear, *Yonnondio*, this man speaks with the voice of all the *Haudenosaunee*. Hear their answer. Open your ears to what they say. The Seneca, Cayuga, Onondaga, Oneida and Mohawk say that, when they buried the hatchet in the middle of Fort Cadaraqui, in the presence of your predecessor, they planted the tree of peace, in the same place, to be there carefully preserved, so that, instead of a house for soldiers, that fort might be a house of merchants; that, in place of arms and munitions of war, only beaver and merchandise would enter there.

"Hear, *Yonnondio*, take care for the future, that so great a number of soldiers as appear here do not choke the tree of peace planted in such a small fort. It would be a great loss if, after it had so easily taken root, you were to stop its growth and prevent it from covering your country and ours with its branches. I assure you, in the name of the *Haudenosaunee*, that our warriors shall dance to the calumet of peace under its leaves and shall never dig up the hatchet unless their brothers, *Yonnondio* or *Corlaer,* shall either jointly or separately try to attack the country which the Great Spirit gave to our ancestors. This belt preserves my words, and this other, the authority which the *Haudenosaunee* have given me!"

Then Garangula told Le Moyne to speak, explain his words, and omit nothing.

After Le Moyne had translated, La Barre grew red in the face. He jerked out of his chair and stalked into his tent. The next morning, Sean and Aernout, with all the sachems, returned to Onontague.

Once there, Sean and Aernout joined the Onondaga, Cayuga and Oneida sachems in a council with the Seneca and Mohawk sachems. Garangula told the story of what had happened in the meeting with La Barre. When Garangula had finished, Adissas rose to his feet and said, "Thank you, Garangula, for telling us what happened in your council with *Yonnondio*. I am appalled by his actions and words. But -- please forgive me -- but I must say that I had told you, when we were meeting with *Corlaer* at Orange, that *Yonnondio* was not to be trusted!"

Garangula grew red in the face but, before he could respond to Adissas, Aernout stood and said, "*Corlaer* forbade you to meet with *Yonnondio*! Yet you did so! And, you saw how he treated you like children! When will you learn that only the English are your brothers? When will you learn that the English, unlike the French, wish no ill will toward the People of the Longhouse? What do you think *Corlaer* will say when I tell him that, contrary to his wishes, the sachems of the Onondaga, Cayuga and Oneida treated with *Yonnondio*? He would be right to say that we should abandon you to your fate. He would be right to say that we should not care what the French may do to you!"

Garangula was blustering, not knowing what to say, when another Onondaga sachem, Carachkondie, stood and said, "Aerie, we are sorry and ashamed. Now we understand that the governor of Canada is not as great a man as *Corlear*, and we are vexed for having given the governor of Canada so many fine wampum belts."

Aernout responded, "I see, Carachkondie, that you now understand that *Corlaer* had only the best interests of the Five Nations at heart when he told you to avoid *Yonnondio*. I am pleased that you have this understanding and that it has come at so small a price. But, burn it into your memories that *Corlaer* was right. Never forget that only *Corlaer* has your best interests at heart!"

With that, Aernout turned and, with Sean, walked away from the council.

"Aernout," whispered Sean. "Was it necessary to embarrass Garangula in front of the other sachems?"

"Aye, lad, it was," he replied. "And, I would do it again. Dongan told the old fool not to meet with La Barre! I told him the same thing, but still he did it. That La Barre insulted him and I embarrassed him is no less than he deserves! Come, lad. We've done all that we can here. It's time we return home. When I returned from Albany, I came by horseback to save time. I brought an extra mount and, so, we will be riding home."

With that, they saddled and mounted their horses and left the Onondaga castle behind them.

Chapter 24

As soon as they arrived at Caughnawaga, Aernout sent one of the children who had been playing outside the gate to ask Cahaiadoirs to join them. He told the boy to go directly to the old sachem, to speak only to him and to tell no one else that they had arrived. Promising, the boy ran off. Soon, he returned with the old man.

"Uncle," said Aernout, "I am pleased to see you well and strong!"

"Nephew," the old man replied, "I am only as well and strong as an old man can be. But, it pleases these old eyes to see you and you, too, Oh-Kahl."

"Uncle," said Sean, "I must ask for your assistance."

"Yes, nephew? What can this old man do for you?"

"Uncle, I must tell Nadie that her daughter, Kai, has been captured by the Huron.

I need your guidance to do so in the proper manner."

"Aiyee!" cried the old man. "The girl was a good girl. She was to be a clan mother. She will be sorely missed. Of course, nephew, this man will help you in this."

Turning to the boy who had summoned him, Cahaiadoirs told him to go to his longhouse and to ask his woman for a certain leather bag. He was to return with it as soon as possible.

Then, the old man explained to Sean that, when an Iroquois is captured it is as though he or she had died. There are certain rituals which must be followed. He said that he, Sean and Aernout would go to the Turtle Clan lodge. There, he would tell Sean what to say and do.

"It is good that you sent for me," he said. "It is proper that such news come from a member of a different clan."

When the boy returned with the leather bag, he was accompanied by Onata, who was Cahaiadoirs' woman.

"Why are you here, woman?" asked Cahaiadoirs.

"When the boy told me what you wanted, this woman knew that someone had died. I thought that my presence might be useful."

"You may be right," he responded. "The daughter of Nadie has been captured by Huron. We must perform the condolence rite."

"Aiyee!" the old woman cried. "Her mother will be heartbroken!"

Together, the small group made its way to the Turtle Clan lodge. After ascertaining that

Nadie was inside, Cahaiadoirs led them in. The old man approached Nadie and, standing in front of her, took three strings of wampum from the pouch. At the sight of the wampum, the other people in the lodge began to moan and gathered around Nadie who, by now, understood what was happening and had a stricken look on her face.

Cahaiadoirs said to Nadie, "Sister, it grieves me to tell you that your daughter, Kai, is now a prisoner of the Abenaki. I offer you this old man's condolences and those of all our people."

"Aiyee!" screamed Nadie as she fell forward onto the ground. Screaming, crying, she tossed and rolled around in the dirt. The other clan members who were present began to cry and wail, as well. Sean, bewildered, just stood there, not knowing what to do.

Onata embraced Nadie and helped her rise to her knees. Her face was covered with dirt, and her tears made tracks down her cheeks.

Then, Cahaiadoirs held out one of the strings of wampum. As Nadie took it from him, he said, "When a woman is grieving, the tears blind her eyes so that she cannot see. With these words, I wipe away the tears from your eyes so that now you may see clearly."

He then held out the next strand of wampum. When Nadie had accepted it, he said, "When a woman is grieving, there is a blockage in her ears, and she cannot hear. With these words, I remove the blockage from your ears so that you may once again have perfect hearing."

While Cahaiadoirs was speaking, two clanswomen poured water on the cooking fires in the longhouse.

Finally, the old man gave her the last string of wampum, saying, "When a woman is grieving, her throat is stopped and she cannot speak. With these words, I remove the obstruction from your throat so that you may speak and breathe freely."

Sobbing, Nadie clasped the three strings of wampum to her breast while other members of the clan, still crying and wailing, began rubbing dirt over their bodies and hair.

"I want to know how this happened," sobbed the woman.

By now, Sean, too, had started crying but, at a nod from Cahaiadoirs, he approached Nadie and said, "Aunt, your daughter was a true *Ganienkeh* woman."

"Of that, I have no doubt," said Nadie, with a hard edge in her voice. "I said that I want to know how she was captured!"

In response, Sean told her the whole story. He told her how Kai had insisted on accompanying him to the Seneca lands. Of how helpful she had been on the trip. How she had saved his life. Why he and the two Seneca warriors had left her behind when they saw the enemy canoes. And, finally, he told how they had discovered that she had been taken by the Huron.

When he was finished, Aernout said to Nadie, "Sister, I grieve for your loss. But, from what Oh-Kahl has said, you and your clan should be proud of your daughter and always remember her for her strength of character."

"Thank you, Aerie," said Nadie. "And, thank you, uncle," she said to Cahaiadoirs, "for performing the condolence ceremony."

Then, turning her gaze on a still crying Sean, she said. "You, Oh-Kahl, were her chosen man. It would please this old woman if you would join us in the mourning ritual."

"I would be honored," said Sean.

Cahaiadoirs said to Sean, "The mourning ritual will start tonight and will last for ten days."

"That is all right," said Sean. "I want to do this. You understand, don't you Aernout?"

"Aye, lad," said Aernout. "Do what you feel you must do. I will see you when you return to Albany."

Turning to leave, Aernout said, "Oh, I will ask the boy to take care of your horse and belongings."

"Thank you, Aernout. Please tell him that he will be rewarded."

"No, Oh-Kahl," said Cahaiadoirs. "No reward will be necessary."

With that, Cahaiadoirs, Onata and Aernout left the longhouse.

With the help of one of the clan's warriors, Sean prepared himself for mourning. He rubbed dirt into his skin, clothes and hair, and used his knife to cut tufts of hair from his head.

That night, the entire castle participated in what Sean found to be the most elaborate wake he had ever seen. Although there was no body over which to keep vigil, the Iroquois believed that customs, especially those surrounding death, needed to be followed, or terrible things would happen.

First, every resident of the castle came to the Turtle Clan longhouse to offer their condolences. In the face of the wails, groans and lamentations that filled the longhouse, they gave lavish gifts, which had been saved for just such a situation, to assuage the anguish of the mourners.

Then, at midnight, a feast was held, with food provided by women from the other clans. During the meal, each person who knew Kai stood and spoke about her, their memories of her and what she had done. Cahaiadoirs, as the highest-ranking person in the castle, retold Sean's tale of Kai's last days and embellished on Sean's suppositions regarding her bravery in defiance of her Huron captors.

For ten days, Sean and the members of Kai's clan remained in deep mourning, secluded in the longhouse. They continued to smear themselves with dirt and lay, face down, on their mats, enveloped in their robes, silent or replying with only an exclamation to those who addressed them. During this period, mirrors and any other objects which might cast a reflection were hidden. There were no fires in the longhouse. They ate their food cold, and left the longhouse only at night, and as secretly as possible.

On the tenth day, Nadie came to him and said, "Nephew, thank you for remembering my daughter with us. Now, you must go."

"Are you sure, aunt, that I should go?" he asked. "Is there nothing more I can do?"

"No," she replied. "This woman and some close family members will continue to mourn. For us, the mourning period will take a year. We must also decide if we will require that the war chief send warriors to attack the Huron and steal a young girl to take my daughter's place. I don't know if I want that. An adopted daughter would not be able to follow me as clan mother, and I do not know if it would make me feel any better knowing that a Huron mother was feeling as much pain as this woman does.

"But," she said with a sigh, "this is not something that you need to worry about. It is not expected of you. You are not of our people. You have other duties. You must go."

"I thank you for allowing me to be with you at this sad time," said Sean.

"I thank you, nephew, for being with us and for bringing my daughter happiness," she replied.

Sean left and went in search of Cahaiadoirs. When he found him, the old man sent for the boy who had his belongings and was caring for his horse. He tried to give the boy his hatchet as a reward, but the boy refused. Cahaiadoirs explained that the boy could not accept because what he had done was in condolence for Sean's loss.

Sean thanked the boy and, carrying his pack, walked down to the river. There, he removed his dirty clothing and washed himself.

Using a small trade mirror, he shaved and tried to cut his hair more evenly.

When he was finished, he bade farewell to Cahaiadoirs, thanked him again for his help, and rode away from Caughnawaga.

Over the next three days, Sean had ample opportunity to reflect on his relationship with Kai. He remembered her smile, her laugh, her obstinacy. Too, he remembered how she felt in his arms, and how much he would look forward to seeing her each time he returned to Caughnawaga.

He knew that he loved and wanted to spend his life with Laurentje but, at the same time, he knew that the beautiful Mohawk woman would always hold a special place in his heart.

By the time he reached Albany, and had ridden through the west gate of the palisade, he knew that he was finished mourning and that it was time for him to move on with his life. It was time to start anew. He had a woman whom he loved and wanted to marry, so he rode directly to the Staats' home to tell her.

Laurentje answered his knock at the kitchen door and exclaimed, "Sean! You're home! I am so glad to see you!"

He gathered her in his arms, kissed her and held her while he focused his thoughts.

"Laurentje," he said. "I need to speak with Major and Mistress Staats. Are they at home?"

"Yes, they are. But they are just eating dinner. Do you really need to speak with them right now?"

"Yes. I do," he emphasized. "Please. Could ye just ask them if I might have a moment of their time?"

"Of course!" she replied and rushed off leaving Sean standing on the back step.

Moments later, she returned and led Sean into the Staats' dining room.

"Well, young man, what is so important that it couldn't wait until I had finished my dinner?" demanded the major.

"Now, major," said his wife, "I am sure that Sean has his reasons. Let the young man talk and don't go scaring him!"

"Major, Mistress Staats, I want to ask for your permission to ask Laurentje to marry me."

"Marry you? When? She has more than four years still remaining on her bond!" exclaimed the major.

"Yes sir, I know. But I have come into possession of an extremely valuable piece of land near Schaghticoke. When I sell it, I will be in a position to buy her bond from ye."

"I don't know..." said the major. "Mistress Staats! She is your servant. What do you say to this?"

"Why, major," she replied. "I have been waiting for this since the first time this young man visited our home. Although I must say that I hadn't expected it to happen so quickly. Of course, young man, you have our permission to speak to Laurentje about this."

"Th, th, thank ye Ma'am, sir!" Sean stammered. "Laurentje, can I speak with you?"

Taking Sean's hand, Laurentje let him lead her through the house and out into the yard.

Finally alone, Sean said, "Laurentje, my lovely lass, I love ye. Would ye give me the honor of becoming my wife? As I told Major and Mistress Staats, my prospects have tremendously improved and I am now in a position to take care of ye properly!"

"Oh, Sean!" she exclaimed. "I love you, too! Of course, I will marry you!"

With that Sean took her into his arms, kissed her and said, "My love, ye have made me the happiest man on the face of the earth!"

Historical Background

The key events described in *Primitive Passions* actually happened. In the mid-1680s, the fur trade at Albany had ground almost to a halt, as the Iroquois could find fewer and fewer beaver in what is now upstate New York. In order to keep themselves supplied with arms with which to fight their enemies and the ironware which they had come to value, the Iroquois were forced to attack French trading parties. They raided those going to the Great Lakes for weapons and trade goods and those returning from the Great Lakes for furs which they would then trade at Albany.

In addition, representatives of William Penn did try to buy the Susquehanna Valley and fur traders from Pennsylvania did make minor inroads among the Iroquois. In response, the Albany magistrates and traders, including Aernout C. Viele, used subterfuge to stymie

Penn. The Iroquois did "suddenly" remember that they had given the Susquehanna Valley to the English.

The French, meanwhile, were doing all that they could to prevent the Dutch and English from usurping the fur trade of the western Indians while trying sway the allegiance of the Iroquois or, failing that, ensure their destruction. Governor La Barre did launch an attack on the Seneca, and his invasion did end ignobly with his force stricken with fever.

Throughout, the Iroquois believed that they could delay choosing sides until they could determine who was stronger – the French or English. For example, no one, least of all the Iroquois, really believed that the Duke of York's Arms on their gates would stop the French. But, if they did, then it was proof that the English were stronger than the French. It was a diplomatic game the sachems would play with varying success until well into the 18th century.

The French Jesuits, while trying to "save the savages," often played the role of *agents provocateurs* on behalf of the government of New France.

As the events described are real, so are most of the characters. Among the English such well-known personages as Robert Livingston, Col. Thomas Dongan, Major Patrick MacGregory and Lord Howard are real. All of the Dutch characters, including Aernout Viele, his immediate and extended family, really existed. Real people among the French include Governor La Barre, the French Jesuit, Father De

Lamberville, and the French officers, de Salvaye and Le Moyne de Longueuil.

All of the Iroquois sachems who spoke at the Albany councils -- Odianne, Tekanista, Thanohjanihta and Adissas -- actually did meet with Dongan and Lord Howard as described, and Garangula, the primary Onondaga sachem, did boldly rebuke Governor de La Barre in their meeting at La Famine. The quotes are accurate as recorded, although I have updated the language.

About the Author

JOHN M. CAHILL was born in Pittsfield, Massachusetts, and grew up in the history-rich Berkshire Hills. He earned a B.A. in Journalism and Political Science from the University of Massachusetts at Amherst and enjoyed a successful and rewarding career in public relations and social marketing with New York State government. It was while working and living in New York's Mohawk Valley that he took an interest in the history of 17th-century New York and began to explore the relationships and interactions of the Dutch and English fur traders with their Iroquois neighbors and their French adversaries. He lives with his wife in Vienna, Austria. This is his first novel and the first volume of *The Boschlopers* saga.

www.ingramcontent.com/pod-product-compliance
Lightning Source LLC
Chambersburg PA
CBHW061614210726
48287CB00001B/132